tl

we wanted

a novel by

kelsey kingsley

copyright

Cover: Danny Manzella
Editor: Jessica Blaikie

This book is dedicated to me—

To the kid who was dying to see the Foo Fighters live,

To the woman who finally did.

This is the life you wanted.

Never change.

It just is.

a note from the author

ear Reader,

Sometimes inspiration comes as a trickle. Little moments, memories, and songs come together, fueling my imagination, until I finally have enough inspiration to put my fingers to the keys and write.

And other times, inspiration rushes at me with such a force, it leaves me winded and emotional. A single moment—a song—can leave me with enough inspiration to write an entire book. This story is a perfect example of that.

It all happened when I saw the Foo Fighters play "Everlong."

I've been listening to this song for over twenty years. I have loved it for most of my life. But sometimes we love a song without ever *really* listening to it. We can hear it repeatedly and never fully grasp the depth to its meaning, and that was very much the case with this.

On July 14th, 2018, I finally listened.

1

It hit me as though I'd never heard it before. I felt the emotion, I felt the love, and I knew I needed to write this book about a snarky drummer named Sebastian and his little witch.

What I didn't know was how much I would end up loving this story. How fun it would be to write these characters. How sad I would be when it was over.

But for you, it's only the beginning.

I'm jealous.

I'll see you at the end.

Kelsey

1

tabitha

"Mrs. Worthington, I'm sure your chinchilla will be perfectly fine during the open house," I insisted, while I kept the phone pinned between my ear and shoulder and slapped together the saddest excuse for a peanut butter and jelly sandwich I'd ever seen.

"Do you think so?" the older woman asked worriedly and I could practically see her feathery white brows pinching together. "Maybe I should remove Sandy from the house. I wouldn't want to stress him out, you know?"

"Of course not," I grumbled, stuffing the sandwich into a baggie and then a paper lunch bag. Pulling the phone away from my ear, I threw my head back and bellowed, "Greyson! Let's go!"

While I waited for the telltale sounds of his heavy footsteps against the treads, I tipped my forehead against the cool surface of the refrigerator and pressed the phone back to my ear. "Sorry about that, Mrs. Worthington. Just trying to get my nephew ready for school. Every day is a battle."

"Oh, I understand, Tabitha," she replied, stressing her sympathies in every inflection. "How is he?"

"It's an adjustment," I answered robotically, because that was the fastest response. It allowed for fewer questions and less conversation, and that was perfect. It wasn't something I wanted to talk about.

"I can only imagine. That poor boy."

That poor boy. A selfish niggling wormed its way into my brain with the sentiment. I did feel terrible for him. Losing his mother suddenly, within a year of losing both his grandparents, had, of course, been rough on him. Nobody understood that more than me. But just once, I would've appreciated a *poor Tabitha. Poor Tabitha* lost both of her ill and elderly parents within months of each other. *Poor Tabitha* had to bury her older sister just two months ago. *Poor Tabitha* couldn't sell the one house she had taken on in the past year.

Poor Tabitha.

I shook my head to push away my selfish mental whining. "I know," I replied, sighing into the phone. "It's been a tough time for both of us, but we're getting there."

But first, we had to get to school. "Greyson!"

With another apologetic groan, I brought the phone back to my ear. "So sorry. Anyway, I'll stop by the house in just a little while and see what we need to do to get it ready for the weekend, okay? How does noon work for you?"

"Noon is perfect! I'll see you then, Tabitha."

With that, the line went dead and I pocketed the phone. Peeking toward the stairs, I shook my head and cursed my nephew under my breath. It was hard to believe that just two months ago, he and I had been so close. We were buddies, damn near inseparable, but now? It seemed like he was listening less, we were fighting more, and I was one day closer to signing him up for boarding school. And all of this made me feel like the worst person on the planet.

Our therapist had said this type of thing was to be expected. What she hadn't told me, was how much it would hurt when he rolled his eyes or cried when I yelled at him.

He never used to cry. Not until Sam died.

"Greyson, *please*!" I called, resorting to pleading. It always came back to pleading. "You're already late and in another half hour, I will be too. Let's *go*!"

His footsteps thundered down the stairs and right into the kitchen, as though he had just waited for me to start begging. His blonde hair was unkempt, his backpack dragged behind him and a scowl was plastered to his face.

"Thank you," I pushed out with my exasperated sigh and turned to grab the paper bag. "I made you—"

"Great," Greyson mumbled, snatching the bag off the counter and throwing it unceremoniously into his backpack. "Let's go so you can stop your bitching."

Our therapist told me I shouldn't let him talk to me like that, even if it did come from a place of sadness and anger. "Greyson, what did I tell you about cursing at me?" I scolded, following her instructions in a stern, even voice.

"Like I give a shit," he replied, a bold challenge displayed in his tone. "Let's go."

God, give me strength. I pressed my eyes shut and pinched the bridge of my nose as he barreled out of the kitchen to the front door, swinging it open and leaving the house. I was trying to be patient and understanding, but every day brought me closer to a place of being fed up.

Maybe today would be that day.

***

"You have such an eye for this," Mrs. Worthington complimented as I carefully positioned the vase of silk tulips on a living room end table.

With a kind smile plastered to my face, I laid a book next to the vase and stood back to marvel at my masterpiece. It was the little things that helped sell a house. Some people believe it's the bigger picture—a redesigned landscape, a knocked-down wall, a refurnished living room—but sometimes all it takes is the turn of a couch and a vase of fake flowers.

"This looks good," I assessed, nodding confidently. "I think we'll sell this weekend. My guess is, three offers."

God, I hope so.

"Oh, that would be fantastic," Mrs. Worthington clutched at her chest, a watery smile on her face. "I really do hate to give the place up, you know."

I did know. She'd only mentioned the fact three-thousand times since I took her on as a client at the beginning of the year. "I know you do." I smiled sympathetically, nodding as I laid the throw pillows just-so on the couch. "If you can avoid sitting on the couch until after Saturday, that would be perfect."

"Of course, dear." She bobbed her head in agreement before continuing, "Mr. Worthington and I always wanted to have a family in this house. It's meant for that. But," she sighed sadly, "it just wasn't in the cards for us, I guess."

I couldn't say it was a sentiment I could ever sympathize with. Children were never something I wanted for myself; I was always a better aunt. But, I could warp my own failed life dreams to relate to hers, and I nodded my understanding.

"I bought my house right before Brad left," I replied, reminding myself of the personal heartache. "Double-sinks kinda suck when you're on your own."

What a crappy year it's been.

"Brad is such a jerk name," Mrs. Worthington sneered with a disapproving shake of her head.

"I wish someone had told me that before I let him propose," I laughed, before clapping my hands together. "Okay! So, Saturday, I'll bring by some coffee and doughnuts. I'll have Greyson with me, if that's okay. He has drum lessons immediately after, so I figured—"

Waving both of her wrinkled hands, Mrs. Worthington dismissed my apologetic tone. "Stop, honey. I never mind when your nephew is around, you know that. He's a good boy."

8

It's true; Greyson was a great kid, for everybody else. He used to be for me too, but now …

"Thank you," I replied gratefully. "Well, I think that's everything for today. Do you need me to run you through anything? Or I could just call you tomorrow with some reminders?"

With a shake of her head, the older woman flashed me with a warm smile. "Nope, I think we're good. Thank you so much for everything, Tabitha. I know what you're going through, and it honestly means the world to me that you're still willing to sell the place."

As I grabbed my bag from the easy chair, I slid it onto my shoulder and smiled. "Believe me, the distraction is more than welcomed."

***

"Hey Grey," I greeted Greyson as he slumped into the passenger seat. "How was school?"

"Oh, just great," he grumbled angrily, slamming the door shut and resting his elbow against the window ledge.

"Well, that doesn't sound so wonderful," I countered, driving away from the curb. "Can you please put on your seatbelt?"

He muttered something unintelligible, but he listened, and strapped himself in with an irritated huff. Without another word, he turned up the volume on my current playlist to listen to a Foo Fighters song we were both fans of. I decided to be brave as I smiled at him.

9

"Hey, remember when we went to see the Foos together?" I asked, reaching over to tap my knuckles against his thigh.

"Yeah," he brusquely replied, fixing his gaze out the window.

"Those were some good shows," I reminisced, all at once wanting to cry and also hating the world for dulling those happy memories with bad ones.

Greyson didn't reply. He continued to stare out the window, scratching his fingers against the ledge and pinching, releasing, pinching his lips. I knew those ticks; he wanted to cry. I hated myself for hoping he wouldn't. Just for one day, I hoped we could get through without any tears or shouting. I could handle banter. I could handle his attitude. But I didn't want the grief.

We drove down the streets of Hog Hill, New York toward my farmhouse-style abode in the suburbs, I tapped my fingers against the steering wheel as the next track began to play. A song by Seether called "Broken." Sam loved this song. She and I had seen them together once, years ago, before Greyson was born. Before I forced myself to grow up. During her days of batting her lashes to get backstage to sleep with members of the band.

I reached over and skipped the song.

***

After dinner, I headed to Greyson's room to corral his dirty clothes from off the floor. I wasn't surprised to find him at his laptop, playing the latest in his arsenal of

10

video games, and I announced my arrival with a knock on the doorframe.

"Hey, Grey."

Glancing over his shoulder and taking a momentary pause from his dragon slaying, he grunted. "Oh, hi."

"I'm just gonna, uh," I gestured toward the blanket of clothes over the floor, "clean these up and throw some laundry in the wash, okay?"

"Uh-huh," he grumbled, turning back to his game.

"It's fine, Grey; I don't need help or anything," I muttered begrudgingly, bending over to scoop clothes into my arms. I dumped them into the laundry basket at the door.

"I'm in the middle of a tournament, Aunt Tabs," he groused, thrusting a hand toward the computer screen and I raised my hands in surrender.

"I didn't say anything," I defended, grabbing another few shirts and dirty socks in my arms before spotting a discarded sheet of paper under his bed. "Is this homework?"

"Huh, what?" Greyson asked, turning to look at the paper in question just in time for me to grab it. "Wait, give that to—"

Before he could snatch it away from me, I was already reading. "Adoption form for … little orphan Greyson?" I thrust the paper toward him. "What the hell? Who gave you this?"

"Relax," he grumbled, tearing it from my hand and throwing it into the wastepaper basket. "It's just a joke."

Tears poked and prodded at the back of my eyes as I shook my head. "Oh, really? It's a joke? You find it funny?"

Flashes of light and the sounds of swords clanging came from his computer, but the game was now forgotten as he swiveled around in his chair. Crossing his arms over his chest and scowling pitifully, he replied, "Will you just *relax*? My friends did it—"

"Oh, okay, your *friends*," I snickered. "So, you think it's okay for your *friends* to tease you about your mother dying? Is that it? Because if you do, please, just let me know and I'll make sure to crack those jokes all the time—"

"No!" he shouted, thrusting his fists against the arms of the chair. "No. Okay?!"

Pursing my lips, I cocked my head. "No, *what*?"

"I don't think it's fucking funny, okay?" The tears brimmed his eyes, his hands unclenched and pushed into his hair.

I had pushed him again and I wasn't proud of it. Stepping toward him, I asked gently, "Grey, do they do this a lot? They bully you?" Sniffling and wiping a hand under his nose, he nodded. "Why don't you tell me about this stuff, kid? I can't help you if you don't tell me."

"And what the fuck am I going to tell *you*?" he snapped, screwing his face with anger and upset. "What are *you* going to do to fix this shit? Huh?"

I wiped a hand over my forehead. "I could talk to your teachers, or the parents' of these kids, or I—"

"You can't do a fucking thing," he gritted through clenched teeth as he thrust himself to his feet. "You don't know what this is like for me. You don't know what it's—"

Shaking my head incredulously, I dropped my arms to my sides. "Oh, I don't?"

"No! You *don't!*" His fists pumped—clenching, unclenching—as his face reddened and his pulse quickened.

With a bitter snicker, I reached my breaking point. "Greyson. I lost *both* of my parents *and* my sister in less than a year. And on top of that, my fiancé dumped me, I've been trying to sell a fucking house for the past *seven* months, and my nephew won't even *try* to help me make this shit work. So, okay, maybe I have no idea what it's like to go to school and have my shit-headed little *friends* make fun of me for losing my mom and growing up without a dad, but *I'm an orphan too*, Greyson!"

A rush of tears zigzagged over my cheeks, to drip from my chin and plop onto the carpet. With a frustrated groan, I turned on my heel and hurried from his room, forgetting entirely about the laundry basket by the door. My room was down the hall from his and I got there quickly, throwing the door open and slamming it behind me. Before I knew what I was doing, I balled my fists and screamed.

The noise was unintelligible and sounded foreign to my ears. I hated myself immediately for losing my cool so thoroughly and completely, but oh my *God*, I didn't know what else to do. He was being bullied in the cruelest of ways and he wasn't talking to me. His way of communicating was by fighting. And what the hell was I supposed to do about that?

13

I pulled in a deep, controlled breath and forced myself to calm down to a more rational realm of thinking. Greyson was just a kid, and I was supposed to be the adult here. I was in control, I called the shots, and with another breath, I tried to think of what Sam might've done.

My sister never won any Mom of the Year awards. Her methods were often immature and irrational, but she did love her son and almost everything she did, she did for him.

A pile of boxes from her place were still stacked in the corner of my room, waiting to be gone through. I hadn't been given the chance, since having to quickly move her things from the apartment she and Greyson had lived in. It had all been stuffed into boxes, without a thought about organization, and in the corner of my room they had remained. I don't know why I thought the answer to my problem might've been in there, but it was the closest thing to having my sister with me and guiding me. So, I went for it.

The first box was stuffed with clothes. The marriage of her cheap perfume and cigarettes clung to the fabrics of shirts, jeans, and waitress uniforms, and tears met my smile. God, for years, I had begged her to quit smoking. I never thought I'd one day miss the smell so much, and I brought one shirt to my nose and sucked in the scent. I wished I could permanently implant it into my memory, knowing all too well that it would never stay.

Carefully placing the box onto the floor, I opened the second. Immediately I remembered her closet full of storage. Some Christmas decorations, a safety lockbox, and a small stack of envelopes rubber-banded together were all that was left of the pile of junk she had kept in there. I already knew the lockbox contained a couple of emergency credit cards and a few important documents, but the envelopes snagged my curiosity.

The rubber band snapped; age had made it brittle. Three envelopes laid in my hand, all with the return address of someone named Morrison only a few hours away in New York.

Opening the first, I was surprised to find a handwritten letter. Barely legible, in sloppy cursive.

I took a deep breath and moved to my bed to read.

Sam,

I tried calling you the other day a few times and didn't get an answer. I hope you don't think I'm acting like a stalker by finding your address, but I had to try and get in touch with you. I have things I want to say, and I don't know how else to say them.

So, I know you told me you were getting an abortion, and I know I said I would support you in that. Obviously, if that's what you really want to do, I'm cool with it. But, the more I think about this shit, the more I think I'd also be fine with trying to make something work. Like, you and me, raising the kid. I mean, I know I told you I didn't want to be a father, but after I thought about it, I realized I could be a pretty good dad. I could even be a good husband. I'm making good money, I have a house, and I could support you and the kid. Maybe one day we could get married, and we could be a real family.

What do you think? Obviously, this is all up to you. You do whatever you think is best. I'm just saying, we could make it work. I want to make it work.

I hope you write back, and I really hope this is your address.

-Sebastian

Sam,

I sent you a letter a few weeks ago and never got a response. I tried calling you again and got no answer. So, I don't know if you've already gotten the abortion and you're just ignoring me or what, but I thought I'd send another letter to make sure you're okay. I've been thinking a lot about you and the baby. I've actually been playing really badly—you guys are a fucking distraction.

Please let me know you're okay.

-Sebastian

Sam,

It's been a month since I sent my last letter. It's been about two months since I heard from you at all. I guess I have to assume you had the abortion, and you don't want to hear from me.

Or maybe this isn't even your address, haha. God, how fucking crazy would that be?

Anyway, in case this is you, I'm sorry about all of this shit. I'm sorry you went through everything alone. I wish you would've at least let me be there; I would've made time for you, if you had asked. I hope you have family to turn to. I hope you're okay.

I'm including a check with this letter, because at this point, I don't know what the hell else I can do.

I promise I'll leave you alone now. Have a good life, Sam. I hope it's everything you wanted.

-Sebastian

2

sebastian

"Ladies and gentlemen, give it up for Sebastian Moore, killing it on the drums!"

Banging my head, I rocked my drum solo for a modest thirty seconds, before falling back in place with the bass and guitars. Devin O'Leary, front man and genius behind this whole thing, wished the crowd a good night and a safe drive home. We jammed for a few more seconds, and then …

After one, two flams, and a crash of the cymbals, I stood up from my throne, thrusting my sticks over my head and feeling like I'd just run a marathon and destroyed it. Devin ran toward me, his guitar slung around his back and his hand outstretched, and after pocketing my sticks, I slapped him five.

The four of us took the stairs and entered the backstage of Madison Square Garden. It was our last night opening for Devin's hero, the one and only John

Mayer, and we had *killed it*. The band's Instagram followers and Facebook likes had been blowing through the roof since the beginning of the tour. It was our biggest break, and we were headed places, *fast*.

"Seb," Devin said breathlessly, clapping a hand over my back, "what the hell did you do back there, during the 'Better Man' cover?"

Wiping the back of my arm across my forehead, I nodded. "Oh, yeah, sorry about that. I was just in the zone and rolled with it. I know we didn't rehearse it like that, but—"

Tyler Meade, our bass player, shook his head. "Fucking hell, bro. Don't apologize for that shit! That was *amazing*! That thing you did with the—" He mimicked the polyrhythm with a few mouth sounds and some movements of his hands.

Devin nodded affirmatively. "It was fucking *sick*. It made that song even better, if that's at all possible."

Kylie O'Leary, Devin's wife and our manager, approached with a grin and a leap into her husband's arms. It was customary. At the end of every show, the two of them would spend about fifteen seconds making out, expelling the adrenaline and completely forgetting that we were there.

Devin made an attempt to feel her up, and she brushed his hand away. "Not in front of these idiots," she scolded lightly, and the rest of us erupted in a cacophony of chuckles.

"Oh, please, don't stop on our account," Ty mumbled good-naturedly. "Olivia's already almost a year old, isn't she? Time to get started on number two."

Kylie's feet met the ground as she reached out to playfully shove Ty. "The bus is barely big enough for all of us, and you want to add another baby to the mix?"

"Aw, come on, Ky," I wrapped an arm around Devin's shoulders. "You're gonna let the big guy down. Plus, you're in the rare position of having traveling babysitters. Don't you wanna take advantage of that?"

"He's got a point, baby," Devin agreed, nodding enthusiastically. "There's three of them, so we should have at least three kids, right?"

"Could add a keyboardist, and then there'll be four," Chad suggested with a shrug.

"Great!" Ty laughed, clapping his hands. He took Kylie and Devin each by an arm and nudged them together. "Go on. As you were."

"I hate them," Kylie mumbled with a lighthearted giggle, and Devin laughed as he shoved Ty away. "Maybe you guys can focus on your own love lives instead of focusing on *ours*, okay?"

I groaned and rolled my eyes. "Hard not to focus on yours, when you flaunt it all the goddamn time," I teased, leaning in to kiss Kylie's cheek before gripping Dev's shoulders in my hands. "Come on," I grinned. "Last night of the tour, dudes and dudette. Let's party."

"*Party*?" Ty scoffed. "Sebastian, man, you go ahead and have fun. I need to pass out for the next twelve hours before my flight back home tomorrow."

"Dev, Chad?" I extended my arms to my friends, hoping one of them would accept the invitation.

"Skypin' with my girl tonight," Chad muttered with a shrug, and Dev shook his head before replying, "We've

23

spent the past three nights doing nothing but work; I need to relax."

I love these guys. After years of making sweet music together, they are the extended family I always wanted, and there wasn't much I wouldn't do for them. But fuck, they make it difficult to live the life of the carefree bachelor.

***

"You heading to bed already?" Devin asked, hoisting his daughter Olivia onto his hip. "Not gonna pick up some chick to keep you company?"

He was teasing. My casual coupling had been kept to a minimum since touring with the Partridge Family. Usually only when we were stationed in one spot for a few days, and I had the time to make a connection with someone, in a hotel. Older age and touring with a married couple had done that to me—made me crave a connection.

I held a hand up on the way to my bunk. "Already got Miss Right over here, bro. I'm good."

Kylie threw her head back as she opened the refrigerator and pulled out a bottle of breast milk. Just another fun thing I'd learned to live with.

"Can you remember this is a *family bus* and *not* a frat house?" she asked.

"Family shares stuff, Ky," I reasoned with a shrug. "And I just wanted you guys to know that I won't be lonely tonight."

24

"I'm *so* glad," she chided with a roll of her eyes. "Remember Livy isn't far from talking. Last thing we need is for her to start repeating some of this crap."

The bathroom door opened at the end of the hall and Chad emerged with a magazine in hand.

"Yo, speakin' of crap," he announced in his Texan accent, "I'm warnin' y'all right now: that bathroom is filled with toxic fumes and you might wanna keep your distance."

Devin, Ty, and I erupted in a chorus of laughter while Kylie huffed a groan.

"Chad," she whined. "Did you at least spray the air freshener?"

"You asshole," Ty groaned with a grin, slumping further into the couch. "I *told you* to stay the hell away from those nachos. They looked fucking nasty."

"It's the IBS, guys. I can't help it." Chad rubbed a hand over his stomach while I bit back an immature laugh.

With the bottle in hand, Kylie took Olivia from Devin's arms. Her walk down the hall was interrupted by a dry-heave, and Chad's cheeks flared with his suppressed chuckle.

"I think Daddy and I need to have another girl," we heard her muttering to Olivia, and the three of us turned to Devin with suggestive grins. "We need to up the estrogen in this place," she added as the bedroom door closed at the end of the hall.

"Sounds like she's on board with our plan for the second one," Ty laughed, waggling his brows and nudging Dev with the toe of his boot.

25

"Yeah, yeah," Devin groaned, flopping down next to Ty. "You should bring your wife and daughter on tour with us. Ky would appreciate the company."

"I would if Carrie didn't have school," Ty mentioned with a sigh. The lonely lilt to his voice was evident, and I pursed my lips sympathetically with my own distant ping of longing stabbing at my heart.

"Homeschool is a wonderful thing," Chad nodded, sliding onto a bench at the table. "Best thing my parents ever did for me."

"Yeah, and have *you* guys teaching her?" Ty lifted the corner of his mouth into an amused grin. "I don't think so."

"Well, the second I ask Ali to marry me, I'm bringin' her along," Chad replied with an affirmative nod.

"How long you guys been together again?" Devin asked, using a guitar pick to scratch behind his ear.

Chad puffed with pride as he said, "Six years."

Ty and Devin both groaned in unison as I shook my head. Chad raised his hands in a questioning shrug.

"Man, shit or get off the pot," Ty nodded, and then added, "And uh, I don't mean literally."

"Huh?" Chad drew his brows together and folded his arms on the table. "Whatcha talkin' about?"

Leaning against the wall, I pointed a finger toward the youngest member of our group. "Chadwick—"

"I really hate when you call me that," he groaned. "It's not my name."

"Right. My bad." I nodded apologetically before continuing, "Chaddington Bear, I have never been

26

married nor will I probably ever be, but even *I* know that you've been stringing that little lady along for too long. If you like it, put a ring on it, or you know, walk away and find someone else to, uh … *occupy* your time. Plenty of chicks love that Southern thing you got going on."

Chad groaned as Devin glanced up at me and smirked around his chuckle. "You're one seriously eloquent motherfucker, you know that?"

Spreading my arms wide, I leaned toward him. "Someone's gotta tell him like it is. Might as well be me."

Patting my hand against the wall, I announced, "And with that piece of advice, gentlemen, I'm heading to bed to jerk off and fall into a coma. None of you better wake me up tomorrow before eleven. Good. Night."

With their mumbled wishes for good sleep behind me, I walked to my bunk and hoisted myself inside, closing the curtain and flipping on the light. I fumbled around for my headphones and cellphone, and scrolled through my library of music.

I had a playlist for everything. Working out, cooking, eating, and jamming. Sleeping was no exception and with one tap of my finger, the Foo Fighters' "Walking After You" began to drift at a soothing volume through the noise-cancelling headphones.

With an even exhale, I slipped easily into a state of relaxation, gripping the phone to my chest. Every breath brought me closer to my home and being alone.

I hated to admit it, but fuck, I was dreading it.

The town car dropped me off at the door of my house in New York.

"Should I get your bags, sir?" the driver asked, turning to glance at me in the backseat.

"Nah, man; I'm good," I grinned, slipping him a fifty. "Just pop the trunk."

Getting out, I grabbed my suitcases and hoisted them up the gravel walkway. I watched the door as I listened to the car back out of the driveway. It was this exact moment when I wished there was someone on the other side to open the door and greet me. A butler or a maid would have probably sufficed, just having someone happy to see me. A fucking goldfish, even. But there wasn't anybody. Nobody there to hug or kiss me, and there was certainly nobody there to open the damn door.

I dropped the bags at the door and fished my keys from a pocket. I had bought this place back when I started making a living doing what I loved. I'd been a kid back then, only twenty years old, and I was eager to be on my own. It was a modest house, especially compared to what I was making now, but how much space did one guy really need?

"Honey, I'm home!" I shouted from the door, before answering in a high-pitched tone, "Oh, Sebastian. I've missed you so fucking much. I can't wait for you to spend a whole week buried between my legs." And I rolled my eyes at myself, because next to pathetic in the dictionary, you could find a picture of me. Sebastian Moore.

The bags were dragged inside and left next to the stairs as I walked toward the couch. My mom, bless her, had stopped in on a regular basis to bring in the mail and to keep the place dusted and vacuumed. I found the pile of mail on the coffee table, starting to land slide onto the carpet.

"Bill, bill, bill," I chanted, picking up envelopes and discarding them to the floor. "Junk, junk, bullshit catalog, bill …"

I sighed, quickly moving through months of amounted crap, until I reached an envelope that had fallen to the floor. It was handwritten, and whoever it was had used my birth name, *Sebastian Morrison*, in the address.

"Huh," I muttered to nobody, and ripped it open.

Sebastian,

You have no idea who I am, but my name is Tabitha Clarke. I found a few letters from you in my sister Samantha's things and I thought I'd reach out to you.

Samantha. My eyes stared at the name, unblinking and startled. I hadn't even thought about Sam in—fuck, well over a decade. But there were some things, other things, I could never forget.

From what you wrote, it seems that my sister never replied to you, and I'm truly sorry for that. Because while you were made to believe that she had an abortion, she did in fact have the baby—a little boy. His name is Greyson, and he is now fifteen years old. I thought you'd like to know.

I have to admit, I'm also writing for selfish reasons. You see, Sam was killed in a car accident two months ago. After losing both of my parents earlier this year, I have no other family, and therefore nobody else to help raise Greyson. Because you are apparently his biological father, I wanted to invite you to step in. He's going through a horrible time, between losing three members of his family and being bullied at school, and I could really use the help.

I do realize how odd and abrupt this invitation may seem. You are ultimately a stranger to us and I have no idea if you are a good person. But your letters from sixteen years ago seemed sincere and I'm taking it on good faith that you're still that man.

I've included my phone number. I'm hoping you'll call.

-Tabitha

What the fuck. Before I realized what was happening, my hand unclenched the letter on its own accord, like it was on fire, and it went drifting to the floor at my feet. This woman, Tabitha, from some place called Hog Hill, New York was telling me that I had a kid. A son.

I have a fucking son.

I hadn't thought about Samantha Clarke in well over a decade. Fifteen years, apparently. But with those

30

words, I remembered the phone call in which she told me she was pregnant. I remembered it like it had happened yesterday. The sweaty palms, the dry throat, and the feeling that the world was falling apart around me. I was a kid myself, on the fast lane to the life I wanted, and becoming a father had never been part of the plan.

I didn't have to worry about it though, she'd said. She was getting an abortion, being only nineteen herself with zero prospects for the future. I told her I would respect her choice to do whatever she wanted and left it at that, while the overwhelming sense of relief coalesced with something else: *guilt*. And that guilt eventually manifested into an overpowering need to provide, and that was when I knew, I *did* want that kid.

I wrote to her after she ignored my calls, but I never heard back. I assumed she'd gotten the abortion and wanted to put the whole thing behind her, and so, I had left her alone.

"What the fuck," I uttered aloud, reaching down to pick the letter up again. "Sam is *dead*?"

My eyes scanned the letter again. She'd died in a fucking car accident? I dropped the piece of paper to the coffee table, thrust my fingers into my hair, and held my head in my hands. I had so many questions, so many things I wanted to know. Why the hell hadn't she told me? Why had she done it all on her own? But above all else, I wanted to know about *him*. Who was he? What does he look like?

"I have a fucking kid," I mumbled, and immediately, I grabbed my phone.

3

tabby

"Mrs. Worthington, you really don't need to worry about Sandy," I pleaded with the old woman as she bustled her way back to the chinchilla's room.

I still couldn't believe the damn chinchilla had its own bedroom. This is obviously what happens to old ladies who lose their husbands and don't have grandchildren.

Is this my future?

"I'm just going to have a peek at him, Tabitha," she called back in a sing-song tone that told me there would probably be kisses and cuddles involved in that *peek*.

Just then, a couple walked through the front door of the old Victorian property. Their gaze immediately soared to the vaulted ceilings, grins overtaking their young faces at the awe-inspiring dose of natural light that swept the room. They were the kind of people I kept an eye out for, not folks like the long-haired and tattooed Prince of Grunge that walked in earlier. People like that wandered in off the streets for the free coffee and doughnuts, but *this* couple? They had interest, and interest meant potential sale.

"Good afternoon!" I approached with a beaming grin, holding out a manicured hand. "Thank you *so* much for stopping in. I'm Tabitha Clarke, agent and owner at TC Real Estate."

The young man gripped my palm in his. "Sam," he responded with a friendly smile and my heart flinched at the name. He placed a hand at the small of his partner's back. "This is my wife, Margo."

"It's a pleasure to meet you, Sam," I slipped my hand from his and nodded toward the pretty blonde, "and Margo. Are you looking to buy?"

She bobbed her head excitedly. "We just got back from our honeymoon in Belize, and we're looking for a house in the area."

Perfect. Newlyweds. "*Well*," I enthused, welcoming them into the home with a sweep of my arm, "this is the perfect place to begin your new life together. The homeowner actually told me that she and her late-husband—"

"Excuse me," Sam interrupted with a grimace. "Did you say … *late*-husband?"

Fuck.

Moistening my lips, I nodded hastily. "Uh, yes. They had bought the house—"

33

Sam reached out to grip the shoulder of his new wife. "I'm sorry, Mrs. Clarke. We don't want a house that was owned by a dead person."

Margo nodded apologetically, frowning and reaching for her husband's hand. "We want a house with history, but not *that* much history," she explained flimsily, and I fought hard against the roll of my eyes.

"The home *was* built in the late-1800's," I reminded them. "It clearly states that in the newspaper listing."

Sam nodded. "Right, but … we just …" He looked to Margo for backup.

"We just thought everybody had moved out before they had passed away. I'm so sorry for wasting your time," and before I could give them my card, they turned and walked out the door.

Son of a bitch. The day wasn't going nearly as planned, and I couldn't put my finger on what exactly I was doing wrong. The place was staged beautifully, the coffee was fresh, and the doughnuts were fluffy. Greyson was hanging out with Sandy the chinchilla, so I couldn't even blame his less than chipper attitude for scaring potential buyers away.

I kept telling myself that it was just an off day, but dammit, I wanted to sell this house. I *needed* to. I was desperate for the boost to my confidence and I had no idea where else I was supposed to get it, if not from making this sale.

I tipped my head back and allowed myself a moment to groan. I ran my hands over my face, just as the pocket of my nicest black pants began to vibrate. My personal phone erupted with the chorus of the Foo Fighters'

"M.I.A." and I pulled it out. The number was unknown, and I rejected the call.

"I swear, I get more spam calls than—" Just as I was pocketing the phone, it again began to ring. Same number. "What the hell?"

Clearing my throat, I accepted and pressed the phone to my ear. "Hello. This is Tabitha Clarke. May I ask who's calling?"

A throaty chuckle drifted into my ear and I narrowed my eyes. Before I could ask the no-name caller what exactly was so funny, they replied, "You know, in a world of bullshit callers who are just *dying* to phish for your information, do you really think it's the smartest thing to answer with your *name*?"

It was a man's voice. Warm and smooth. If I wasn't too busy being taken aback, I might've marveled in the attractive quality of his tone.

"Excuse me?" I replied brusquely. "Who *is* this?" I certainly had no idea. I'd remember a voice like that.

"Right, I probably should've answered with that first. My bad. No filters." He cleared his throat. "Here, I'll give you a hint: You wrote me a letter."

My eyes widened and I smiled with the realization that I was actually talking to Greyson's father. "Oh my God, is this Sebastian Morrison?"

I couldn't believe my letter had gotten there so fast. I mean, it'd been several days since I had written it and dropped it in the mail, but I never expected a phone call so soon. He must've only *just* received it.

"Well, it's Sebastian *Moore* now, but yeah, that would be me."

Sebastian Moore? Was he married and changed his name? I wondered if I should ask, and then thought better of it. It wasn't any of my business. I didn't know him and he knew even less about me. So, instead, I prepared myself to jump right into asking him when we could meet, when he started talking again.

"Yeah, you're probably wondering about that. So, it's nothing crazy or anything, just when I was younger, I went by Sebastian Morrison, but my manager thought I'd get more jobs as Sebastian Moore. Sounds better, right?"

Well, that piqued my interest, as I headed toward the kitchen. "More jobs?"

A moment of silence clouded the space between his line and mine before he answered, "Wait. So, you know nothing about me?"

"Not really," I shamefully replied, kicking myself for not thinking to do a Google search on this guy.

"Hm," he grunted, probably judging me for the very thing I was berating myself for. "I'm a drummer."

Of course, he was a musician. Sam always had a thing for musicians, especially the drummers. "They keep the rhythm better," she'd tease me, and I'd roll my eyes at her. And I rolled my eyes to the ceiling then, asking her why it couldn't have been an accountant or a doctor.

"Of course you are," I muttered, not intending to say it aloud.

Sebastian hit me with that throaty chuckle again. "What the hell does *that* mean?"

Laying a hand over my eyes, I winced. "Nothing. I'm sorry. Um, so you got my letter?"

"I did, and as you can imagine, I kinda shit myself when I read it," he replied just as another young couple walked through the door.

Dammit. Professionally, I should've been running to greet them, but desperation was taking over and I wanted nothing more than to speak to Sebastian.

"One moment," I said politely into the phone before lowering it to my shoulder. I approached the couple and quietly introduced myself. "Tabitha Clarke, realtor. I just need to take this important business call for a few minutes, but if you need me, I'll be right in the kitchen."

"Thank you very much," the young woman replied with a pretty smile, hooking her arm around the young man's before they took themselves on a tour of the house.

I ducked into the kitchen and put the phone back to my ear. "Sorry about that. I—"

"Real estate, huh? *That* sounds like fun," he mentioned sarcastically, obviously having overheard. "I bet you've seen all kinds of shit."

"Uh, what?" I stammered, laying a hand on the cool granite countertop.

"How many cat ladies have you dealt with?"

What the hell is this guy on? "I don't—"

"Hoarders?"

"I'm sorry," I interjected, pressing my fingers to my temple. "Can we please not talk about my career right now, and instead discuss the reason for my writing to you?"

"Right," he replied, his voice gruff. "Sorry. So. I have a kid. That's unexpected."

37

I nodded. "I can only imagine how shocking this must be for you. I ... I honestly have no idea why Sam wouldn't have—"

I was interrupted by the sound of rustling and glass clinking on glass. "*Fuck*," he grumbled into the phone, and then added, "Sorry. Can I call you back?"

"Uh, I—"

"Yeah, I know. Really inconvenient timing, I got it. But listen, I thought I could have this conversation without alcohol, but I really don't think I can. I need to run to the store and grab some."

Part of me wanted to roll my eyes at the interruption, but then, I couldn't say I blamed him. "Yeah, sure. I should be getting back to work anyway. Maybe you can give me a call tonight, around six?"

"Oh, Tabby," he chuckled lightly, using a nickname I hated and hadn't heard since I was a child. "It's a date."

***

Mrs. Worthington held Sandy, all nestled in the crook of her arm as she stroked the soft fur along his back. "I'm worried I'll never sell this darn house," she sighed with a gentle shake of her head.

"Don't worry," I assured her. "Sometimes offers come in a day or two later. It'll happen."

Honestly, I wasn't sure who I was lying to more; her, or me.

Not a single person had expressed interest in the place. A few stragglers had walked in, searching for a free doughnut or a cup of coffee. A handful of couples showed up too, but not a single one approached me with a serious offer. A few took brochures but that was where the intrigue stopped.

Hope was dwindling.

Greyson grabbed for another doughnut and I held out a hand to stop him. "Hey, we'll be eating dinner soon."

Rolling his eyes, he reached over my outstretched hand. "I'll eat doughnuts for dinner."

"You're killing me, Grey," I grumbled with a sigh, laying my hands over my face. "Anyway, Mrs. Worthington, don't worry. I *will* sell this place, even if it's the last thing I do, okay? Trust me. I've never failed a customer yet."

But wasn't there a first time for everything?

The white-haired woman smiled and continued to stroke the chinchilla. "I trust you, honey. Go home and get some rest. I'll call you tomorrow."

Collecting my paperwork, bag, and nephew, we left and drove home in silence. Silence was better than fighting, and when we got home, I offered to order a pizza to save us the inevitable dinner argument. Greyson grunted his agreement before running upstairs to get some drum practice in.

Dropping down to the couch, I ordered a pepperoni pie and laid my head back. Staring at the ceiling, I let myself slip into the painful place of missing my sister.

She had made life difficult on me by having Greyson. From the very beginning, I felt a responsibility to be the stable sister, to always be someone the kid could lean on when things got rocky with his mom. But even through the self-imposed pressure, I always loved her. We had a good time together, and she'd been my best friend.

My phone startled me, as Sebastian's name popped up on the screen.

"Mr. Morrison," I promptly answered, smiling politely. "Thank you so much for—"

"Okay, Tabby," he began with a breathy chuckle, "can we drop the formal bullshit? I don't know how to do this crap, let alone talk like I'm in a faculty meeting or whatever."

Stunned by his abrasiveness, I blinked and sat up straight on the couch. "O-oh, uh, sure. Sorry. This is usually how I handle busin—"

"*This* isn't business," he interrupted.

"I guess you're right," I agreed softly, nodding. "So, um, what should we—"

"Why did you write to me?"

My lips pressed into a tight line at being interrupted for the second time. "I already explained that in my letter."

"Right, I'm looking at it right now. You're having a difficult time with the kid. He's had a rough year, and so have you—I got it. But you didn't *explain* it to me."

My lips tipped downward into a scowl. "I wrote to you because I need *help*. I have nobody to turn to, and I'm sorry that you were—"

"Don't apologize for it," he cut me off *again*, and my fist clenched. "I'm just asking, what is he doing? Is he standing on the roof and screaming fuck the world? Is he setting the place on fire? Or is he just being a pain in the ass kid who lost his mom?"

Wiping a hand over my face, I shook my head. What the hell did it matter? Did this guy think he was some kind of teenager whisperer? "*O-kay*. Um, well, he's having a really tough time in school. Kids are bullying him. He's completely lost interest in everything other than his video games and music, he won't listen to a word I say, we fight all the damn time, and he's … I don't know. He cries a lot. He's never been an emotional kid like this, and—"

"Tabby, the kid lost his *mom*."

"Can you *please* stop interrupting me? It's incredibly rude," I finally snapped.

"Sorry. You're just saying all this shit to me and I think you think he's acting fucking weird or something, but the kid *lost his mom*. He's *mourning*. I mean, I've never dealt with a kid whose lost nearly everybody within a short span of time, but he sounds pretty fucking normal to me," Sebastian prattled on with a nonchalant tone.

I had spoken to the man for all of a few minutes and I already couldn't stand his casual confidence. "I'm not saying it isn't *normal*," I pushed through the phone. "I'm saying that I've been having a difficult time trying to help him and still maintain my position at work. I have …" I wiped a hand over my mouth, unable to believe that I was actually about to confess these things to a man I didn't even know, but I continued. "I have had my life flipped entirely upside down in the past year, and I haven't been given the fucking *chance* to handle shit

41

myself, let alone for him. I am in over my head and I just need some help. I thought that, if you had *any* interest in being involved years ago, then maybe—"

"Yes," he replied curtly and kindly, and I froze, my hand pressing against my heaving chest.

"What?"

"Yeah, I'll help. What do you need?"

"Oh, uh …" The truth was, I hadn't thought this far into it. I don't think I expected him to be agreeable. "Well, um, maybe you'd like to meet, and we can go from there?"

"Definitely," Sebastian replied enthusiastically. "You guys are in Hog Hill?"

"Uh, y-yes," I stammered. "But we could come to you, if that would make things easier. I don't know what your work schedule is like, or—"

"Nah, I have nothing going on right now. How's tomorrow?"

Startled, I mentally ran through my itinerary. "Uh, tomorrow? Wow, that's … soon. I need to talk to Greyson about … all this. But, um, I guess tomorrow could work. I'll be in the office early in the day, but that'd be great, if you don't mind the drive. How about you call me when you're close and we can decide on a place to meet?"

"Sounds good, Tabby," Sebastian replied. "What's the kid into, by the way?"

I shrugged. "Um, video games and music. Drums."

Sebastian chuckled, and I tried to ignore the way it made me feel. Warm. Almost good. "Well then. We'll get along just fine."

4

sebastian

"*I just wanted to tell you that I'm pregnant. I thought you'd like to know,*" *she spoke quietly into the phone, as though she was trying to prevent someone from hearing.*

"*How the fuck are you pregnant?*" *I nearly shouted, my eyes straining against their sockets. I had used a fucking condom. I always used a condom.*

"*It just happened, I guess. It's not your fault,*" *she insisted, but it had to be. She hadn't touched the thing. Nobody ever did. Just me.* "*And anyway, I've decided to get rid of it.*"

"*Then why the fuck did you bother to call me?*" *I snapped angrily.*

"*Just to tell someone, I guess.*"

I jolted from my bed with a gasp. My fingers stabbed through my hair, gripping and pulling. Anger pushed through my veins in a flurry as I struggled to control my breathing.

"You fucking *lied* to me," I said to the dark, empty room. "Why the fuck did you lie to me?"

Nobody answered.

We had been young, and fatherhood was never something I'd considered for myself. I would never attempt to deny either of those facts. When Sam had called me with the news, I was angry. I was scared. But when she mentioned the abortion? I felt sad. Heartbroken, even. I didn't try to talk her out of it. I didn't make any attempt to influence her decision, but all I could think was, "That's my kid in there, and I don't get a say in this."

I mourned that baby for months before my busy life helped me to move on with distraction after distraction, until I just didn't think about it much anymore. But, every now and then, I'd think about that time I was almost a dad. When I almost had a kid.

What a mindfuck it was to learn that, while I'd thought he was gone, he was out there in the world, living his life.

***

"So, wait a second, dude …" Ty was silent for a few seconds before continuing, "You got some chick pregnant years ago, and you found out *yesterday* that he's been alive all this time, and you're driving up to see him *today*?"

His voice flooded the interior of my Range Rover, and I nodded in reply. "That's the gist of it, yeah. Crazy, right?"

45

"You know, I have no problem imagining you knocking someone up, but the idea of you as a *parent* is just … really fucking with me right now." I could picture my friend shaking his head with disbelief.

"*You*?! Bro, imagine how *I* feel!" I was laughing in spite of the churning in my stomach as I drove down I-95 toward Hog Hill. The GPS told me I had another fifteen miles to go before reaching my destination. Fifteen miles wasn't a whole lot.

"And his mom's dead, you said?"

I nodded sadly. "Yeah, she got into a car accident a few months ago apparently."

"So, who's the kid with now?"

"His aunt." I thought about Tabitha Clarke. The professional and polite tone she'd used both times I spoke with her, until her brief moment of weakness. I'd heard the breaking in her voice as she begged *me* for help; a stranger. She was desperate, and I'd felt bad.

"Did you look them up on Facebook?" Ty asked skeptically.

Chuckling, I shook my head. "Nah. Probably should've, right?"

"Uh, what the fuck, man. These people could be taking advantage of you right now."

I guess it was a possibility. I'd never considered that could be the case, not when Tabby knew the things I had written. But wasn't it possible that she'd found the letters I'd written to Sam and decided to use it against me? I still hadn't spoken to the kid, and had no proof he even existed.

But the desperation in her voice had been real.

46

"I think I'm good, but I'll text you the address, just in case," I told him with another chuckle.

"Yeah, well, good luck. I'm going back to bed. Later, *Dad*," he teased before hanging up the phone.

I shook my head, casually snickering as I turned up the volume on the Foo Fighters' "Walk." But deep down, I wondered what it'd feel like for someone to seriously call me *dad*.

Wondering if he—*Greyson*—ever would.

***

"Tabby Clarke." I held the phone to my ear, speaking cheerily as my heart hammered wildly in my chest. "I have arrived in your tiny town. Did you know you have a little over two-thousand residents here?"

"Sure. Thank you for that," she grumbled. "I'm at the office. Um, maybe you could wait at this coffee shop on Main Street? It's close to where I work. Do you even drink coffee?"

"My middle name is Folgers," I joked, peering out the windshield at what I was sure was the coffee shop in question.

On Main Street ... I was on Main Street, according to the GPS. I turned to the left and right, looking for the real estate agency she worked at, and quickly spotted it. TC Real Estate. *TC*—Tabitha Clarke. Maybe I could just take a walk down there and peek through the window. Check this Tabby Clarke out. Make sure she was a woman in her thirties and not a creepy lady looking for a thrill.

47

"Great. Okay. Can you be there in about twenty minutes?"

Looking back to the coffee shop directly in front of me, I nodded. "Yep. I think I can manage that."

"Excellent," she replied. I could imagine her talking to her clients this way. Sickeningly chipper and falsely positive. "I'll see you then."

She hung up and, as I stuffed my phone into my pocket, I mocked, "Excellent."

Getting out of my truck, I considered just walking into the coffee shop and waiting, and perhaps that's what I should've done. It would've been the more courteous thing to do, after already making the arrangement with Tabby. But God, my curiosity was barking and I wasn't in the mood to sit still.

So, I walked.

I headed in the direction of the real estate agency. A brick exterior with painted white pillars framed the white door. Stopping out front on the other side of the street, I squinted my eyes, taking in the classy, just-as-white interior, and the woman sitting behind a desk.

"Hello, Tabby Clarke," I muttered under my breath, shoving my hands into my pockets.

Well, she wasn't particularly gorgeous, but she was on the upper-end of average. Dark brown hair pulled into a neat twist at the back of her head. An immaculate, business-like sense of fashion, and a pencil pinched between two long, manicured fingers.

She wasn't bad, but she'd be easy to resist. That was a good thing.

With an assessing nod, I told myself to walk back to the coffee shop. I glanced toward it and its whimsical sign hanging above the door, and then looked back to the realty office. It couldn't hurt to walk in, I figured. She wouldn't know who I was, unless she had Googled my name, which was a likely possibility. Still, it felt safe to just wander in, pretend to be someone else for a moment, and then hurry back to the coffee shop.

"Unless she realizes I'm the same guy," I mumbled to myself as an old woman walked down the sidewalk behind me.

"Excuse me?" she asked, stopping to take me in.

Turning to face her, I noticed her scrutinizing stare aimed directly at the knot I'd twisted my hair into. "Oh, sorry. I was just talking to myself."

"Mm," she grumbled with a shake of her head before continuing on her way. "This town's going straight to hell."

Well, aren't you a ray of sunshine?

I turned back to the realtor's office and decided to go for it. What was the worst that could happen? She'd realized that I'd been spying on her? I could just tell her I was making sure she wasn't fucking with me. That was the truth, after all.

I headed across the street and walked right through the door without hesitation, sliding my sunglasses off and breathing in the scent of freshly cut flowers and perfume. It was clearly a woman's office. Organized, clean, and pretty, and I nodded my approval.

"Can I—" Tabby began, her words cut short as I turned to face her. "*Whoa*."

49

"Hi," I said with a grin, in a voice I hoped screamed I was looking for a home.

"You look like a *model*," she gushed, flattening her hands on her desk as her lips parted with surprise. "Oh my *God*. I can't believe I just said that. I swear I'm a happily married woman, oh my God …"

Married? I was almost certain Tabby wasn't married. "Uh, maybe you could help—"

"You know what? I don't think I should. You are just too …" She shook her head. "Let me just get Tabitha for you, okay?" The flustered woman, apparently not Tabby, stood up from her desk and raked her eyes over me from head to toe. "Oh my God, you're *so tall.*" She squeezed her eyes shut. "Get a grip, Jessica."

Jessica hurried away, disappearing behind a door with a frosted window. Painted, white lettering read *Tabitha Clarke* on the glass and I nodded slowly, stepping closer to the office.

"Tabitha, oh my *God*, you have to get a look at this guy out here," Jessica enthused, and I stifled my chuckle. "He looks like Thor's hotter brother."

Well, that's a new one.

"*Seriously*?" came Tabby's voice without the distortion of a cellphone speaker. "Is he looking to buy or sell?"

"I … I didn't ask, okay? I couldn't say anything to him. You know how I get around gorgeous guys. I just … I can't even with them."

Tabby sighed in the way I would've expected her to. Impatiently. "He can't be *that* good-looking, Jess, come on."

Wheels scraped against solid wood and footsteps came closer to the door. A shadowed silhouette came into view and I quickly turned around to study pictures of house listings on the wall behind me. I noted that her name was only associated with one, and as the door opened, I started to wonder what the hell I'd been thinking, coming in here instead of the coffee shop.

"Excuse me," she said in a friendly but assertive voice. "So sorry to keep you waiting. My associate is a little, uh, preoccupied with other clients."

When I turned around, I found myself wishing Jessica had in fact been Tabby. Because *this* woman would most definitely be a distraction, with her form-fitting black top and hip-hugging, wide-legged black pants.

"It's fine," I replied, my lips curling into a smile, and her features immediately fell with instant recognition.

"*Sebastian?*" she questioned, crossing her arms over her chest and tipping her head to cascade her long, auburn braid over a shoulder. She made no secret of looking me over, narrowing her eyes and pinching her lips, as I casually stuffed my hands into my jeans pockets. "*Why* are you here?"

"You *know* him?" Jessica chimed in from behind Tabby as she peered over her shoulder. "How the hell do you know *him*?"

Never being one to bite my tongue, I shrugged with nonchalance and tipped my head back to admire the ceiling. "I saw the office, so I thought I'd stop in."

"This is *incredibly* inappropriate," Tabby reprimanded. "I asked you to wait for me at the coffee shop and you *deliberately*—"

"Do you talk to everyone like this?" I asked, dropping my gaze back to hers. Using my dislike toward her tone to cover the fact that I very much liked looking at her and her big emerald eyes.

"Excuse me?" Her arms crossed tighter.

"Do you talk to everyone like they're little kids?"

With widened eyes and puckered lips, Jessica slid back to her desk with the stealth of a ninja, revealing that few people crossed Tabitha Clarke. I smirked, cocking my head and holding Tabby's stare.

Watching the contracting muscles of her throat as she swallowed her pride, she inhaled and exhaled with the forming of a forced little smile. "I just like things to go according to plan."

Her tone was tense and controlled. She was angry, trying to disguise it with a tight-lipped grin, but her feelings were made apparent in the reddened tips of her several-times-pierced ears. Flitting my gaze to the hoops curving around the outer shell of each ear, I quickly counted. Seven in each. A high number for a straight-laced professional.

Curling my lips into a lopsided smile, I nodded slowly. "Then allow me to apologize for inconveniencing your schedule, Tabby. I'll just be on my way and meet you in," I lifted my arm to take a peek at my watch, "fourteen minutes."

A hot flame flickered in the irises of her green eyes, as fiery as the red in her hair. I was knowingly pushing buttons and it was reckless, given the stakes. She held the key to a relationship with the son I never knew existed, and here I was, playing with fire.

Backpedaling, I cleared my throat. "I could order for us, while I wait," I offered, emphasizing the kind lilt in my tone with a nod of my chin. "Anything in particular you'd like?"

Inhaling another dose of calm, she bobbed her head once. "A low-fat vanilla latte, please."

"You got it." I turned on my heel, dropping my gaze to her feet. Pointy beige stilettos that could probably kill me if she tried.

Nodding politely at Jessica, I tapped my fingers on her desk. "Nice to meet you, Jess. See you around."

She nodded slowly, following my every step with lust-filled eyes. "Bye, Thor."

5

tabby

"Who is *that*?" Jess blurted, her gaze still glued to his ass as he jogged across the street.

"It's a long story," I grumbled through clenched teeth. It really wasn't. There was nothing long in simply stating that he was the recently discovered father of Sam's child. But getting into it meant to further linger on the situation and I had other things to mull over.

Like, how he was exactly what I hoped he wouldn't be.

"Oh no, Tabs. You can't have a guy like *that* walk in here without dropping some details. *How* do you know him?"

"Sam used to know him," I loosely explained, heading back into my office.

"Ooh," I listened to Jess drawl from her desk, bouncing the rubbery eraser of a pencil against the wooden surface. "Yeah, that makes sense. He looks like a Sam kinda guy."

Truer words had never been spoken.

I wasn't surprised that, sixteen years ago, my sister had met a rocker with tattoos, long hair and ripped jeans, and had a one-night stand. It's what she did back then, before having Greyson forced her to slow down a little. But what surprised me was that this guy *still* had the long hair and ripped jeans. I guess there wasn't much he could do about the tattoos painting his arms and God knows where else, but there wasn't much to separate this man from a boy.

What I hated even more, was how good he made it look, how *easy*. How it was simply a part of who he was, on the road or otherwise. Nothing had forced him to grow up. He was allowed to live in a permanent bubble of adolescence for all of eternity, with nothing but some fine lines at the corners of his eyes to give away the decades of life.

I was jealous. I hated being jealous.

"Okay, but seriously though, Tabs. Did you get a glimpse at his ass?" Jess stood in the doorway of my office, gripping an energy drink in her palm.

"Do I need to remind you that you're married?" I grumbled, dropping into my office chair and rifling through some papers on my desk.

"My husband doesn't have an ass like that," she reasoned, sipping her drink before pursing her lips. "Doesn't hurt to look, right? You think he's single?"

55

"I have no idea, Jess." I huffed my irritation and pulled out the guest list from the open house.

Eleven people in all had shown up to check out Mrs. Worthington's house. Several had shown a vague interest in it, and I thought at least a couple of them would call today with an offer. None of them had. The phone had been silent all day save for the call from Sebastian. All wasn't lost, not yet, but the inkling of hope was fading at a rapid pace.

"I need to sell this house," I muttered to myself, forgetting momentarily that Jess was still in the doorway.

"Maybe you could give it to Alex?" she offered gently, wincing apologetically. She knew how much I hated to give up, so much that I never had yet. But after more than six months of trying to sell the damn place, I guess she knew as well as I that the clock was ticking. Sooner rather than later, I'd have to admit defeat.

"Maybe," I agreed reluctantly. "I just can't understand what's wrong with this place. I don't get it."

"It's a beautiful house," Jess sympathized with a slight shake of her head. "I'd offer to give it a shot but—"

Jess didn't like selling the old homes. There was more convincing involved that she could never handle. Bargaining wasn't her strong point, and because of this, she stuck with new construction.

"No, it's okay," I released a rueful sigh and checked the clock on the wall. "I guess I should head down to the freakin' coffee shop."

I hated the tone of my voice. I should've been grateful that this guy, a total stranger, had driven all this

56

way to meet with me. I just couldn't shake that I'd expected so much more from the attractive voice on the phone. Like some initial semblance of maturity upon meeting.

"Okay," Jess nodded, heading back to her desk as I stood up to grab my purse. "Don't come back pregnant, okay? Although if you did—"

Groaning under my breath, I left my office, sliding my bag over my shoulder. "You really have no idea how unfunny that really is."

"I'm just saying, that guy could easily impregnate me by just *glancing* in my direction," she defended, holding her hands in front of her chest as she sat down. "That's *all* I'm saying."

***

Sebastian sat on one of the coffee shop's puffy leather couches, his knees spread as far as they would go, tapping his fingers against his thigh while scrolling through his phone. I pinched my eyes closed, held my head high and made the decision, once and for all, to be nice.

Walking through the door, I approached him with confidence, outstretching my hand and inclining my head. "Sebastian."

At the sound of his name, he turned his head and stood up to reach out and grasp my hand. "Tabby," he greeted me with a nod of his head, squeezing my palm in his. Just firm enough to be assertive and strong. "Sorry about that before."

57

I allowed myself a search of his eyes, seeking sincerity in his gaze and finding it within the melted chocolate pools of his irises. "It's okay," I replied, my gaze unwavering. "Let's sit."

Releasing my hand from his, he waited as I sat down, shocking me with the gentlemanly gesture. I crossed my legs and reached toward the latte he had generously bought for me.

"Thank you," I raised the cup to him as he sat beside me. Close enough for his knee to brush against mine.

"Oh," he shook his head, lifting a dismissive hand. "It's fine."

Taking a sip, I enjoyed a moment of refreshing silence. A chance to quickly rehearse my next words, and allow myself a few seconds to fall into the calm of the acoustic café music.

"This is a fucking great song," Sebastian blurted, tearing me from my serene coffee moment.

With a harsh swallow, I put the mug back on the table. "I don't know it."

"Mm," he grunted with a thoughtful scowl, pointing one finger into the air. "This is John Mayer. You gotta know John Mayer."

With a single bob of my head, I replied, "I do."

"This one's called 'Slow Dancing In A Burning Room.' I've heard this song nearly every fucking night for the past few months," he informed me, nodding his head to the tune. "It's a good one, but you know what's funny about it?"

I shook my head without the least bit of interest in what he was saying. "What?"

With a chuckle that wormed its way through my ears and into every part of my body until it reached my toes, he replied, "Every single night, I'd watch couples in the crowd start making out and slow dancing to this like it's some beautiful love song. But it's not. It's about a relationship that's falling apart." He closed his eyes and sang a few lines in a husky voice that made talking feel like sex, then added, "But damn, it's a fucking great song."

Clearing my throat, I shifted my thighs, and pushed my brain beyond the focal point between my legs. "You're a, uh … groupie of his?"

Quickly snapping his eyes open, he shot me a narrowed glance. "A *groupie*? I told you, I'm a drummer."

"I know that," I replied brusquely. "But you said you've heard that song every night, so …"

One side of his perfectly symmetrical mouth curled upward as he shook his head. Criticizing me with a smile. "I play for the band that opened for him, sweetheart."

I wanted to berate him for the bold use of a pet name. His superior tone left a heated dread coiling in my belly, warning me against getting closer to him. But I didn't scold him; I couldn't. Not after I'd already acted like a control freak at the office.

Pursing my lips and swallowing the vile words rising in my throat, I tipped my head, eyeing him with intrigue. "What band?"

"Ever heard of Devin O'Leary?"

"Uh, yes, actually. I have," I widened my eyes, surprised by the strange turn of events. "He's Greyson's favorite."

Sebastian cocked a brow as he leaned forward, pressing his tattooed elbows to what were probably tattooed knees. Eyeing me intently, I imagined him undressing me with those chocolate-covered eyes, peeling back the layers to find the screaming girl inside. I could've been dressed in a parka and ski pants and I still would've felt naked and vulnerable.

"Get the hell out."

"Seriously. He loves him. And you're ..." Recollection practically smacked me in the forehead. "Wait a minute. You're *that* Sebastian Moore?"

"Is there another I don't know about?" His teeth sunk into the fullness of his bottom lip, now thoroughly amused by my surprise and amounting excitement.

"No, no, no," I chanted, shaking my head and pressing my hands to my cheeks. "Greyson is *obsessed* with you. You don't even understand. He started playing the drums several years ago because of *you*."

Twisting his mouth into a contemplative frown, he slowly bobbed his head. "You're serious about this?" He lifted his eyebrows with the question.

I nodded eagerly, knowing for certain there was no way I was letting this guy get away. Even if my body did want me to get a restraining order and move two countries over.

"He loves you," I stated plainly.

"Well, shit," he replied, stunned and startled. "When the hell do I get to meet him?"

6

sebastian

My own eagerness surprised the shit out of me. I knew I had entertained the fantasy of family, someone to greet me at home after a long quarter-year on the road. But I thought that's all it was—a fantasy. I never expected that the moment it became a reality, I'd be so ready to jump into the daddy role.

Apparently, Tabby wasn't so eager to toss me into it either. I read it in the tight downward curl of her lips and tense cock of her head. The swaying of her stilettoed foot had stopped and now it was still. Frozen.

The woman was a goddamn statue.

"*Or*," I backpedaled, "I could wait."

She reanimated with a shake of her head. "No, it's not …"

Her words faded into the Counting Crows tune now playing in the background. I could imagine what she

61

intended to say: *It's not you.* But it *was.* I was a stranger. The kid didn't know me. I'd been absent from his life for fifteen years. How the hell could I expect to just drop myself into his life now without warning?

"I think we should ease him into it," she decided after a few moments of silence. "He doesn't need to know right away that you're his—"

"Oh, so when do you think that'd be a good idea, exactly? When he's already attached? 'Cause God, that'd be fucking awesome. 'Oh, hey, kid, by the way! You know, we've been getting along swimmingly for the past six months, and I thought I'd just break it to you over s'mores, that you're also my kid. Oh, what's that? Yeah, I've been lying to you. Uh-huh, yep, your aunt thought it'd be—'"

With her lips pressed firmly together, she shut me up with a single glance. It didn't take a body language specialist to know that Tabby didn't like being told what to do. I couldn't imagine how this woman, designed to thrive in her structure and control, was managing with a fifteen-year-old kid. It'd been a while since I was that young, but fuck, I remember enough to know I was a little rebelling bastard. The talking back, the power struggles, and the hormonal outbursts.

"I get it," she practically growled under her breath before releasing her fiery exhale.

She reached forward and daintily picked up the porcelain cup. As she sipped lightly, I was scheming. Plotting ways to unravel all of those tightly bound layers and reveal the disaster undoubtedly underneath. To dirty her up and make her live. She needed a slice of greasy pizza. A big fucking hamburger. Buffalo wings. Hard-shell tacos. God, some cookie crumbs would've been refreshing right about now, just to see her relax, as she placed the mug back on the table and repositioned her carefully crossed legs.

Or maybe, she really just needs to be fucked. I swallowed and blinked away the thought, hoping my dick would get the memo.

"Maybe you're right," she admitted with a notable amount of reluctance. "Maybe it'd be best to just … get it over with right away."

Pressing my hand to my chest, I tipped my head with exaggerated compassion. "Tabby, I know that must've taken so much for you to say. Thank you. Just …" I wiped away a phantom tear. "Thank you so much."

One groomed brow twitched as her emerald eyes squinted in my direction. I wondered what her laugh sounded like. If she had one.

"You drive your bandmates insane, don't you?" she asked astutely, shaking her head.

I shrugged, quirking my lips into a smug grin. "It's a gift."

"Sure it is." So curt. So sharp. "Maybe you could meet Greyson tonight, if you aren't busy. He'd probably love it."

"Ah, well, I thought I'd head downtown for some good ol' cow tippin', but if you're gonna twist my arm, I guess I could clear my schedule," I deadpanned with a straight face, and hot damn, there might've been the faintest glimmer of amusement twinkling in those gemstone eyes.

63

"Great. I pick him up from school at three, so maybe you could meet us for dinner," she said, reaching for her purse and pulling out a planner.

"Wait, are you actually penciling me in?"

"I don't want to forget," she explained pointedly, pulling a pen from the spiral binding.

"You would actually forget dinner plans a few hours after making them?" I cocked a disbelieving brow, but when she turned to me with her stony expression, I relented. "Well, shit. Okay. You know, they have these cellphone apps that help with memory loss. My mom—"

"How does five work for you?" Her words carried along her irritated sigh.

Gripping the back of my neck and squeezing, I tipped my head. "Hmm … yeah, I guess I can fit you in between watching the grass grow and—"

"Great." She snapped her planner shut and stuffed it back into her bag before turning to me. "Can I be very honest with you for a moment?"

"God, *please*," I breathed with relief. "I thrive on honesty. Unless I'm bullshitting."

"I'm sure you think you're charming and funny, and I'm fairly certain this obnoxiously arrogant, rock star thing gets you laid on a regular basis," she raked her scrutinizing glare over me. "But in the short time I've known you, I can very plainly tell that you reached the age of thirteen and there, your personality and maturity have stayed. If I wasn't at my wit's end, I honestly wouldn't want you anywhere near my nephew. But, because I'm desperate, I'm willing to give this a chance."

I raised my eyebrows with honest intrigue as she continued, "But you are on a probation period, Mr. Morrison or *Moore*—whatever your name is. So, if you do *anything* to influence him negatively or hurt him in *any* way, I reserve the right to demand you remove yourself from his life. And I really don't care how much he admires you professionally. The last thing that kid needs is for some flaky man-child to break his heart. Do you understand me?"

By all accounts, I should've been infuriated by her feisty little speech. I should have stood up and announced that the next time she saw me, it'd be in court. Yet I wasn't mad, nor was I going to make any threats. Because, underneath that cast-iron exterior, was a woman who cared about her nephew and only wanted to help him. And because she'd been so refreshingly and beautifully honest.

Leaning toward her, the creak of leather slicing through the silence around us, I brought my eyes within centimeters of hers. Our foreheads nearly touched and the bitter coffee floating on her hot breath tickled against my lips, so strong I could almost taste it.

"You should let yourself be honest more often," I whispered, as I watched the unrelenting stone in her features begin to chip.

***

Hog Hill was, for lack of a better phrase, total shit.

The town had a coffee shop, one real estate agency, a library, an Italian restaurant, and a drive-thru burger joint I'd never heard of called Billy's Beef & Buns. That was the extent of their exciting downtown, while the rest of the place seemed to consist of mostly farmland, a few blocks of appealing suburbia, and a Wal-Mart.

No wonder a kid around here would go insane. There was nothing to do, unless they had some killer afterschool reading programs at the library. But I wasn't holding my breath.

Finding myself a bench near the library, I sat down, outstretched my legs and pulled out my phone. After dialing Devin's number, I pressed the phone to my ear and waited for my friend to answer.

"Yo man, missing me already?" Dev chuckled.

"You know it, baby," I replied with a grunted laugh of my own. The friendly banter was short-lived though as I thrust a hand into my hair and tipped my head back to stare at the cloudless mid-May sky. "You got a minute?"

"Yeah, sure. I'm just watching TV while Livy takes a nap."

"No Ky today?" I closed my eyes, enjoying the warmth of the sun on my face.

"Nah, she's shopping with her friend Brooke," he explained. "So, what's up?"

I was moments away from admitting my current state of affairs to another person. There was a surreal element to the whole ordeal, like it was happening to someone else and I was just an innocent bystander, looking in from the outside.

"So, uh ... I kinda found out that I have a kid," I announced unceremoniously.

Devin's laugh burst through the phone. "What the fuck, dude! Are you serious?"

I felt every muscle and bone in my throat shift as I swallowed. "Yeah, I'm serious, man."

Composing himself and coughing, Dev replied, "Get the hell out of here. What happened?"

"Uh, well, about sixteen years ago, I got a chick pregnant. She told me she was having an abortion, but apparently, she didn't." I shook my head, still in disbelief that this was my reality. "She died two months ago, and her sister found me."

"Holy fuck," Devin muttered after enough moments of silence to leave me feeling sick. "Where are you?"

"The greatest place on Earth," I joked. "Hog Hill, New York."

"Where the hell is that?" he grunted around a chuckle.

"Exactly," I muttered, shaking my head. "This chick, the sister, Tabby, is apparently having one hell of a time with the kid. I guess she thought I might be able to help, and I'm really hoping I can. I just kinda don't know what the fuck I'm doing."

"Ah, bro, you'll be fine," Dev assured me. "Just be yourself. Any kid would love you. I mean, Livy does."

I grunted. "Yeah, well, Tabby doesn't seem to agree. She chewed me out for being an immature, washed-up, arrogant asshole just a little while ago," I laughed, thrusting my hand into my hair.

Devin joined me in laughing. "Wow. She's a bitch?"

"Kinda, but you know, it also turned me on," I admitted, still laughing. "Doesn't help that she's smokin' hot, man. She's got this sexy professional thing going on."

"Jesus Christ," he chuckled, his laughter quelling. "Keep it in your pants."

"Yeah," I agreed reluctantly, nodding. "You're probably right."

A tinny baby's cry came through the phone and my mouth curled into a smile. *Livy*. Devin sighed. "Gotta go, Seb. Keep me posted, okay?"

I nodded into the bright sunshine. "You got it."

"And hey, good luck," he concluded, hanging up.

I grunted with a bob of my head.

Good luck. Yeah. I was gonna need it.

7

tabby

"Do you need booze?" Jess asked, standing in the open doorway of my office. "'Cause you really look like you need booze."

The heels of my palms continued to press into my eyes as I groaned. "I don't need alcohol, Jess."

"I know you're *saying* that, but you really, really look desperate," she insisted. "You know, my brother smokes weed when he gets too stressed out, and let me tell you, it does the trick. Sometimes getting high is *exactly* what you need to—"

Dropping my hands to my desk, I stared at her with incredulity. "I'm *not* stressed."

Jess pressed a hip into the doorframe and cocked her head, pursing her lips with a dose of her own disbelief. "Yeah. Right. And Alex isn't a flaming homosexual."

"Loud and proud, honey!" Alex crowed as he approached Jess, taking a place next to her in the doorway. "Look at our poor little girl. I think cocktails are in order, what do you say?"

"I *can't*," I persisted, shifting my glare from one employee to the other. "I have dinner plans tonight."

Jess's jaw flopped open. "Oh my God, tell me you're going out with Thor."

"Thor?" Alex asked, pinching his brows.

With a zealous twirl on her heel, Jess pressed her palms against the lavender breast of Alex's button-down dress shirt. "You missed it. This guy walked in earlier looking for Tabitha. He had to be *at least* six-two, with a blonde man-bun, *gorgeous* brown eyes, ink *everywhere*, and muscles for days. Total panty-dropper."

"Jeez, Jess," I gawked with a shake of my head. "Why don't you just paint a picture for us?"

"Oh, please do," Alex nodded encouragingly. He dipped his head to stare into Jess's eager eyes. "Did you happen to snap a pic of this fine specimen?"

An exaggerated pout puffed out Jess's bottom lip. "I didn't. I was too busy committing his ass to memory, sorry."

Alex turned to me expectantly. "But you're going to dinner with him?"

"I never said that!" My tone jumped an octave and my two colleagues simultaneously cocked their heads. Busted. "It's not what either of you are thinking."

"Well, I mean, sex is good at relieving stress too, so …" Jess shrugged innocently while her eyebrows jumped with the suggestion.

70

I'd be lying if I said I hadn't thought about it. I might've adopted a life of reserve and structure, but I'm not dead and I'd have to be to not pick up on Sebastian's appeal. He oozed of danger and risk—everything exciting—but there wasn't a single characteristic I'd picked up on thus far that said he was a good idea.

Because he wasn't.

"Knock it off," I demanded, my tone hard and serious. "He's not here for me, okay?"

"Oh?" Jess questioned, crossing her arms to ward off the sting of my reprimand. "Then why exactly would a gift from the Nordic gods be walking into your real estate office in Middle of Nowhere, New York?"

I stood up from my desk with more gusto than necessary, sending my chair rolling toward the wall. "Because he's Greyson's fucking father, that's why. I found his information in some of Sam's stuff, and asked him to come here to help me with him, okay? There will be no booze, there will be no pot, and there will certainly be no sex. Now, please, I have some shit to deal with before I have to pick up Greyson and then deal with *his* bullshit before we meet Sebastian for dinner."

It didn't take long for the embarrassment to hit me. My emotions were usually so disciplined but lately I could feel the control slipping from my grasp. It wasn't any surprise that all areas of my life were struggling, and I reminded myself that this was exactly why I had requested help from Sebastian.

Neither Alex or Jess left the office. They just stared with grimaces fixed on their faces.

Clapping a hand to my forehead, I pressed my lids shut. "I'm sorry, guys," I breathed, voice thick with apology as I dropped into my chair.

"Honey," Alex soothed, rushing into the office and around my desk. His gentle hands squeezed my shoulders. "Don't apologize. You've been taking quite the little journey through Hell. We know that, and we understand."

"I know you know," I heaved a sigh and let my head droop forward. "But it doesn't excuse taking it out on you."

"Hold on just one second." Jess hurried away from the office door. I listened as she rifled through some things, while Alex's hands worked expertly at my shoulders. When Jess returned, I wasn't surprised to find her wielding a mini bottle of Grey Goose. "Here. I was saving this for my next sale, but you obviously need it *way* more than I do."

I couldn't remember the last time I had indulged in a drink, whether to numb the pain or otherwise. Every time I thought I might, something diverted my attention and called me away from indulging in a moment of weakness. Now, staring at that tiny bottle of vodka, I thought about my list of responsibilities for the day. Plot the next move on the Worthington house, return a few phone calls, pick up Greyson, and meet Sebastian for dinner. Every single one of them picked away at my nerves and every one added another increment of unneeded stress.

But there was vodka, and it would help.

I outstretched my hand. "Give it here," I demanded with the faintest hint of a grateful smile.

Cracking it open, Jess stepped forward, dangling the open bottle from her fingertips. "I will give this to you, but first you have to promise me something."

"What?" I whined, ready to snatch the bottle away from her.

"You're taking this weekend off."

Flitting my gaze from the bottle to her eyes, I scowled and shook my head fervently. "I can't do that!"

"Yes. You. Can," Alex insisted, squeezing my shoulders with every syllable. "We can handle things over here. You haven't taken time off in ... well, shit, I can't remember the last time you took a break."

There was truth in that. Even throughout the tragedies of the past year, I never took an entire day off work. Between funerals and wakes, I was always stopping into the office and checking on business. Even if it was only to make sure we had enough paper cups at the water cooler. Anything to tear me away from the emotional hell I would never allow myself to succumb to.

"I don't know, guys," I sighed, unable to submit that easily.

"It *isn't* a suggestion." Jess shook her head, waving the bottle in front of my eyes. Hypnotizing me with liquid courage. "I don't care if all you do is binge *Outlander* and get completely plastered. You're taking a long weekend to do what you haven't been doing all year."

"Oh, it's a *long* weekend now?" I grunted bitterly. "And what is it that I haven't been doing?"

Alex lowered his lips to my ear and whispered, "Taking care of *yourself.*"

"Fine," I groused, snatching the bottle away from Jess's waving hand. "I'll take the weekend."

"And you're not allowed to call," Jess tacked on, pointing one little finger at me.

With the bottle tipped to my lips, I narrowed my eyes at her. "We'll see."

***

While parked outside of Greyson's school, I lifted my planner to scan over the scribbled appointments and reminders.

After indulging in the miniature bottle of Grey Goose, sipping it slowly while listening to music with my door closed, I had focused on the Worthington house. During the months I'd spent trying to sell the place, I had become emotionally invested in it. The more I lingered on it, the sadder it made me. When I looked at it and its solid brick exterior, I couldn't imagine anybody not falling in love with it; I certainly had. Stepping inside, you couldn't help but gasp at the beauty in every inch of craftsmanship that went into constructing the home from the inside out. From the winding staircase in the entryway to the delicate floral design in the parqueted floors, it was all utterly breathtaking.

Hell, if I had the money, I'd buy it myself.

In real estate though, the problem was always what was hiding within the walls. The weighted sadness hidden in the framework was something you couldn't fumigate or exterminate. No contractor on the planet possessed the ability to remove the fingerprint of tragedy and history, and I was convinced that every potential buyer could feel it.

Initially, I thought it was just me. Being no stranger to the heavy burden of loss, I picked up on it right away, as I stepped inside from the creaking old porch. I knew immediately that Mr. Worthington had died in that house, joining the other ghosts that dwelled in every groan of a floorboard or squeal of a door hinge. Things like that didn't bother me. It added history and character, but I soon realized that I was very alone in feeling that way.

I sighed and closed my planner. The perfect buyer was out there. I just wasn't sure that I was the one to find him or her, and the thought of giving up felt like treason.

Greyson wrenched the car door open and practically threw himself into the passenger seat. Spotting the slip of paper clenched in his hand, I immediately assumed it was another ill-mannered joke from his so-called friends. I wrenched it from his grasp and widened my eyes immediately at the bold black letters printed on the grey paper.

"In-school suspension?" I gasped with exasperation. "Greyson! What *happened*?"

"Nothing," was his muffled reply, his fist pressed to his lips as he stared out the window.

"Uh, well, excuse me but this doesn't look like *nothing*," I snapped in reply. "You're going to tell me right now what you did to get yourself suspended."

Greyson twisted his neck abruptly, bitterness searing the eyes that suddenly looked so much like Sebastian's. "I got into a fight, okay? I punched—"

"*You punched someone?*" My exhale barreled from my chest, leaving me empty and aching. "Why? Why the hell would you do that?"

Greyson wasn't a violent kid. Never had been. For him to act out physically only meant that he'd been pushed past his breaking point. And I hadn't seen it coming. How had I not seen it coming?

God, Sam, what the hell am I doing to him?

"Because ..." His explanation faded with the crack in his voice. His eyes brimming with tears and lips pinching with the determination not to give in.

"Grey." I reached across the car, gripping his knee and squeezing reassuringly. "I'm not mad, okay? Just tell me what happened."

"Jason called Mom a whore." His whisper seemed to echo through the car's interior. The muscles in his throat worked as he tipped his head against the seat to stare at the ceiling. "So, I fucking punched him. Okay? That's what happened."

Another deflating exhale escaped my tired lungs as I slumped into my seat. *Whore* was such a harsh word, and the guilt of having accused my sister of being one myself swept over me. Memories of the night she announced her pregnancy plundered my mind with the terrible things that were said. The knee-jerk reactions that came in the form of hurtful insults.

"Greyson ..." Volume couldn't reach my voice past the lump of foreboding emotion. "I hope you know that's not true."

"Yeah, well," he sucked in his emotion, replacing his tears with a face of stone, "she was fucking his dad that night, so I guess he would know better than me."

I couldn't help my gasp. I knew Sam had been out with a guy that night, and thanks to the toxicology report, I knew she'd been drinking with him. What I didn't know was that she'd been with the father of a kid from Greyson's school, and I twisted my lips with a quick snap of anger. My sister had gotten around, God knows, but she'd always seemed to keep her impulses in check around the school parents.

Lifting a hand to my mouth and clutching my lips in its grasp, I stared out the window toward nothing at all, still gripping the in-school suspension notice in my hand.

"We've had one hell of a year, Grey," I found myself saying, disbelief shaking my head.

"Yeah, no shit," he mumbled, dropping his gaze to the twisting fingers on his lap.

"I wish I could tell you it was going to get better," I replied ruefully. "But I have to tell you something."

Greyson turned to me with the pain of someone beyond his years. "What?"

I reached out with a trembling hand and brushed a spray of blonde from his forehead. I made an attempt at a brave smile only to grimace in anticipation of an outburst that would likely send our world into yet another crisis, and I whispered, "I found your dad."

8

sebastian

Tabby had planned to meet me at Poco Bella, the Italian restaurant in town. It was positioned only a few storefronts down from her office, and as I walked from where I'd parked the truck, I noticed the darkened windows of TC Real Estate. I wondered what she and Greyson were doing to occupy themselves in the stretch of time between school and meeting me at the restaurant. I wondered where they lived, what their house looked like, and what it must be like to have someone to come home to.

Opening the restaurant door, I was struck immediately with the collision of garlic and tomato sauce. A low, grumbled complaint came from my stomach as I gave the hostess my name and the size of my party, and took a quick glance at the bar. It was tempting to spend the wait filling my gut with liquid bravery. But, remembering Tabby and her close-mindedness, I thought better of it. Last thing I needed was for her to accuse me of being a drunk.

So, instead I sat down in the restaurant's dimly lit waiting area, tapping my fingers to an ironic cover of Billy Joel's "Piano Man," played only with an acoustic guitar. I glanced at my watch three times in a thirty second span, bouncing my knee and wondering if I should've brought something for the kid. A gift, a peace offering, a bribe. *Something*.

I realized I was nervous. When the hell was the last time I'd honestly been nervous about anything? Sure, I used to be, back in the beginning of my music career. I would look out into the crowd from backstage and want to puke on whoever or whatever was closest to me. It was stage fright at its finest, but after performing a few hundred times, I had worked my way through it until it was now second nature.

Hell, even the brief situation with Sam hadn't made me nervous. Panicked? Yes. Sad? Yes. Heartbroken? It was the only time I ever was. But *nervous*? Nah. No reason to be. What was done was done.

But meeting this kid … I was nervous about that. What if he hated me? I know Tabby said he admired me, and that I was the reason he took drum lessons. But, liking someone as a hero and as a person, are two completely different animals.

"Sebastian?" I looked up to find the hostess clutching three menus under one arm and sweeping the other toward the dining area. "Your table is ready."

"Awesome," I replied with a cheerful façade, standing up on jelly legs and following her through the open doorway.

Three place settings were presented to me at a round table and my heart sped up to a canter. No matter where I sat, I'd be next to both of them. Outnumbered. Tag-teamed.

"Is everything okay?"

I glanced beside me at the young brunette, her big blue eyes fixated intently on my face. She was cute, most likely legal, and if I wasn't focused so hard on holding the coffee I'd consumed earlier in my stomach, I probably would've hit on her. A little innocent flirting would've done me some good. Just to give myself a distraction. But God, that vanilla cold brew just wouldn't stop threatening.

"Yeah, everything's great." I grinned confidently, pulling out a chair and sitting myself down. "Could I maybe get some water?"

"Of course," she replied with her own smile and a bow of her head as she doled out the menus. "I'll send your waitress over right away."

"Perfect." I opened the menu with a grateful smile in her direction before turning my gaze to the items listed in scrawling cursive. *Fancy.* I guess Hog Hill needed its upscale joint to play contrast to Billy's Beef & Buns. Billy's was probably more my speed, to be honest. But I had let Tabby pick, and this place seemed right up her high-brow alley.

After settling on the filet mignon, I puffed out a sigh, and checked my watch for the sixth time since I'd arrived. Tabby said five and it was now a quarter after. The woman didn't seem like the type to sleep in, let alone miss an appointment, even if it was with a long-haired hoodlum like me. I questioned if I should call her and make sure we were still on, when the door to the restaurant opened some feet behind me.

My sense of hearing was acute, listening intently to the shuffling of feet and the hostess asking how many were in their party.

"We're meeting someone," I heard Tabby say, and that was my cue.

With a tightly knotted bundle of nerves clawing at the walls of my gut, I pushed out my chair and stood from the table. I might've been a dick, but I wasn't without manners, and I turned to face the door.

"Ah, there he is," Tabby told the hostess, stepping forward to greet me with a handshake, but my eyes weren't on her.

They were on the kid.

Tall and blonde, with a familiar cut to his jaw and dark brown eyes. It didn't matter that I couldn't for the life of me remember what his mother looked like. This kid was every little bit my clone, at least on the outside, and I couldn't help the sobering wash of warmth that overcame me at the sight of him.

Hell, I might even call it love at first sight.

"Sebastian," Tabby injected my thoughts with her sharp tone, and I reluctantly diverted my eyes from him to meet her gaze. "It's good to see you again."

This woman was probably good at a lot of things. Like, being neat and proficient. But lying was not one of them. A muscle in her smooth jawline twitched as I accepted her outstretched hand.

"You're late." I couldn't help myself. The jab had landed at my feet and I grasped it.

Sliding her hand from mine, her wry smile didn't meet the narrowed glare in her eyes. "We had some issues to deal with first. Took longer than expected. But thank you for waiting."

The dirty look in her eyes transformed itself into something pleasant as she turned her head to face the kid still standing near the door. His face remained tipped downward, unable to look at me. I was closer than I thought I'd ever be in the physical sense, but this inability to accept my presence made me feel further than I had when I thought he was gone.

"Sebastian, I want you to meet Greyson," Tabby introduced with waving fingers reaching out to him.

I watched the expansion of his chest as he finally slid his eyes upward to take in my face. God, it was impossible to deny the resemblance. Every second I stared at him, it rattled my soul a little more. Knowing that he'd been a fan of mine made me wonder if he had ever noticed it himself.

"Hi, Greyson," I rasped breathlessly. When had my lungs stopped working? Forcing an inhale, I stepped forward past Tabby and extended my hand. "I'm really happy you're here."

Greyson eyed my hand but didn't take it. "Aunt Tabs says you didn't know I existed."

I dropped my hand to my side, clenching it into a fist as I shook my head regretfully. "No, I didn't," I admitted.

"Why don't we sit?" Tabby suggested hastily, moving to grab Greyson by the arm and pulling him gently toward the table. "I'm sure you have tons of questions to ask Sebastian, right?"

"Just one," he mumbled as he dropped into a chair and wrenched his arm from his aunt's grasp.

"Yeah?" I lifted my brows questioningly, as I pulled out Tabby's chair, shocking the crap out of her. "What's that?" I asked, sitting down between them.

Narrowing his eyes to barely open slits and lowering his dark blonde brows, he asked, "Did you love my mom?"

The question hit me like a knife to the ribs. Stabbing. Twisting. I dropped my shameful gaze to the table as Tabby gasped.

"*Greyson*," she hissed through clenched teeth. "That's not appro—"

I shook my head, laying a hand over her shoulder. The touch startled her and halted her words. "No, it's fine," I said. "It's an honest question, and I want him to feel comfortable to say whatever the hell he wants."

Lifting his chin triumphantly, he dared me to answer with eyes that perfectly mirrored my own. "Well? Did you?"

"No," I answered bluntly, without any attempt to soften the blow.

"So, she *was* a whore," Greyson replied, turning to his aunt. "I was suspended for nothing."

84

"Greyson!" Tabby's green eyes flashed with embarrassment and anger.

Holding my hands up from the table, palms out, I narrowed my eyes at him and Tabby. "Whoa, wait a minute. *What*?"

As if I wasn't there, Greyson kept his glare on his aunt. "Mom *was* a whore," he repeated with a tenacity that disturbed me. "She slept around. Jason said so, and he was right."

Tabby's mortification was overpowered by her frustration. "You will not talk about your mother like that, do you understand me?"

"But you can't say it isn't true!" Greyson shouted at her.

Turning to me, he screwed his mouth up and glowered with something dangerously close to hatred. "Do you even remember her, you asshole?"

Never before had I faced penance for my fondness for casual sex. I wasn't a complete bastard, *no means no* and all that. I enjoyed sex with women who enjoyed it as much as I did. A mutual understanding to enjoy each other without any strings attached. But now, I sat across from a consequence—a proverbial string—of all those one-night stands. Their faces had all faded from my memory, including hers, but this kid's face was my own. It was a sudden and bitter reminder of a night I had long forgotten.

"Not really," I replied hoarsely.

With those two little words, Greyson pushed away from the table and stood up. He walked to the door and left the building. I managed to keep my cool, straight-

85

faced façade, with only my thundering heart giving away my persistent nerves.

Tabby turned abruptly, staring at me with earnest disgust. "You couldn't even *lie*?"

"Oh, yeah, you know, you're right," I pinched my brows and nodded thoughtfully. "I should've told him that his mom and I were madly in love with each other and that I've dreamt of her every night since we—"

"Okay," she growled under her breath, gripping the edge of the table. "I get it. But you didn't have to answer him *at all*."

"Maybe not," I agreed, shifting my gaze from the empty seat to her face. "But here's the thing, Tabby; I spent a very long time wishing he was alive so that I could talk to him, period. So, if I have the chance to answer one of his questions, as shitty as the answer might be, I'm going to, and I'm gonna do it honestly."

Her features loosened as she laid her palms on the table. Her stare was fixed on the window, and I turned to peer over my shoulder, to see Greyson standing with his back against the glass.

"He punched a kid in school today," Tabby admitted, her tone tight and constricted.

"Why?" I asked, looking back to her with a raised brow.

"The night Sam died, she was driving home drunk from this other kid's house after sleeping with his father. The kid called Sam a whore." She bit her upper lip, scraping a bit of her lipstick away. "Greyson got himself a week of in-school suspension."

That little bastard.

Something primal whispered from deep within me. Something that only spoke for my parents or sisters, until now. I clenched my fists on the table, not caring that Tabby could see my blanched knuckles.

"What'd they do to the little shit who said it?"

Tabby shrugged a shoulder, pressing her lips together. "Nothing, I'm guessing. I didn't go inside to ask." Her throat bobbed with her swallow as she straightened her slumped shoulders and lifted her chin. "Now you see, though. You see how much he's struggling."

I nodded, unrolling my fists and tapping my fingers against the table. "I do."

Smoothing her top over her stomach, she looked to her hands and away from me. "Maybe you could …" She swallowed again, mustering her courage. "Maybe you could talk to him. Convince him to come inside and eat, and then we'll see what happens from there."

With another glance over my shoulder, I watched the shudder of his shoulders. The kid was crying, just as she said he did. The cracks in his tough disguise were huge, even if he didn't think so with his bold choice of words, and I saw in him someone who was even more alone than me in an empty house.

"Yeah," I nodded. "I'll try."

Just to see what happens.

9

sebastian

"You know, I gotta say," I muttered, stepping outside and squinting up at the sun. "This town fucking blows."

Greyson turned briefly, only to look at my shoes, and then looked back at the sidewalk beneath his feet. I figured any acknowledgement was better than none at all, so I stood beside him, my back pressed to the window.

"I grew up in a shitty little town like this a few hours away from here," I continued, revisiting my small-town childhood for his sake. "Reputations take a long time to die in towns like that. Even now, when I go back to visit my parents, everyone that recognizes me talks about the stupid shit I used to do when I was a kid." I bumped my shoulder against his. "That's why I changed my name from Morrison to Moore. Well, okay, not really, but still. It *would've* been a good reason."

"I really don't care about where you grew up," Greyson grumbled, shooting me with a sideways sneer.

"Hey, well now, there's something we have in common already."

"Whatever," he muttered. "You don't have to do this shit, you know."

"What shit?" I crossed my arms over my chest.

"Bond with me, or whatever you're trying to do," he snickered, lifting his head and stabbing me with his steely glare.

"I'm not," I insisted with my best I-don't-give-a-shit shrug. "I'm just coming out here to make it look like I'm talking to you, because your aunt asked sort of nicely. Whether you come back inside or not is entirely up to you. I don't really give a fuck either way."

"If you didn't give a fuck, you wouldn't have called," the kid replied with the beginnings of a smug grin tugging at his lips.

Nodding slowly, the corners of my mouth tipped downward. "Touché. But if you've already figured out that much, then you must be smart enough to know your mom was no whore."

The comment got to him and a muscle in his jaw twitched. "I know that already."

"Then why'd you let that kid get to you? You could've walked away, ignored him or whatever."

"Because she was my mom!" he shouted, pushing away from the glass.

He took two steps away from me, crossing his arms and standing at the edge of the sidewalk. He waited there, eyeing the line between sidewalk and street, as

89

though he was making the decision to stay or run. When he finally turned around, I saw his expression etched in stone with only the tears brimming in his eyes giving away any emotion.

"I had enough of hearing it," he added. "They've been saying shit most of my life, about her or me not having a dad, and I couldn't take it anymore."

Nodding, I looked him in the eye. "Never said I blamed you, kid. I would've done the same thing." *And you do have a dad*. The words nagged at the tip of my tongue, but I choked them down with a fervent swallow and let myself grin as I asked, "You wanna eat? Because, I don't know about you, but I'm fucking starving."

***

I'm a people person, a people *pleaser*, and there are very few times in my life where I recall the silence being awkward.

Well, it was awkward now.

Tabby silently prodded at her chicken parmesan with the tips of her fork. Greyson scrolled through his phone in between lifting his gaze to me, making sure I was still there. Making sure I was still *me*. I wished there had been an instantaneous comfort between us. You see it sometimes, on those TV shows where the long-lost parent is reunited with their child. They hug, they cry, and they sit down and talk like they never missed a beat. Why couldn't that have happened for us? Why did it feel so unfair that it hadn't?

Sweeping my gaze around the restaurant, I huffed with a weighted breath. If I wanted any semblance of a relationship to form, I needed to connect with these people, and I knew there was no way that was happening with Tabby. Not yet. The woman was sexy in an off-limits kind of way, and we had nothing to talk about. Nothing to bond over.

Besides, I wasn't there for *her*.

So, I clung to the only thing I knew I had with the kid.

"Okay." I hit my hand to the surface of the table, drawing both of their attentions to me. "Favorite drummers. And … go!"

Greyson hesitated, glancing from me and back to his phone, before licking his lips. "Uh …"

"Okay, I'll go first," I offered, steepling my hands and tapping my fingers together. "Dave Grohl, Taylor Hawkins, Chad Smith, and Carter Beauford."

"No Travis Barker?" Tabby chimed in with a challenging squint of her eyes.

Well, this is interesting.

I smirked. "Barker's cool. Fast. Not a favorite though."

"Him or his style?" She folded her arms over her chest, tipping her head.

"His style isn't one I try to channel myself into, no," I countered. "You're a Blink fan?"

Shrugging a shoulder, she tipped her mouth into a questionable smirk. "They're okay. I was just asking. A guy I used to date back in the day was a huge fan of

Blink 182 and Travis Barker. He said he was the best drummer on the planet."

"*Nobody* is the best drummer on the planet." I leaned back in my chair. "Greyson, man, I'm still waiting."

Swallowing, he shrugged and shook his head as though he was clueless, but then he said, "Dave Grohl, Taylor Hawkins, Tony Royster Jr., and, um …" His eyes lifted, settled on mine, and dropped with embarrassment. "You."

"Shit." I grinned, pushing a hand into the length of my hair. "That's quite a list to be included in. Tony Royster? I mean, *shit*, I don't hold a candle to that kid."

"Uh, you come pretty close," Greyson disputed, quirking his lips into a disapproving frown. "I mean, *I* think so anyway."

"Well, thank you." I bowed my head, lifting my mouth into a lopsided smile. "You're a Grohl and Hawkins fan, too. See, I knew I liked you, kid. Didn't know we had the same taste in music, though. You like the Foo Fighters?"

That finally triggered something and detonated the bomb of excitement. Greyson lifted his eyes to mine, nodding adamantly. "Hell yeah!"

"Awesome," I nodded thoughtfully. We were getting somewhere. "Top three favorite Foo songs."

"Oh, crap," Greyson muttered, hit with a nearly impossible question. "Uh … okay, I think I'd pick 'My Hero,' 'Everlong,' and 'Gimme Stitches.' What about you?"

"A couple of classics and an unlikely pick." I nodded, impressed. "Okay. I'd have to agree on

'Everlong.' That song is … about as perfect as a song can get. I'm really into 'Aurora' and 'Arlandria' too. 'Stacked Actors' is up there, but we're just doing three."

Greyson bobbed his head with enthusiasm, practically bouncing in his seat. The difference from before was night and day, and I wondered when he'd last talked about something other than his issues.

"Okay," I said. "Favorite—"

"Wait," Tabby spoke up, leaning forward in her seat. "Why don't *I* get to answer?"

Folding my arms onto the table, I cocked my head. "Well, if you have three favorite Foo songs, then by all means, Ms. Clarke."

Pursing her lips and looking to the small pendant light hanging just above the table, she drew in a deep breath before saying, "Hmm … well, it *is* a tough question, and it usually depends on my mood. But I'd say, on any given day, 'Have It All,' 'M.I.A.,' and 'February Stars' would be my three all-time favorites. *Although*, I will say, 'Everlong' is probably my favorite love song in the world."

Well, shit. Miss Prim and Proper was a fan. A *real* fan. Not just someone who enjoyed a few of the singles, but someone who listened to the albums.

I sucked my teeth, nodding slowly. Taking in the piercings hugging her ears and all of that red hair. "Color me impressed, Tabby."

"Aunt Tabs took me to see the Foo Fighters for my birthday a few years ago," Greyson chimed in while I continued to assess her and all of her layers.

"Oh yeah?" I asked, glancing toward him. "Which show?"

"Citi Field," Tabby told me before cutting a small piece of chicken and popping it into her mouth. "We stayed overnight in New York City. Grey had never been to a concert before."

I'd been to both. "Which night did you go to?"

"Both." There was a bit of conccit in the way she said it, like she was bragging. "We were in the first few rows."

I knew what she was doing. She was showing off, showing me up, but her attempts were snubbed by my curiosity and the growing excitement in my pants.

Nodding, my smirk never fading, I replied, "So was I."

Greyson's jaw nearly hit the table. "You were there?"

"Kid, don't look too surprised. I have seen the Foo Fighters thirty-seven—"

"Forty-two for me," Tabby lifted a hand, and dammit if her smirk wasn't playful.

***

Outside of the restaurant, Tabby was pacing the sidewalk, talking to someone of importance on her cellphone. She kept holding a finger up to Greyson and me as her conversation continued.

"Is it always like this?" I grumbled through the side of my mouth.

With a tired nod, Greyson groaned. "Mm-hmm."

"Mrs. Worthington, I know you wanted to keep the sale of the house more local and community-based, but I think we might have a little more luck if we went to the internet," Tabby prattled into the phone, waving her free hand this way and that. "Yes, I know you don't have a computer ... I know; it's outside of your—well, yes, of course I would oversee the whole thing."

The woman didn't know how to leave her work at the office. That much was abundantly clear, and yet she wondered why the kid wouldn't connect with her. I scoffed to myself, shaking my head with irritated aggravation as she made another pass. I wouldn't call myself an expert with kids, but this was a no-brainer.

A text chimed through on my phone and I slipped it from my pocket. I smiled at Devin's name, missing my friend.

Devin: Hey bro, how did it go with the kid?

Me: Still going. Waiting for his aunt to stop bullshitting on her phone.

Devin: Aunt, huh? The hot one?

From the corner of my eye, I made sure that Greyson wasn't reading my texts before replying.

Me: Man, you have no fucking clue.

Devin: She still think you're an asshole?

Me: Probably. But she's been to forty-something Foo Fighters concerts. I was ready for her to suck my dick right there.

Devin: LMAO. Impressive. Hope you didn't tell her that.

Me: Nah. Kept it to myself.

Devin: Aww. My little boy's growing up.

Devin: How's the kid?

Me: Not sure. He's got that brooding teen thing down pretty well. Except he actually does have shit to brood over.

Me: Gotta go. Aunt's off the phone.

"My client," Tabby told me needlessly as we each pocketed our respective phones. "I've spent nearly a year trying to sell her house."

"Is that a long time?" I asked, not knowing the first thing about real estate.

"It's long for me," she stated matter-of-factly, but the confidence in her tone couldn't hide the glimmer of disappointment in her eyes.

Clearing her throat, Tabby turned to Greyson and reached her hand out to squeeze his shoulder. "We should get back home, kiddo. It's getting late and you have homework."

"Whatever," he muttered in a low, rasped voice as he pushed away from the building and walked toward where I assumed they had parked.

"Are you going to say goodbye?" Tabby warned, pressing a fist to her cocked hip.

Greyson threw a wave over his shoulder as he continued to walk. Tabby huffed irritably and turned to tip her head back, looking up to my eyes.

"Thank you for dinner," she replied with a small, polite smile. "You really didn't have to pay. We could've split—"

"You're kidding, right?" I scoffed and shook my head. "It wasn't a big deal."

With another sigh, she tucked her purse under her arm and extended a hand. "Well, thank you again, Sebastian. I hope Greyson can see you again soon."

Clasping my fingers around hers, I didn't shake. Instead I just held her hand, heated palm to heated palm, and a side of my mouth lifted. "What are you doing tomorrow?"

Taken aback, she pulled her hand from mine, laying it at her side. "*Tomorrow*? I … well, Greyson has school, but I suppose you can see him afterward. Isn't that a lot of driving in only a couple of days though? You don't mind?"

"I'll just stay at a hotel," I shrugged with nonchalance. "I have nothing going on right now."

"O-oh," she stuttered, surprised and flustered. "Do you, um, need the address of a good one in the area?"

"Nah." I shook my head. "I'll just Yelp that shit."

Tabby nodded once. "Well then, I'll make sure Greyson is ready after school."

"Awesome." I tipped my chin, meeting her eyes with mine. "Have a good night, Tabby."

"You too, Sebastian."

10

tabby

"Y ou're seeing Sebastian again after school," I told Greyson, as I stuffed another sorry-looking peanut butter and jelly sandwich into a paper bag.

"Why?" He dropped into a chair at the kitchen table and poked at the corn muffin I'd given him.

"Why not?" I countered with a dash of impatience.

"You don't like him," Greyson snickered, glancing over his shoulder.

"That's not true." It was very true.

"Yeah, okay." Sarcasm dripped from his voice as he turned back to the muffin.

Hurrying to the mirror beside the front door, I swiped on a coat of lipstick and blotted my lips together as I begrudgingly allowed my thoughts to drift to Sebastian.

I wasn't proud to admit that he had lingered in my mind long after I'd fallen asleep the night before, bringing on dreams I would rather keep to myself. My body reacted to him in ways that I found eerily familiar. While we think we leave the past behind, the past never truly leaves us. Types don't change as much as we think they do, and Sebastian was my type through and through. He reminded me of my youth, before work and age and tragedy. He reminded me of guys I used to date, while also reminding me of why I no longer allowed myself to fall victim to those lustful feelings.

Men like him are trouble. They don't want serious. They don't want forever.

Still, Sebastian had surprised me. For someone with the maturity level of a child, he had handled himself well with Greyson, albeit somewhat abrasively. I'd have to talk to him about his choice of language. Greyson might've picked up on some choice words from his mother, who's idea of discipline was having cake for dessert instead of ice cream, but that didn't mean it was appropriate for Sebastian to speak so frankly.

Capping my lipstick, I turned back to Greyson as he basically pecked at the muffin. One crumb at a time.

"Hey, come on," I urged him, hurrying toward my briefcase on the counter. "We need to get going."

"Fine," he huffed, cramming half of the muffin into his mouth as he stood up and threw the other half away.

I felt the creases between my brows forming as my lips curved into a frown. He stood there, staring at me. Challenging. Daring me to scold him for wasting food, for acting out. But, I remembered our therapist and what she had said about allowing him to bully me, or to egg me on, and I squared my shoulders and let it run over me.

Pick your battles.

"Let's go." I pulled my briefcase from the counter and led the way to the front door.

***

"Alex, we're putting the Worthington house online," I announced, as I walked through the door of the agency.

"Oh, *finally*," he groaned, rolling his eyes dramatically. "What'd you have to do to convince her?"

"I lit some candles at Church and promised to never say the Lord's name in vain again," I muttered, my words dripping with sarcasm as I hurried into my office.

"You know, I was just thinking to myself about how hilariously unwitty you are," Alex quipped, his tone dry and flat. "I'm genuinely curious here. That old lady looks at the computer like it's the damn devil."

"I know," I emphasized, dropping into my chair and unclipping my briefcase to pull out my laptop. "But I told her how this area just isn't pulling the number of potential buyers as we'd hoped for from local paper listings alone."

"And that did it?" He tipped his chin, eyeing me with doubt.

"Okay, *and* I promised to run out and grab Sandy a new cage today before stopping by the house," I relented with a roll of my eyes. Alex cackled. "Hey, it was worth it. We'll definitely find a buyer now. I do need for you to

100

run the listing on the usual sites, though. Can you manage it?"

"Honey, just give me the pics and info. Anything to help lighten your load. You're doing enough as it is," he replied softly.

I smiled gratefully. "Thank you." Reaching into my briefcase, I pulled out the sheet of paper with the information he'd need. "And I'll forward the pictures to your email."

"Perfect. I'll get those up today." Alex gave me an affirmative nod, hugging the paper to his chest. "Now, before I run along and do that, why don't you tell me about your dinner with the baby daddy?"

The mention of the words *baby daddy* sent Jess running into my office with enough gusto to help her win a marathon.

"Yes, yes, *yes*! How is Thor?" she asked, her voice thick with enthusiasm and desire.

"Can you stop calling him that?" I grumbled, shaking my head as I powered on the laptop.

"Ooh, she's already getting defensive. I *love* it." Alex exchanged a knowing look with Jess and I resisted the urge to throw my stapler at him.

"Dinner was *fine*," I divulged vaguely, looking from Alex to Jess. "You do realize that I am only the middle man here, right? I'm acting as the mediator for him and Greyson, to help them develop a relationship. That's all."

Alex tipped his mouth to Jess's ear. "So she says," he grumbled in a volume I could hear loud and clear, and Jess giggled airily.

"I'm going to pretend that you didn't say that." I narrowed my glare at them before loosening my brow and picking up my phone. "Now, if you'll excuse me, I need to find a chinchilla cage in the area."

***

Heading out toward my car, I spotted a flash of golden hair from the corner of my eye and turned, assuming immediately that Greyson had skipped school. I wouldn't put it past him, and as I opened my mouth to begin the lecture of the century, I promptly closed it.

"Well, if it isn't Tabby Clarke," Sebastian crooned, holding a to-go cup from the coffee shop in his hand. "Where are you off to in the middle of the workday?"

"Off to see a client," I replied without any intention to keep the conversation moving as I hurried toward my car.

I was horrified to find Sebastian following me, taking long, easy strides to keep up with my power walk. "The one with the chinchilla?"

Faltering in my steps, I turned to him with an accusatory and suspicious glare. "How did you know she has a chinchilla?"

"You were on the phone last night," he explained easily with a shrug.

"Oh. Right." I pulled in a deep breath and continued on my way to the car.

Sebastian kept up.

"So, can I come?"

102

His questions were forward and disconcerting. He didn't know me from a hole in the wall and I don't care how popular he was in the world of music—I didn't know all that much about him either. It rattled me, that he would rather jump straight into forwardness than work his way up to a place of comfort.

"Um, I don't think that's appropriate," I stammered, pulling my keys from a pocket as I approached my car.

"God, you don't think anything's appropriate," he laughed. "But, in this case, you're probably right. I mean, obviously, you're working," he offered with a shake of his head. At himself or at me, I couldn't be sure. "*But ...* I've never pet a chinchilla before and I hear they're *really* fucking soft."

He was unrelenting and infuriating. I turned to insist that he stand down and find something else to keep him occupied until Greyson was out of school, but instead, I made the mistake of taking him in. The breadth of his shoulders, the leather jacket concealing them from my curious gaze. His t-shirt, stretched over the hard-cut muscles of his chest and smoothed over his flat stomach. He had kept his hair down today, instead of that stupid knot, and the gentle late-spring breeze lifted the golden strands from off of his neck. The tattoos imprinted to his skin there winked at me with every gust of wind, and it was a test of my willpower not to launch myself at him.

"The fact that you've never pet a chinchilla doesn't make the situation any more appropriate," I pressed, standing my ground.

His lips twitched to unveil a playful grin as he said, "You must've driven your sister insane."

"Excuse me?" I spat, crossing my arms, my keys dangling from my fingers. "I thought you didn't remember my sister," I accused with a narrowed, stony glare.

"Honestly, no. I don't. When you've slept with as many women as I have, you stop remembering."

"Oh, well, that's *lovely*," I grumbled under my breath, shaking my head. "What a great influence you are."

"Never said I was," he replied pointedly, waggling his brows and smirking smugly. "As I was saying, I don't need to remember your sister to know what type of girl she was. She was bold enough to approach a bunch of guys in a band and agree to a one-night stand. That takes balls, and the fact that you won't allow me to accompany you because it's inappropriate, tells me you have none. So, like I said, you probably drove your sister absolutely insane."

Scouring rage and disgust engulfed my veins in fire. My cheeks burnt with the evidence of my anger and I clenched my fists against my sides. Taking one step forward, my toes nearly touched his as I tipped my head back to glare confidently into his eyes.

"You know absolutely *nothing* about me," I growled, my words pouring like lava from my mouth.

Dipping his head to stab my gaze with his, his features contorted with smug victory. "And yet, I seem to know *exactly* how to get underneath your skin," he boasted before standing again to his full height.

Sucking in breaths to calm myself back down to a reasonable temperament, I dropped my eyes to the pavement beneath my feet.

That's when I noticed our shoes.

It was silly, noticing something as mundane and everyday as *shoes*, especially ones so common. But, both pairs of identical Converse pointed toward each other— black canvas, scuffed and dirty white capped toes—and it irritated me to think it might mean something. That perhaps it had been fate pushing me to uncharacteristically change my shoes in the middle of the workday and switch from my usual heels to something more preferred.

"If you want my honest opinion—"

"I don't," I interjected, still staring at those sneakers.

"Okay. That's fine. But I'm giving it to you anyway."

I pulled my eyes from the ground to look up at him, staring expectantly and hoping he'd get it over with fast. I was already late, no thanks to this nonsense.

At the lift of my chin, he smiled, deepening the lines creasing the corners of his eyes and the sides of his mouth. He smiled a lot. It was apparent in how natural he wore the grin. I didn't know what that was like anymore.

"I think you had to grow up really fast. Probably before you were ready," he assessed with a critical eye, although the grin never wavered. "I think, at one point, you were maybe a lot more like your sister than you let on."

The statement, though true, left me jarred and wondering just how wide those holes in my heart really were. How was it so easy for him to peer inside like that and know something I'd tried so hard to leave behind?

"How do you know that?" The question floated along a whisper, unable to raise my voice. I was too startled. Too shaken.

Pulling a hand from his pocket, he didn't falter in lifting his fingers to tuck some hair behind my ear. His fingertips were rough and callused against my skin, but his touch was expertly gentle, as he slowly traced the curve of that ear. His gaze held mine tightly and my pulse quickened, throbbing at the base of my throat with every beat of my panicked heart. The collection of hoops clicked together with the movement, until he reached my lobe, where he lingered. Gently pinching the skin between his fingers and moving in closely to inspect.

"These are gauged," he determined with a nod, his smirk unrelenting.

I jerked my head back, pulling away from his touch. Unnerved by my sudden movement, he slipped his hand back into his pocket.

"I think somewhere in there, Tabby, there's a badass just dying to come out."

"I'm a badass just the way I am," I countered with my own smirk, untucking the hair from behind my ear.

"Yeah, I'd agree with that," he nodded, sincerity in his eyes, "but I don't think this stuck-up attitude comes as naturally as you'd like to think it does."

I can't keep doing this. I grabbed my phone from my pocket and checked the time. I was going to be late to meet with Mrs. Worthington, and realizing I wasn't

106

going to shake this overanalyzing bastard, I turned to unlock my car and get in.

"Are you coming?" I snapped at him.

With an obnoxious bout of forced enthusiasm, he clapped his hands together, jumping on his toes. "Do you *really* mean it?" His voice oozed obnoxiously with sarcasm and something almost endearing.

"Oh my God, just get in the car," I responded with a dramatic roll of my eyes.

Sebastian rounded the car to get into the passenger side, and as soon as he was seated, his knees hit the dashboard. "What the hell kind of car is this?"

"You can move the seat back," I needlessly instructed.

Reaching to the floor between his legs, he found the lever and pulled, sending the seat back as far as it'd go. And his legs still looked uncomfortably bent.

"Looks bigger on the outside," he muttered, opening the door. "Yeah, this isn't gonna work. Come on, Thumbelina."

"What did you just call me?"

"Thumbelina. You know? Tiny fairy?" He got out of the car.

"Uh, where are you going?" I called after him before he could shut the door behind him.

"We're taking my car," he informed me, as he headed in the direction of a silver Range Rover, before repeating, "Come on."

Something told me I was going to regret this.

11

tabby

"Mrs. Worthington, I am *so* sorry I'm late." I rushed to explain, as I ran into the house with Sebastian on my heels, carrying the new chinchilla cage.

"Oh, Tabitha, where else would I be?" The old woman waved a dismissive hand, her smile never fading. As her sparkling blue eyes lifted to the blonde hulk behind me, she beamed. "Is that Sandy's new abode? Oh, thank you so much for picking it up!"

"Of course! I'm always happy to help, you know that," I reminded her, ensuring my loyalty to the job, and to my friend.

"Will you introduce me to your … companion?" she asked. I had wondered when she would.

With a strengthening breath, I turned to flash hardened eyes at Sebastian, hoping he'd get the memo to behave himself. The sun did nothing to save us from the heat and after hoisting the cage into the trunk of his car, he had stripped the leather jacket off, showcasing the tattoos muraled over his arms. It was difficult not to be distracted by them—tattoos were always a weakness of mine—but I forced myself to keep my gaze upward as I touched a light hand to his arm.

"This is my friend Sebastian." The word *friend* felt wrong on my tongue. It was a lie, but was the truth any better? "He came along to help with the new cage."

"Oh, how nice. Thank you so much, Sebastian. I *do* love that name, you know," Mrs. Worthington replied, folding her hands against her middle. "Mr. Worthington always wanted a son named Sebastian."

"Mr. Worthington has good taste," Sebastian's voice rumbled luxuriously from behind me, and I suppressed a groan.

"He did," Mrs. Worthington nodded with a rueful little smile twitching at her lips. "Can I get either of you something to drink?"

I opened my mouth to speak. "N—"

"Water, please, young lady," Sebastian spoke up. "It's as hot as Satan's scrotum out there."

At the crude comment and his sickeningly charming arrogance, my lips pulled between my teeth, and I bit down with embarrassment, disgust, and anger. On the ride over, I had warned him to behave and keep his mouth shut. I didn't know the man very well, but I already knew him well enough to know he was incapable of following simple directions.

But then, Mrs. Worthington erupted with a bubbly chuckle, a sound I wasn't sure I'd ever heard from her in all the time I'd known her. My anger washed away as her cheeks tinted rose and knotted fingers pressed to her lips.

"You remind me of my Thomas," she sighed wistfully. "I'll be right back."

I watched her turn and move toward the kitchen, giggling all the way. Sebastian stepped around me into the entryway and placed the box onto the wooden floor. When he stood, he took a moment, sweeping his eyes around the wood-paneled walls, the crown molding, and inlaid floors.

"Hot damn," he uttered breathlessly. "This place is a fucking masterpiece."

His appreciation for the craftsmanship was evident in the way his hand gingerly laid over the staircase's newel post, tracing his fingertips over the carved swirls and twirls.

"Yeah, it is," I agreed solemnly. "Too bad nobody wants it."

"Anybody who can afford this house and doesn't buy it, is an idiot," he stated bluntly.

His dark blonde brows drew together and his eyes narrowed, peering up the open stairway and into the hallway above. Nodding slowly, he turned to me with an expression I hadn't yet seen.

"Did the old guy die here?"

"Wow, you picked up on that." I blinked away the evidence of my shock as I cleared my throat. "Yeah, he did. Last year. Mrs. Worthington's niece wants her to move in with her family in Pittsburgh, but she needs to sell the house first. Apparently she believes that her late-husband is scaring potential buyers away."

Sebastian's mouth stretched with a slow grin. "A haunted house, huh? That's fucking badass."

"It's not haunted," I mumbled, shaking my head.

"Then what do you call it?" He tipped his head with intrigue. I rolled my eyes, but my lips remained sealed. "Yeah, just like I thought; you got nothin'."

"I'm just not convinced that the spirit of her dead husband is to blame for the lack of offers," I whispered harshly.

With a suspicious glance around the room, Sebastian bent to lower his eyes to mine. "Don't say that so loud. You don't wanna piss the old dude off," he warned in a husky voice that shouldn't have sprouted goosebumps along the back of my neck, but it did.

"Oh, shut up." I shoved against his chest, startled immediately by the ungiving, firm muscle under my palm.

A heated shiver trickled over my spine and I urged myself to calm the hell down. Tensing the muscles of my face into an expression of indifference, I pointed to the cage and then toward the back of the room.

"Sandy is right through that door, if you don't mind taking that in there," I instructed just as Mrs. Worthington returned with a tall glass of water, frosted with condensation.

"Here you go. Drink up," she cooed, doting on him as though he was someone to her.

"Thank you, sweetheart," Sebastian replied, gratefully taking the glass from her and drinking it down in two strong gulps. Wiping his mouth with the back of his hand, he sighed appreciatively. "I'll go put that cage together. That way, you ladies can get straight to business and I can play with the chinchilla. Everybody wins."

I so badly wanted to hate him for being so arrogantly sweet. The trouble was, I could tell it wasn't an act. This was just the way he was, and although it was irritatingly immature, I almost found his demeanor to be refreshing. A break in the morose monotony of my life.

Almost.

"That would be lovely, Sebastian. Thank you so much." Mrs. Worthington smiled, reaching a hand out to briefly touch his elbow. "And by the way, I do appreciate all of your body art. Very tastefully done. I see some of these young people with silly little trinkets doodled all over their skin, but yours are stunning."

Raising his forearms, he twisted them from back to front. "What, these old things?" Bowing his head, he smiled gratefully. "You have a good eye for fine art."

The old woman was *swooning*. Staring at him like he was sent to her by God Himself. As Sebastian turned toward the kitchen, Mrs. Worthington eyed me over her shoulder with those glittering blue eyes of hers.

"If I didn't know any better, I'd say he looks a lot like Greyson," she commented with a gentle smile.

"That would be because he's Greyson's father," I admitted without apprehension. It was the truth and she'd guessed accurately.

"How lovely that he's in the boy's life," Mrs. Worthington declared with a glowing smile.

Sebastian returned to the foyer, bending to hoist the cage into his arms. From behind, Mrs. Worthington and I shared a moment of our own silent appreciation for the way his jeans hugged his ass perfectly. Tailored to fit, no doubt, and we watched him walk toward the closed door at the back of the room. The shifting and bunching of his t-shirt, stretched over his back and biceps, was almost the equivalent to a striptease. Tantalizing. Hypnotizing.

How lovely, indeed.

***

"Is there anything I have to do with this … computer hullabaloo?" Mrs. Worthington asked, screwing her face up and showing her blatant distaste for technology.

The woman didn't even own a TV. Her entertainment consisted entirely of reading, gardening, and knitting.

"Not a thing," I told her gently, laying a hand over her knee.

"You know, I just would've preferred the house go to someone local, preferably someone *familiar*," she persisted.

I'd heard her say this six times over the past hour, but still, I continued to nod with the patience of a saint. "I know, Mrs. Worthington. But the residents of Hog Hill already live here, and not a whole lot of people are reading the Hog Hill Gazette."

I chose to leave out the fact that nobody in town had the money to afford such a big and beautiful house. It was the only mansion within town lines, and the majority of the town folk were upper-middle class, at best.

"But the ads in the papers …" She offered a rueful smile and shook her head. "I thought it would be better

113

than announcing it to the world. I-I don't want the place to be torn down and turned into some mini-mall."

"I know." I nodded sympathetically. "But I promise I will make sure whoever gets the house respects its integrity. You know I would never sell it to someone who didn't."

"Oh, honey, I know." She nodded firmly, to herself more than me. Her eyes flitted skyward and clasped her hands over her heart. "I just wish we'd had children. This wouldn't have been a problem then."

Sebastian intruded on the business conversation, reminding me that he was still there. Sandy was nestled in the crook of one muscular arm, as the opposite hand stroked along his back and tail.

"Softest thing in the fucking world," he confirmed with a shit-eating grin. He lifted Sandy to eye-level and grinned unabashedly. "Tabby, have you ever held this thing? He's such a sweetheart."

There was something strangely endearing about this grown man holding the little critter to his nose and nuzzling it.

"Yes, I've had the pleasure a number of times," I told him, unable to stop my smile as I turned to Mrs. Worthington.

"I'm getting one," Sebastian declared, hugging Sandy to his chest. "This is definitely happening."

"I've always had pets," Mrs. Worthington nodded solemnly. "I need the companionship. Something to be happy I'm home."

Inviting himself to sit at the table, Sebastian dropped into the chair beside me, ruffling Sandy's little head. "Bet it was nice when your husband was alive."

"Yes, it was." Mrs. Worthington smiled with that tinge of sadness that was always present whenever she spoke about him. "It was just the two of us with a dog for many years, and when he passed, so did our dog at the time. I got Sandy shortly after."

Sebastian nodded, looking at the furry animal tucked into his chest. "Sucks being on your own, doesn't it?"

Mrs. Worthington met his eyes, and whatever she found there brought her to rest her knobby hand against the torn knee of his jeans. "It certainly does."

"Why didn't you have kids?" he asked, and I could've smacked him. Who asks something like that? How did this man not have *any* filters?

But Mrs. Worthington burst just with a somber laugh and held her hands up into the kitchen air. "Do you see this house around us?"

"Hard to miss," Sebastian replied, quirking his lips and stroking Sandy.

"Well, it's not cheap, and because Thomas never believed in keeping a working wife, he instead worked himself to the bone. He was always very career oriented, and not very in tune with his wants for a family when we were younger and able. It wasn't until it was too late that we realized how much we would've enjoyed having children of our own," she explained without hesitancy, folding her hands over her lap and nodding regretfully.

"Hm," Sebastian grunted with a thoughtful nod.

"Anyway," I hurried to interject, "I hope that soon, we'll have a buyer for the house and you can move in with your niece. It'll be good for you to have family around."

"Yes," Mrs. Worthington nodded kindly. "I hope so too. I just hope the house goes to someone who will—"

"I know," I cut her off with a glance toward the clock. "It'll be fine, I promise. But right now, Sebastian and I really need to go pick up Greyson from school. I'll see you in a few days, okay? I'll call if I have any updates."

"Oh, of course!" She reached out to take Sandy from Sebastian's arms.

"Mrs. Worthington, thank you so much for letting me chill with this little dude," he said, petting the critter with an affectionate smile. "I can cross chinchilla holding off my bucket list now."

"Sebastian, you are welcome to visit him any time," Mrs. Worthington replied, pressing a hand to his jaw. "And please, call me Jane."

12

sebastian

"I can't believe you asked her about her lack of children," Tabby groused from beside me. The woman sure loved to complain and suck the fun out of everything.

"Why is that so hard for you to believe? I was curious, so I asked." It was perfectly reasonable to me. How was anybody supposed to learn about anything or anybody if they were too afraid to ask simple questions?

"Because it's *rude*! A woman can do whatever the hell she wants without having to answer to some man she doesn't even know!"

Her shrill tone rang above the Foo Fighters' "Learn to Fly" and without a moments hesitation, I pulled to the side of the old country road. Nothing but fields and a small cluster of trees surrounded us on both sides. Tabby looked around with curiosity and panic mingling on her features.

"Okay," I began, resting my arm over the back of her seat, "first of all, if you ever yell over Dave Grohl again, I'm kicking you out of the car and making you walk the rest of the way. Hell, maybe there's a Holstein around here you can hitch a ride from, but you're not riding with me."

Tabby only blinked her incredulity. A fine line formed between her shaped brows, and I touched the spot with my thumb, rubbing it away and surprising her with the touch. She responded by backing away toward the window.

"Second, how *exactly* was it rude? It's not like I said, 'Yo, Mrs. W., I have a deep-seated issue with broads who don't procreate the way the Lord intended them to. So, what the fuck's the deal with that?' No, I asked a genuinely honest question, and she *chose* to answer."

Shaking her head, Tabby scowled and folded her arms over her chest. "It's inappropriate to ask people things like that about their personal lives. Maybe she had an illness that prevented her from conceiving. You don't know."

"Then she was free to use her own discretion and not answer," I replied in a low, graveled voice. "How else are you supposed to get to know everybody you meet?"

"You don't have to get to know *everybody*," Tabby countered, her tone sharp and challenging.

With consideration, I tipped my head. Maybe she was right about that. Maybe my desire to know

118

everybody, to loosely befriend everybody, had diminished all want to learn everything about only one. But wasn't that what made so many people like me? My uninhibited interest in everyone I met? Wasn't that what made me the most popular member of the band, next to Devin?

"Maybe not," I nodded thoughtfully.

"It doesn't make you less lonely," she added, and when I cocked my head at the statement, she snickered with triumph. "I'm observant too, Mr. I Want A Chinchilla."

"Hey!" I shouted defensively, gripping the steering wheel and pointing a stern finger at her. "That thing was really fucking cute and soft, okay? Nobody said a damn thing about being lonely."

"But you did. With all that crap about having someone to come home to."

Fuck. I did *say that.*

She leaned across the center console toward me and I swallowed. "And the next time *you* shout over Dave Grohl, I'm kicking you out and stealing your fancy car."

Satisfied with having the final word, Tabby fell back into the seat, crossing her legs and folding her arms over her chest. If I had turned all of my attention to putting the truck back onto the road and driving to Greyson's school, I might not have noticed the crimson flush splotching over her cheeks. I might've missed the lick of her lips, or the fluttered palpitation in the base of her throat.

But I didn't.

I picked up on every one of those hints that this was more than just a heated dispute between two opposites.

119

This was a dance. Flirtation. I wasn't sure she could honestly acknowledge it for what it was yet, but the evidence was written clearly in every nervous twist of her fingers and every bite of her bottom lip.

She wanted me. Or at least her body did, and whether or not I'd give it to her …

Well, I hadn't decided yet.

***

"Where's your car?" Greyson asked, scanning his eyes over the Range Rover.

"Sebastian is too gargantuan to fit into my very normal-sized car," Tabby explained with a sarcastic bite.

"Your car *is* pretty tiny," he disputed, and I held my hand up to him.

"High five, kid. I knew you couldn't sit comfortably in that thing."

To my surprise, he didn't leave me hanging. Acting as though it was an inconvenience, his hand clapped against mine, while his lips twitched with a smile.

I opened the back door for him as he asked what we were doing for the night. I could only shrug, because, well, what the hell do you do in a town called Hog Hill, anyway?

"Any suggestions, Thumbelina?" I looked to Tabby, raising an eyebrow and flashing her a lopsided smile.

She hesitated, her attention occupied by weaving her long hair into a neat braid. The auburn rope hung over her shoulder, glistening under the sunlight in tones of copper and ruby, and it took every ounce of my

120

willpower to not pull the rubber band from the end. To not let it cascade in waves against her back and shoulders. To not thrust my fingers into it, tangle it around my hands, and mess it up.

"Um, well, maybe Sebastian wants to see your drums," she offered to Greyson as she then climbed into the car.

His drums. Why hadn't I thought about that? Was there a better way to bond with him than the thing I knew best?

I ran to the drivers' side and glanced into the backseat. "Uh, yes. Let's do that."

"Sure," Greyson grumbled, painting his face with indifference.

I drove Tabby to her car, where she and Greyson left my truck to drive themselves home. I followed, once again finding myself alone and realizing how nice it was to have other people drive with me.

***

Tabby's house was exactly what I would've imagined. Neat. Orderly. A Pottery Barn catalogue had thrown up all over her kitchen and living room, and the air was lightly scented with Fresh Linen and Seaside Escape, as proven by the candles on her coffee table. But with a watchful eye, I hunted for little hints of the secret parts of herself. They were well camouflaged, buried within the makings of a *Better Homes & Gardens* spread, but they were there. The leopard print pillow on the easy chair by the window. The multi-colored collection of Chucks hidden on a low shelf in the front entryway. The leather jacket hanging in the closet, just noticeable through the barely jarred door.

Tiny pieces that she couldn't quite let go of from a previous life.

"Greyson's room is upstairs," Tabby told me, catching me perusing the shelves of records in her living room.

"Ah, right." I nodded, sliding one out, checking the title. "Quite a collection you have here."

She had a bit of everything, from Marley to U2 to The Clash, all in alphabetical order. Her record collection was kept like everything else in her life I'd seen so far—neatly. But unlike her arsenal of Converse, or the leather jacket in the closet, she kept these on proud display. They were dusted and treasured, kept on shelves that encompassed an entire wall of her living room.

"Thanks," she quickly said, taking the record from my hands and putting it back in its place. "I've been collecting for years."

"Obviously." I grinned, taking another from the shelf. Nirvana's *In Utero*. "This is a great album."

"Yes, it is," she agreed, plucking it from my grasp and sliding it back with her other Nirvana albums. "Greyson's waiting for you."

"God, you really don't want me looking at these, huh?" I teased, grabbing another and turning it over. Metallica's *...And Justice For All*. "God, I haven't listened to this in forever."

"I just don't want Greyson thinking you don't have an interest in him." She took the record from me and held onto it. Maybe thinking that if she didn't put it back, I wouldn't grab another.

"Maybe I have multiple interests," I countered, teasing.

Clutching the album to her chest, she pinched her lips and lowered her gaze to the beige carpet. "I don't even know what that means."

"What it means, Tabby, is that maybe I want to get to know Greyson *and* you."

"You have absolutely no reason to get to know me outside of the bare minimum," she stated wryly, sliding the record back onto its shelf. "You should be more focused on getting to know your son."

Leaning my hip against the shelves, I folded my arms and shook my head. "You know, here's the thing; I refuse to believe you're as reserved as you're making yourself out to be. I've seen enough to know that at the very least, you and I could be friends, so why you're resisting that so much, I have no idea. But something you need to know about me is, I don't give up easily." And as though I were setting out to challenge her and her protests against being my friend—or otherwise—I grabbed another record. The first album my hand landed on and pulled it out.

The cover pushed me to cock my head, to draw my brows together and narrow my eyes. *Mask the Raven*, the first album of the first band I was ever in, Saint Savage. We were a metal band comprised mostly of a few guys from Scranton. A friend of mine had hooked me up, and we'd gone on to do some great things before splitting up and moving on. It was the band I was in when I met

Greyson's mother, and before Tabby could snatch the record from my hands, I held it up out of her reach.

"You were a fan?" I asked the question as another piece of information registered. We'd only sold the vinyl records at shows. Realization lit like a bulb as I eyed her suspiciously. "Were *you* at that show?"

She knew the one. That was made apparent by the sudden streak of red blossoming against her cheeks as she jumped, attempting to swipe the record from my hand. The fragments of information clicked into place, and although some parts were still hazy, some things were starting to make a little more sense.

"Take it easy, Thumbelina," I said gently, handing the album to her. "So, can I take a guess at what happened?"

"Oh, well, it's not like I can stop you anyway, so go right ahead," Tabby mumbled, putting the album back. She stared at the shelf, unable to look at me, but why? Embarrassment? Shame?

"Okay." I bobbed my head once, and turned to pace the living room floor. "So, you and your sister were both big fans of music. Maybe it was something you bonded over and you'd go to shows together. *You* went to enjoy the music—hell, maybe you both did, but your sister preferred the other perks of being a groupie. Like, hooking up with band members." I glanced over my shoulder to find she'd turned to watch my back. "Stop me if I'm wrong."

With a quick shake of her head, she croaked, "Keep going."

Hmmm … "Everything was fun, everything was great. Until one day, you go to this metal concert. You like the opening act and you buy their album. They're super approachable, because they're small and just the opener, but you don't meet them. Your sister does. She gets pregnant, and all of a sudden, everything that you thought was fun isn't anymore. You don't want to be her, so you force yourself to grow up, because—"

"Are you coming up here or what?" Greyson called from upstairs, interrupting my spiel.

Before I responded, I turned from my pacing and eyed Tabby. I took in the furrowed creases between her brows, the rapid movement of her throat as she swallowed, and the strength of her arms as they tightened around her middle.

Bingo.

Maybe I wasn't spot on. Maybe I had missed something. But for what it was worth, I'd figured her out.

"Yeah," I called back, heading toward the stairs as I pointed a finger at her. "Can we continue this later?" I gave her a few seconds to respond. I didn't think she'd accept my request, but then she faintly nodded.

I smiled reassuringly at her, even though she didn't look much like smiling herself. Because the thing was, despite how much her body might've wanted me and mine her, I really did want to genuinely know her. We were going to know each other for a long time, as long as Greyson wanted me in his life, and at the very least, we should get along.

Understanding her was the first step in the right direction, as far as I was concerned, and I hoped she'd grant me the privilege.

13

tabby

As Sebastian ran up the stairs to hang out with Greyson, I exhaled with a heaving gust. My hands scrubbed over my face as I grappled for the strength to continue the conversation.

How the hell had he figured all that shit out? That's the part I didn't quite understand. Had he known all along, or was that stupid album really that much of a giveaway? Either way, it freaked me out to know he now knew at least the majority of the situation. And he wanted to know the rest. It didn't actually hurt to tell him, not when he already knew so much, but it would require a dose of courage I didn't know I had in me.

"I need a drink," I muttered to myself as I hurried into the kitchen to scour my meager collection of wine.

I rarely drank. Too much of my life had required me to keep a level head. But, every now and then, I appreciated a glass of something. Now was one of those times and I grabbed for a bottle of wine my ex-future mother-in-law had gifted me last Christmas.

How strange it is, to find ourselves suddenly clouded by memories we hadn't given a moment's thought in months. I remembered her then, my ex-fiancé's mother, and the uncertainty in her eyes as I unwrapped the bottle. She knew I didn't drink much, but she had seen the bottle at her local liquor store and it reminded her of me. "The design looks like the windows at your office," she'd said with a reluctant smile. I told her I loved the thought and that the bottle was gorgeous, because it was.

I miss her.

My lips pinched tightly as I uncorked the bottle and filled a glass to the halfway point. For a year after getting engaged, I'd grown so accustomed to the idea that she would be a woman I'd know for the rest of her life. Hell, that was the case for his entire family, but when he'd let me go, I had to let the rest of them go as well.

Bringing the glass to my lips, I sipped lightly. It was good. A little sweet, a lot fruity. A satisfying burn scratched at my throat as it slid down and instantly heated my belly. I hated moments like these. Moments that reminded me of all the people and things I'd lost in the past year. It always just seemed so much better to ignore it all.

Sebastian's boisterous laughter floated down the stairs and lingered in the air around me, pushing my melancholy thoughts aside until I couldn't think of anything but what they were doing upstairs. I hoped Greyson was having a good time. I hoped they were bonding over something they had in common. I hoped for all of these things because what I wanted for myself had nothing to do with what I wanted for Greyson, and that was for him to have a good relationship with his father.

***

My wine glass was empty and I found myself marginally relaxed. A steady beat of drums and cymbals crashed through the ceiling and into my ears, as I sat in my armchair, eyes closed and numb enough to feel happy.

Then, my business phone rang.

Grabbing it from the table beside me, I checked the number. Unknown.

"Hm," I grunted shortly before answering it. "Hello?"

"Hi there. Is this Tabitha Clarke?" a man's voice replied.

"This is she." I sat up straighter, hardly registering that the drumming from above had now stopped.

"Good evening! My name is Roman Dolecki. So sorry to disturb you at home, at such a late hour, but your assistant gave me your number and said it would be fine to—"

"Excuse me. My … assistant?" I took a glance at my watch. It was nearly six o'clock.

"Ah, he said his name was Alex Lewis?"

"Oh, right. Yes, of course."

At that point, I figured things out. He was calling about the listing, and so soon! I allowed myself a grin of triumph. Granted, this wasn't a sale, but how amazing was it to already be gaining traction in just a few hours of putting the listing online?

"What can I do for you, Mr. Dolecki?"

Clearing his throat, he began, "Well, Ms. Clarke, I'd like to first introduce myself. I'm an entrepreneur living in New York City, and I'm looking to relocate somewhere, uh, quieter."

"I see," I murmured, grabbing a pen and notepad from my briefcase to scribble his name along the lines.

"I was just browsing earlier for houses in your area, when I came across the Worthington house—that is what you're calling it, correct?"

I nodded to myself. "Yes. Isn't it gorgeous? The pictures really don't do it justice."

"I can only imagine," he practically hummed with delight. "I'd love to see it myself, and I plan to, but unfortunately I'm unable to leave town for another couple of weeks."

"Oh, well, I can't guarantee that there won't be any offers made before then," I said regretfully. If we were already receiving interest within a few hours, what was to say there wouldn't be more in a few days?

"I figured as such," he replied with a friendly lilt to his voice. "I'm not asking to put a hold on the listing. But I was hoping that it would perhaps help my case if I used you to also sell my home in the city."

"W-what?" I was genuinely taken aback. Was it possible that he was serious? I was *hours* away, living in a middle of nowhere town in upstate New York. Surely

130

there were more experienced, more accessible realtors living in Manhattan.

"I took the liberty of reading your history via your website. I'm very impressed with your experience and the work your agency has done. I know I could work with someone more local, but it's always easier if the buy and sell are handled by the same realtor. Plus, and please don't take offense, I also feel less likely to be taken advantage of by a small-town girl than a big shot from the city," Mr. Dolecki explained in that convincing tone you expect from lawyers and salesmen.

I wanted to protest, because it did seem a little ridiculous to me, but he did raise a compelling argument. It *was* easier if I handled both, and although it was several hours away, I supposed it wasn't completely out of the question to take a day trip down to meet up with him.

But what about Greyson? And the niggling thought irritated me in the most shameful way.

"Mr. Dolecki, can I think about it? Unfortunately, I do have other responsibilities in my life that would interfere with me traveling at the moment. And while I know that New York City isn't—"

"Ms. Clarke, if family is an issue, I will personally pay for a hotel room for you, your husband, and children."

Footsteps thundered down the stairs and I dropped my pen at the abrupt cacophony of noise.

"O-oh, no, I'm n-not married, and I don't—" I stopped myself before I could tell him I don't have children, just as Sebastian swung into the living room. "Actually, I have custody of my nephew."

"Hey, do you mind if I order a pizza?" Sebastian asked, and I shot him an irritated look, while I pointed at my phone. "Oh, *sorry*," he drawled quietly. "God forbid someone does you a favor."

The dig was personal. Too personal for someone who had only just met me.

"Well, Ms. Clarke," Mr. Dolecki replied, a sense of pleasantry in his voice that I appreciated in comparison to Sebastian's brashness. "I would be happy to put the two of you up. In a hotel, I mean. Is this weekend okay?"

"Uh …" God, it was so sudden. I did want to sell the damn house, but I had only just answered the phone, and now he wanted me to travel to the city. And on my agreed weekend off, no less. "Would you mind if I thought about it?"

"Oh, of course! I'm sorry for being so forward. I'll admit, I instantly fell in love with the house from the pictures and got excited. But, please, take a day or two to think things over. I know it's a lot to ask."

"Thank you so much. You can expect a call from me within the next twenty-four hours," I replied gratefully. I jotted down his work and home phone numbers, and wished him a good night before hanging up.

When I laid my phone down on the coffee table, I looked up to find Sebastian still standing there, staring at me expectantly. I tried to remember what exactly it was he had wanted and when I came up empty, I asked him to repeat himself.

"Oh, don't worry about it. Greyson already called for the pizza," he responded. "Who was on the phone?"

It wasn't any of his business, but I still found myself saying, "Someone saw the listing online for Mrs. Worthington's house and loved it so much he called right away."

Impressed, the corners of his mouth turned downward with his nod. "Wow. That's fucking awesome. Why did he care if you were married?"

"What?" I asked, tucking the notepad back into my briefcase. "He didn't—"

"You told him you weren't married, so I assumed he asked."

The audacity of this man was something else. "He didn't *ask*. He *offered* to pay for a hotel for my husband and I, if I had one, so I told him I didn't."

"Hm," Sebastian grunted, narrowing his eyes with suspicion. "Why would you need to stay in a hotel?"

"Oh my God," I breathed out with my sigh. "If you really *have* to know, he lives in New York City, and would like to meet me to discuss the sale of his house."

"Oh, well, you don't need a hotel then." He nodded as though agreeing with himself. "You and Greyson can stay with me."

I blinked up at him, thoroughly exasperated. How the hell could he possibly suggest something like that? We had only just met him. We hardly knew him. Staying in his house over the weekend seemed foolish and risky, and so, I found myself shaking my head.

"That is definitely not a good idea."

"Oh yeah? And why not?" He folded his arms over his chest as Greyson walked into the room, phone in hand.

"Pizza's coming," he mumbled.

Sebastian asked him how much it came to, and just as I stood up to grab my purse, he held a hand up to stop me. "I got it," he said, pulling his wallet out and handing Greyson a few bills. "Tell the guy to keep the change."

Greyson nodded and wandered out of the room, leaving Sebastian and me alone once again. He stared at me, waiting for my reply with his head cocked and fingers tapping on his bicep.

"Sebastian, you only *just* met us. You can't expect me to feel comfortable staying in your house," I explained, unsure of why I even needed a reason.

"Yeah? And you're just going to go meet this random guy who only just called you? Alone?"

"This is business!" I shouted with an exasperated shake of my head. "You can't compare—"

"You're right." He smirked. "It *is* different. You actually know who I am. Plus, Tabby, didn't you want me to help with Greyson? This is a perfect way to start, isn't it? I could hang out with him while you're doing business, and it's a lot easier for me to do that in a place where there's, uh, actually shit to do that doesn't involve tractors and haystacks."

I hated that he was actually making sense, not to mention that it might be good for Greyson to get away from this damn town for a couple days. And, remembering what Jess and Alex had said, maybe it would be good for me too.

"I'll think about it," I told Sebastian, and he grinned brighter than I ever would've expected.

"That's all I ask."

14

sebastian

"Welcome to my humble abode," I exclaimed, running down the steps of my porch to greet Tabby and Greyson.

"It's so small," Greyson grumbled, getting out of the car and looking up at my house with enough disgust to set the thing on fire.

"What the hell were you expecting, the Taj Mahal?" I asked with an eye roll.

I really wanted to hug them, after not seeing them for a few days. It had weirded me out, to feel so alone without their company, after only having it for a short period of time. And it wasn't exactly the best company a guy could get, if I'm being honest. But good or not, it felt real, and that was better than any type of company I could get from random chicks.

Still, I didn't hug them. Instead I offered Greyson an awkward shoulder slap, and Tabby denied me the air-kiss I attempted by hurrying away. *Whatever*.

"Be nice, Grey," she reprimanded lightly. "It's very nice of Sebastian to let us stay here for the next couple of days."

"Yes, it is," I agreed, grabbing their bags from the trunk of Tabby's car. "I'm practically a saint, really."

Without any reply, I led them into the house and to their rooms. It was only a four-bedroom house, with the third room converted into a drum studio and the fourth used for storage, so I gave Greyson the choice of bunking with Tabby or taking the couch. I figured there wasn't any chance of him wanting to share with me, and I was certain Hell would freeze over before I ever got Tabby into my bed.

"Great. I came all the way here to sleep on a freakin' couch," Greyson grumbled, crossing his arms and scowling.

"Dude, I haven't even shown you the couch I'm talking about yet," I pointed out, leading him toward the basement door.

Tabby followed as I brought him to the basement den, or what some would call a man cave. A sixty-inch TV and a shelf of video game consoles was the first thing you saw as you came down the steps, followed by the large, leather sectional, complete with the biggest fucking lounge I could find at one end. It was big enough for me, at six-three, to lay on comfortably, so Greyson would have no problem.

137

When I turned to assess his reaction, I saw his wide-eyed enthusiasm as he wandered over to the bar and refrigerator.

"I stocked the fridge with snacks and drinks. There's also a microwave behind the bar over there." I smirked, dropping his suitcase on the floor in front of the cushioned ottoman. "Does this suit you, Your Highness?"

"Uh … this is okay," he muttered, but the expression on his face told me it was more than okay. He was impressed, and dare I say it, happy.

"Just wait until you see my drum studio," I told him, jumping my brows and winking. "You can play whenever the fuck you want without bothering the old battle-axe over here."

"Hey," Tabby growled from behind me, and I turned to grin at her. "And by the way, there better not be any alcohol in that bar."

"What?" I dropped my jaw. "You mean tequila and vodka weren't a good idea?"

"Sebastian," she gritted through her teeth.

With a snicker, I rolled my eyes. "You must think I'm a fucking idiot, Thumbelina," I said, nudging her toward the stairs. "I saved all the booze for us."

"Ha-ha," she drawled. "Greyson, I'm going to let Sebastian show me my room. Are you okay down here?"

Turning back to look at him, he was already in the fridge and pulling out a can of soda. "Uh-huh," he murmured before heading to the couch and dropping down.

"Remote's on the seat next to you." I pointed, and he nodded absentmindedly. Turning back to Tabby, I chuckled under my breath. "I think he's fine."

Heading up the two flights of stairs to the second floor of the house, I grimaced when we reached the hallway.

"Okay," I announced, pushing open the first door. "This is your room. I know it isn't anything fancy like whatever swanky five-star hotel that dude wanted to put you up in, but … Well, you can check it out."

With a sigh, Tabby entered the room. I waited in the doorway, as she took in the King-sized bed, complete with the new bedspread I had my mom help me pick out. She ran her hand over the mountain of pillows and turned around to face the TV on the opposite wall, hanging above the dresser now topped with a fresh bouquet of flowers.

"Sebastian," she uttered, her voice tight as she walked toward the vase of brightly colored tulips. "Did you actually get me flowers?"

"Would you call me a presumptuous dick if I said yes?" I cocked a brow as she looked toward me.

"No," she replied, shaking her head. "I would say that's very sweet and thoughtful of you. They're beautiful, thank you."

"You're welcome," I said, reaching my hand up to grip the back of my neck. "Is the room okay?"

And, in that moment, it became my favorite room in the whole fucking house. Because, for the first time since I met her, it was *then* that she smiled at me. Not a slight twitch of her lips, not a polite curve of the mouth in the presence of her nephew. This was a genuine, all-encompassing grin that creased the corners of her eyes and lit her entire face with an ethereal glow. And all I could do was stand there in the doorway, wondering if it was just my heart that had stopped, or if it was time altogether.

"It's perfect," she nearly whispered, her voice hushed against the impact of her smile.

What the fuck is happening? My exhale left my lungs in a gust of uncertainty, while my inhale puffed me up with pride for making her happy. For making her *smile*.

"Cool," I responded, not knowing what else to say. "Uh, over here …" I walked away from the door to head further down the hallway. She followed. "This is the bathroom."

I pushed the next door open. Tabby's eyes lit up with another dose of shock as she stepped inside, taking in spacious wide, glass shower stall.

"Well, this is nicer than mine," she complimented, running her fingertips over the vanity countertop.

Chuckling, I leaned against the wall. "Surprised?"

"Uh, yeah," she said, laughing airily. "A little. I didn't think it'd be so … *clean*."

Laughing and pushing a hand through my hair, I decided to mention, "If you want to take a bath while you're here, there's a jacuzzi in my bathroom."

All remnants of happiness withered from her face as she screwed her features up with disgust. "I don't even want to know what's happened in there."

"Uh, aside from jerking off about seventy-thousand times, nothing," I countered, narrowing my eyes with a smug smirk. "You're the first woman aside from my mother and sisters to ever be in this house."

"Oh, like I'm going to believe that," she snickered, shaking her head incredulously. "Seriously. You don't need to lie to impress me. I don't give a crap."

"Well, clearly you do, if you're making accusations like that. And I'm telling you, I don't let the women I sleep with know where I live. That's the *last* thing I need," I groused, folding my arms over my chest.

"You let my sister know where you lived, after sending those letters," she argued, pinching her lips with a victorious smirk.

"That was different," I insisted, my tone wry.

"Oh, yeah? Well, how do you know you don't have a whole tribe of children out there that you just don't know about?" she shot back. "Or better yet, how do you know a thousand women haven't gotten rid of pregnancies that *you* made happen?"

This little fucking witch. How could she go from being so grateful to being so fucking nasty in a matter of minutes?

I can handle a lot. I could banter with the best of them, and I enjoy it, especially with her for some reason. But that comment … That was a low blow, considering she had read the letters I'd sent. She knew how I had felt back then, and she was using it against me.

"You know what, Tabitha?" I shook my head, edging away and turning to cross the hall to my own room. "Go fuck yourself."

141

I heard the sharp intake of her breath from behind me as I threw my door open and let it slam shut. Crossing the floor to my bed, I stopped and pinched the bridge of my nose. *Fuck.* It took me a second to realize that what I was feeling wasn't even anger. No, that pinging ache in my stomach wasn't fury or rage; it was the feeling of being insulted and hurt—by *her.* For reasons I couldn't yet understand, I hated that she thought that way about me.

A soft knock came to the door. "What?" I growled, pinching harder.

Tabby came in, quietly stepping into the room. "Hey, I, um … I didn't mean that. I shouldn't have said it."

"Whatever," I grumbled.

"God, you sound just like Greyson," she laughed gently, awkwardly.

Reluctantly, I turned around to face her. Guilt was painted over her face like a timid mask, all doe-eyes and pouty lips. Not knowing what to do with her hands, her fingers twisted together, and she looked up at me with what I assumed was the hope that I'd forgive her.

"I'm sorry." Her words floated on her weighted breath. It was something I doubted she said very often.

"Don't sweat it," I muttered, inhaling and exhaling the remainder of my hurt away.

Her eyes skittered to the side and eyed my bed. I had to admit, having her there, in such close proximity to where I slept, injected enough sexual tension into the air to suffocate me. If I wasn't absolutely terrified of her screaming and clawing my eyes out, I might've tossed her down right there.

"I should unpack," she announced abruptly, the moment she realized I'd followed her gaze.

"Sure," I nodded, hoping she didn't catch sight of the obvious hard-on beginning to strain against the zipper of my jeans.

She turned around to head back across the hall when she stopped. "By the way, I can't believe you actually put me across the hall from you."

Calm down, dick. "Why's that?"

"Just seems very presumptuous of you," she mocked. "Almost seems like you're expecting something to happen."

Fucking relax. "I guess it does almost seem that way."

She glanced over her shoulder and if I wasn't mistaken, I thought I detected just the hint of a flicker burning in the center of those emerald eyes. But without another word, she exited the room. I heard the door across the hall gently close, and not caring if she heard, I released a primal, guttural groan.

Maybe she was right. Maybe this was a terrible idea.

Or maybe this is exactly what you both need.

15

tabby

I don't know what I'd expected from Sebastian's house. I guess, if I really thought about it, I'd pictured an embellished bachelor pad. Leather and leopard print everywhere. Maybe a stripper pole or two. Beer on tap. Something I might've seen on MTV's *Cribs* back in the day.

But this? This was a modest home with a small gourmet kitchen and a mahogany dinner table. High-backed dining chairs and tasteful, yet masculine, wall art. This wasn't at all what I would've pictured. Not by a long shot.

I didn't imagine he'd decorated himself. On several occasions now, he had mentioned a mother and sisters. As I cut a piece of steak, I wondered how much they'd helped to furnish his house, and I hated to admit, the thought was endearing.

"How's the steak?" Sebastian asked, as I slowly chewed, watching him and trying so hard to figure him out.

"Very good," I complimented. "You cooked?"

"Mm," he nodded, swallowing a bite of baked potato. "I almost always cook at home, unless I'm going out to eat with my family."

Greyson's face shadowed with disbelief. "*Always*?"

Chuckling, Sebastian bobbed his head. "Always. You gotta understand something, okay? When I'm on the road, it's a pretty even split between home-cooked meals and grabbing shit on the run. And that's only been since *I* started cooking and Kylie joined us. Before that? It was all room service and fast food. I get so freakin' sick of fried crap, it's not even funny."

It made sense, looking at him again and the definition of muscle cut along his arms, flexing and shifting as he cut his steak. Nobody could look like that and survive off a diet of fast food and chain restaurants. But knowing he cooked meals himself, and ones of this caliber, impressed me beyond reason.

Again, not what I expected.

"Tomorrow, Mom said she'd bring over a lasagna," Sebastian informed us with the smallest hint of a smile.

"Your mother?" I asked needlessly. Of course he was talking about his mother. Who else would he refer to as *Mom*?

Nodding, he stabbed a piece of asparagus. "Yeah. I kinda told her about Greyson and she, uh, wants to meet him." Awkwardly, he shoveled the asparagus into his mouth, diverting his eyes and clenching his fist around his fork.

Sliding my eyes to Greyson, I detected just the slightest bit of apprehension on the surface, clouding something that might've been excitement. He never did have much of a relationship with my parents—his grandparents. By the time he was older and could remember them, they were old, crabby, and in poor health. Knowing he had another shot at having grandparents that might hold an interest in him was a good thing. I hope he understood that.

"Is your father alive?" I asked Sebastian, and he nodded.

"Oh yeah," he replied with enthusiasm. "He'd come by tomorrow too, but one of their sows just gave birth, so—"

"Sows?" Greyson asked, raising a brow.

"Yeah," Sebastian laughed. "My parents are farmers. They have pigs and cows and chickens and all sorts of shit."

This man and all his surprises. "You were raised on a farm?"

"Don't look so shocked, Thumbelina," he chuckled. "I look fucking amazing in a pair of overalls."

"Oh, I'm sure," I replied sarcastically.

"Anyway," Sebastian continued, eating more of the asparagus, "Dad's tending to the piglets. So, he won't be by tomorrow. He's—"

"Well, maybe we could go over there on Sunday," I suggested, offering a surprise of my own.

Both Sebastian and Greyson turned to me, startled.

146

"Seriously?" Sebastian asked, thrusting a hand through his hair. "I didn't think you'd want—"

"I think it'd be fun to check out a farm," I offered, when really, I was just curious about the people who had raised him.

Letting it settle in, Sebastian nodded. "Well, we can definitely do that, if Greyson's cool with it. I'm sure my sisters would be there too, and their husbands and kids."

Propping my chin into the palm of my hand, I asked, "How many kids do they have?"

"I'm an uncle times nine." He puffed with a noticeable amount of pride before sipping at his beer.

"I thought you didn't have much experience with kids," I reminded, eyeing him with skepticism.

"Yeah, I don't, really. I don't see my sisters all that often these days. They're so busy with their own lives, and I'm so busy with mine …" A rueful look clouded his eyes as he shrugged, and I wondered how someone like him could be so lonely.

***

Greyson turned down Sebastian's offer to jam in his drum studio, and instead, immediately headed downstairs after dinner. He was playing *Street Fighter 5*, he said, and wanted to get back to it. The moment he closed the basement door behind him, I was so aware of how alone Sebastian and I were, as we cleared the dinner dishes.

"So," he began, closing the dishwasher, "it's just us. What the hell should we do?"

"Um, well, I should probably prepare for my meeting with Roman tomorrow," I informed him, wiping my hands on a dish towel.

"Do you do anything but work?"

The accusation pricked at my nerves. "Of course I do."

"Really? Because I've known you for several days now and I'm not sure you pay attention to anything that isn't work."

Anger flared in my gut. "I care about other things. I care about Greyson, and—"

"I didn't mean that you don't care about Greyson, or anything else," Sebastian defended himself, folding his arms over his chest and leaning against the refrigerator. "Of course you do. But when was the last time you did anything *with* him?"

"Um … we had dinner last—"

"No, that doesn't count," Sebastian interrupted, shaking his head. "Tabby, I don't know much about kids, but one thing I *do* know is that they're not going to respond to you if you don't make them feel important. That's just basic human shit."

The nerve of this man. I gawked and sputtered before spitting out, "I do make him feel important! Are you kidding me? I didn't have to take him in. I didn't have to ruin everything for—" My voice stopped abruptly as I realized what I was going to admit. What nobody else knew.

Sebastian shook his head, smirking with intrigue. "Oh, I don't think so," he said, reaching out and gripping my shoulders, before steering me into the living room.

"You don't start saying some shit like that and not get to finish."

Hands still on my shoulders, he pressed until I sat on the couch. From a mini bar, he grabbed a bottle of whiskey and two glasses, and I shook my head adamantly.

"No way," I told him as he began to pour. "I don't drink whiskey."

"You do tonight," he smirked.

"No, I really … I can't handle whiskey. It gets me really drunk, and it gets me drunk really fast."

"You ever think that you could benefit from getting really drunk, really fast?" He handed me one of the glasses and when I refused to take it, his gaze softened. "One drink, Tabby. Just one."

Sighing, I relaxed and took the glass from him, tipping it to my lips. The whiskey was smooth, warm, and tasted like sin.

"So, you owe me a story," Sebastian declared, leaning back against the couch.

I didn't need to ask what story he was talking about; I knew, remembering our conversation from the other night. The night when he found his old band's album on my shelf.

Turning the glass in my hands, I gazed into the amber liquid like a reflecting pool. "I don't … I don't know if I can talk about it," I admitted with a rueful chuckle. "I've never told anybody."

Leaning forward to rest his elbows on his knees, he nodded. "Yeah, I get that. Before this week, I had never told anybody else about what happened with Sam."

Startled, I turned to him. "Really? Nobody?"

"Nope. I didn't think I had a reason to. I thought she had gotten an abortion, so what was there to tell?"

My throat constricted around the realization that maybe Sebastian and I weren't so different. For a long time, we'd both harbored more than one person should have to carry.

"But you were practically a kid, and having to handle all of that by yourself? You didn't even tell your parents?"

Shaking his head, he rolled the glass between his hands. "Why? So they could mourn what never was, too?"

Taking a deep breath, I nodded, understanding. And then I began to tell my story.

"I asked Sam to go to the Fist Fest with me. She wasn't the biggest fan of metal—*I* was—but we went to concerts together all the time, regardless of music genre. I was mostly going for Heavy Chains—do you remember them?" I lifted my gaze to find his, and he nodded. "I was a *huge* fan of theirs. But anyway, the band that went on right before them was awesome and I knew I wanted their record. But, since Heavy Chains was playing right after, I didn't know when I'd get the chance to run out to the merch table. So, Sam offered."

I took another sip of the whiskey, letting it roll around on my tongue to dissolve my worries before swallowing. "I was sixteen years old," I felt the need to clarify, to emphasize the next part of the story, "and Sam didn't come back to me for an hour."

Sebastian's brows lowered. "Those festivals get really fucking crazy. She left you alone for that long?"

The irony made me chuckle bitterly. "Yeah, no shit. And I knew the second I saw her what had happened, because that's what she always did. Sometimes it felt like she couldn't go anywhere without hooking up with some guy. I never faulted her for it, you know, she was young and having fun. But that night, I was pissed because she'd told me she would be right back. I couldn't even enjoy the band I went there for because I was too busy worrying about where the fuck she'd gone."

The guilt that blanketed his face surprised me, as though it was somehow his fault. "Tabby … that's … that's fucked up."

I shook my head, not wanting to hear it from him. Not wanting him to take the blame for something he was clueless about. "I got over it. I mean, I was pissed that she didn't even bother to get my album signed by the band," I laughed bitterly, "but I got over it. Until a couple of months later of course, when she found out she was pregnant, and then it all changed.

"Nobody was surprised that Sam had gotten knocked up. I think we all knew that it was only a matter of time," I explained. "She told my parents she didn't know who the father was, but she told *me* that it was a guy from Saint Savage."

"So, you had to carry that weight for a long time," Sebastian chimed in, and I nodded.

"I thought about trying to contact the band, but I didn't know how. And even if I did, what was I supposed to say? I didn't know *who* she had slept with. She never

151

gave me a name or anything," I said, feeling the need to explain why I'd never tried to find him sooner.

Tipping his eyebrows with understanding, he shook his head. "I never said I blamed you."

"I know, but …" I sighed, sipping again. "I felt so guilty. About that, and that our parents had no idea, and … I don't know. The whole situation was fucked up, and it was around that time I realized I had to grow up. I couldn't keep hanging out with her like that. I think part of me was afraid I'd end up like her. And she never did grow up, you know. She was always hooking up with guys—less frequently, because of Greyson, but she still did it. She held down a couple jobs waitressing, but it was a revolving door, and she and Greyson were moving in and out of apartments while she treated him more as a friend than her son, and—"

"And so, you've always had to step in as the authority figure," Sebastian interjected, an understanding sparking in his eyes.

I nodded. "Yes. I had to, to be there for Greyson when she decided she needed one of her *dates*. And that's … that's how she fucking died, too. She was drunk, coming back from sleeping with someone else, and wrapped her fucking car around a telephone pole." Without warning, I gasped, sharply inhaling my sob. "And it was just … the last fucking thing I needed."

It sounded so selfish, I knew that. I hated myself for saying it out loud, but when I looked to Sebastian, I was surprised to find not an ounce of judgment or sympathy in his gaze. All there was, was understanding.

152

"Did you know I was engaged?" I asked him, searching his eyes and wondering how it was possible for someone's irises to never end.

"I didn't," he replied, shaking his head.

"Yeah," I nodded, sniffling. "I was marrying this accountant from Harrisburg. His name was Brad."

"Brad and Tabitha," Sebastian mocked with a hoity-toity lilt to his voice. "That doesn't even sound right."

"Nothing about us really was," I admitted with an ounce of shame. "I liked him a lot. He was a really good man, and he stood by me through the deaths of my parents and my sister. He helped with everything and I really thought I'd hit the jackpot with him, even if we never felt quite right. I thought it was just the stress of everything I was going through, you know? But then, when he realized that Greyson had moved in and wasn't leaving …" I pressed my fist to my lips, holding in another sob. A burst of anger. The vile disgust.

"He ended things because of that?" Sebastian guessed, a dash of his own anger tinting his words.

I nodded. "We never wanted kids."

"Neither did I," Sebastian fired back, angry at a person not sitting there, "but plans change."

"Yeah, well," I sighed, clutching the glass and knocking the rest back, "I didn't get a choice in the matter. But he did."

Snickering, Sebastian finished his own drink and poured another. "Well, you're better off now," he grumbled, shaking his head. "Piece of shit. Better to happen before you were legally bound to him."

"This is true," I nodded solemnly. "That's what I've tried telling myself, and at least we hadn't started planning the wedding yet, but it did suck."

"Well, of course it did." He sank further into the couch, holding the glass between his legs. "You thought you had everything planned out, and then something dropped into your lap and changed it all. I get that."

It was as simple as some unseen person changing a lightbulb in the room, but with that statement, I saw Sebastian in a different light. Maybe he had chosen to remain perpetually in band t-shirts and leather jackets, while I'd stuffed mine in a closet, only to be worn on weekends. Maybe he was unashamed of his painted skin, while I kept my one tattoo hidden. However, in other ways, we were very much the same—both of us living a life we thought we had sorted, only to find that there was so much out of our control.

"Well," he said after a few moment's silence, "I'm sorry you've had a shitty year, but for what it's worth, I'm glad it brought you my way."

Rolling my lips between my teeth, I propelled myself into overanalyzing every word and inflection of that statement. The way he said it, without an iota of sympathy, made it seem that he really wasn't sorry, because it brought me here. And then, there was that … *I'm glad it brought you my way*. What did that mean? Was he generalizing *you*? Did he mean Greyson *and* me? Or …

I licked the whiskey from my tucked-in lips, finding some semblance of courage in the lingering remnants, and with them, I acknowledged the tension between us.

Had it been there since we met? I was attracted to him—that was for damn sure—but had I known it immediately, or had it taken its time settling in? It was only days ago, but I couldn't remember anything other than my irritation. Had there been something else, underneath all that? Had my attraction derived from a place of disgust and I wanted him simply because of how angry he made me? Or was it that he reminded me of everything I'd been denying myself over the years, in my frantic determination to grow up?

"It's too quiet," Sebastian announced, drinking from his glass and standing up. "Let's go."

"W-where are we going?" I stammered, following orders as I pulled myself to my feet.

"Upstairs." Grabbing the bottle of whiskey, he headed toward the stairs. "Bring your glass," he glanced over his shoulder and winked, "just in case."

His room was across the hall from mine. I still wasn't sure he hadn't done that on purpose. He could've set me up in the basement. He could've given Greyson his room and taken the couch himself. Instead, I was on one side and he on the other, with an entire floor between us and responsibility.

And funnily enough, it wasn't Sebastian I didn't trust.

16

sebastian

"You ever play before?"

I placed my full glass of whiskey and the bottle onto a table next to my DW Collector's Series kit and sat down on the cushioned leather stool, lowering the seat until it was uncomfortable. I grabbed one of the sticks resting against the snare, and watched her as the birch spun between my fingers.

Tabby was standing with her back to the closed door, her fingers clutched around her empty glass. "No," she replied, shaking her head. "Greyson rarely plays around me, let alone lets me try."

"First time for everything," I said with a lift of my lips. I scooped both sticks into one palm and held them out to her. "Come on."

"You want *me* to play?"

"Yep." I stood up, walking around the kit and encouraging her to take the sticks.

Reluctantly, she handed me the glass and accepted the sticks in trade. I welcomed her to sit on the throne with a grand sweep of my arm. She rolled her eyes, but accepted the invitation, walking around and sitting down.

Positioning myself behind her, I crouched down and lifted her feet, placing one on the bass pedal and the other on the hi-hat pedal.

"Heels up," I instructed with a smile, not oblivious to the intent way she stared at me as I maneuvered her body. Like a doll.

Standing up, I took one of her clenched hands and pulled the stick free. I manipulated her fingers around the stick, positioning her grip just so. I was satisfied to find her mimicking with her other hand and nodded my approval.

"You're a good student," I praised, gripping her forearms and positioning the tip of one drumstick against the snare; the other against the hi-hat.

"Thank you. All my teachers thought so." She surprised me with a fluttery giggle. *She's nervous.* "I'm going to suck *so* badly at this. I have zero coordination."

"Nah," I insisted, shaking my head. "It's your first time. I'll be gentle."

Tabby sucked an inhale through her teeth at the blatant insinuation I wasn't at all sorry for.

Kneeling behind her, I said, "We'll do something totally basic. We won't even worry about the pedals yet, okay, so put your feet down." I pressed her Chuck-covered feet against the pedals with a hit of the bass drum and the closing of the hi-hat. "Just like that. Keep them there. What you're gonna do is up here …" I covered her wrists with my hands and felt the beat of her pulse beneath my fingertips. "You're gonna hit the snare twice, hi-hat once. Like this …"

Bum-bum-chh. I moved her hands, playing the simple beat, with my chest to her back and my temple to hers. God, was this only a ploy to get closer? Yes and no. Mostly yes. But she was tense and desperate for a release I wasn't sure she'd accept through sex. The next best thing I could offer was this—the only other thing I could offer.

I assisted her again—bum, bum, chh—and she leaned back a little into my chest. I smiled, nudging her forward.

"No slouching," I scolded teasingly.

"Sorry," she muttered, poking her tongue between her lips.

With a reluctance nagging at my nerves, I released her wrists and sat back on my heels. "Okay, Thumbelina. Flying solo now. Try it."

"Oh God," Tabby groaned, throwing her head back.

The words. The toss of her hair. A dirty sequence of images flashed through my mind and I had to pinch my eyes shut and shake my head to chase them away.

"Come on. Just try it once and I'll let you off the hook."

With another low groan and a deep breath, she bobbed her head to the tune I'd instructed. Then, with stiff arms and gritted teeth, she made a solid attempt.

Bum. Bum. Chh.

158

"See?" I grinned, absurdly proud over something so basic and lacking in skill. "Not so bad, right?"

Tabby looked over her shoulder, beaming with pure joy. "Oh my God, I feel so completely stupid for being this happy."

Chuckling, I moved to kneel beside her. "Wanna really blow your own mind?"

"Hell yes," she grinned with confidence, suddenly uninhibited.

"Okay, with each hit of the hi-hat, you're also gonna hit the bass. Think you can do it?" And although she eyed me warily, I talked her through every step, puffing her up with confidence. Then, ten minutes later, she was playing with both sticks and a pedal. She played like a toddler taking their first steps—nervous and unsure—but still she played and the excitement emanating from her swallowed me whole, and I grinned with her.

"I can't believe I did that," she sighed happily, handing me the sticks.

"Told you." I smiled encouragingly.

"Now, you play," she directed, standing up and pressing her back to the wall behind the kit.

"After what you just did? Hell no, I don't think I could stand the humiliation." I shook my head profusely, crossing my arms.

"God, you're an asshole," Tabby muttered around a sigh.

"I'm just teasing. You really should be proud," I insisted, adjusting the height of the stool. "I just don't want you to feel bad. I don't want you to compare what you—"

"Sebastian," she drawled impatiently.

"Fine," I grumbled, already quirking my lips and itching with the anticipation of playing. I positioned my feet on the pedals and pointed a stick over my shoulder at her. "Now, my beautiful assistant, I need you to do me a favor."

"What's that?" Tabby asked lightly.

Guiding her with the stick, I instructed, "Over there is an old-ass iPod sitting in a speaker dock. Be a doll and hit play."

With a grudging sigh, Tabby pushed away from the wall and walked around the drum kit. I followed her with hungry eyes. The enunciated sway of her hips in skin-tight jeans. The lift and drop of her shapely ass. The heart-shape it took on when she slowly bent over to eye the device, ensuring I was sufficiently aroused and shifting uncomfortably on my seat.

After turning on the music, the room filled with the Foo Fighters and I was instantly disappointed when she stood up and turned to face me. A coy smirk shaping her lips. "By the way, I know you had the remote next to you."

Well, isn't this interesting. "Oh yeah?"

"Mm-hmm," she nodded, crossing her arms.

"But you still chose to indulge me, huh?" I cocked a brow.

She sighed and lifted her gaze to the air, listening. "I love this song," she mentioned lightly, ignoring my comment.

"Who doesn't?" I nodded, lifting my lips into a lopsided smile, as "Everlong" filtered through the air. "It's my absolute favorite."

"To play, or to listen to?"

"Both." I smiled as I reached to the side and grabbed a chair from the corner of the room, pulling it over and patting the seat. "Come. Sit."

Tabby eyed me intently as I stopped the song with the remote and got it ready to play again, pausing while I waited for her to situate herself. I expected her to gingerly sit herself down, crossing her legs and folding her hands in her lap. But she all but shocked the shit out of me when she kicked off her Converse and pulled her knees to her chest, perching her feet at the edge of the seat. Her toenails were red and black.

"Those are my favorite colors." I tapped the end of one stick to her biggest toe, and she hid her smile behind her knee as she nearly whispered, "Mine too."

Grabbing the remote again, I pressed play, holding her gaze as the first guitar notes drifted through the speakers and I positioned my sticks, waiting for my cue. I could practically play this song in my sleep—it'd been one of my most-used since its release in '97—and I was able to drift along through the heat of her gaze during those first few hits of the hi-hat. But after those introductory notes, my music pulled me in and my concentration took over, just as the base drum kicked in.

I gritted my teeth, exercising the muscles in my arms with the tedious taps of the hi-hat, broken with the hit against the snare. Each chorus was led with a whip of my hair, banging my head to the beat, as I sang along on

161

autopilot to one of the most romantic songs I've ever known. And, with every kick of the bass and beat of a tom, I felt her eyes on me.

It wasn't until the lull in the song, where all but the guitar stops, that I looked back to Tabby. With sweat beading against my forehead and hair in my face, I knew exactly how I looked, and yet her stare held nothing but the same hunger I'd been feeling all goddamn day. Her feet were now on the floor, as she teetered closer to the precipice of the chair. Ready to lunge.

My hands were begging to drop the sticks, to throw them across the room and pull her onto my lap, but I wasn't going to. This was her call. Whatever she wanted, I would give, but she'd have to tell me first. She'd have to show me. The woman was so fickle, and I watched her as I finished playing, waiting for the moment when she would change her mind.

It didn't come.

With the final guitar riff, I laid the sticks onto the snare, and Tabby was on her feet, her hands reaching out to grasp the sides of my face. The song was on repeat—it usually was while I practiced—and as it began again, she was tipping my head back, bending her neck, and pressing her lips to mine faster than I had a chance to react. Her need for control was immediately startling and so fucking refreshing, as her tongue coaxed my mouth open, diving in to acquaint itself with mine and my teeth and the inside of my lips.

Finally catching up, I responded with a groan. She tasted like whiskey and mint, fire and ice. A perfect combination of what I knew to be her. Reaching for her

162

arms, I pulled her down to straddle my lap and tugged at the band holding her hair in place. It slipped away and all of that red came undone, cascading over my hands in waves. I thrust my fingers into it. Tangling, twisting, tying myself to her as our mouths opened wider, our tongues delved deeper, and I was almost certain she could swallow me whole if she tried.

It was when Tabby moved her hips against mine that I think her trance was broken. One press of my desperate erection between her legs and she was shaking her head, unthreading her hands from my hair and moving backward to stand up.

"We need to stop," she abruptly decided.

I opened my eyes, finding she hadn't yet, and replied, "Okay."

"I shouldn't be doing this. I … I have my meeting to prepare for," she proclaimed, making excuses.

Still, I nodded, and still, I sat. "Okay."

Stepping backward once more, her eyes still shut and unable to look at me, she nearly knocked over a cymbal stand. I reached out with an urgent grasp, stopping the teetering chrome from crashing to the floor, and chuckled.

"Easy there, Thumbelina."

That was when she opened her eyes, now taking me in, and I allowed myself the moment to look at her. *Really* look at her. Her striking emerald eyes and her ruby hair in waves against the smooth pallor of her face. With the black shirt she wore, the tight jeans and the red and black polish on her toes, she looked like a punk-rock Disney princess. With "Everlong" on repeat, I felt that, for the first time since meeting her, I was seeing this woman for who she truly was.

And she was beautiful.

"W-what?" she stuttered, tangling her fingers together over her stomach.

I shook my head. "What?" I repeated.

"What are you looking at?"

"You are fucking gorgeous," I blurted out, without a single care to hold my tongue. I never had before—why start now?

Shaking her head, she pulled her eyes away from mine. "You're only saying that now because I just made out with you."

"No," I protested, grabbing her hands and putting a stop to the nervous twisting. "I'm telling you you're fucking gorgeous, because you are. The fact that you made out with me was only a bonus, and it was a good one, but I promise, Tabby, I never say anything I don't mean."

Her gaze narrowed skeptically. "Why do you call me that?"

"What?"

"Tabby."

"Should I not call you Tabby?"

"No, it's fine." She hummed thoughtfully, dropping her gaze to our hands, still linked together. "I think I'm gonna go prepare for my meeting tomorrow."

"Okay."

"Good night, Sebastian," she said, pulling her hands from mine and moving quickly toward the door.

"Night, Tabby," I responded.

164

As she left the room, I grabbed the remote and stopped the music.

17

tabby

I didn't want to say that I was avoiding Sebastian. To avoid him would've been immature and pathetic.

But I was avoiding Sebastian.

He woke up before me, much to my surprise, so I waited on the other side of my door until he went downstairs, before I stealthily tiptoed toward the bathroom door. Quietly closing it behind me before taking a quick shower and hurrying back to my room.

Roman called while I was curling my hair.

"Ms. Clarke," he greeted me, with the sound of a smile framing his voice.

"Hello, Mr. Dolecki," I replied in the same friendly, albeit professional, tone. "How are you this morning?"

"Excellent. Looking forward to our meeting. I realize we probably should have arranged these details earlier in the week, but would you like me to send a car to pick you up?"

"No, that's all right." I wrapped a section of my hair around the heated wand. "I prefer to drive myself."

"A woman in control," he mused with a throaty chuckle. "Does noon still work for you?"

"Yes," I nodded to myself in the mirror, releasing the now-tight curl and lifting another section of hair. "That works perfectly."

"I hope you bring your appetite. Antonio's is my favorite spot in the whole city."

"I looked at their menu last night," I fibbed. *I was making out last night*. I cringed. "They look delicious."

"They are," he agreed politely.

We finalized the details—he would get us a table, I would meet him at the restaurant—before hanging up just as I finished my curls. With a gentle raking of a brush through my auburn hair, I loosened the strands to emphasized waves, pinned two front sections back, and froze it all in place with a shot of hairspray.

Turning to grab my clothes from their garment bag laying on the bed, a heavy knock came at the door and my guts tied into knots.

"Who is it?" I called in some effort to keep my voice light and without anxiety.

"I'll give you one guess," Sebastian spoke through the door, and to still a whimper I wasn't proud of, I clapped my hands over my face. "You don't have to open the door. I just wanted to tell you there's food downstairs if you're hungry."

Shaking my head against my palms, I replied, "Nope. Not hungry."

"Oh. Well. I kinda made a shitload of food, so …" The gentle tapping of fingers against the door echoed into the room. *Go away, go away, please go away.* "It's fine. You don't have to—"

"I'll grab something before I leave," I fibbed. This was becoming a habit.

Pushing myself through the motions of getting ready, I unzipped the garment bag and listened for the sound of his footsteps walking away. But I never heard them. I began to wonder, as I pulled out the pencil skirt and frilly top, if he had instead levitated down the stairs. When my curiosity had gotten the better of me, I walked to the door and swung it open. I wasn't surprised to find him still standing there, his back pressed to his door across the hall.

"Oh, hey," Sebastian said with a casual grin, but there was no hiding the concern in his eyes. "I figured you'd have to leave eventually. Didn't think it'd be in a towel, though."

He gestured to the fluffy, dark blue towel wrapped around my body, the end came to just my middle thigh.

"I was just about to get dressed," I explained, wishing I had brought my robe and putting on my most effective irritated face. "Why are you waiting outside my room?"

"Because we should talk," he stated plainly, crossing his arms over his chest.

"No, we really shouldn't." I made a move to close the door, when he stepped forward and shot his hand out to press against it. With an impatient sigh, I shook my head. "Sebastian, I have to get ready for work, okay? I need to go."

"*You* kissed *me*," he reminded me, ignoring my protests, "and whatever you want that to mean is totally fine with me. I don't read into shit like that. If all you want is to make out with me on occasion, or if you never wanna touch me again—it's all cool with me. But I want to know why you're now avoiding me."

He was an infuriating mass of man, blocking me from closing the door to my room and stopping me from getting ready to leave for work. The audacity of this display of immaturity was proof enough as to why kissing him was a very bad idea. He was a man-child without any sense of responsibility.

"*Why?*" I snapped, pinching the towel to keep it from falling, and he nodded. "Because what happened *never* should have happened at all, *that's* why."

Sebastian's lips quirked with amusement, correlating with the crinkles at his eyes. "So, you think that avoiding me is going to make me forget that your tongue was in my mouth. I gotcha."

"That's not what I said," I disputed, shaking my head and pinching my eyes shut. Words quickly filled my mouth and I spat them out before thinking. "I never should have kissed you. I was caught in a moment of weakness, not to mention the fact that I'd had a glass of whiskey, and then acted on it. I'm having a difficult time processing it, because I *know* it was wrong, but I'm also afraid that if I look at you, I'll create all of these reasons why it *isn't* wrong."

169

"I see." I opened my eyes to find that his hand had left the door and his arms were now crossed over his chest. "Why can't you just let it be what it is?"

"What do you mean?" I asked impatiently, ready to shut the door and be on my way.

"You said it yourself; it was a moment of weakness. You don't have to complicate it by thinking about right or wrong or whatever else."

"But it *is* wrong," I felt the need to clarify.

"No," Sebastian insisted with a blunt edge. "It's not anything. Don't label it. You could've just said to me, 'Hey, shitface, I know I was dry-humping you last night but I never wanna do it again, okay?' And I would've said, 'Yeah, no problem,' and that would've been it. But then, you went and *made* it something by avoiding me. No need to do that with me."

It hadn't occurred to me that I was the one making it weird, and then all at once, I realized I'd been the reason it'd gotten weird in the first place. He hadn't kissed me. He was flirty, yes, but he wasn't the one shoving his tongue down my throat. Still, the fact remained, that I didn't do this type of thing. I'd *never* done this type of thing, not like my sister.

"I didn't realize that was an option," I admitted, dropping my gaze.

"The hell, Tabby? You think, since you kissed me, it means we're bound to some unspoken laws or something?"

"Well, I don't exactly do this kind of thing, do I?" I didn't mean for it to sound like an accusation, but wasn't that what it was? This was what *he* did, it's what my *sister* did. Still, I shook my head, pressing my fingertips to my forehead. "Sorry. I didn't mean it like—"

Sebastian chuckled. "Kissing me doesn't automatically change who you are, contrary to popular belief," he said in a low, gravelly voice, reading my thoughts.

My resolve to be a stony, unrelenting statue melted as one lithe finger curled under my chin to tip my head up and back. His eyelids fell to half-mast, grabbing a hold of the green in my eyes to melt into the brown of his, before bending to dust his lips over mine. So quick, I might not have registered that it happened at all, if it weren't for the lightning strikes against my heart and the thundering of my pulse.

"See?" he whispered, his sweet maple syrup breath hot against my skin. "Still you."

And just like that, he stood back and declared that I needed to get ready for my meeting, as though I hadn't told him several times since opening the damn door. He walked away and down the stairs, casually calling to Greyson and asking if he wanted to jam later. Acting so nonchalant and as though he hadn't refreshed a memory that'd only just begun to lose its vivid luster.

He was wrong, I realized, as my fingertips moved from my towel to my buzzing lips. I *was* different. Changed with a kiss. And I had no idea how I was going to get through that meeting.

***

"Jess, what can you tell me about Roman Dolecki?" I asked through the Bluetooth in my car. I had attempted some research the night before, to ensure I knew about the potential new client, but the problem was my brain. It wouldn't focus on anything but the drummer across the hall.

"Uh, well, he's secretive as fuck," Jess snickered. "I couldn't find many decent pictures of him, which is strange, given the stature of the projects he's been involved in. A lot of big stuff; the rebranding of sports arenas, the brain behind a few up-and-coming social media outlets, and a business shareholder in a few restaurant chains. His name isn't exactly well known, but he's a pretty big deal apparently."

"Interesting," I muttered, letting loose an exhausted sigh.

Driving in New York City sucked. There's a reason why so few people living there own cars. I was grateful that Sebastian lived just outside of Manhattan, in a small suburban town only a twenty minute drive from the city line. But right now, as I waited for a small sea of people to cross over Broadway, I wished he had gotten himself a loft within the city limits instead. Then I could've walked, or taken a cab and have been done with it, instead of spending over forty minutes in bumper-to-bumper traffic.

"He's pretty accomplished for a guy of his age, too. He's only forty-one," Jess informed me. "So, you can take that bit of info for what it's worth."

"What am I going to do with that?" I guffawed. "'Oh, Roman, good for you for making something of

172

yourself before your prime. Now, buy this house, for the love of God.'"

"Well, I mean, I wouldn't say it in *those* words, but … complimenting people helps," she offered.

"I'll see where the conversation takes us," I gritted as I hit the horn, beeping at a cab that insisted on cutting me off. "God, I should've agreed to letting him send a car."

"Yeah, probably," Jess agreed. "Oh, and before I forget, you're not doing any more work tonight, right? I mean, we gave you a pass with the meeting because it made sense, but you did agree to the weekend off."

"Yes, Jess," I groaned, rolling my eyes. "I know. I'm going straight to Sebastian's house after this, to eat some ice cream and watch some crappy TV."

"Good," she replied happily. "And speaking of Thor, how was his house last night?"

"Uh …" All brain function stopped as I zeroed in on that one memory. The taste of his tongue. The feel of his hair between my fingers. "G-good."

"G-good?" she mocked around a bubbly laugh. "What the hell does that mean?"

"It means it was good." I bit my lip, nearing the restaurant. "He cooked dinner and it was really nice. I had a drink, and—"

"A drink? What did you drink?"

You know you don't have a reputation for indulging in alcohol when your friends gasp and immediately ask what you had. "Whiskey."

"You can't handle whiskey," Jess speculated. I could practically hear the gears in her brain turning. "You had a drink with Thor?"

"Can you please stop calling him that, for crying out loud? It's ridiculous. And I'm almost th—"

She gasped. "Did you guys *do it*?"

"Oh, gee, Jess. How mature. *Did we do it* ... you know, we *are* adults. We're not kids in high school or something. You can just say—"

"You're rambling. Why are you rambling?" Her voice was full of mischief. Like she knew something I didn't.

So I decided to indulge as I pulled into a parking garage. "Because I kissed him last night, okay? I kissed him, and then I made things weird by avoiding him this morning. Then, *he* made things even weirder by kissing me again to prove a point or something, and—"

"Whoa! Wait a minute! *You* kissed *him*? Tabitha Clarke, I'm impressed!" Jess was downright giddy and I could hear Alex squealing in the background. "I'm putting you on speaker. Alex wants in."

Why did I say anything? "I don't have time for this, guys," I grumbled, parking the car and unplugging the phone. "I'll talk to you later, okay?"

"Honey, don't you *dare*," Alex responded. "You will tell me if that man kisses as good as he looks, and you will—"

I hurried through the parking garage to the street as I groaned. "It was a moment of weakness. I was drunk," I lied, "and it's *never* happening again. Forget I said anything. Now, I'm hanging up. I'm at the restaurant. I'll tell you later how it goes with Roman."

I hung up before they could respond and walked down the sidewalk to the quaint Italian restaurant. With a deep, cleansing breath, I forced all thought of Sebastian and his lips from my mind and focused entirely on the job at hand: finding a buyer for Mrs. Worthington's house. I walked through the door, taken immediately by the scent of freshly baked garlic bread and the sound of traditional music.

"Table for one?" the hostess asked with a beaming smile, and I shook my head.

"I'm meeting Roman Dolecki," I informed her, clutching my briefcase to my side.

"Ah, yes, of course. Please, right this way." I followed her into the dining room and to a table in the far corner. "Mr. Dolecki, your guest has arrived."

A man of about six-feet in height stood, smoothing down his silk tie over a crisp button-down shirt. Dark, nearly-black hair shone under the warm glow of overhead lights, and at the sight of me, his deep-brown eyes glinted with delight. A smile stretched his lips, encased by a blanket of stubble, as dark as the hair on his head.

"Ms. Clarke," he bowed his head to me before extending his hand. "It's a pleasure."

"Mr. Dolecki," I greeted him with a warm smile, sliding my palm against his. It was smooth and warm. Not the hands of a worker. *Or a drummer.*

"Please, Ms. Clarke; call me Roman." His voice was velvet and every word was gilded in gold.

175

"Okay, Roman," I replied, pulling my hand from his. "And you may call me Tabitha."

"All right then," he smiled, gesturing toward my chair. "Tabitha."

Not Tabby.

18

sebastian

"Okay, so this is my kit," I said, stretching my arms out toward the seven-piece DW Collector's Series kit with a tobacco stain burst finish and the Devin O'Leary logo emblazoned on the bass drum. "And this, is yours."

I didn't think it was possible to get any big emotion from Greyson, but his eyes damn near popped out of his head as he lunged into the room and bolted straight for my kit.

"Holy shit," he gushed, running around and gingerly sitting down on the stool. "These are your *real* drums?"

"Well, I didn't pull them out of my ass," I laughed.

"Holy shit," he repeated, running his hand over the glossy wooden shell of a tom before reluctantly standing. He slowly edged toward the seven-piece Pearl Export set. "This is *mine*?"

"I mean, if you want it, sure," I said nonchalantly.

"You already set it up for a lefty," he mentioned breathlessly, sitting down on the leather stool.

I nodded. "Yeah, I noticed you're left-handed. I can play both, so that's no biggie if you need to mirror me."

The ragged breath Greyson drew in worried me. Was the kid going to cry? I hardly knew what to do with a kid at all, let alone one that was crying. Was he pissed at my attempt to impress him in the only way I truly knew how?

"You, uh … you really want to play with me?" he asked, looking up at me with an expression I couldn't begin to read.

With a shrug, I ran my finger over the edge of a cymbal. "I mean, you're fucking good, man; I'd love to jam with you. And I thought I'd offer to teach you some stuff, if you were interested."

Greyson exhaled and his lips twitched before he shrugged. "My, uh … my teacher said there's something new to learn from everybody."

I nodded. "Your teacher's a smart guy. I actually learned this new stick trick from my tech a few weeks ago. I've been traveling with the guy for three freakin' years and I only just picked this thing up." I grabbed a pair of sticks resting on the rim of one of my drums and held them up. "Wanna see?"

Greyson's eyes lifted to mine and he shrugged. "Yeah, sure. I mean … whatever."

***

178

I never thought I'd have a kid of my own, let alone one I could share my passion with. I'm not sure there's anything in this entire universe that could make me feel more alive than that.

I wished he was smiling as much as me. I wished he laughed more when I cracked a joke, or snapped a drumstick in half after hitting the snare's rim too hard. But it was okay, because he was there and he was enjoying himself more than he would've a few days ago when we first met.

"Okay," I said breathlessly, sweat dripping from my forehead, "I need to fucking rehydrate. Let's take a break."

"How much do you practice?" he asked, swiping his arm across his brow.

"Oh, fuck, kid. Uh …" I squinted up into the light, trying to pull the numbers. "I don't really time myself or anything, but it's usually a few hours a day when I'm not in the studio or on the road."

Greyson nodded intently, taking in the tiny sliver of information. "I can't practice too much."

"Why not?" I asked, laying my sticks down and getting up to walk to the door. "You should be practicing as often as you can."

"Yeah, but Aunt Tabs doesn't let me unless I've done my homework, and, you know …" He shrugged, as though that were a good enough finish to his sentence.

"Well," I said, sighing and opening the door, "you do need to practice and hone your skills. But you should also be doing your schoolwork too. Education is important."

179

"Why?" He followed me down the stairs. "You didn't go to college."

"No, I didn't." I walked across the living room to the kitchen, talking over my shoulder as I went. "Not every path leads to college, and I'm a firm believer that you shouldn't push it if it genuinely isn't for you. No sense in blowing that type of cash on a degree just because society tells you to."

"See? That's what I tell Aunt Tabs," Greyson replied, nodding enthusiastically as I opened the refrigerator and grabbed a couple bottles of water. "I don't need no education."

"Hold up, Pink Floyd," I interjected, raising a finger while closing the fridge. "Just because I knew I didn't want to go to college, doesn't mean I didn't keep my grades up in school."

"Why does it even matter?" he grumbled, taking a bottle from my hand.

"Because the reality is, kid, you might not go on to do what I do. You might play your first show and realize you fucking hate performing in front of people. Which is cool. It's not for everybody. But then what? What if you decide to become a music teacher? Or open up your own studio? You're gonna need that education then, and if you don't have it, well ..." I cocked my head and grimaced. "Can't be that teacher if you're a high school dropout, you know what I'm saying?"

Greyson's brows knitted together, his brow crumpled with thought, and he nodded. "That makes sense."

Maybe I'm not so terrible at this dad shit after all. "But hey, if that first show goes well, I have connections out the ass, so you'll be set for fucking life."

Then he grinned, uncapping his bottle. "You better hook me up, man."

Man. I would've given my right arm to hear him call me Dad. But I settled for the smile and the bonding experience.

"You're a lot cooler about this shit than Aunt Tabs," he muttered, after taking a sip of water. "You explain it better, instead of just getting mad."

Folding my arms against the counter, I sighed and carefully selected my words. "Yeah, but you know, your aunt's trying really hard to do what's best for you. You've both had some shitty stuff happen recently."

"Yeah," he mumbled, casting his gaze toward something distant. "She doesn't want me though."

There'd been times in my life where I'd wondered about my own sense of compassion and whether or not I still had a heart, or if it had been hardened by the road. But that moment reminded me of the organ still thumping in my chest, as it pulsed with an ache too real to be phantom.

"Greyson, she does," I nodded assuredly. "She just wants to help you."

"Yeah, by making *you* want me instead," he snickered, shaking his head.

For a second, I actually wondered if he was right, until I remembered there wasn't much a teenager said that wasn't a gross exaggeration of the truth.

"Well, I'm sure that's not true," I said, my tone sure and firm, before I decided to add, "But if you ever want to get a break from her, you can always come and hang out here. I'll keep your ass in check, and let you beat the shit out of my drums, okay?"

Dark brown eyes met mine, searching for the assurance that I was serious. That I wanted him. That he wasn't a burden.

Then, he nodded. "Cool," he said simply, unsuccessfully hiding his smile.

With a glance at the clock, I noted the time. It was a little after four in the afternoon. My mom would be over soon. Where the hell was Tabby? I knew I shouldn't be keeping tabs on her, but she'd already been gone for nearly six hours. How long did business meetings usually take? And why the fuck did I even care?

Because she kissed me.

The thought made me smirk, and I turned to grab an apple from the opposite counter, letting Greyson get a good look at my back while I stewed in my thoughts.

Why did it matter if she kissed me? Plenty of women had kissed me. Hell, most of them had done a lot more than just kiss. It never made me feel at all like I had to keep tabs on them. More often than not, I never had a way of staying in touch with them in the first place. So, what the hell was it about *her* that gave me that feeling? Why did I care?

The front door opened and that only meant one thing.

"Bastian!" My mom announced her arrival with her signature shout.

182

I spun on my heel, staring at Greyson. "That's my mom," I whispered to him. "You ready?"

Greyson shrugged. He had no idea what he was in for.

"In here, Mom," I called, leaning against the counter and eyeing the doorway.

"I brought your lasagna and I made some Itali—" Her voice caught in her throat at the sight of the fifteen-year-old boy. A shaking hand covered her mouth as she stepped forward, approaching him warily and eyeing him with the worry that he might be a mirage. "Oh my God, you're *real*. You're a real boy."

My ridiculous brain danced with images of wooden puppet boys and I shook my head, pushing a hand through my hair. "What were you expecting? *Pinocchio*?"

She looked to me and shrugged with the tray of lasagna and loaves of bread still in her arms. "W-well, I … I don't know, Bastian! I thought you were kidding! I never know with you," she practically screeched, turning to Greyson before saying, in a much friendlier tone, "I never know with him. He's always calling me with one ridiculous thing or ano—"

"What? I never do that," I disputed.

"There was that one time when you called and told me that you broke your sister's leg and—"

"I was twelve!" I laughed. Greyson was staring at me, jarred and unsure, and I shook my head at him. "Don't worry. My mother's insane, but she's harmless."

Mom walked over to me with purpose, swatting at the side of my head with a loaf of garlic bread. "Don't

183

you tell him I'm insane. Do you really want that to be his first impression of me?"

"You don't need me to say it, Mom. You're doing just fine on your own," I winced, rubbing at the spot on my head and rolling my eyes back to Greyson, only to find him smiling. "Greyson, this is my mother, Ronnie. Mom, this is Greyson."

With her eyes fixed on him, my mother slid the metal tray onto the counter, and clapped her hands over her heart. "Hi Greyson," she uttered in a whisper, her voice immediately choked with emotion.

"Hey," he replied, surprising me with a friendly tone to his voice. Surprising me more with his smile.

"Bastian didn't tell me what a handsome boy you are. God, will you just look at you? You look just like …" She turned to me, looking into my eyes and revealing the tears in hers. "Well, you look just like your father."

"That's what my mom used to say," Greyson said, and both my mother and I turned to him with a mutual gasp.

"Oh, honey, I'm *so sorry* about your mother," Mom spoke over me as I found myself asking, "She did?"

With a smile directed at Mom, he thanked her with a politeness I hadn't seen in him before. Then, when he diverted his attention to me, he answered, "Yeah. I don't … I don't think she wanted me to hear it, but she'd say it to Aunt Tabs sometimes."

I nodded. "Right."

"Didn't you say his aunt was here? Is she eating with us?" Mom busied herself with preheating the oven and unwrapping the loaves of bread.

"Uh, I don't know when she'll be back, but—" The broken chime of the doorbell pierced my eardrums as the three of us winced in unison. "Fuck, I really have to fix that thing."

"We both know you're not fixing shit," Mom muttered under her breath. "You might as well pay someone—"

"I'm not paying someone to do something I can do myself," I shot back at her as I headed toward the door, opening it to reveal an exhausted Tabby. Her high-heeled shoes from the morning had been replaced with a dirty pair of Converse. "Thumbelina, lovely for you to join us."

"Oh, you're not going to ask how the meeting went?" she chided, pushing past me and into the house, before dropping her briefcase on the floor like she lived here.

"So sorry, sweetheart. Please, tell me; how did your meeting go? Can I take your coat? Rub your feet? Should I fix you a cocktail?" I quipped, smirking at her as I closed the door and headed back into the kitchen.

"Oh, ha-ha," she drawled while following me, only to gasp at the sight of my bustling mother. "Sebastian, why didn't you tell me you had company? I wouldn't have—"

"Been so rude? Yeah, I wanted my mom to hear how you talk to me before she tries to set me up," I told her with a grin before making the introductions.

"Tabby," my mom grasped Tabby's hand between both of hers, "it's lovely to meet you, and aren't you gorgeous! Bastian, isn't she just stunning?"

"Smokin' hot, Mom," I agreed halfheartedly, but meaning every word, as the oven announced it was sufficiently preheated.

"Wow, your mom is so nice, *Bastian*. That's surprising," Tabby quipped with a teasing smirk as I opened the oven door to shove the lasagna in. "What happened to *you*?"

Mom released Tabby's hand only to grip her shoulders, smiling the way she had when meeting my sisters' husbands. Like she knew something we didn't. Some sixth sense only mothers are bestowed with. It took everything in my power not to tackle the woman who had birthed me, pick her up like a football, and send her sailing out the front door.

"Trust me, my boy was raised with my three daughters. He sure knows how to push buttons, but underneath all that? He is as sweet as a newborn calf," Mom assured Tabby, squeezing her shoulders and making me increasingly more uncomfortable with every tick of the clock.

"The barnyard analogies, Mom. Seriously." I scoffed, shaking my head.

"It's what I know," she shrugged, never taking her eyes off Tabby.

Speaking over my mother's head, I looked Tabby in the eye. "You'd never know this woman was raised in the heart of Brooklyn. Just, you know, throwing that out there."

I waited for Tabby's usual jab in my direction or a roll of her eyes, the things I had come to expect in the short time I'd known her. The stuff that might've happened before she upset the balance and kissed me, before I then egged her on and kissed *her*. But they didn't come.

Tabby's eyes left mine, settling on my mom's as she took the older woman's arm and led her into the living room. She beckoned Greyson to follow, before bombarding Mom with questions about my sisters and our upbringing. All with a startling amount of genuine interest. I'm not sure she realized what she was doing by asking questions, and then asking some more between nods of her head and sweet smiles. But I knew exactly what was happening, as I watched the clock and timed the lasagna and garlic bread.

I'm in so much fucking trouble.

19

tabby

In my line of work, it's necessary that I possess the ability to get along with anybody and everybody. I know how to make everything they say look interesting. I know when to smile, to nod, to tip my eyebrows with concern. I'm a professional, and I am always in tune with my social cues.

This was what I had prepared myself for when meeting Sebastian's mother. I had known she was coming over, and from the moment I met her, I had every intention of putting on my "game face" and appeasing her until she was gone.

In my line of work, I also find myself in instances where I genuinely become friends with the client, as was the case with Mrs. Worthington. I don't know why I hadn't anticipated this also being the case also with Ronnie Morrison.

"Well, now I know where Sebastian gets his cooking skills from," I complimented, finishing my second piece of lasagna.

The praise wasn't also meant to boost his ego, but he puffed his chest and reached out to clap his mother on the shoulder, gripping and shaking. "She had to give me something other than this amazing hair."

"I do wish you'd cut that mop," Ronnie quipped, brushing his hand away. "You always have it in that stupid knot."

My laugh burst from my lips and Sebastian narrowed his gaze at me. "Sorry. Nobody looks good with a man-bun."

"That's not true," he countered, pointing his fork at me with a raise of his brow before turning it on his mother. "And by the way, missy, I don't *always* have it in a *stupid knot*. I let it down when I'm playing. It looks badass, and the ladies love it."

"I don't need to know about you and your *ladies*," Ronnie snorted, waving a frantic and dismissive hand. "And you shouldn't be talking about that garbage with your son around anyway. You don't want to be a bad influence on him."

Immediately, Ronnie had taken to Greyson for who he was in the family: her grandson. *Sebastian's* son. While it was something I was still getting used to, there hadn't been any resistance period for her. It just was. And Sebastian seemed to teeter on some invisible line, not yet ready to commit to titles and formal names. Maybe he was just afraid of scaring the kid away.

"He's fifteen, Mom," Sebastian grumbled.

189

"Yeah, and do I need to remind you of what I was catching *you* doing at fifteen?" She shook her head, stifling a smile as she turned to Greyson. "You can assume that if he's done it, you shouldn't."

Greyson's eyes sparkled with laughter, flitting his gaze between Ronnie and Sebastian. "What were you doing at fifteen?" he asked, challenging Sebastian with a grin I hadn't seen in months.

"Don't you dare answer that," Ronnie scolded her son, as Sebastian raised his brows before uttering a stern, "Don't you worry about what I was doing. Just worry about yourself."

I think Sebastian doubted his ability to mature and be a father just as much as I did. I think maybe he also thought he was too far gone. His eyes met mine, as though looking for my approval and reassurance—as though it mattered—and I offered him a smile and a gentle nod.

"Come *on*," Greyson laughed, grabbing another piece of garlic bread.

"Nope," Sebastian shook his head.

"Man!" Greyson whined, the volume of his voice ringing through the dining room. I giggled under my breath. "I need to know what I've gotta do to get into the lifestyle."

"What lifestyle, honey?" Ronnie asked him, not using the brash tone she used with Sebastian.

"You know," Greyson responded, "rock and roll."

I shook my head. "Greyson, you don't need—"

"What was I saying earlier?" Sebastian interjected, his steely glare aimed across the table at the scowling, shrugging teenager. "I told you to focus on drumming and your schoolwork. Right?"

"Yeah, but what does that have to do with, like, girls and stuff?"

Sebastian's eye roll piqued my interest. "Let me tell you something about all that, okay? *Girls and stuff*? That shit is a distraction. Nobody really gives a fuck about how many chicks you've slept with. Nobody behind the scenes is saying, 'Oh, yeah, that dude Greyson's banged six hundred women.' No. Behind the scenes, they're talking about how well you play and how well you play with others. Trust me. Nobody wants to work with a fucking douchebag, okay? Don't be a fucking douchebag."

Greyson grumbled, slouching in his chair and resuming his dinner. Ronnie smiled at her son, an aura of pride clearly emanating. Sebastian just continued to eat like he hadn't just made the most brash, most enlightening speech either of Greyson's parents had ever made before. And me?

I was wishing for the control to repel him.

***

"I love your mom," I told him, after Ronnie had left.

"She likes you too," he replied, his tone unmoving as he loaded the leftovers into the fridge.

"A lot of people like me, Sebastian. Believe it or not," I teased, resting my back against the counter.

191

He closed the refrigerator door and eyed me with a blend of irritation and skepticism. "Why would you think I wouldn't believe that?"

"Because you don't." My arms crossed over my chest, and I watched the deep line between his brows form. "You like to push my buttons. You don't like *me*."

Sebastian scoffed. "You have no idea what you're talking about."

"Oh, I don't? Since I met you a few days ago, you've done nothing but taunt me. Honestly, I have no idea how you turned out the way you did when your mother is so wonderful."

Slowly licking his lips and studying me with a critical eye, Sebastian shook his head. "Remember how boys would pick on the girls they like in Kindergarten?"

With a light roll of my eyes, I turned to grab my phone from the counter. "Don't try to act like your immaturity is your own special way of showing that you like me. That's the most pathetic thing I've ever heard."

"I *do* like you," he insisted. "It might not be in a romantic way, but it's sure as hell in a friendly sort of way, and *definitely* in an 'I'd love to fuck you' way."

The abrupt mention of sex pushed my legs to involuntarily lock as my spine shivered with excitement. *Calm the hell down.* "How do you do that?"

"Do what?"

"Say the things you want to say when you want to say them." I turned around to face him, my phone in my grasp. "I can't do that."

Sebastian shook his head. "I don't always want to say them, but they're always better out than in." He

192

stepped forward, dipping his head to seek my eyes. "And, this is your cue to say, 'Oh, Sebastian, I like you too. Let's be fuck buddies.' 'Cause I'd really like that."

"You're disgusting," I snickered, shaking my head.

"Why is that disgusting?" He cocked a questioning brow.

"Because it's *wrong*," I countered with incredulity.

"There you go again, putting those right and wrong labels on shit." He shook his head, chuckling gently. "You're not a kid, and neither am I, despite what you want to believe. Adults can have sex if they want to, without it being anything more than sex. It just *is*, Tabby."

There he went again, *it just is*. I didn't understand how he could do that; live his life so carefree, without any worry of consequence. But then, look at what happened when he did act with maturity and thought. I reminded myself that he *had* attempted to do the right thing, to be an adult when the time called, and my sister had denied him the privilege of growing up for his son. But he *had* tried, and I wondered, was that more mature than the life I was living, where I denied myself every pleasure presented to me?

Would it kill me to let go, just this once?

Grasping for the surge of electricity I'd held the night before, I stepped forward. My feet weren't my own and my legs were foreign, driving me forward nearly against my will. The toes of my Converse met the white-caps of his, and his fingers pulled the barrette from my hair, tossing it to the floor, before threading themselves between the strands as his neck craned. Concealing the rights and wrongs of the moment with his mouth over mine, I stood on my toes and looped my arms around his neck. He was so tall, so much taller than five-foot, and I had to balance on the balls of my feet. To balance the time our tongues spent in my mouth and his, to increase the pressure of lips on lips, to let go and drown in something other than responsibility and the forever lingering pain of my grief.

My grief. Where did *that* come from? I hadn't thought about it in weeks; I couldn't. When could I? I was always too busy. Too busy with work. Too busy with Greyson—*shit. Greyson.*

I untangled my tongue from Sebastian's and began to pull away as he shook his head. "No, don't stop," he urged, pressing kiss after kiss against my lips.

"We need," my words muffled, "we need to," another kiss halted my words, tongue met tongue, moan met moan, until another reluctant withdraw, "*Greyson.*" And then, he understood.

One, two, three more kisses against my lips, and he groaned, pulling away. "*Fuck*, I think I'd be totally content just kissing you."

The feeling was mutual, but I wouldn't say it. He could say whatever it was that passed his mind, but I wasn't there yet. Maybe I never would be.

Wrapping his arms around my waist and tearing a gasp from my lungs, he lifted and unceremoniously tossed me over his shoulder like a sack of potatoes. He carried me, despite my repeated protests, toward the stairs, taking them two at a time. And with every step my complaints faded, first into light giggles and then a bubbly laughter I couldn't control, even if I wanted to.

I was having fun. *He* was fun.

Not right, not wrong.

It just is.

20

sebastian

With the door closed and the lock secured, I threw her onto my bed. As she landed, all of that auburn hair fanned against the navy blue of my blanket, her knees propped up and parted, her arms went overhead and her face flushed with excitement and laughter, I suddenly remembered that no woman had ever laid there before.

I never thought I'd realistically have another first, not at thirty-six with a lifetime of experience already under my belt, but here I was. Instantly sober and taking in the titanic profundity of the moment.

Tabby grinned unabashedly, the remnants of her laughter lingering in the lines around her eyes. "What are you looking at?"

Backpedaling from what could've been a mood killer, I knelt to the floor at the foot of the bed and proceeded to pull her sneakers off. "I'm looking at you."

"Oh yeah?" She twirled a strand of her hair around a finger, tempting me with the view of watching her from between her spread legs. "And what do you see?"

What do I see? For days I'd been trying to peel back every one of her stony layers, searching for that girl she used to be—*and still is*—underneath all that hardened skin and professional attire. I'd been trying so hard to see everything she could be, and there, in her business suit and Converse, with auburn hair in a chaotic halo around her head, and a coy smile on her face, I couldn't help but feel victorious.

"Everything," I stated simply.

"Oh, you see *everything*, huh?" she laughed nervously, doing me the favor of undoing her pants as I finished dropping her shoes to the floor.

"Yep," I nodded.

"Are you saying *I'm* everything?"

It was a jab, a playful tease. Nothing to look into as she lifted her ass and shimmied out of her beige pants, revealing a pair of smooth, porcelain legs. Women had made comments like that to me before. It had never been special, but now, maybe it was. Because I started to wonder, for the first time in my life, if anybody could be everything to me. And, what was it about *her* making that comment that made me wonder?

"Maybe," I laughed, standing up and peeling off my t-shirt, tossing it aside and undoing my jeans.

"Jesus Christ," she lifted onto her elbows to gawk at my bared torso, "I've never seen anything that looked like that in real life."

I glanced down at my crotch. "Just wait until it's out of my jeans. It'll really blow your mind then."

"Not *that*," she muttered around a giggle as she clambered to a kneeling position. I watched her eyes widen as her palms pressed against my chest, splaying her fingers over the hard-earned muscle and working their way down to my stomach. "Holy crap, you actually have abs. I mean, it's not a six-pack, but—"

My laugh startled her, and she raised her eyes to mine. "So sorry to disappoint. I promise to do a thousand crunches a day from now on, my queen."

Her mouth dropped with horror as she shook her head. "Oh my God, no! I don't even like six-packs."

"Bullshit! What woman doesn't like ripped abs? I've seen the fucking book covers on the shit you women read," I grunted, teasing with a raised brow. My jeans unzipped, and dropped to my ankles.

"Okay, first of all, that's not what *I* read, and second of all, I *don't* like six-packs. I like *this*. Definition without being … fake." She lowered herself, sitting back against her heels, still smoothing her hands over my stomach. She watched, as though she was drawing her own tattoos against my skin, leaving her mark, and branding me. "Fuck, I guess I like you."

"Oh God, that must be terrible for you to live with," I laughed, kicking off my shoes and jeans. I stole her hands away from my body and jumped to the bed, landing on my back and rolling her to lay against me.

Still in her neat button-down shirt and still undeniably sexy as hell. "Tell me, Thumbelina; what can I do to make it better?"

"You can shut up, for one," she laughed, dipping her mouth to mine as my eyes closed and she ghosted a peck on my top lip, bottom lip, both lips.

Holding my chin in her hand, she turned my head and pressed her kisses against my bearded cheek, memorizing the line of my jaw with closed lips, before trailing over my neck to my collarbone and chest. In bed, I believed in equal opportunity, always giving as much as I took, and I didn't plan on tonight being any different. But God, her lips were so damn soft, now fluttering over the flinching muscles of my stomach, moving down, down, further down with every painful, passing second. I kept my eyes closed, allowing myself a selfish moment to relish in the first nearly-timid touch of her lips against me through the fabric of my briefs. I gasped, as though I didn't see it coming, following with an inward moan.

"If you start with that, I can't promise I'd ask you to stop," I told her, my voice gruff and primal.

"Not until you say when, right?" she whispered, unsure of herself and her words, and I opened my eyes.

She had made a reference to "Everlong," our song— *wait,* our *song? What the hell is that shit?*

I looked down over my chest and stomach, to her. Biting her bottom lip, her lithe nude-nailed fingertips stroking gently over the waistband of my underwear.

"Not even then," I replied, equally unsure of myself and my own stupid words, because seriously, what was with that *our song* shit? I outstretched an arm. "Get up here."

Nodding fervently, she raised onto her knees, coming toward me and unbuttoning her shirt as she went. Slowly, slowly, *so* fucking slowly, revealing a hint of skin, a flash of bra, the bejeweled end of her bellybutton piercing, until the shirt opened, and her arms slid out. Now, I could have stared at the lace bra concealing her rounded breasts, the definition of her own lean stomach, or the winding roadmap of her hips and waist and thighs.

But my eyes were on the black feathers inked to her shoulders.

"Turn around," I commanded, and with a bite of her lip, she nodded and complied.

It was a crow, its wings spread, spanning the width of her shoulders. The detail was beautiful, every feather so real I thought I could touch the downy softness. I sat up, unhooked her bra and pressed my palm to her back, sliding over the ridged hills of her spine until I could touch the bird's talons, its beak, its wingspan.

"You're surprised?" she asked, lilting on a giggle.

I shook my head, moving to my knees and wrapping my arms around her waist. I buried my nose into her neck, nestled my impatient dick against her ass, and whispered, "Not even a little bit."

"Hm," she nodded with a sigh, tossing her bra aside then turning in my arms. Before she could press her chest to mine though, I caught the glint of the barbells piercing her nipples. So many fucking layers. "It just is, right?"

What she was referring to, I had no clue. I couldn't begin to delve too deep into that head of hers as I pushed

200

her back against the bed. I shucked her panties and my briefs to land somewhere on the floor. Because I had told her not to think about rights and wrongs, so I was meant to commit to that agreement as well.

But it wasn't easy, when our bodies joined together and I shuddered like I was a fucking virgin who'd never been touched before. I was different, immediately changed, and unsure of what kind of magic she possessed or if I should fear for my life. *It just is, it just is, it just is* … I chanted in my head, lying over her and holding still as my head bowed, pressing my forehead to hers. Settling into the new beat of my heart, and realizing there really are rights and wrongs, and this was …

Well, I didn't really fucking know.

Tabby wrapped her legs around my waist and forced me deeper, until I thought she became me and I was her, and I wondered why the fuck I was still there with the witch with the emerald eyes and auburn hair?

Gripping my shoulders, she pressed her lips to my jaw and whispered, "I didn't say when."

***

So, this is what it feels like to sign your soul over to the devil. I nodded to myself, my arm still wrapped around her bare, tattooed shoulders. *I mean, if this is the end of the world, it's not terrible. I could live with it.*

Tabby sighed languorously, pressing her multiple-pierced ear to my heart, as she drew an arc—back and forth, back and forth—over my chest with lazy fingertips.

"I've never let myself do this before," she mentioned in a voice shadowed with sleep. Her first words spoken since chanting my name like some sort of incantation. Casting her spell, ensuring nobody would ever utter my name like that again.

Witch.

"Do what?" I stared at the ceiling, committing the line of her jaw to memory with only my fingertips.

"Fuck without feeling," she whispered, her words wrapped tightly around an impending giggle. "I get it now. It's so ... *freeing*. It's like, a, um ... like an outlet."

A dull ache started in my chest as I nodded. "Told you."

Then I asked her, strictly out of curiosity, "What was it like with your ex?"

Tabby lifted onto her elbow, looking down at me with a questioning glare. "Look, I don't have an extensive backlist or anything, but I'm pretty sure you're not supposed to talk about other people you've slept with right after sleeping with someone else."

I laughed, lifting a hand to brush the hair from her face and tucking it behind her ear. "You don't have to worry about hurting my feelings with that stuff. No strings attached. Seriously, I wanna know."

"*Why* do you want to know?"

"Why do you ask so many damn questions?" I laughed, shaking my head. "I'm just curious. I've never fucked *with* feeling before." *I don't think so anyway.*

Tabby sighed, pulling herself up to sit beside me. She was unashamed of her naked body, sitting tall with her breasts displayed to my wandering eyes. Most women would cover up after doing the deed, hide themselves away as though they could erase the sins of our time together. But Tabby? She acknowledged that I knew her now and embraced it.

"It was, um …," she bit a thumbnail, searching for the word, "comfortable? I guess that's the word for it."

I shook my head against my pillow. "No, that's not what I mean. You're talking about how it was after you had been together for a while, right?" She shrugged, then nodded. "Yeah, no, that's not what I meant. The first couple of times, what were they like?"

"Well, I don't know—"

"Tabby," I interrupted, propping myself up against the headboard, "this isn't a difficult question. The first time you had sex with Barney—"

She laughed and rolled her eyes. "His name wasn't—"

"William, Scott, Fred—whatever his name was, it doesn't matter," I sighed, pulling my hair back and into a ponytail at the base of my neck. "The first time you slept with him, were there fireworks? Did you hear a marching band? Did a unicorn take a big fucking dump in the middle of the bed? What was it about that time that confirmed you wanted to fuck that *one* dick for the rest of your life?"

Tabby blew out an exhale through pinched lips and puffed cheeks. "Wow, okay, um … I guess it was that it just felt *right*, as lame as that sounds. I mean, I had been with one other boyfriend before him and it was okay, but it never felt quite like *that*."

Then I dared to ask, "But how do you know when it *feels right*? What the hell do people even mean when they say that?"

She looked over me, right above my head. Toward the wall and beyond. Her eyes sparkled with what I knew to be heartbreak. That was one feeling I could recognize.

"I guess, um," her lips pressed firmly together as she shrugged a shoulder and forced a smile, "when they feel like home? Or, uh, when you can't imagine ever wanting to be with another person after them?" She wiped an escaped tear from her cheek and I outstretched my arm.

"I'm sorry for asking," I said gently, wrapping my arm around her shoulders as she settled against me again.

"No, it's fine," she whispered, shaking her head, although tears kept slipping down her cheeks.

"Is it, though?"

Some cross between a sob and a laugh pushed through her lips as she shook her head. "No," she admitted, "I don't think I've been fine in a really long time."

"You can, uh, talk about it, if you want," I offered, not intending to sound as awkward as I did.

Tabby shook her head, sniffling and laying her head against my shoulder. "No, it's okay. I just … um, can I sleep in here tonight, maybe?"

Narrowing my eyes toward the door, I cocked my head. "Uh, yeah, sure. I'll just stay across the—"

With a watery laugh, she shook her head again, wrapping her arm around my waist. "I don't want you to leave, you moron. Sleep with me."

204

My exhale could've woken the dead. It practically left my chest concaved and my lungs shriveled. "Yeah, we can do that," I agreed awkwardly. "Can I piss first, or uh …"

"Oh, right, go ahead."

Tabby rolled off me, and I got up from the bed quicker than if the damn thing were doused in gasoline. I watched her slip underneath the sheets, settling against the pillows with tears continuing to zigzag slowly over her face. When she met my eye, she smiled apologetically and wiped at her cheeks.

"I'm sorry about … this. This probably isn't what you wanted." She bit her lip, diverting her gaze from mine.

"No, it's cool. I'd rather you get it out than forcing yourself to just deal," I replied honestly, and turned abruptly to walk into the bathroom. I closed the door behind me and immediately leaned my forearms against the vanity, looking over the double sinks into the mirror.

I felt different. Hell, I even *looked* different. A round or two of meaningless sex had a way of leaving me satisfied, ready to crawl back to the tour bus or my bed and nod off and sleep for twelve hours. But this? I was shaken, not stirred, with my heart bumping maniacally in my chest. What did she say about feeling at home? That's *not* what this shit was. This was like being left out in the rain, under a torrential sky of thunder and lightning, and begging to be let in.

I gripped the counter, staring into the eyes of the man in the mirror. He stared back angrily, pressing into my mind that he wasn't a one-woman kind of guy. He didn't date, didn't go for seconds, and he sure as hell didn't share the same bed.

But fuck, it didn't sound all that bad, did it? I mean, scary as hell, sure, but not *bad*.

I went back to her after taking the promised piss. Eyes closed and breathing evenly, I thought she was already sleeping, but as I climbed under the sheets, her arm reached out for me.

"Hey, you okay?" she asked groggily.

"I've never done this before," I confessed.

"What?" Her hand smoothed over the hair on my chest, and it was like being pet. It was nice.

"Slept with someone." It sounded ridiculous and I chuckled, shaking my head. "God, that makes me sound like such a pussy."

"Wait, like … never? You've *never* spent the night with a woman?"

"Nope," I laughed. "I've always slept alone, unless you count camping trips with my sisters. But I was like, eight or something."

"That's crazy," Tabby said, disbelief in her tone. "Well, I guess this is a night of firsts for both of us, huh?"

I tipped my head to rest my cheek against her hair and chuckled. "Yeah, I guess it is."

She settled against my shoulder, sighing contentedly, and I closed my eyes. The bed was an incubator, percolating with our combined warmth, and the gentle push and pull of her breathing lulled me closer to the brink of sleep. Until I remembered something important,

206

something I should've asked before I started thinking with my dick.

"Hey," I nudged her cheek gently with my knuckles, "how did your meeting go today?"

"Oh, it went really well," she replied, tightening her hold around my waist. "Roman's really nice."

Something else came to join the new and unusual sensations already corroding my veins. "Roman, huh? Not *Mr. Dolecki*?"

"He," she yawned, "prefers first names."

I'm sure he does. "You're gonna sell his house?"

Tabby nodded against me. "Yeah. I have to come back in a week or so to take a look around the place, prep it for the sale … you know, that kind of stuff."

"That means you'll be back," I stated, choosing to focus more on that than the sudden first-name basis.

"Yep," and with that, she tipped her head back, disturbing me from my resting spot to kiss my jaw. "Goodnight, Sebastian."

I returned the kiss to the top of her head. "Goodnight, Thumbelina."

21

tabby

I woke up with a wistful sigh against a pillow that wasn't mine. Hell, so much wasn't mine, I quickly realized. An arm, draped over my waist and heavy with sleep. A bristled chin, tucked into the space where neck meets shoulder. A splash of yellow blurring into red. A chest, blanketed in curls and heaving with every breath, pressed to my back.

Sebastian.

For a man who had never slept in the same bed with a woman before, he certainly seemed to know what he was doing. Wrapped around my body like a koala, there was no chance of me leaving the bed without waking him up, but did I really want to leave? Yes. Well, not really, but yes. I needed to pee, and I needed to make sure Greyson didn't find out about this. But otherwise … no. I didn't want to leave. He felt, smelled, and looked good.

Strong arms, strong legs, and toned everything else. I wanted to stay and stroke the hairs on his arms until he woke gently, but *God*, I needed to pee.

"Hey." I lifted my hand and nudged against his chin. No response. "Sebastian?" Another nudge and his lips twitched.

He grunted awake, with his temple still kissing mine. "I hate being woken up," he mumbled, his voice fuzzy with lingering sleep.

"Yeah, but I have to pee."

"So, go pee," he grumbled irritably, rolling the other way to release me from his hold.

I'm not sure what I expected from a morning after. We both knew this was a no-strings type of deal. A means for release—of stress, grief, whatever—but I guess I wasn't expecting his tone to be so brash and rude. Like he *wanted* me to go. I felt rejected as I sat up, looking over my bare shoulder to watch him settle on his back, with his arms outstretched. I stood up then gasped when his hand hit my ass, and I turned around to find his lips stretched into a smirk.

"You better be coming back when you're done." There was a more coherent sound to his voice, now lifted with happiness, and I smiled.

"I'll be right back."

Naked and not caring, I walked to the bathroom adjacent to his room. He hadn't been lying about the jacuzzi tub. It was big—room for two—and there were two sinks in the vanity. This house was obviously meant for a couple. A strange purchase for a guy hell-bent on remaining single forever.

It dawned on me, perhaps that wasn't always his intention. Or maybe his mother had insisted he buy a house that could one day accommodate a family, or at the very least a wife—*just in case*. Still, I believed him when he said he'd never had a woman in this house, and it wasn't lost on me that the only reason he allowed me here was because of Greyson.

I went back to his bed, happy to find him awake and waiting for me. He stretched his arms out, already luring me back with wiggling fingers, and I collapsed into him. Funny, when just a few days ago, all I wanted was to run away.

"I think you're a witch," Sebastian said, his voice clear and deep.

I giggled. "A witch, huh?"

"Yes." He nodded, stroking his fingers over my back and shoulders.

"And why do you think that?"

"Well, for starters, your name is witchy as fuck, okay. Don't deny that."

When was the last time I'd laughed this much after just waking up? "It kind of is, yeah."

I glanced at him to find his face twisted with thought. "Actually, you know what? You and your sister *both* have witchy names. Were your parents, by any chance, Merlin and Sabrina? Because that would make a shitload of sense right now."

"No." I was bubbling with little bursts of giggles, twisting my fingers into his chest hair and closing my eyes. "Their names were Charles and Josephine."

"*O-kay*. So, your parents were British royalty and they had witches for daughters. Got it." He kissed my forehead. "Anyway, aside from your name, there's the fact that I have never in my life slept quite like that, and I sleep pretty well even on a bad day. I mean, I sleep like a fucking log, but last night was …" He shook his head, sending an exhale out with a gust. "Last night was crazy. I feel like I've slept for a week."

"I feel pretty good too," I told him, acknowledging how foreign it was to feel so refreshed.

"Well, yeah, I would think so," he snickered. "I mean, you came, how many times? Fourteen, fifteen?" I snorted and clapped a hand over my face as he chuckled. "You're so welcome, by the way. And that's another thing too, actually."

"What is?" My voice traveled with my laughter, as I moved my hand lower over the tight and tattooed skin of his stomach.

"The sex." He was nodding again, staring up at the ceiling thoughtfully.

"Please do not tell me it was the best sex of your life," I groaned, tracing my finger over the strip of dark blonde hair, a pathway from navel to groin. "You don't need to lie to me like that."

"I won't lie," he promised. "I won't lay here and tell you I've never been with women who knew what they were doing. Because let me tell you, Thumbelina, I've had some *incredible* sex in my time."

"Uh-huh," I grumbled, rolling my eyes. "So, if you've already had the best of the best, then what was so special about me?" I might've been fishing for a

211

compliment, but what girl didn't do that from time to time?

"It was memorable."

The severity of his voice brought me to lift my head and look directly at him. His face was sincere and straight, without any sign of laughter or joking evident on his lips or in his eyes. "What do you mean?"

"I mean, I've been with so many women, that I don't remember any of them. Like, after a while, you stop remembering every cup of coffee you drink when you drink it every day, you know? That's how sex is for me. It's nothing, it's ... it's coffee." He shrugged, playing at nonchalance while his arm tightened around my shoulders, pulling me closer and squeezing my arm. "But last night wasn't like that."

His heart was pounding like thunder against my ear. "What made it different?"

"I wanna do it again," he stated so plainly, and I tipped my head back to catch his eyes.

"What happened to no strings?"

"I didn't say anything about strings," he pointed out, winking. "I'm saying, you and I are going to know each other, we're going to *see* each other, and I figure, as long as I'm not on tour, and you're available, why the fuck not?"

Why the fuck not, indeed. "So, you're saying you want us to be ..."

"Fuck buddies, friends with benefits, whatever you wanna call it. Or we can just, you know, not call it anything and just let it be what it is." His voice was so

212

casual, like he was talking about what he ate for breakfast or what his plans were for the day.

"I figured it was a one-and-done type of thing," I confessed.

"Yeah, well …" He let the words linger in the air. They hung there and made me question what it was that should follow. There were so many possible options, so many things that could've slipped in place of the silence, until he finally added, "Neither of us said when."

***

The three of us drove in Sebastian's Range Rover to his parents' place in Tarrytown. Greyson was excited, passing by the Sleepy Hollow town sign and asking Sebastian what it was like to grow up so close to the legendary town.

"Lame," he laughed. "I didn't get into it the way other people did. But Halloween was always fun."

Greyson made him promise they could do something together for Halloween. I glanced at Sebastian, hoping he wouldn't make a promise he couldn't keep. I didn't know what his schedule looked like months from now. I only knew he was off for the summer months, and after that, well, who knew.

He caught my questioning glare, and reading my mind, told me, "Even if I'm not here, I'll fly him out to wherever I am."

"Really?" Greyson gripped the backs of our seats, pulling himself forward. "You're serious?"

"Hell yeah," Sebastian said with enthusiasm.

213

I glared at him with a warning. "Uh, school?"

"Access to jets, baby," he waggled his brows at me, and I groaned, rolling my eyes. "But seriously, if he misses a day or two of school, would that really be the biggest deal?"

"No, I guess not," I conceded, sighing. "But you have to keep your grades up, okay?"

It felt wrong, using Greyson's budding relationship with his father as a bargaining chip, but Sebastian nodded his agreement. "Yeah, that's a good idea, actually. Keep your grades up, and we can do cool shit. Do shitty in school, and you're stuck cleaning my gutters and polishing my drums. Deal?"

And to my amazement, Greyson nodded as he sat back into his seat. "Yeah, okay. Deal."

Sebastian lifted his knuckles to me, and I tapped mine against his fist. I turned toward the window, smiling to myself as we pulled into the long, winding driveway of his parents' farmhouse. Just a few days ago, I never would've expected this man-child of a rock star to be an actual help with Greyson, let alone a tentative parent, and a help to *me*. I knew we—*I*—had a long way to go, but hope was suddenly a reality, and I knew it was because of him.

22

sebastian

"Oh my God. There's a *pig* on the *couch*," Tabby hissed from beside me as I cracked the front door open.

"Yes, Tabby, I'm not blind," I muttered in reply before calling into the house, "Mom? Dad? Anybody? We're—"

"Bastian!" Dad ran into the living room wearing his mucked-up overalls and carrying a little pink piglet in his arms. "Come in, for crying out loud! You don't need to wait for an invitation, you know that. Jeez Louise, kiddo, it's like you're a stranger around here."

I pushed the door open the rest of the way and stepped into the house. "Yeah, yeah. I know. I just didn't wanna walk in while you guys were, I dunno, naked or something. Don't need to be scarred like that again."

"Did you say hi to Mildred?" he asked me, gesturing toward the fat, sleeping potbelly pig on the couch.

"Hi Mildred," I grumbled, lifting a hand in a halfhearted wave.

Satisfied, Dad caught sight of the woman beside me and the kid lingering behind us, and I imagined what a stranger would think, looking at us. They'd assume we were a family, two parents with their child, and the corners of my mouth twitched at the thought. Dad knew better though, and he stepped toward us with his rosy-cheeked grin.

"Here, kid, take a piglet," he said to me, shoving the squirming little thing into my arms before pulling Tabby into him without warning. "You must be Tabby. I'm John."

"Tabitha," she corrected, voice muffled by the bib of his overalls. She hugged him though and with warmth and comfort. "Sebastian's the only one who insists on calling me Tabby, and I hate it."

"Ooh, watch this one, son," Dad laughed, releasing her from his grip. "She's got claws."

"Trust me," I chuckled, smirking coyly and catching Tabby's eye. "I've already had the pleasure."

She blushed, and I'm pretty sure I was too, as I dropped my eyes back to the piglet. Scratching it behind the ears.

"And *this* handsome young man must be Greyson." Dad's voice was coated in affection. "Are you too old for a hug?"

Hugging the grunting little pig to my chest, I watched Greyson as he took in the sight of my dirty father. His balding head, baseball-mitt hands, and cheery smile. I wondered what Tabby's parents—his other grandparents—had been like. Judging by his reaction to Mom and now Dad, I guessed they weren't overtly affectionate. He responded with a rapid shake of his head and released a wobbly exhale as Dad wrapped his arms around his shoulders. Greyson settled against him, hugging stiffly before letting go and stepping back, crossing his arms and brushing his hair from his eyes.

Dad touched the ends of his shaggy blonde hair. "You're like your father with this long mop," he scoffed affectionately. "Burgers and dogs okay with you guys?"

Greyson shrugged as Tabby nodded. "That's great," she replied, smiling politely. "Thank you so much for having us."

With one thick finger, dirt haloing the nail, Dad pointed at her. "That's the last time you'll treat yourself like a guest in this house, young lady. As my grandson's aunt, you are officially a part of this family, and you are *always* welcome here. Got it?"

She faltered for a moment, his comment had shaken her. Hell, it had shaken me, too. But she bobbed her head once, smiling and blinking away the tears collecting in her eyes. "Got it," she said, her voice tight.

"Excellent. Now," he turned to Greyson, "your aunts, uncles, and cousins are out back, so come on. Might as well get the introductions out of the way now, so you can get into the fun stuff."

Greyson looked immediately intimidated, and I laughed. "Dad, don't scare him away. I only *just* got him to not hate me."

217

"I never *hated* you," Greyson protested, shaking his head and scowling.

"Bullshit, kid," I eyed him skeptically.

"I'm cool," he said to my dad, and with a triumphant glare from my father, he led Greyson to the backdoor, leaving me with a piglet and my Thumbelina.

My Thumbelina? What the fucking hell?

I turned to her, proffering the squirming baby. "Wanna hold him?"

"It *is* cute," she conceded, holding out her arms. I handed him off to her and as she stroked his head, she commented, "So, your parents keep a pig in the house."

Glancing toward the still-sleeping Mildred, I nodded. "Yeah, they went a little crazy after my sisters and I all moved out. Empty nest syndrome or some shit. I think it's insane, but … you know …" I shrugged a shoulder and turned away from the snoring pig.

Tabby hummed before saying, "I don't think they're crazy. Actually, I think they're pretty amazing."

"Yeah, they're not bad," I relented, nodding. "I got pretty lucky, I guess. What were yours like?"

With a halfhearted shrug, she held her gaze on the pig in her arms. "Um, they were okay. I mean, I loved them—they were my parents, you know?—but they were older when they had us. My dad was fifty-one when they had Sam, my mom was forty-two, and I'm three years younger than she was."

"Wow." I crossed my arms, genuinely interested. "And they both died this past year?"

A shadow of sorrow was cast over her features as she smiled, still petting the piglet. "Yeah. Dad was

218

eighty-four and died a week before Thanksgiving. Mom was seventy-five, had cancer, and basically decided to give up after Dad was gone. She died in January."

Jesus Christ. "I can't imagine loving someone so much that I'd just give up on life if I didn't have them anymore," I muttered, looking to the wall and finding myself faced with a picture of my parents on their wedding day. How convenient. "My parents married when they were nineteen," I divulged. "I'm the youngest of four, and they had me when they were in their late-twenties, and I'm now thirty-six, so that gives you an idea of how long they've been together."

Tabby nodded. "I bet your parents would be lost without each other too, then. They probably don't even remember being apart."

I shook my head. "No, probably not. My sisters are all the same way, too. My oldest sister married her husband when she was twenty, and the other two weren't much older than that."

"So, you're the black sheep," she teased, reaching out and poking my stomach, letting her hand linger there for a moment before pulling back. The woman was obsessed with my stomach.

"Yep," I nodded. "They actually have a black sheep out back named Bastian."

"Oh, shut up," she grumbled, taking the first step to head in the direction in which my dad had taken Greyson. "Anyway, my parents weren't the most affectionate. I mean, they loved us and all, and they cared for Greyson, of course. But, they believed in a, uh … a more *distant* affection, I guess. Or maybe they were just too old to be bothered, I don't know. But, um …"

With a shallow gasp, she stopped in the middle of the dining room, facing the French doors that led to the backyard. "I'm glad Greyson has this now. We never did, and I know that, even though Sam never wanted you involved for whatever reason, I know she'd be happy that he has a family."

I looked through the paned doors at my three sisters, their husbands, and their slew of children, all greeting Greyson with hugs and handshakes. Two of my nephews were somewhere around his age, about his height and clapping his shoulders with enthusiasm, encouraging him to follow them. He went, and fuck me, I choked up.

"I was thinking …" Tabby began with a deep breath. "Maybe when school lets out, you'd want him to stay with you."

I looked to her abruptly, remembering what Greyson had said about her not wanting him. "Tabby, I just met him a few days ago. I don't know if he's ready for that."

But she shook her head adamantly. "I'm not saying definitely. We have about a month until then. But, I mean, if he wants to, then what do you think? It would be helping me out a lot, now that I'm dealing with the sale of the Worthington house *and* Roman's—"

Somewhere after she mentioned Roman, I stopped listening. Why did she call it the Worthington house, as a title, and not *Jane's* house? Why did she call it Roman's house and not the Dolecki house? Why in the fucking world did I even give a shit what she called it?

"—could be good for you too," she concluded, turning to face me.

Not having a clue what she'd said, I only asked, "And where would you be?"

"Uh, well, I'd be at home, unless I was working at Roman's, in which case I'd be ..."

"With me," I finished, not even caring about the possessive tone in my voice.

"While I'm not working, yeah, sure. Probably."

A summer. Two and a half, maybe three months of Greyson and Tabby. Months of life inside my house, months of having someone to come home to.

I found myself smiling and nodding. "Yeah, this sounds good. If Greyson wants to."

***

"Tabby, I *love* your hair," Mel gushed, boldly undoing Tabby's braid and running her fingers through the auburn strands the way I had just this morning.

"Ugh, I love your *shirt*," Dinah chimed in, bouncing Jen's new baby on her hip. "I miss when I had a cute body."

"Yeah, seriously, I *love* your body. Don't have babies," Jen groaned, rolling her eyes toward her husband Greg.

What I gathered was, my sisters loved Tabby. They were all immediately infatuated with everything about her. I hung back with my brothers-in-law, watching the lovefest from afar, as I slowly nursed a beer. Greg shook his head at his wife and turned to the rest of us.

"Can I remind you guys that *she's* the one who insisted on having kids? I would've been totally cool with getting a dog," he grumbled, reaching into the cooler for his second beer. "But no, *she* needed a family. She thought it would've been *so sad* to not procreate."

"Dude, you're preaching to the choir," Steve agreed, nodding. "I mean, I love my kids. They're cool, but I mean, I could've done without the orthodontist bills." Both of Steve and Mel's sons had gotten braces at the beginning of the year. It was college or straight teeth, but Uncle Sebastian was going to help where he could. "I'd always thought you got off easy," he chuckled, jabbing my ribs with his elbow, "but uh …" He nodded his chin toward Greyson.

"Give me a break," I grumbled around a laugh. "I think everybody was kinda waiting for this to happen eventually. I can't spread my seed around without *someone* getting fucking pollinated, right?"

The trio of brothers-in-law laughed, shaking their heads, and Greg said, "At least you can laugh about it."

I didn't mention that I'd known about Samantha's pregnancy years ago. There wasn't a point to getting into that story. It would only make them think poorly about Greyson's mother, for keeping me in the dark for fifteen years, and what purpose would that serve?

"So, what's her story?" Matt asked, tipping the neck of his beer toward Tabby.

Every bone and nerve in my body tightened as I caught the hungry look in his eyes. "What do you mean?"

"She's hot," he commented.

222

Matt, like the others, was a loyal son of a bitch, and I knew he'd never stray from my sister. That's not why my eye began twitching. It was that part of my brain that had pulled that *our song, my Thumbelina* shit out of nowhere. Apparently, it also didn't like other men calling her hot.

"Yeah," I agreed with a quick jerk of my head, my fist clenching and unclenching at my side.

"Oh, look at him, getting all defensive," Greg teased, shoving against my arm before dropping down into a plastic lawn chair.

Steve snorted. "You're gonna crush that beer, bro."

I hadn't even noticed my white knuckles around the amber glass, and I loosened my grip. "I'm not getting defensive," I insisted, keeping my gaze on Tabby.

"Aww, guys, our little boy finally has a crush on a girl." Matt emphasized a pout, wrapping his arm around my shoulders and pulling me against him. "God, we've been waiting for this day since … well, shit, I actually can't go that far back in my memory. Fuck, I'm getting old."

"Yeah, you are." I shoved him off, tipping the beer to my lips.

"Whoa. He's not denying it. What do you think it means?" Greg shifted his eyes between Steve and Matt. "Should we be scared? Because, guys, I'm scared."

"Oh, fuck off," I chuckled, shaking my head. "There's nothing to confirm or deny. She's just Greyson's aunt."

"Oh, that explains everything," Steve grunted as Mel approached him. He pressed a kiss to her temple, but her eyes were on me.

"Tabby is *uh-mazing*," she gushed, telling me what I already knew.

"She's cool." I shrugged, dropping my gaze to funnel all thoughts into the open mouth of my beer. Hell, maybe I could just let that little hole suck me right in. I could disappear and get the hell away from all these eyes on me.

"*Cool*?" Mel parroted, her tone riddled with disbelief.

I lifted my eyes back to hers, squinting and shaking my head. "I bring a kid home like he's a freakin' puppy or something, and all you people can talk about is the woman he comes along with?"

"Oh my God, he's getting defensive." Mel clapped her hands against her heart, turning to stare at her husband. "Honey, my baby brother is getting defensive *over a girl*. Do you know how—"

"We know," Steve chuckled. "It's sweet."

With an aggravated huff, and knowing I wasn't helping my case, I trudged away from them to stand with my dad at the barbeque. They could speculate all they wanted—I didn't care—but Christ, you'd think I was Greyson's age, with the way they were behaving. It's not as though I'd never brought a woman home before—

Except I haven't.

Dad glanced at me. "You okay?"

"Uh, yeah, why?"

"You look a little pale to me," Dad commented, nodding. "Ask your mother—she'll *know* if you look pale."

"I'm fine." I wasn't fine. "Just tired." Not tired. Totally rested, actually.

"Ah, yeah. Must still be weird, sleeping in your bed after months on the road, right?"

"Yeah," I fibbed, nodding and trying my best to look convincing as I shifted my gaze across the yard toward Tabby.

She was talking to Mom, Jen, and Dinah, holding one of the younger kids, one of Mel's, I think—why could I never keep all those rugrats straight? She was laughing, and just like that, I had to know what they were laughing about. I wanted to hear her, maybe laugh with her. I walked over, abandoning my dad with his hot dogs and burgers, and approached, tunneling my vision only on Tabby.

Witches have that effect on men, right?

"Hey, ladies," I casually interjected, standing between my sisters.

"Oh, look, it's our little baby brother," Dinah teased, standing on her toes and reaching her hand to pull the rubber band from my hair. The blonde mop spilled over my shoulders as she pocketed the elastic. "I hate that stupid bun."

"Another point for me!" Tabby cheered, raising her arms above her head.

I scowled, shoving the hair out of my face with a thrust of my hand. "Not a single one of these people approves of my awesome head of hair, just so you know. They can't help that they're all jealous as hell." I jabbed my thumb over my shoulder at my bald father. "That guy especially."

225

"Oh, you." Mom swatted at my chest with her hands and I brushed her away with a light chuckle. "Leave your father alone." She glanced at Tabby and sighed. "He hoped that, when he finally had a boy, he'd inherit his hair genes. John has been balding since his twenties."

"And instead, he got Fabio," Jen teased, rolling her eyes and Tabby grinned broadly around a giggle.

"*Fabio*—I like that one. My friend calls him Thor," she told them.

"Ah, yes," I nodded thoughtfully. "I remember Jessica fondly. She treated me *so much better* than you did when I first met you. You were so mean."

"You had it coming," Tabby defended, quirking her lips into a smirk.

"He probably did," Jen backed her up. "He's been a pain in the ass since he was born."

Dad announced not long after that dinner was ready. Mom arranged us around the long picnic table they used for such occasions, putting Greyson in the middle of Mel and Steve's two oldest sons. He was having such a good time, and that reminded me of the assholes he was hanging out with at school. The ones who made fun of his mother and teased him for not having any parents. A sense of pride for my family rolled over me. That they could embrace this kid they didn't know, who looked an awful lot like me, even the younger ones who undoubtedly had their questions.

The rest of the kids—ten in all—were arranged in age order at one end of the long table, with the adults at the other. Couples sat in pairs, and Mom insisted that Tabby and I should sit together. I told her it wasn't necessary, if Tabby wanted to sit beside one of my sisters, but Mom was persistent. It was almost as though the woman could smell the residual effects of sex still clinging to our skin and hair, despite the shower we had taken together before heading over.

"Greyson, you okay down there?" Tabby called, sitting down beside me without batting a lash. He waved her away with a disgusted expression before turning to Johnny, one of Mel's boys. "Wow, did you see the look he just gave me?"

I laughed. "Yeah, have fun driving home with him in the morning."

"In the morning?" Tabby turned a startled expression to me. "I have to head home *tonight*. I need to be in work tomorrow. I have lots of stuff to do, with this new job."

Not wanting her to see my disappointment, I nodded, and grabbed for some corn on the cob. "Oh, okay, that's cool. Makes sense."

"Yeah, but hey, obviously you can come by to see Greyson whenever you want," she mentioned, loading up her plate with macaroni salad, a hamburger, and some fruit salad.

I grabbed more corn. "Maybe I'll do that." And maybe I'd also stop by her work in the middle of the day to act out my fantasy of office sex. "I could stay at the motel again—"

"Why?" she asked abruptly. "I live in a four-bedroom house. Why wouldn't you just stay with us?"

"I wasn't sure that was an option?" The uncertainty in my voice made the statement sound like a question and Tabby rolled her eyes as I grabbed for another corn cob.

"We're past the point of being strangers, Sebastian," she grumbled, rolling her eyes. "For *obvious* reasons, and I think you know what I mean."

"Oh, no, I don't think you've made it clear enough," I retorted, easily falling back into our banter. "Maybe you should spell it out for me the way you did last—"

It was at that point I realized our end of the table had fallen silent, with every pair of shifty eyes now inconspicuously aimed at us, as though we'd never notice them listening in on our conversation. I swallowed, and looking down at my plate, noticed that I'd been mindlessly taking ears of corn out of the bowl. Six now sat on my plate, stacked like a pyramid next to the burger I'd grabbed before sitting.

"Jesus," I grumbled under my breath, and looked up to ten pairs of eyes scouring right through me. "What the hell are you all looking at?"

"Oh, nothing," Mel chided in the sing-song voice she never stopped using. Her lips quirked into a little triumphant smirk and I resisted the urge to kick her under the table.

"You better be eating all that corn," Mom scolded, pointing a finger at my plate. "And *maybe* you want to keep some private matters *private*."

The awkward silence that blanketed our end of the table lasted all but a few minutes before conversation picked up again. Tabby talked to my parents about farm living, the guys talked to me about life on the road, and my sisters talked about getting the kids together to go to

Hershey Park. It was at that moment when their mouths stopped moving in unison, as though a spark struck them all at the same time, and they turned to me.

"What?" I asked, looking between the three of them while freaking out internally. "You guys aren't going to try and blow my hair out again, are you? Because remember the last time you did that, I looked like fucking Fabio—"

"Sebastian," Dinah uttered with excited urgency, "you have a kid now."

I swallowed. "Well, I mean, he didn't just happen. He's been alive for fifteen years and—"

"No," Jen interrupted. "You should come to Hershey Park with us. Bring Greyson."

I can imagine my face perfectly displayed the horror I was feeling. "Oh no. Absolutely not." I shook my head adamantly. "I'm not attending Mommy's Day Out to talk about mani-pedis and tampons while the kids go on roller coasters, or whatever the hell you guys do. No way."

"But you never do stuff with us!" Mel whined, throwing her head back.

"Because I don't want to talk about how cute Ricky Martin is, or whoever the hell it is you guys like now," I reasoned, diving in to eat every last kernel of corn off my plate. "You guys have a good time and—"

My ears perked up to Greyson's laugh at the end of the table, and I turned to watch him, frozen and unblinking. He was holding his stomach, leaning over his plate and laughing so hard, tears were brimming his eyes. Why hadn't anybody told me that would be the most amazing sound I'd ever hear? Not even my first set of

229

DW Collector's Series drums had sounded as beautiful to me as the purest form of his laughter.

He was accompanied by Johnny and Travis, the three of them sounding so similar as they laughed about whatever-the-hell it was, and Tabby tipped on her segment of the bench, pressing her arm into mine.

"He hasn't laughed like that in months," she whispered loud enough for me to hear. "Maybe all year." Her words caught in her throat, blocked by clotting emotion and she raised her hand to her mouth before excusing herself from the table.

I turned to my sisters, and took a bite of corn as I asked, "So, when are we going?"

23

tabby

"There she is," Jess announced my arrival the moment I walked through the door. She pressed a cup of coffee into my hands on my way to my office. "How was your relaxing weekend off? With *Thor*?"

"Oh, it was nice," I mentioned lightly, heading toward my desk and sitting down.

Alex and Jess stood on either side of the doorway, arms crossed and eyeing me skeptically.

"*Nice*?" Alex scoffed, slowly blinking his disbelief. "That's a word people use when they don't want to get into it."

"Yeah, girl," Jess agreed. "We need more details than that."

If they were asking me for a more descriptive word explaining the goings-on of my weekend, they weren't going to get it from me. I didn't even know how to describe it to myself, let alone them. Fun? Scandalous?

"At least tell us how Thor was," Alex begged, pressing his palms together. "Pretty please?"

How he was. My eyes snapped open and I shot them with a steely glare. "What? What do you mean?"

Alex shrugged. "How was his house? Did he look just as delicious in his pajamas as he does in those jeans? Does he cook?"

"Oh," I breathed with relief, shaking my head. "His house is nice, and he cooks really well. He was, um … surprising, actually."

Jess stepped toward the desk. "Wait, what did *you* think he was talking about?"

I swallowed against the anxiety tightening around my throat. "I thought you were going to bring up—"

"You mean *the kiss*?" she asked, planting a hand against her hip. "You said you were drunk and it wasn't going to happen again, so we figured it wasn't a big deal. *Unless* …"

"No, you're right," I brushed her off hastily, opening my briefcase and sipping at my coffee. "Now, I need to get back into the swing of things here, guys. So, if you could just—"

Alex raised his hands into the air and shook his head. "Oh no, honey. Hold up just a second. You came back to work a new woman. I don't know why I didn't notice this the second you walked through the door. Jessica, will you please assess our fearless leader and tell me what's different about her?" He walked to stand beside my desk, gesturing his hands toward me like he was a model on a gameshow.

I told myself there was no way they could tell I had indulged in an uncharacteristic night of meaningless sex. It had been over twenty-four hours since I'd shared a bed with Sebastian. I'd had two showers since then, four spritzes of perfume, and a whole night of sleep separate from him. And still, I found myself afraid they could tell, afraid they'd want details, afraid they'd see me differently.

"It's her hair," Jess nodded after a moment of assessing. "You never wear your hair completely down like that."

"*Bingo.*" Alex ran his long fingers through the lengths of my hair, humming with delight. "God, lady, your hair is *gorgeous.* That weekend must've done you some good, because this is a new, free you. I *love* it."

Relief lifted a massive weight from my shoulders and I sat up a little higher, smiling. "It really was great. Sebastian has one of those waterfall showerheads in his bathroom, and it really is as luxurious at it sounds. I should have one installed in my place, but who has the time for that?"

I sighed, remembering the shower we had taken after fully waking up on Sunday. The way he had insisted on washing my hair, which seemed like such a silly thing at the time. I was a grown woman fully capable of washing my own hair, thank you very much, and that's exactly what I had told him. But he wanted to, and although I rolled my eyes and felt ridiculous, I found that it was one

233

of the simplest joys I'd experienced in recent history. Just having someone else wash my hair.

I had smelled like him all day, at his parents' house and even driving home. I had avoided showering again until I woke up this morning, just to keep his scent around me a little longer. I'd told myself that the one and only reason for my hesitation, was simply that he smelled good. Nothing more.

"What's that face for?" Jess accused, tipping her head and jutting her hip.

"What?" I asked, focusing my eyes onto the papers on my desk. "What face?"

"You disappeared for a second," she mentioned gently, nodding. "You had this little smile on your face. You looked the way my dog did the day he got his paws on a dead squirrel in the yard." Jess and her husband had adopted a Lab puppy a year ago who had a penchant for retrieving everything he could, including the occasional deceased animal. Can't take the Retriever out of the Labrador, they always said, and they were right.

"Oh, I, uh, was just thinking about how crappy my shower is in comparison," and that wasn't entirely a lie. "You really wouldn't think it'd make that much of a difference, but it actually does."

I cleansed my mind and body with a deep inhale and a full exhale, tapping my fingers against my desk. "Okay, guys, seriously. I need to get to work in here. I need to call Mrs. Worthington and Roman and get the ball rolling on these sales."

With an exaggerated yawn, Alex excused himself from the room and Jess stepped toward the desk. "What's the plan with that?"

Pulling out a stack of paperwork and shuffling it into neat piles, I replied, "Well, I could technically make the sale on the Worthington house now. Roman could move in right away, while I sell his Manhattan house remotely."

"But?" Jess offered expectantly, pinching her lips.

"But, I want him to meet with Mrs. Worthington before I make any decisions. She has approved or disapproved all potential buyers thus far, and I want her to be as involved as humanly possible. Roman can be in the area, he says, in a few weeks, so they'll be able to meet then. Unfortunately, that means I'll be sitting on this deal for at least that long, but there isn't much else I can do in the meantime." I shrugged. "Honestly, I don't know why he can't be here sooner than that. It could be a day trip for him, just to meet the old woman for a few minutes."

Jess hummed, bobbing her head. "He's a busy guy."

"Yes, he really is," I agreed.

I was disappointed when Jess grabbed the chair across from me and pulled it close to the desk. I really did have work to do, things to think about, but I knew her gossip face when I saw it, and I braced myself.

"What's he like?" she whispered, leaning forward over the desk.

"Who, Roman?" She nodded eagerly, and I instantly felt my cheeks flush. "He's actually kind of amazing, honestly."

"Oh God, is he one of those men that *oozes* wealth? Because I just got this feeling, and with a name like that? *Roman Dolecki* ..." She released a groan that would've been inappropriate had it not been the two of us in my office. "Yes, *please*."

"Pretty much," I laughed, shaking my head and taking another sip of coffee. "And he's so nice," I added.

Edging closer over the desk, Jess asked, "Is he hot?"

And because the conversation was distracting her, and myself, from any thoughts about the weekend or Sebastian, I nodded. "Uh, yes. Incredibly."

***

"How was your drive home?" Roman asked, his deep voice caressing my ear through the speakerphone in my office.

Jess was in the doorway, dramatically fanning herself, and I rolled my eyes. "It was good," I nodded, pulling out my planner from my briefcase and flipping it open to this week. "We didn't head back until late last night, so there was almost nobody else on the road."

"Ah, those are my favorite times to drive." I could picture him, cocking his head and rubbing one manicured hand against his stubbled chin. "I should take you out in my Ferrari sometime. There's really something about driving at night with the top down."

My eyes lifted to Jess, who had already tipped her head to one side like a confused dog. "Oh, um, I'm sure that'd be lovely."

236

I wasn't sure how to take the comment. Was he being nice? Was it flirtatious? Or was he simply showing off? It was too vague to tell.

Clearing my throat, I tapped the little box marked *Saturday* in my planner. "So, Roman, I have this weekend free to come out to see your home. I know it's such short notice, but does that work for you?"

I listened to the tune of mouse-clicking and keyboard-tapping until he hummed thoughtfully. The sound could've made a nun's toes curl. "I would need to shuffle a few things around, but I should be able to make it work. Saturday, you said? What time?"

"Around noon?"

Another hum and my cheeks flushed. "Noon it is. I'll let my assistant know."

I jotted *Roman* into the box. "Excellent."

"Indeed," he agreed. "Can't wait to see you again, Tabitha."

"I'm looking forward to it as well." I made sure my smile was wide as I said goodbye to him, leaving him with a good impression, even if he could only hear it. Jess was nearly a puddle when I looked back to her and chuckled, shaking my head. "You are absolutely ridiculous, you know that?"

"I'm sorry if thirteen years of marriage has made me hot for any guy with a deep voice and a laugh that could melt butter," she shot back with a flip of her hair before heading back to her desk.

***

237

Monday rolled into Tuesday, and then Wednesday brought a surprise visit from Sebastian. He stopped by my office and requested my house keys while I was still processing the fact of him being there at all.

"Why didn't you tell me you were coming?" I demanded to know, fishing the keyring from my purse and pulling off the spare key to the house that I'd given to my ex once upon a time.

"You told me I could come whenever I wanted," he reminded me, slipping his sunglasses off and dropping into the chair on the other side of my desk. "Also, I kinda feel like I'm wasting even more time just sitting around at home."

"Wasting time?" I slid the key across the desk. Giving it to him was tied to a commitment and I was shocked by how easily I gave it away.

Nodding, he grabbed the shiny piece of metal and put it onto his own key ring. It felt symbolic and oddly permanent, until three little words popped into my mind: *It just is*.

"Yeah, I mean, haven't I wasted enough already?"

"You mean with Greyson?"

"Yeah," Sebastian said simply, continuing to bob his head as he dropped his keys on my desk. "I got to thinking last night that I've been robbed. Of time, you know?"

I gave him a small sympathetic smile. "Yeah," I nodded, "I can understand that."

He gazed at me across the desk, his deep brown eyes taking me back to moments when we were both naked. With a flicker of recognition, he leaned back in his seat, reached behind and gave the door a nudge. It drifted shut, not quite clicking in place, but for one moment, I hardly cared as he stood up and rounded my desk. Pressing both hands to the arms of my chair, he caged me in, lowering his mouth not to my lips but to my neck. There, he kissed me with closed lips, filling his lungs with my scent and sighing with what I only knew as relief.

"Work Tabby smells different from Weekend Tabby," he muttered against my sensitive skin.

"It's a different perfume," I replied in a whisper, and he kissed my neck again, this time with his tongue. "I have two," I kept talking. "One for work, and one for—"

His tongue traced the curve of my ear, flipping every earring in its wake, and I shuddered with a flutter of my eyelids.

"You have too many rules," he assessed, speaking between kisses against my jaw and my lips.

"You don't have enough," I countered, allowing myself the smallest of smiles while my body wanted to lean back and spread my legs. He called me a witch, but what did that make him?

"I have plenty of rules, thank you very much." He chuckled, peppering my lips with a series of small kisses and nuzzling his nose against mine.

There was an affection in the way he kissed me now. It wasn't the urgent slip of a tongue—my own fault on Friday night—and it wasn't the desperate need to fuck that we'd experienced on Saturday. This was Sunday Morning Sebastian. He who declared we should be a regular thing. He who washed my hair.

"Oh really?" I challenged. "Name three."

239

"Okay," he smirked and pressed his lips to mine. "One, I don't give women my number. Used to, not anymore." He kissed my chin. "Two, I never spend the night with a woman I've been with." Slowly and holding my gaze, he lowered to his knees. "And three, I never sleep with the same woman twice."

Hooking his hands behind my calves, he pulled me to the edge of my chair. "Just because I'm breaking them all for you, Tabby, doesn't mean they're not there."

***

After dinner, Sebastian and Greyson hung out in Greyson's room, playing with his drums while I cleaned up. Sebastian had made enchiladas, enough that we'd have leftovers for the next night or two.

This is nice, I found myself thinking as I climbed the stairs to my bedroom. But what about this was nice, exactly? Was it having Sebastian here for Greyson? Was it having someone else to rely on? Was it simply *him*? Maybe it was all of the above, and choosing felt like choosing a favorite pair of Chucks. They were *all* comfortable, and they *all* felt good. Not for any particular reason, other than they just were.

I took the time to take a long, hot shower, fantasizing about our afternoon tryst in my office. We were never caught, Alex had been out of the office and Jess was on her lunch break, but the risk had still been there. I'd never done something like that before. Not even close. The most daring I'd ever been was making love to my ex in my parents' house, one night when he was staying in town. However many rules Sebastian was breaking for me, I was breaking so many more for him, and I smiled to myself, remembering every touch of his tongue and lips as though it were happening again right there in my shower.

After slipping my arms into my robe and tying the sash, I left the bathroom to tell Greyson it was almost time for bed. When I entered the room, Sebastian was tuning his drums.

"You guys having fun?" I asked, leaning my hip against the doorframe.

Sebastian glanced up at me, his eyes feeding on what he knew to be naked under the robe, and I unsuccessfully hid my coy grin.

"If you consider twisting lugs for hours and hours on end, then sure, having a *blast*," he grumbled, shifting his glare to Greyson, who threw himself back against his bed.

"Oh my God, man, I told you, you don't have to do it," he groused, flipping his arms above his head. "And it hasn't been *hours*. You've only been doing it for like, fifteen minutes."

"Fifteen minutes of my life that I'm never getting back, my friend," Sebastian teased, lifting his lips into a half-smile as he tapped a drumstick against a tom. "I'm just glad you don't have a sixteen-piece kit, or I'd be jumping off a bridge right now."

"I said you don't have to do it," Greyson mumbled with a shrug.

"No kid of mine is playing drums that sound the way these just did," Sebastian replied, and Greyson groaned, rolling over on his bed to face him, watching.

I observed them for a couple of minutes in silence. Sebastian, making sure his son's drums sounded as good as they could. Greyson, studying his every movement the way a kid might watch his dad change the oil in a car. It was quiet, but it was bonding, and it was happening quicker than I expected it to.

"You have any drum keys?" Sebastian asked Greyson, setting the last drum back on its stand.

Greyson shook his head. "I lost the one I had."

"What do you tune with, then?" Sebastian sat up straight on the stool.

"I found a socket wrench and I use that." Greyson sat up and opened the drawer in his night stand, producing a small wrench and handing it to Sebastian.

"Why didn't you tell me you didn't have one?" I asked him, mildly irritated. "I would've gotten you, um, keys." I had absolutely no idea what I was talking about.

Greyson only shrugged before looking back to Sebastian as he turned the wrench over in his hands.

"This is fine. It's the right size to use without messing up the heads, assuming you know what you're doing. But here," Sebastian stood up and fished something out of his pocket, producing his fist to Greyson, "open your hand." Greyson complied, and Sebastian dropped two silver tools into his open palm. Use those, and if you lose them or you need help, let me know. Okay?"

Greyson nodded, looking at the keys in his hand. "These are DW," he commented, examining them closely. "Do you get like, five-thousand of these?"

Sebastian chuckled warmly, reaching up to set his hair free from the elastic. Golden strands spilled out over his shoulders and one hand smoothed it all out. Was this a mating dance, I wondered? Because, with every rake of his hand through the thick mane, I felt my knees growing weaker and the fire between my legs burning brighter, stronger.

"Since the endorsements started, it kinda feels that way, yeah," he answered Greyson.

"Endorsements?" I asked, allowing myself a selfish moment of wanting to be included.

Sebastian turned his head with a little lift to his lips, as though suddenly reminded I was still there. "In a nutshell, I'm paid to advertise for specific brands. So, for example, my drums are DW and my cymbals are Zildjian. I'd be using this shit regardless, because it's what I love, but when they approached and asked to endorse me, I was like, fuck yes. Now, I'm always set until the contract runs out or they sign me on again."

I nodded, genuinely intrigued. "So, that must mean you're pretty good, right?"

Greyson scoffed. "Oh my God, Aunt Tabs," he groaned, shaking his head.

"What?" I asked, darting my eyes between him and Sebastian.

Sebastian only smiled, tipping his head and looking at me as though I was the most adorable thing to walk the planet. "Yeah, I'm pretty good."

Greyson sat up abruptly. "That's basically the biggest understatement *ever*," he groused before looking to me. "He was voted as one of the top ten greatest drummers of our time in *Drum Planet*."

"Oh, so that's *really* good then?"

"Aunt *Tabs*!" Greyson groaned with blatant embarrassment, flopping against his pillows. "I can't even with you."

"Good," I shot back, laughing, "because you need to get ready for bed. It's already ten and you have to wake up in seven hours."

"Uh-huh. Get out of my room then," he grumbled, then turned to Sebastian. "You gonna be here in the morning?"

Sebastian nodded, sliding his gaze toward me. "Yeah, I'll be here."

"Cool." Greyson nodded, sitting up and finding his pajamas on the bed. "Night."

"Night, kid," Sebastian said, reaching out to maybe touch Greyson on the shoulder, maybe the head or arm, but he pulled back abruptly and turned to leave the room.

"Goodnight, Grey," I said softly, pulling the door closed and turning to Sebastian, luring him to my room with my eyes. Once the door was shut behind us, I warned him immediately, "You can't sleep in here tonight."

Sebastian threw his head back and whined, "Tabby! Why not?"

"Oh, God," I groaned, pulling back the comforter on my bed. "You know why."

"Nope," he shook his head, dropping his hands to the button at his waist, "I really don't. Because all I'm thinking right now is how badly I need to fuck you. I'm not thinking at all about what's happening after that."

"Okay, well, first of all, you're going to put the brakes on that until we know Greyson is sleeping," I stated pointedly, sitting on the edge of my bed and crossing my legs.

Ignoring my demands, Sebastian unzipped his fly and eyed me questioningly. "And how exactly are we supposed to know if he's sleeping? You gonna go in there and check? Because, babe, let me tell you something. My mom made that mistake with me *once* and she never opened my door again."

Wiping my hand over my eyes, I released a controlled exhale. "He falls asleep pretty quickly, but it takes him about fifteen minutes to get ready for bed."

"Wow, you have everything down to a fucking science, don't you?" He kicked his sneakers off and let his jeans drop. "Okay, Father Time, as you were saying, why can't I enjoy the pleasure of sleeping with you?"

"For a guy who'd never gone to sleep with a woman before, you certainly like doing it a lot," I grumbled, smirking and shaking my head, and forcing myself from lowering my gaze to his blatant arousal.

"Let's just say I didn't realize what I was missing out on, okay?" He pulled his shirt over his head and dropped it unceremoniously to the jeans at his feet.

I couldn't say what was more impressive about his physique, his upper body strength, or lower. His calves and thighs were all sculpted by the same artist as his shoulders, chest, back, and arms—his music. It felt like a sin to have him there in my room, nearly naked and jumping to my bed with his arms outstretched, but it was a blessing to watch him and know that, even for a fragment of time, he was mine to enjoy.

"Greyson can't know about us, and if he sees you leaving my room in the morning …" I shook my head as he reached for my waist, wrapping his arms around me and pulling me to him. "That would be so wrong."

"There you go with that shit again," he mumbled into the fluff of my robe, his voice lilting with his smile as a callused hand slid up over my naked thigh, slipping closer and closer to the part of me that wanted him the most. "You weren't saying anything about it being wrong when I had my face buried between your thighs this afternoon."

I swallowed and licked my dry lips. "Well, whatever it is," I pressed between shallow breaths, "I don't want him knowing about it. Is *that* wrong?"

His hand stopped just at the juncture between thigh and groin, the very tips of his fingers brushing against my most sensitive of parts, sending my nerve endings into a fucking frenzy. It took every last bit of my willpower to not grab his hand and demand he do things I would've been ashamed of just a week ago.

"Yeah," he finally agreed, nodding his head against my back. "You're right. He shouldn't know. That'd probably be confusing as hell for him."

"It's not … not that," I sighed, moving his hand from my legs and turning to face him. He looked up at me from the bed, and I wondered if I'd ever again see

246

someone this beautiful lying beside me, when we were done with whatever *this* is. "I mean, it *is*, but I also don't want to make things more awkward when this inevitably ends. Bad enough you and I will have to know each other for the rest of our lives, because of him, but we don't need to make it awkward for him."

Sebastian nodded, sincerity searing his gaze. "No, you're right. I get it. But you know what that means, right?"

"What?" I asked, unable to stop myself from touching his face and pushing my fingertips into all that hair.

"You'll just have to find a reason to stay at *my* place all the time, and we'll lock him in the basement." He grinned, pulling himself up and tackling me.

"Great plan," I giggled. "Speaking of which, I need to stay over this weekend, if that's okay—"

"Lucky me," he uttered around a moan, clasping a hand at the nape of my neck and pressing his lips to mine. "Business meeting?"

"Mm-hmm," I hummed against his lips. "Meeting Roman at his house."

As his tongue slid deftly into my mouth, I almost missed the hesitation in the otherwise fluid movement. But I didn't. He had faltered for half a second, his tongue frozen at the precipice between his mouth and mine, at the mention of the other name. Was he *jealous*? He had no reason to be, none whatsoever. We weren't together, and Roman was only a client—but what other explanation was there?

I tugged my tongue from his hold on me. "Sebas—"

"Has it been enough time yet?" he whispered before snagging my bottom lip between his teeth and opening my robe.

24

sebastian

It only took a few weeks for me to know exactly why you should never sleep with the same woman twice. I'd had my suspicions after the first couple of times with Tabby, but over the span of those three weeks, I now knew for certain.

I was addicted.

I'd considered on multiple occasions that it was just her way, being a witch and all, but a group text with my buddies, Devin, Ty, and Chad, had proven that it was a widespread epidemic:

> **Me**: What are you fuckers up to?
> **Devin**: Changing Livy's diaper for the third time in the past two hours. Prunes = bad idea.   Never again.
> **Ty**: Could've told you that.

249

Ty: Carrie's got a dance recital today.

Me: Precious. Pics of you in a tutu please.

Chad: I'm spending the day with my girl's parents. Kill me.

Devin: You put a ring on that yet?

Chad: No.

Me: Gonna drop the Beyoncé lyrics in 3 … 2 … 1 …

Chad: Fuck off.

Me: Anybody gonna ask me what I'm doing? Or have we forgotten our manners?

Chad: We don't need to ask.

Devin: We all know you're off to fuck the baby momma's sister again.

Ty: Or cook her dinner, lol.

Me: Guys, seriously. It's bad. I'm telling myself I'm over here to help Greyson pack for staying at my place for a couple of months, but all I can think about is how many times I can get her off. Something's wrong with me.

Ty: Welcome to the world of monogamy, bro.

Me: lol, we're just fucking, dude.

Devin: And cooking dinner, and going out together …

Me: With Greyson!

Devin: Oh, sure. Whatever you gotta tell yourself.

Chad: So … when are you gonna put a ring on THAT?

I tossed my phone against the dashboard. I wasn't going to waste my red light on a question like that.

250

Fucking Chad. He'd been with the same woman for *six years* and he had the audacity to ask that of me after sleeping with one for three *weeks*?

I had told Greyson that I would pick him up from school on his last day, and then the two of us were going to head to Mrs. Worthington's house for dinner and chinchilla snuggles with Tabby and Jane. I pulled up to the curb and got out to lean against the side of the Range Rover, waiting for school to be let out, when a soccer mommy waiting at a mini-van caught sight of me.

"I haven't seen you around here before," she casually mentioned, walking over to me with a friendly smile planted firmly to her face, but there was no mistaking her wandering eyes.

"Because I've never been here before," I replied with the obvious.

"Well, are you a father?"

I was still getting used to saying it aloud, but I nodded without hesitation. "I am. Otherwise it'd be pretty creepy for a middle-aged guy to be hanging around outside of a school, wouldn't it?"

She laughed with a blend of flirtation and discomfort. "Yeah, I would say so." She extended her waif of a hand. "Cindy Schaffer."

We shook. "Sebastian Moore."

"Who do you belong to?" Cindy asked, pulling her hand back and flipping her hair over her shoulder.

"*Belong* to?" I scoffed.

I was about to run through a speech about being an independent man and not *belonging* to anybody, when

251

she giggled with obvious intent and laid her hand against my arm.

"I mean, who is your child?"

My eyes dropped to that lingering hand. Instinct told me to check for a wedding ring, only to find none. Pulling my eyes back to her face, I quickly made an assessment: single divorced mommy looking for a thrill.

"Greyson Clarke."

The hand still hadn't left my arm, as a cocktail of sympathy and shock flickered over her gaze. "You're … Greyson's father? I wasn't aware—"

"Yes," I replied shortly, finding myself exceedingly aggravated with her hand on my arm and those fingers, now beginning to stroke lightly. Nobody but Tabby had touched me in over three weeks and I wasn't liking it.

"I'm … I'm so sorry about his mother." A judgmental note struck that word: *mother*. "I'm Jason's mom. He's friends with Greyson."

I remembered that name. *Jason*. "Wait a second," I hardened, brushing her hand off my arm, "*Jason*? His dad was screwing Sam, wasn't he?"

My brash question startled her. She looked around us for obvious onlookers, as she gave her head a tiny shake. "Um, well, they had seen each other a few times—"

"Right. That's what I thought," I nodded, crossing my arms over my chest. "Cindy, do me a favor, okay, and tell Jason's dad, that if Jason ever calls Greyson an orphan or his mother a whore ever again, I'm going to personally pay him a visit. Can you do that for me?"

The doors to the school opened up and a flood of students spilled out onto the curb. I should've been watching for Greyson, but I was too busy glaring at Cindy. Her mouth opened and shut repeatedly, like a damn guppy, before she turned without another word and hurried back to her mini-van. I spotted Greyson, who had already seen me talking to her, as he walked over.

"Hey," he mumbled, glancing toward her. "Why were you talking to Jason's mom?"

"Just introducing myself." *And letting her know you're not a fucking orphan.* "How was the last day of school?"

Relief curved his lips as he nodded. "Good."

"Good," I repeated, gripping his shoulder. "Come on, let's go."

***

Keeping our special relationship under wraps was becoming exceedingly more difficult as time went on. My instincts told me to greet her with a kiss, talk with my arms wrapped around her waist, hold her hand when she was frustrated with work, and yet, I couldn't do a damn thing. Not with Greyson around.

The kid wasn't an idiot. I did wonder occasionally if he ever picked up on it, perhaps when Tabby's eyes met mine and the lingering glances did the talking.

"Sebastian, if you ever decide to stop drumming, you really should do something with your cooking," Jane complimented, treating herself to another chicken kebab.

"You could have a cooking show," Tabby chimed in, plucking a slice of grilled zucchini from the skewer. "You could even incorporate music with food."

I leaned back in the patio chair, tipping my head to face the evening sky. "Beats and Eats."

Greyson, with his mouth full, pointed excitedly over the table. "Eat the Beat!"

"I like it," Tabby commented, tugging her bottom lip between her teeth and nodding. "We should make this happen. When are you retiring?" She reached over to nudge her knuckles against my arm. Every touch from her was an electric fire, straight to my heart.

"From music?" I raised my brows incredulously. "Thumbelina, that ain't ever happening, but if one of you wants to follow me around in the kitchen with a camera, we could get something going on YouTube."

"That's even better!" Greyson shouted. "Then you don't need to follow any TV rules. You could curse all you wanted and—"

"Oh, great. This idea just went to hell," Tabby groused, shoving her chair out from the table. "I need to give Roman a call."

Oh God, that fucking guy. "Why?" I found myself asking. "We're eating."

Turning to face me, her eyes squinted and her jaw ticked. She replied, "Because I told him that I'd call now. I'll be right back."

"It can't wait until after?" I challenged, pressing my lips into a firm line. "Is it really more important than the four of us having dinner together right now? I mean, I don't know, but I'd think you'd want to have dinner with

254

us before we don't see you for a week. Maybe that's just me though." I shrugged casually, and reached out to grab another kebab from the center of the table.

Tabby shoved her chair back in. "Fine," she snapped, continuing to stare at me. "I'll call him after."

Jane laid a hand over Tabby's. "Family always comes first, honey. Work comes second."

"See?" I pointed my skewer across the table. "That's exactly what I was thinking."

As we were cleaning up after dinner, Tabby stood in the doorway of Jane's magnificent kitchen and crooked a finger, beckoning for me to follow her. "I need to talk to you," she demanded in a voice that told me I was either about to receive a serious beating, or the most furious sex of my life.

"What's up, dearest?" I asked, a sarcastic bite to my tone as I followed her into Sandy's chinchilla room.

Tabby closed the door behind her, then prodded a firm finger into my chest. "Listen to me right now, Sebastian. You have no right to dictate when I should or should not work. I am trying very hard here to sell two houses, one of which is several hours away. So, when Roman, who is a very busy man, for your information, wants to talk to me at a specific time, I *need* to talk to him *then*. Do you understand me?"

Standing tall and brushing her finger from my chest, I nodded. "Yeah, I understand you. You're saying that your job, *Roman*, is more important than celebrating the fact that your nephew managed to get through this schoolyear, despite everything he's been through."

Her mouth dropped open, anger singeing the embers in her eyes. "How dare—"

"Wait." I held up a finger. "I just remembered something else," and she sighed, gesturing for me to get on with it. "You're about to have two months all to yourself. Two months to sell houses, call Roman, meet with Roman, do whatever you want to do with Roman—"

"What the fuck is your problem with Roman?" Tabby interjected, pinching her brows and tightening her lips. "Any time I mention him, you get like this."

"I don't have a problem with Roman," I insisted, and I think I almost believed it. "But I *do* have a problem with you allowing him to cross over into the time you should be devoting to your family. I don't care how fucking busy or important his life is. *Nothing* should be more important to you than that kid and knowing that, by some fucking miracle, he still passed this year."

I struck against something inside of her with that. I knew it by the way she laid a hand against her chest, before covering her mouth with the other. I thought maybe I had pushed it too hard. After all, Greyson had suffered the same heartache she had. They were both coping and dealing with the losses, and who the fuck was I to criticize the way she handled it from her end? Hell, maybe work was *how* she coped.

Noticing the tears clinging to her lashes, I shook my head, ashamed I'd been such a thoughtless asshole. "Tabby … Fuck, I'm sorry. That was a dickish—"

"No," she shook her head furiously. "No. You're right. You're absolutely right."

256

I shuffled my feet against the dirty chinchilla floor. "Can I, uh, get that in writing?"

"Shut up," she groaned, blinking the tears away. "All I've had as a distraction has been work. I know I haven't been the most attentive to Greyson. But, …" She emitted an aggravated huff, shaking her head. "You know, I know I haven't said it, but, thank you."

"You're thanking me for pissing you off?" I tipped my head, eyeing her questioningly.

"No, idiot," she shook her head, stepping toward me and wrapping her arms around my waist. "I'm thanking you for helping us so much."

This was my favorite. When she hugged me and pressed her cheek to my chest, and I quickly wrapped my arms around her shoulders, kissing her hair and pulling in the scent of flowers and spring. "How the hell have I been helping *you*, other than bestowing upon you the gift of my magic dick?"

She laughed gently. "I don't even know sometimes. Things just feel better when you're around, I don't know how to explain it."

"I told you," I chuckled, resting my chin against the crown of her head, "it's my magic dick."

With a groan, she pulled away from my embrace, encouraging a swelling ache to flood my chest. I caught a twitch at the corner of her mouth and asked, "What?" What was she smiling about, what was so funny, *what what what*.

"No, it's stupid," she brushed it away. But then she bit her lip and tipped her eyes to the ceiling, giggling lightly.

257

"Come on, you can't look like that and not tell me," I laughed, reaching out to pull her against me. Just for a few seconds longer, before we had to go back to our land of make believe. "What were you gonna say?"

She squirmed and shoved against my chest before relenting with a touch of my lips against hers. A sigh lifted her body into mine, her fingers grasping my shirt, as she melted into my kiss. And just as quickly, she mumbled a protest and wriggled from my grasp.

"Not here," she insisted, and with a weighted sigh, I nodded. "But what I was going to say is," her hand lowered to cup my groin for all of a nanosecond, "a witch needs her magic wand."

And she released me, walking backward toward the door and biting her lip, until she realized I wasn't following. "Aren't you coming?"

Squeezing my eyes shut and thinking about anything but her on my dick, I grumbled, "Trying not to."

In a fit of stifled giggles, she left the room, leaving me to allow the blood to travel north. Moments later, Jane came in carrying Sandy, and she smiled broadly at me.

"What are you doing in here?" she asked, passing Sandy to my open hands.

"Oh, Tabby and I were just talking. Thought I'd hang out in here for a few minutes and pray to the chinchilla gods that you'd be done with him soon." I lifted the little guy to my face and grinned.

"You can just ask to hold him whenever you want, you know," she said, opening his cage and filling his food dish.

"But then I'd be getting in the middle of your business. I don't know what you guys talk about. It might be important." I scratched Sandy between the ears and ran my finger down his nose. "That'd be rude and then he and I wouldn't be buddies anymore."

"Oh, I don't think you'd have to worry about that," she chuckled, unhooking his water bottle from the side of the cage. Her sparkling blue eyes made a quick glance at me before returning to the job at hand. "So, did Tabitha tell you Roman's coming by in a couple weeks?" she asked, twisting off the cap and reaching for a bottle of distilled water.

"Here? To see the house?" I stroked my hands delicately over Sandy's back.

"Mm-hmm," she confirmed with a slow bob of her head. "Have you had the pleasure of making his acquaintance yet?"

"Can't say that I have," I grumbled, trying so desperately not to let on that my nerves were ticking with anxiety. "Have you?"

Pursing her lips, she filled the bottle and shook her head. "Nope, can't say that I have. Should be interesting to see what Tom thinks of him."

Tom was Jane's late husband, and she was convinced that he would only allow the person who *deserved* the house to remain there.

"Hm," I hummed with intrigue. "I'd sure like to see if Tom sends Roman out on his rich ass in a whirlwind of poltergeist fury."

With a look of sparking mischief, Jane twisted the top back onto Sandy's water bottle and grinned. "What are you doing in a couple of weekends?"

***

"Okay, so," I opened the door and flipped on the light switch, "if there's anything you wanna change, that's cool. Just let me know."

When I'd bought the house years ago, it'd been advertised as a four-bedroom home. One of those bedrooms was now mine, another was reserved for the rare guest, and the other two had been used for a drum studio and storage. But after Greyson had started hanging out in the basement den, I thought it was time to move the storage to the attic and give the basement bedroom to him.

Mom and Tabby helped pick out the bedding, although both of them had insisted he didn't need a Queen-sized bed. But come on, the kid was sleeping on a Twin at Tabby's place. I could at least give him some space to toss and turn on at mine.

"You mean I'm not sleeping on the couch anymore?" he joked, walking into the room, wearing a grin I felt in my heart.

"Nah. I figured it was time to upgrade your accommodations," I laughed, crossing the room to the closet and opening the door. "You've got room for your clothes and shoes, and if you need anything, we can go shopping, or uh, I can give you my credit card and you can order some stuff online. Whatever."

Greyson shook his head with disbelief. "You would just give me your credit card to do whatever I wanted?"

"Uh, you act like I wouldn't be monitoring the fuck out of that shit. If I saw any charges coming in from Bangin' Babes or whatever-the-fuck dot com, you can bet your ass I'd get a taste for what it's like to ground someone," I challenged, daring him with a smirk.

"Why would I pay for porn when I can just get it for free?"

The youth of today really have no idea how good they have it. When I was his age, I was stealing my sisters' Cosmo magazines.

"That's my boy," I clapped him on the shoulder, and headed toward the door. "I'm fucking tired and don't wanna cook, so I'll just order a pizza tonight, okay? You can get unpacked and whatever."

He nodded. "Yeah, pizza's good."

"Damn right, it is. And it's way better than that upstate pizza you've been suffering with," I bobbed my head. "Oh, and by the way, I didn't bring your drums down here 'cause I'd have to soundproof the room. If you really want to practice in here, that's fine, we can do that, but—"

Greyson shrugged. "Nah, it's okay."

"You're sure?" I tipped my chin to my chest, watching his reactions. "I don't wanna—"

"No," he shook his head, "I wanna be able to play with you."

The admission was a Cupid's arrow to my chest, and I fought my smile, not wanting to put him on the spot or make the moment awkward. It was a struggle, but I nodded and kept my lips from grinning.

"Okay, cool," and I left to order the pizza and revel in being wanted. By my kid.

25

sebastian

"How have you boys been this week?" Mom asked, bustling into the house with a tray of my dad's famous barbeque ribs. "Things going well? Is he pissing you off yet, Greyson?"

Greyson shrugged. "It's okay."

It was Thursday. Tomorrow, we would be heading back to spend the night with Tabby before meeting with my sisters at Hershey Park on Saturday morning.

"Good," she replied, pressing her hand to his back. "Are you hungry? You can grab some ribs—"

"I'm gonna go play *Street Fighter*," he cut her off, and headed straight to the basement.

Mom looked to me, both of us wincing when the door shut behind him. "So, I take it things aren't going so great?"

I folded my forearms against the counter and pursed my lips with consideration. How could I adequately describe the week we'd had in a way that she'd understand, without having witnessed it herself?

There seemed to be a pattern in this new life of mine. Greyson and I would spend time together, playing drums or video games, or watching movies. We'd laugh, have a great time, and then there'd be a lull. A moment between movies, a quiet minute in the grocery store, a few fuzzy seconds while we waited for the next song to play, and his mood would dim. Instantly, he'd shut down, shut me out, and walk away. I often wouldn't see him again until the next day.

"Things are fine until they're not," I mumbled, shrugging and tapping my fingertips against the counter, before adding, "They're more fine than not though."

"Well, that's good," she encouraged, standing across from me. "Hon, you can't expect for things to be perfect in just a few weeks. Nothing ever is."

"I know that." I sucked in a frustrated gust of air, holding it before exhaling my discouragement. "I just wanted to have a better report for Tabby, I guess. I didn't want her to worry about him over here."

"Have you been talking to her?"

I nodded, tracing the speckles in the stone. It'd been nearly two weeks since I'd seen her, and I hated how badly I missed her. How badly I felt dependent on her. "Yeah, we text all the time."

"Then I'm sure she already knows how he's doing," she assured me, and she was right. I gave Tabby updates on the regular. She knew about his flip-flopping, and she

264

had even expected it. Still, it didn't make me feel like any less of a failure at this whole single parent thing, and I wondered if maybe I wasn't cut out for it after all.

"I bet you're excited to see her again, huh," Mom teased, nudging her hand against mine and grabbing my attention.

"Sure," I shrugged, overselling my nonchalance. "It'll be nice."

"*Nice*," she mocked with a tip of her head. "Can I remind you that I carried you in my belly for forty-one weeks?"

"God, I don't envy you," I mumbled, shaking my head with a chuckle.

"You didn't want to leave, and after twenty-six fucking hours of labor, I finally had my boy and he was already a literal pain in my ass," she snickered, reminding me for the thousandth time that she broke her tailbone while giving birth to me.

"Still sorry about that," I pouted.

"You lived with me for a little over eighteen years before you moved out, and I spent that time, and all this time after, learning everything there is to know about you." She raised a finger, poking the center of my chest. "You can't hide a damn thing from me. Remember that."

"I'm not hiding anything," I quirked my lips.

"Okay, then you'll admit that you have feelings for Tabby."

I lifted my arms off the counter and huffed at the accusation. "If you mean we're *friends*, then sure."

265

"Well, I already know you're friends, but that's not what I meant." She poked my chest again. "You *like* her."

Mimicking, I poked her forehead. "Not like that," I smirked, emphasizing every word with another poke between her brows.

Narrowing her eyes and shaking her head, she pressed her lips into a firm line and brushed my finger away. "You can deny it all you want, Bastian. Just don't forget that I know you better than you know yourself, and I know I've never seen you like this before. Not even during your Christina Aguilera phase."

"That wasn't a phase, Mom. I still beat it to Christina Aguilera." It was almost the truth, aside from the fact that I hadn't jerked off to anything but memories of Tabby since our first time together.

She smacked my arm. "Don't be disgusting."

I shrugged. "Just being honest."

"Well, if you're in the mood to be honest, then why not admit that you like her?"

"Fine," I practically sneered, not entirely sure of why I was suddenly getting so defensive. "If I'm being honest, then how about this? I *really* like sex with her. That's fucking great."

Mom pinched her lips and shook her head. "You know I didn't need to hear that."

Guilt struck my gut. I dropped my head, staring at the floor. "No, probably not. Sorry."

With a disgruntled sigh, she waved an arm in the air. "Whatever. You're adults. It's none of my business. I just hope nobody ends up hurt in that situation."

266

Me too.

***

"So, then," I told Greyson, as we pulled up to the curb outside of Jane's house, "I'm coming out of the bathroom stall, right, and there's Grohl at the fucking urinal. And all I could think was, my fucking *god* is taking a piss right after I just took a shit. Most embarrassing moment of my fucking life."

"Get the fuck out of here," Greyson laughed, staring at me with wonderment. "What did you do?"

"What did I *do*? Kid, I didn't do *anything*. I just went to wash my hands, hoping to Christ I'd just disappear."

"That's fucking crazy, D—" My heart stopped as he caught himself. Was he going to call me Dad? God, I wanted him to call me Dad. More than anything. "Did he say anything?"

"Yeah, actually. He said, 'Hey, you're Sebastian Moore, right?' and that on its own was enough to make me piss myself. But then he had to go ahead and say, 'You should try this shit you spray into the bowl before you take a dump. It helps a lot.'" I bubbled with laughter at the memory.

"You're kidding me!" Greyson exclaimed, continuing to laugh.

"Not even a little bit," I insisted with a shake of my head. "Hell, I *wish*. You don't want your god talking to you about bathroom etiquette, trust me."

With a puff of my cheeks and a long-winded sigh, I eyed the house, knowing Tabby was behind those walls. It felt like I hadn't seen her in months, when it was really only a couple of weeks. Would I be able to control myself?

"Ready, kid?" I asked, smacking my hand against his thigh before getting out of the car.

The two of us walked through the wrought iron fence and up the porch steps, and before I could ring the doorbell, Jane threw the door open. With Sandy clutched to her chest, and whispered, "He's here."

"Who?" Greyson asked.

"Mr. Dolecki," Jane hissed, thrusting Sandy into Greyson's arms before grabbing me by the wrist. "Sebastian, you need to get a load of this guy."

She dragged me toward the back of the house, through a hallway and into a room that she'd told me Mr. Worthington used as a library. There, we found Tabby, perched on the arm of a chair, giggling and talking with a man in what was undoubtedly a very expensive suit. The way he held his etched-glass tumbler, holding his head up high and leaning over her with a crocodile grin, brought on an immediate sensation of dread. It manifested and coiled through my guts, up toward my lungs, until I swore I could breathe fire.

I didn't realize it before. Didn't know it until I knew his face. But holy hell, I was *jealous.*

"Tabitha! Look who's here!" Jane announced, dragging me further into the room, closer to Tabby and Mr. Fancy Pants.

Tabby turned to look at me. Her hair was pinned up in a complicated-looking twist, her makeup was pristine, and her clothes were pressed and neat. She looked the way she had when I first met her, when all I had wanted to do was mess her up. Now, knowing what she was like without her clothes on, knowing her tattoo and nipple piercings, I wanted to wipe her face, undo her hair, rip those clothes off, and yell at her that this wasn't her. But he didn't know any of that.

"What are you doing here?" she nearly gasped at the sight of me.

Without permission, and without Greyson there to see, I wrapped an arm around her shoulders and pressed my lips to the top of her head. I gauged her body's reaction as I gauged the flat expression on his face.

"I told you we were coming tonight before going to Hershey tomorrow," I reminded her, never taking my eyes off of him.

"Well, I'm work—"

"Tabitha." He spoke with the refinery of someone who had grown up privileged. "Will you please introduce me to your interesting companion?"

Interesting companion. I broke my staring contest with his face to assess myself. Jeans ripped at the knees, sleeveless Metallica t-shirt, Chucks—did he know about *her* collection of Converse?

The contrast between us was startling, I'd give him that. My hair was pulled up in its usual knotted bun, a wreck in comparison to the neat and tidy gelled look he pulled off with pompous pride. My beard was close-cropped and only a bit longer than his, but not nearly as

269

groomed. For fuck's sake, the man looked like he had his eyebrows waxed, and the last time mine had seen any beautification was that one horrific night when my sisters attacked me with the tweezers.

"So sorry, Roman," Tabby rushed to remedy the awkward encounter. "This is Sebastian, my nephew's father. Remember I told you how Greyson lives with me?"

"Ah, yes," Roman nodded thoughtfully, eyeing me up and down with a studious judgment. "I do remember. You're the one who plays with drums, yes?"

Plays with drums. He had sneered the demeaning comment behind something I'm sure he thought looked like a smile.

"That would be me," I extended a hand as I added, "And you're the one who can't decide what you want to do, so you just do *everything*, you little entrepreneur, you."

He chortled condescendingly as we shook. "That's cute. Very witty."

"Sebastian," Tabby cut in, turning her face upward to bore her eyes through me, "Roman and I were in the middle of a business meeting. So, if you could just wait outside, I would really appreciate that."

I smiled tightly, looking from her to Roman, as I nodded. "Right, of course. Pleasure to meet you, Roman."

"Ah, yes, and same to you, Sebastian. I'm sure I'll be seeing you again."

You bet your ass you will. I turned, leaving the room with hostile intent. Jane and Greyson were waiting for me in the kitchen, Sandy still in Greyson's arms.

"Well?" Grey asked. "What's he like?"

"Fucking douche," I assessed abruptly, the words tumbling out of my mouth as though they'd been dying to be released. "What do you think, Jane?"

"Fucking douche," she repeated, nodding.

"So, where's Tom to toss his pompous ass out of here?"

"It doesn't work like that," Jane sighed sadly. "I have to wait for his magic to work. Maybe the bank will disapprove of his request for a mortgage—"

"That guy won't have a mortgage," I told her, shaking my head. "He'll be paying in cash."

"Well, then maybe something else will happen. Another pressing matter, a natural disaster …" She shrugged helplessly.

I could hear their terse laughter drifting through the house, nipping at my ears. What business meeting required him to lean into her the way he was? What could they be talking about, that made her giggle like that?

"Sebastian?" Jane asked, and I snapped out of my ill-fated reverie to find her and Greyson staring at me.

"Sorry," I grumbled, taking Sandy from Greyson's arms and smoothing my hand over his back. "Hopefully something gets in the way of this shit."

Or someone.

***

271

Sighing languorously, Tabby dug her fingers into my chest, rocking her hips and pulling me in. The red tendrils of her hair hung over her breasts to her bellybutton, reaching for my stomach like auburn fingers. Little glints of sparkle caught the light with every back and forth motion, every controlled caress of her groin against mine.

Fuck, I didn't even need to come, I realized, in a trance as she tipped her head back. This was just fine, watching her use me as she wanted, the tickles of hair dancing over my thighs. This was more than fine.

"God, Sebastian," she moaned, her voice lazy and sated, while piercing my skin with her nude-colored fingernails. "I've missed this *so much*."

My hands circled her hips, taking back the control in her speed. "Oh, yeah?"

My palms engulfed her waist, a belt of fingers and ink. She was so small, so delicate, so fragile, and right now, she was mine.

Mine.

Hear that, Roman?

"Mm-hmm," she brought her eyes back to mine and nodded, licking her pouty lips as she bent down to swipe her tongue over mine. "I thought about you every single night."

"Mm," I groaned. "What did you think about?"

"This. Fucking you, and your mouth," she whispered against my lips. "I'd get off, thinking about your tongue."

I growled, capturing her mouth and sweeping inside to collect her taste on the tip of my tongue, to swallow it until it became a part of me. This was all I needed, I decided. Just to be inside her, to curl around her body and cocoon in the nest created by us. This was good, this was *great*, and whatever it was, I wasn't ready to give it up. Not now, not yet, but I felt a darkness looming above the bed. The crocodile smile began to penetrate the veil of passion laying over me, and before I could meet release with release, I lost it.

"What's wrong?" Tabby asked, raising her forehead from mine, searching my eyes. "Are you okay?"

I swallowed. "Yeah, maybe I just need to, uh …"

We changed position and I squeezed my eyes shut. I tried to fight it, to focus, to chase away the dread and the worry. But it wasn't happening. I bent over her, pressing my lips and forehead to her back.

"Sebastian?" She was concerned, looking over her shoulder.

"I'm okay," I assured her, kissing her again. "I think I'm just tired."

I collapsed beside her, half-expecting to see his face hovering over the bed. This feeling was terrible, sickening in every definition of the word, and I bit at my lips out of frustration.

Tabby sat back on her heels, gripping me in her warm, soft hand. "I could do this, if it would help …"

I sighed, touched by her determination to please me and angry that I knew there was no hope of getting there, and I shook my head. "Really, I'm okay."

273

"Are you sure?" She was stroking me gently, without any plan of arousal but to soothe.

I nodded. "Yeah."

"Are you really *that* tired?" She was skeptical. She knew me better than that.

So, I shook my head. "I have some shit on my mind."

Sitting down with her legs crossed, her and all of her naked confidence, she shrugged. "Okay, so talk to me."

I snorted. "Well, okay, for starters, I don't like Roman."

Abruptly pulling her hand from my dick, she demanded, "Why would you bring him up right now?"

"Because I don't like him. He rubs me the wrong way." I folded my arms behind my head.

"Oh, well, great, because right now you're rubbing *me* the wrong way," Tabby growled, clambering from the bed and grabbing her robe. "It doesn't matter if you don't like him, Sebastian. He's my *client*. I'm selling a house to him, and selling one for him, and that's it."

I shrugged, crossing one leg over the other. "Does he know that? Because the way he was leaning over you today ..." I shook my head, pursing my lips. "I dunno, Tabby. Sorta feels like there's more to it than that to me."

"Jealousy doesn't suit you," she sneered, bending over to grab my pajamas. "Get dressed and get out."

"Okay," I shrugged, catching the t-shirt and pants as she chucked them at me.

I pulled them, and she threw the door open. Without a word, I walked out to go to bed. When the door closed behind me, I thrust my hands into my hair and gave a low, internal groan.

What the fuck am I doing? This isn't what I do. This isn't how I handled conflict. I shook my head, turned around and lifted my fist to knock, when the door opened. Tabby was shaking her head, grabbing my hand and pulling me inside.

"This is how we fight, huh?" I asked, as her arms wrapped around my waist and my chin tipped to the crown of her head.

"I think it's sweet you care," she uttered quietly, kissing the center of my chest. "But you don't have to worry about me."

"What if I want to worry about you?"

I tightened my arms around her shoulders, looking off to her bed and wanting nothing more than to lay there. I wanted our arms around each other, drifting toward a sleep where maybe we could also be together in my dreams. That's all I wanted. This. Her.

Fuck. "God, Tabby, what the fuck are you doing to me?"

"What do you mean?" She disturbed my chin's rest as she tipped her head back to look up to me.

"You really are a witch."

She giggled, shaking her head and spearing me with her glittering emerald eyes. "You keep saying that."

"It's better than the truth," I admitted, lifting the corner of my mouth in what I hoped looked like a smile.

"And what's the truth?"

"That you're going to be the end of me."

She hesitated, searching my eyes for clues of something I wasn't sure of, before pulling her arms from around my waist. She pressed her palms to my cheeks, stood on her toes and pressed one sweet kiss against my lips before taking one, two steps back toward the bed. One hand stretched out toward me, grasping my fingers and tugging me back with her.

"What are you doing?" I asked, shaking my head, while allowing her to tow me toward the cloud of sex and dreams.

"I need good sleep," she stated simply, "and I only get that with you."

"What about Greyson?" I cocked my head.

"We both know he sleeps late in the summer," she reasoned with a shrug, dropping down and pulling me with her.

We laid together, facing each other, before the onset of sleep could take us away. There had been a shift on this night, from casual fucking to something teetering toward feelings. I wasn't sure if that was what either of us truly wanted, or if we were simply succumbing to the moment, but I felt them. The emotions. They were there. A discombobulated cluster of confusion and uncertainty sprinkled delicately with something affectionate.

"Maybe it's not the end," she whispered, afraid to speak louder, to tell the truth.

"Sure as fuck feels like it," I laughed, and for a moment, I missed my old life. Before Greyson. Before her.

"Yeah, I know, but maybe it only feels that way because something else is beginning."

"Like what?"

She shrugged. "I have no idea."

Those words served as the end to the night, before she rolled over and turned off the light. She settled her back against my chest and I wrapped my arms around her, sighing contentedly. I breathed in her hair, wrestling between sleep and my thoughts. Roman. Emotions.

It just is.

26

sebastian

"So, Greyson, do you like rollercoasters?" Mel asked as we walked through the Hershey Park entrance.

Greyson shrugged, walking ahead of me alongside my nephews, Johnny and Travis. "I don't know. I've never been on one."

"Oh, man!" Travis exclaimed excitedly. "You're gonna love it."

Dinah sidled up to Greyson. "Do you get motion sickness?"

He shook his head. "No, I don't think so."

She clapped him on the shoulder. "Okay, you'll be fine. Just be warned, these two will be dragging you on everything, if your dad doesn't."

"You like rollercoasters?" Greyson asked me, looking over his shoulder, and I nodded enthusiastically.

"Hell yes." I pounded my fist against Jen's. She was always the other ride enthusiast in the family. "Everyone else is a bunch of wimps," I teased, reaching out and tugging on Dinah's ponytail.

"Sebastian, stop," she whined, swatting me away like I was an annoying, buzzing gnat. "I'm sorry I don't like feeling my intestines in my throat."

Mel nodded sympathetically. "Girl, same."

While all of the kids jumped on the carousel, I hung out with my sisters, watching the kids from the surrounding barricade. Dinah, Mel, and Jen whispered amongst themselves while I listened in, trying to pick up on whatever the hell it was they were saying and failing miserably, with all the amusement park ruckus happening around us.

"Are you guys talking about me?" I finally asked, ducking into their little pow-wow.

"Maybe," Dinah confessed. "Mom told us. Well, she told me, and I told them."

"Told you what?" I narrowed my eyes, turning my gaze onto each of them.

"About you and Tabby," Jen scowled.

"Oh, cool. That was nice of her," I grumbled with a roll of my eyes, making a mental note to strangle my mother.

Stepping forward to point a finger at my chin, Jen continued, "And by the way, I can't believe you're such a disgusting pig. I mean, I think we're all aware of what you do on the road, but with your kid's *aunt*? That's a whole new low."

"Oh, come on, Jen," I groused. "That's not fair."

279

"*How* is it—"

Dinah cleared her throat, interrupting whatever snide remark Jen was about to make. "He's kinda right. Tabby's a big girl and she's obviously okay with it, so …" She shrugged incredulously.

"Thank you, D. I always knew you were my favorite," I wrapped an arm around her shoulders, and just as quickly, she brushed me off.

"That doesn't mean I think it's okay," she tossed in, and I shrugged. "What I just can't understand is why."

"Why what?"

"Why you'd want to. With her." Dinah chewed on her upper lip, eyeing me expectantly.

Cocking a brow, I pulled in a deep breath and stuffed my hands into my pockets. "Uh, you really want me to get into this here," my gaze flitted around the amusement park, "at a family theme park?"

"Keep it vague," Mel suggested, pursing her lips and waiting.

It was easier for me to talk to my sisters than it was my mother. I pulled my hand from my pocket and reached for my neck, gripping and squeezing. "I don't know. We just have … this chemistry, I guess. It just happened and turned into this … *thing*. I couldn't stop it. And to be fair, *she* started it."

"Couldn't stop it or didn't want to?" Dinah questioned.

I took a moment to consider that, and wobbled my head. "Didn't want to."

"So, we were right," Mel smirked triumphantly. "You *do* have a crush on her."

Putting my entire body into an eye roll, I took that moment, in the middle of Hershey Park, to stretch my arms out and say, "Yes, Melanie. I have a crush on a girl. There you go. Congratulations. Are you happy now?"

"*Oh my God*," Jen and Dinah squealed in unison and I groaned, hiding my face behind my palms.

"So, how does she feel about you?" Mel asked. "Why don't you make this thing official?"

"Because she thinks I'm a big man-child and she's just humoring this whole thing until she finds someone better," I rambled. Someone like Roman.

"Well, she wouldn't be wrong about the man-child thing," Dinah muttered as the large group of kids and toddlers approached us. "But, and I'm not just saying this because you're my baby brother, I'm not sure there's anyone better."

***

I'd never realized how much I was missing out on, by not hanging out with my sisters and their kids more often. Johnny, Travis, Greyson, and I rode every rollercoaster in the place, while Jen tagged along every now and then, when her other kids weren't badgering here for this or that. The boys liked having me around to go on the rides—it was better than hanging out with all the girls, they'd said—and *all* of the kids appreciated that I never said no to snacks. My sisters appreciated that they didn't have to pay for anything. And I appreciated the company.

"It's fucking hot as balls," I complained, pulling my shirt off. "I'm hitting the water rides. Who's down?"

"We don't *all* look like that," Mel groaned with a roll of her eyes.

"Who cares how you look?" I asked, balling up my shirt and shoving it into my backpack. "Whether you're fat or not, it's still hot."

"Yeah, well, I'm a little self-conscious," Mel replied, and Jen and Dinah nodded. "Try having four kids and see how good you feel about yourself."

"Four?" I laid a hand over my abs. "Try six, girlfriend. I bounce right back."

The kids laughed while my sisters groaned and rolled their eyes. Then I added, "But seriously, you guys look fine, and anybody who doesn't think so can suck a dick," I laid my hands on the heads of Johnny and Travis, "'cause you made these things and that's a lot cooler than looking like a supermodel."

Mel pressed a hand to her heart. "Sebastian ..."

Jen pinched my cheek. "You can be such a sweetheart. Too bad you're an annoying pain in the ass most of the time."

"Gotta balance it out," I grinned, wrapping an arm around Greyson's shoulders. "But seriously though, you down for some water rides, kid? Because I'm ready to fucking die out here."

Until the sun went down, we rode the rides, ate nearly everything in sight, and by the time we were ready to leave, I was sufficiently exhausted and one hot dog away from barfing. Walking back to our respective cars, we hugged and promised to hang out soon, with my sisters insisting that it was stupid we didn't spend more time together. I couldn't say I disagreed, and thought it was stupid I'd felt that I needed a kid to have an excuse to be with them.

I texted Tabby and asked if it'd be okay to crash at her place again for the night, and she replied with an, "of course." I drove with the hope that I could actually keep *it* up this time and not *think*.

"Today was fun," I commented in the dark of the car, the Foo Fighters playing through the stereo. "I never hang out with my sisters. I don't really know why."

"You're lucky," Greyson mentioned ruefully, and I tore my eyes from the road for just a second to look at him.

"Lucky?"

"You have this kickass family, with your sisters and your parents, and I bet you had grandparents too."

I nodded, feeling oddly apologetic. "Well, yeah, I did …"

"I bet they liked you and did things with you," he continued, slumping against the door and pinning his gaze to the roadside.

"Um, well, on my mom's side, they were a little old and didn't like to do too much," I explained, just for the sake of talking. "But they were nice, and my Grandpa would talk with me sometimes. Grandma just liked to knit things, as Grandmas sometimes do. She'd knit the ugliest fucking hats though, and every Christmas, she'd make me a new one and … I know I *should*, but I don't feel bad that you missed out on *that*. My dad's side—"

"Well, I *do*."

I glanced back to him. "What?"

283

"I fucking *hate* that I missed out on that." He tucked his lips between his teeth, biting and twitching. The push and pull of his breath through his nose was loud and heavy and overpowered the music. "What were your other grandparents like?"

He was going to cry. I scraped my teeth over my bottom lip and ran a hand through my damp hair. "Uh … Well, they were younger than my mom's parents, so they were a lot more active. You would've liked Grampa. He was awesome. Really into music, and he wasn't scared of technology, you know? Like, my dad is terrified of his iPhone, but Grampa was on the computer and downloading music before Dad ever embraced a cellphone. Gramma was a fucking badass too. She actually had a tattoo and took me to get my first when I was sixteen."

Greyson turned to me, disbelief blending with the tears in his eyes. "You've been getting tattoos since you were sixteen?"

I nodded. "Yep. Mom was pissed when I came home with the *Punisher* logo on my arm." I laughed, pointing to the old faded ink. "I've gotten a lot of my older ones touched up or covered over the years, but I won't do a damn thing to this one."

"I want a tattoo when *I* turn sixteen," Greyson told me. It wasn't a question, it was a demand.

I caught his eye and asked, "When's your birthday?"

It was the wrong question to ask. I realized that immediately, when one lone tear slid over his cheek, catching on his lip. "You don't know," he uttered the bitter statement, and what was I going to do? Lie to him? So, I shook my head and said, "No, I don't."

"You're supposed to know." His voice broke, and he cleared his throat, swallowing relentlessly. "You're *supposed* to fucking *know* when my *birthday* is, and she *never* fucking *told you*."

I leaned my elbow against the window ledge, balled my fist and pressing it to my cheek. "Greyson, it's—"

"It's not fucking fair!" he shouted, giving up the fight. "It's not fucking fair. It's not. Why didn't she think I'd want to know you? She knew how to find you, she had your fucking *address*—she *knew*, and she never even gave me the fucking *choice*! Why didn't I get a fucking *choice*?"

I wanted answers to give him. But I didn't have any. "I wish I knew, kid."

"I hate that I'm happy," he admitted in a whisper, his tears unrelenting.

"You're happy?" I couldn't help myself from asking.

He faltered in his nod. "And I fucking hate it."

Everything made sense. His backpedaling. The flip-flopping.

"Greyson, you should *want* to be happy," I told him. "It's *okay* to be happy."

"No, it's *not*," he cried, shaking his head. "The happier I am, the more I stop thinking about her."

Jesus Christ. I never knew that parenthood could be so uplifting and yet so soul-crushing, all at the same time. "So, you think that by being with me, you're forgetting about her," I offered, glancing at him to watch him nod. "Kid, I won't ever let you forget about your mom, okay?"

"Why not? She made you forget about me."

I breathed the words in, clotted my throat with them and struggled to find air. I couldn't drive, not like this, so I pulled to the side of the quiet country road. Leaning my elbows against the steering wheel, I pinched the bridge of my nose, listening to the Foo Fighters sing "February Stars" mixed with the sound of Greyson's tears.

God knows I'd spent time being angry at Sam for what she'd done. God knows I had hurt and mourned. But no amount of anger could take any of that time away, and no amount of guilt was going to change the way things were right now.

"Greyson," I turned to him, laying a hand against his shoulder. He reluctantly looked to me, his face sodden. "Bad shit happens. Unfortunately, that's a part of life, and unfortunately, we just have to deal with it the best that we can. And I think that sometimes, good things come our way in the middle of that bad shit, to help us cope and get through it and become happy again. And I know that, by feeling less sad, you *think* you're forgetting your mom, but I promise you're not. You're just moving past the part that made you sad in the first place, so that you can remember the good stuff again."

Greyson sobbed, and while I looked at him in those moments, with his hair matted against his forehead and the never-ending tears streaming down his smooth cheeks, I thought I could envision him as a little boy. I was reminded of what I didn't know—God, there were so many things I didn't know. I didn't know what his

286

first word was, or if he walked before he could speak. I didn't know what movie he couldn't stop watching when he was a toddler, or how old he was when he lost his first tooth.

How could I possibly be his father, when I didn't even know when he was *born*?

Inadequacy and helplessness sat over me like a two-ton elephant, hunching my shoulders and pressing every last bit of air from my lungs. I couldn't do anything, other than press my hand to his cheek and wish I could be more than just some guy that stumbled into his life.

"I … I miss her, Dad," he whispered around another sob, and just like that, I could breathe again.

My hands clutched to him as he threw his arms around me, pressing his face against my shoulder as he let himself go, gripping my back with his fingers and audibly sobbing. I rocked, closing my eyes and pressing my cheek to his hair, the same color as mine, and all I could promise was that it was okay, I'll make sure it's okay, it's all going to be okay.

And as his tears quelled and his sobs calmed to quivering breaths, he sighed with spent relaxation and said, "I love you."

I couldn't remember the last time I told my dad that I loved him, but I would always remember the first time I whispered "I love you, too" to my son.

27

tabby

"Good night, Aunt Tabs," Greyson said, giving me a hug before turning to Sebastian with a hug for him as well. "Night, Dad."

At the bottom of the stairs, we watched him walk up to his room, and I waited for the door to be closed before looking to Sebastian. His usual fun, exuberant exterior had crumbled away to leave trails of tears streaming in jagged lines over his cheeks and into his beard. With more strength than I knew I possessed, I caught him before he sank to the floor and led him to the couch.

It was only then that I realized I was crying, too.

I didn't realize one little word could have such an effect.

With his arms around me and his head against my shoulder, Sebastian and I cried together without a single word uttered. A blended cocktail of grief and relief spilled out over our shirts and into our hair. Moments passed before he lifted his head and sought my lips, possessing my mouth with a passion beyond friendship and casual fucking. His hands slipped from my back and into my hair, pulling my braid free and transforming me into the unkempt wild woman I could only be for him.

Greyson could've caught us at any time, but I welcomed his hand, cupping my breast over the t-shirt I wore to bed, and I initiated the shimmy out of my pants. Unzipping his jeans, he laid me down, kissing his forehead to mine as we fit together in one, smooth stroke.

"Don't say when, Tabby," he whispered, cupping my face in his palms. "I'm not what you want, I know that. Just don't say when."

"That's not how the song goes." I searched his eyes, meeting his hips with mine, thrust for thrust. "I'm supposed to make you promise *not* to stop if I say—"

He shook his head, lifting the corner of his mouth in a sad smile. "I know better than to promise you anything. Just don't say when. Please. Not yet."

"Okay." I kissed his eyelids and his forehead, smoothing my hands through his hair, and as I wrapped my legs around his waist, I replied, "I won't."

***

We woke up on the couch, puffy-eyed and dry-mouthed. He lifted his head from my breast and kissed me gently on the cheek before getting up and walking into the kitchen. With a glance at my phone, I saw that it was only seven in the morning, and I yawned, ready to head back to bed as Sebastian came in with a glass of water.

"Has he ever said that before?" I asked, as he took a long sip from the glass before handing it to me.

"On the way over here last night," he told me, nodding. His voice was already edging on the brink of tears again. "He told me he loves me," and the depth I was so used to hearing shot up an octave.

Smoothing a hand over his back, I pressed my forehead to his shoulder, kissing his arm. "Oh, Sebastian …"

He sucked in a heavy breath. "I never thought he'd call me his dad. I got so used to being called man or dude. Hell, I don't think he's ever even called me by my name."

"Maybe because he knew it'd be wrong," I offered, stroking my hand down over his arm and lacing my fingers with his.

He nodded affirmatively. "Yeah, probably. That makes sense. I just … I'd thought he was gone for all this time, and to now hear him call me his dad just …" He wiped a hand over his face and laughed without humor. "God, I'm being fucking ridiculous. You're probably like, 'This fucking guy wakes me up to crash at my place, and ends up blubbering like a baby.'"

"No," I pressed, lifting my head and pulling him into my gaze, touching my palm to his cheek. "You're not ridiculous. You're reacting exactly how I would've hoped a decent man would."

His eyes held mine. "You think I'm decent."

"Sebastian, you're more than decent. You are …" I shook my head, stealing away from his stare to look toward our tangled fingers. How could this feel so right, when I knew how wrong it was? "You're everything I shouldn't want."

"And yet, here we are," he whispered in a hoarse voice.

I couldn't reply. I could only nod and stand up, leading him up to my room and hoping Greyson slept in.

***

I walked into work bearing the weight of an identity crisis.

For years, I had worked on reinventing myself and learning to be comfortable in my new skin. I wore the appropriate business attire, I spoke in a polite and acceptable manner. I kept my sneakers and leather jacket in the closet, reserving them only for moments when I could unleash my inner self and be free.

Sebastian made me feel free.

He was fun and honest with himself. He was everything I knew I couldn't be. I needed to avoid the judgements of society in a business world. To live the life of a responsible adult and not fall victim to the same fates and stigmas as my sister, the single mother who could never relax or settle down. And look at what happened to her, proving my point in a twisted heap of metal after one final night of sex and drinking.

It felt cruel and wrong, that if I were to have met him at another point in my life, maybe even at that concert, we could have been so right. We could have been perfect. We could have lived together in a world of rock stars and perpetual youth. And maybe that meant there never would've been a Greyson. Maybe there never would have been the accident that stole my sister's life. But there would have been an us.

And that almost felt worth it.

I sat behind my desk feeling like a specter of myself. A barely-there apparition in a scenario that didn't quite fit. I looked at the paperwork, looked at my briefcase, and wondered to myself how I even got here.

Jess walked into the office with a stack of paper tucked under an arm and immediately pinched her brows. "Hey, are you okay?"

Touching the edge of my desk, I nodded. "Yeah, I'm fine. I just had a long night."

"What happened?" she asked, setting the papers aside and taking a seat.

"Sebastian and Greyson came by after they were at Hershey Park," I told her, creating the scenario and wondering how far I could go before I couldn't say anymore.

"Okay?" She gestured for me to elaborate, because obviously there had to be more.

"Greyson called Sebastian his dad for the first time."

Jess's mouth dropped. "Oh my God, that had to be an emotional thing."

I nodded, already feeling the tightness in my throat and the sting in my eyes. "It really was. And after Greyson went to bed, Sebastian …" A vivid image of a grown man falling apart flashed before my eyes. "He completely lost it."

"Oh, God," Jess sighed ruefully, tipping her head and frowning. "I hate when men cry. Nothing wrecks me quite like that."

"It was rough," I agreed. I leaned forward in my chair, beginning to shuffle things around my desk. Trying to make it feel right. Trying to make it look more like me.

Who am I, anyway?

"Is that it?"

I raised my eyes to hers. "What do you mean?"

"Well, I mean, it's emotional, yeah, but you just seem completely off right now. Did something else happen?"

I placed my stapler next to the tape dispenser, thinking for a second that it looked right, until a second later when it didn't. I shifted them again. Still not right. Maybe next to the paperclips, or maybe—

"Tabitha?" Jess's tone was urgent, tugging me away from my reorganization. "God, what's going on with you?"

"Jess," I cleared my throat, dropping the stapler next to the cup of pens. "Have you ever looked at your life and felt like you don't know who you are anymore? Like, you look around at everything and you wonder how exactly you got there?"

She fixed her thoughtful gaze on the pens and shrugged. "I don't know. I mean, I guess so. I think everybody feels like that from time to time."

"I think I'm going through an existential crisis or something."

"But why? What happened?"

I looked up at her, the woman who I considered to be my closest friend, and asked, "Do you know I have my nipples pierced?"

"Whoa. Okay. I was *not* expecting you to say that just now." Jess blinked a few times, leaning back in her chair. "No, I can't say I knew that."

"Well, I do," I told her, nodding. "And I have this huge tattoo over my upper back, and I am so much happier in my Chucks than I ever am in these stupid heels."

Her smile was sympathetic. "Honey, I don't know a single woman who wouldn't prefer to wear jeans than dress pants to work, but it's *work*," Jess laughed, staring at me as though I had completely lost it. And maybe I had. "I just don't understand why this is a problem. Okay, so you have a tattoo and crazy piercings and you like wearing sneakers. Big deal."

"I can't be a professional adult *and* have the things I really want." My office was a confessional and she was my priest.

"*O-kay*," she drawled, taking in my words with a nod. "What do you want?"

I tipped back in my chair, staring at the ceiling. "Imagine this for a second, okay. Imagine I've moved up in the world of real estate, which is a very real possibility, now that I'm working for someone like Roman. I'm somewhat renown, people in circles know my name, and I'm invited to things where I have to schmooze with business moguls and celebrities. You with me?"

"Uh-huh ..."

"Okay." I pressed my fingers to my eyes and pulled in a deep breath. "Now, imagine my date. Imagine he has long hair that he refuses to cut, imagine he has tattoos on nearly every part of his body, and imagine that he can't keep his stupid mouth shut. How would that look for me? How would it look to go to a very upper-class dinner with a man who doesn't even own a pair of dress shoes?"

Jess's lips parted in a silent gasp. "Oh, shit. You and ..." She didn't dare say his name. Not even *Thor* was appropriate for the moment. "I, um ... I don't know. Are you seriously asking this question right now?"

I simply nodded, having no other words to add.

"Well, the Beckhams make it work," she offered weakly. "I mean, look at David, right? He's covered in ink and Victoria is classy, and—"

"I'm not saying there aren't exceptions to the rule," I interjected, looking back to her with a heated sigh. "But I'm saying, *realistically*, how would it look for me if I'm trying to make connections with people, and my date is blurting out in the middle of a dinner party that he—I don't know!—doesn't like the guy I'm talking to because he *leaned into me*."

She tipped her head curiously. "Did that—"

The door to the agency opened and I shooed her from the office to see who it was.

"Hi, Jessica," came Roman's smooth as silk voice. "Is Tabitha in today?"

Oh, fate. You cruel son of a bitch.

296

"Good morning, Mr. Dolecki. Yeah, she's right in her office. You can go in."

I imagined wiping my entire existence clean in the few seconds it took for Roman to walk from the door to my office, starting from my toes, to the braid draped over my shoulder. I crossed my legs, straightened my skirt, smoothed my shirt and its ruffled collar, and squared my shoulders. Lastly, I propped my chin on an invisible pedestal, holding my head up high and tensing my features. To look proper. To look appropriate.

He appeared in my doorway, crisp tailored suit and perfectly positioned silk tie between the lapels of his jacket. It was hot, too hot for a suit, but he appeared cool and collected as though he walked around in a separate world from the rest of us. One where the sun shone but it was never too hot. Never too hot for suits.

"Tabitha." He said my name the way you would order a dessert. Something that should make you feel guilty, but the desire is too big for shame. "Good morning."

"Roman," I nodded my chin and extended a hand. "How are you?"

We never shook. He simply took my hand and squeezed, holding us together in the air as he said, "I'm great, actually. I have had the pleasure of roaming around town, and I have to be honest—do you mind if I sit?" He gestured toward the chair in front of my desk.

"Oh! Yes, of course. Please," I urged him, releasing his hand.

Roman wasn't a big man, but his power radiated from every pore and puffed him up to the point of being too large for this office. I wondered about his own office, where I had yet to go. How big must it be, to contain a man like this?

"Thank you," he said, finally settled in the seat and crossing an ankle over a knee. "As I was saying, I've found that I absolutely love this town. It's quaint, with a personality the city lacks in greatly."

"Oh, I think Manhattan has plenty of personality," I disagreed diplomatically.

"It does, if you prefer the raucous type," he tipped his chin, a sly grin tugging at the corners of his mouth, "like that *friend* of yours I met on Friday. What was his name?"

The insinuation lodged somewhere in my throat. "Ah, you mean Sebastian."

"Yes. Sebastian." He nodded, interlacing his fingers and hooking his palms around his knee. "If I may be so blunt, I was surprised to see someone like you with a man like him."

The moment was fated. It was no coincidence that this would be happening right after my emotional night with Sebastian and after my conversation with Jess. It was also no coincidence that I would be talking about this with Sebastian's direct opposite. The Yin to his Yang. My past and my present, without any clue of which would be my future.

"Well, he *is* my nephew's father," I reasoned, edging my voice with a warning to tread lightly.

"Right," Roman nodded thoughtfully before waving a dismissive hand. "When I was a younger man, Manhattan was the goal. If I could make it there, I could make it anywhere, as the saying goes, and I did. But I feel ..." Tipping his head to the side, he pinched his lips as though considering what to say next, before dropping his eyes back to mine. "I feel too old for that lifestyle now. The partying, the rush-rush-rush, the stress ... I know you're a little younger than I am, but do you know what I mean?"

It was eerie, to say the least. "If I'm being honest, Roman, I'm not entirely sure what lifestyle is best for me at this point," I spoke frankly.

He smiled with an understanding. "It's difficult to make a decision that could easily have an effect on your entire life, which is why I think I've hesitated for so long to get out of the city. But then, the Worthington house popped up in my search, and I didn't even allow myself to overanalyze it, in the way I might've at one point. I just accepted it, you know? It just was."

I shuddered, not meaning to, as I blinked several times and struggled to process what he just said. The synapses in my brain weren't clicking. It felt like these two men from separate worlds were both having the same conversation with me at once. A metaphorical tug of war that I wasn't sure anybody was truly meant to win.

"Was there a reason you came in here today?" I asked, not intending to sound so agitated and impatient.

"Well, actually, I wanted to ask you to dinner, before I head back to the city."

"Dinner?" I repeated. "To discuss business?"

Roman smiled almost bashfully, tipping his head downward. "Well, I suppose we *could* talk business, but I think I'd prefer to discuss *you* instead."

A bolt of lightning struck my tongue, disabling my ability to speak, as the door to the agency jingled open. A duo of voices, a trio of laughs, and a pair of footsteps. It was all happening so quickly, I couldn't process what was happening, until the doorway to my office was flooded with the forms of Sebastian and Greyson.

"Oh, Roman. Hey," Sebastian immediately greeted, walking into the office to suffocate us all. "Good to see you again, man. Sorry to interrupt—"

"Oh, not at all," Roman replied, not even beginning to hide his irritation.

"Great," Sebastian clapped him on the shoulder. "Nice suit, by the way. What is this? Silk? Cotton?"

"It's a cotton blend, yes." Roman straightened his lapels, cocking his head and staring ahead toward the wall.

"Beautiful. Designer?"

Roman turned to glare upward, and Sebastian tipped his head expectantly. "It's Tom Ford."

"Ah, very nice. I was only wondering because, you know, award ceremonies are coming up. I've gotta figure out who I'm wearing—they say that, right? *Who*? Anyway, last year, at the Grammys, I wore Armani. Nice suit, but God," he turned to me, "that thing was fucking hot as Satan's—"

"Sebastian," I cut him off, pleading with my eyes for him to leave me alone and allow the adults to conduct their business. All the while hoping he'd never leave again.

With his lips parted, he turned to me, staring momentarily as though his thoughts and words had suddenly been forgotten. "Oh, right, yeah. Uh, Greyson and I are hitting the road, so we thought we'd stop by and see you before we left."

"You locked up the house?" I asked, completely ignoring the terse line of Roman's lips and the ticking muscle in his jaw.

"Oh, shit, was I supposed to?" Sebastian turned to Greyson, his eyes widened with mock horror before looking back to me with tired sincerity. "Of course I locked up, Tabby."

I rolled my eyes with a lighthearted laugh. "Thank you."

He nodded. "Yep."

An awkward silence wedged itself into the middle of the room. Roman, with his fingers tapping together irritably, and Sebastian, possibly replaying the moments from the night before, both keeping their eyes on me. These two opposites, both of them wanting me in a way I couldn't quite understand.

I looked up to Sebastian with a smile. "I'll see you guys soon, okay?"

His gaze dropped to my lips. He wanted to kiss me goodbye. A sadness, a loneliness, a longing flickered over his gaze as he swallowed. The secrecy of our relationship—*it just is*—was weighing on him, and I wondered how long we could keep it going, or if we should at all.

He settled for bending over and kissing my cheek, moments before Greyson stepped into the room and mirrored the affection on my other side.

"Bye, Aunt Tabs," he said with a smile, before turning to Sebastian, "I'll be in the car, Dad."

Sebastian nodded, and Greyson left, leaving the three of us alone.

As though Roman wasn't sitting there with us, Sebastian turned his entire body toward me and said, "He's saying it all the time. It's so fucking weird."

"It's a good thing," I assured him, smiling gently.

Roman cleared his throat, and we both turned to look at him. With eyes only on Sebastian, he asked, "Isn't your *son* waiting for you?"

Anger flared in my gut at the comment, but before Sebastian could open his mouth and say something I'd regret for the both of us, I stood up and took him by the arm. Smiling apologetically at Roman, I said, "So sorry about this. Will you please excuse us for just a moment?"

I dragged Sebastian from the room before Roman could reply. I felt Jess's eyes on our backs as I pulled him into the bathroom and closed the door behind us.

"Can I just remind you how much I don't like that guy? He chafes my dick just looking at him," Sebastian casually mentioned, leaning against the wall with his arms folded over his chest.

"Your feelings toward him are irrelevant," I reminded him.

"Why is he here?" he demanded.

"That's none of your business," I stated firmly.

"O-kay," he drawled slowly, tightening his stance. "Then, can I ask why you dragged me into the bathroom? Or is that none of my business too?"

I don't entirely know why, but I felt the need to confess, "Roman asked me out."

Sebastian lifted his eyes to the ceiling, studying the mini chandelier Alex had installed not too long ago. His jaw shifted as he chewed his bottom lip. "Well, can't say I didn't see that one coming," he replied, his voice graveled and unexpectedly emotional.

"You called it." I tried smiling in the way that people in the movies do when in these awkward moments, but I couldn't find it in me. "I think I'm going to accept. Just to see how it goes."

"Yeah, you should," he encouraged, and yet, he still wouldn't look at me. "When am *I* going to see you again?"

I knew what he was really asking. If we were over, whatever we wcre. But I saw no reason to tell him we were done when I was simply having dinner with Roman, so I replied, "What are you guys doing this weekend?"

Dropping his gaze to mine, he tried to smile. He wasn't very successful. "Seeing you, apparently."

I nodded, stepping toward him and pressing my hands to his chest. I felt myself stealing his breath as I kissed him. Would kissing Roman be like this? Would he struggle to regain function over his lungs? Would his heart hammer wildly beneath my hands?

"Get home safe," I whispered against his lips, closing my eyes as he opened the door and left.

303

If Sebastian makes me feel free, how would Roman make me feel?

28

tabby

It felt like a first date, like my first date *ever*, and I guess in a way it was. It was my first date in a new life, one without my parents, without my sister, and without Greyson. I was alone, getting ready in my bedroom and talking to myself the way I would've with Sam, had she been alive.

"This one?" I asked, holding up a slinky black dress to my nearly-naked figure. I wrinkled my nose, tossing it aside and held up the same dress in red. "What about this?"

I imagined what Sam would've said. She would have gone with the red. It was bold, it screamed *look at me, my tits, my ass*. But she would've known ahead of time that the night would lead to sex—her nights always did—and that wasn't what I was after. I didn't do that.

305

Or did I? "Sebastian's different," I muttered to nobody, the profundity of the statement completely lost on me in the moment.

Nothing in my closet seemed right. Nothing worked for the type of night I wanted to have. I wanted nice and casual, with the possibility of more. I didn't want the night these dresses would insinuate; these were the dresses I wore with my ex, when I knew that sex was a sure thing.

I'd wear them for Sebastian. "Oh my God, stop it."

I settled on a knee-length pencil skirt and a black sleeveless top. I double-checked that my tattoo would be hidden without the need for a blazer, made sure my bra was padded enough to conceal my piercings, and selected a pair of black stilettos, before assessing my hourglass silhouette in the full-length mirror.

It would have to do.

Roman picked me up from the house in his Ferrari, the top down as he'd promised weeks ago. After seeing the multi-million-dollar mansion he lived in most days, I felt embarrassed of my little house in a town where this was considered to be on the larger side. And although he didn't say anything, I could feel his judgement when I made him wait for a moment in the living room.

"You have a lot of records," he mentioned casually, his hands tucked into his pant pockets. Perusing the shelves with a skeptic's eye.

"It's a collection," I replied, stating the obvious as I spritzed a bit of my Work Perfume onto my neck and wrists.

"I wouldn't have expected you to be such a rock fan."

I walked across the living room to find him holding the Metallica record Sebastian had held over a month ago. It felt sacrilegious somehow for Roman to be touching the same corner as Sebastian, like two worlds colliding, and I wondered if the universe would explode from their fingerprints merging.

"I listen to a variety." I flashed him a small smile, as I pulled out a Michael Bolton album to prove my point.

Roman chuckled. "I don't see any Sinatra here. I'm a fan of the Rat Pack."

"Well, maybe I'll have to add a little Sammy and Dean."

Lifting his brows, obviously impressed, he asked, "You're actually familiar with them?"

"I told you, I listen to a variety." My smile broadened.

With a hum and a nod, he continued his browsing. "You have so many I haven't even heard of."

I shrugged, holding my hands over my stomach and feeling exceedingly eager to get out of there and to the restaurant. "I used to go to a lot of concerts with my sister. Lots of them were smaller, lesser known artists, and I'd buy their records."

To my horror, he pulled out the Saint Savage album. Sebastian's first band. The album acquired on that fated night. "This looks … violent," he chuckled, examining the black and red cover art of a raven and a bloody heart.

"They were a, uh, metal band I liked a really long time ago," I explained loosely.

307

"Hm," he nodded without a care, and then uttered, "Wow."

"What?" I asked, nervously twisting my fingers.

"This one's signed," he commented, almost impressed.

"No, it isn't," I insisted.

Sam had neglected to get signatures from the band members, as she'd left me alone at the concert where she met Sebastian. But Roman now turned the cover to face me, and there it was, in bold black marker. As clear as if someone had just recently scribbled their name in the upper left corner.

Sebastian Morrison.

"Oh," I whispered, my voice tight with abrupt emotion. "I guess I, uh, must've forgotten about that."

Chuckling, he shoved the album back into its spot and invited me with a heartwarming smile to take his arm. "Ready?"

No. "Yes."

***

Poco Bella was beautiful in the summer, with its terrace aglow with fairy bulbs and candlelight. The adjacent garden was well landscaped, alive and thriving after a long hard winter of snow and death.

Roman was a perfect gentleman, as I already knew him to be. He pulled out my chair and waited patiently for me to sit before seating himself. We ordered our meals, he ordered a bottle of wine for us to share, and as

308

the waiter walked away, he pinched the bridge of his nose.

"I'm so sorry. I didn't think to ask if you drink." Dropping his hand, he smiled apologetically across the table. "Do you?"

I laughed lightly. "I think I can afford a drink or two."

"Oh, thank God," he chuckled, relaxing in his chair. "I went out to dinner with this woman a few months ago who didn't drink any alcohol. I'm not saying that matters to me, but she proceeded to berate me about the caloric value in every glass of wine I drank throughout the night."

"And how many did you drink?" I folded my hands on the table, giving him my full attention.

"Oh, well, after that dinner, I think I had the whole bottle under my belt," and he laughed, erasing any tension that might've been lingering. "*Lots* of calories, but they were worth it."

We didn't drink the whole bottle, it wasn't needed when the conversation flowed lightly and with ease. There was no bickering, no banter, no *heat*. Just genuine conversation between two adults.

We talked about his rapid rise to success, his varied achievements, and the awards that had been presented to him. It was less about bragging, and more to simply run through the laundry list of things that made Roman who he was. He asked about my career ambitions, where I saw myself in ten years, and if I'm being honest, the maturity in conversation felt like a breath of fresh air.

It was nearly impossible not to compare him—*this*—to Sebastian and what I had with him. Here, in this restaurant with Roman, I felt like an adult on a respectable date, while my secret affair with Sebastian seemed childish in comparison.

"I know that maybe it's not the most kosher thing to do, to date your clients," Roman smiled earnestly, reaching across the table to slip his hand over mine, "but I would really like to do this again."

I nodded, pushing Sebastian from my mind. Reminding myself of what I would've done, had he never been in the picture, and so I said, "I would too."

***

"Well, since we've already agreed to a second date, what are we supposed to do now?" Roman smirked coyly, after walking me to the door of my empty house.

I shrugged, the two glasses of wine swirling through my bloodstream, leaving me feeling a little loose and maybe willing to play along if he were to kiss me. "I don't know. I haven't been on a first date in a very long time. I think I've forgotten what happens here."

With a curious nod, Roman drew his brows together and pinched his lips. "I see. Well, I could simply wish you a good night and pleasant dreams, or I could shake your hand, which would be perhaps a little socially awkward of me, but if it's what you'd prefer, we could do that."

I giggled. "Are those the *only* options?"

"*Well*," he stepped forward, polluting the limited space between us with the scent of spice and manly musk, "we *could* hug, which I would appreciate. However, if I were to hug you, I might also feel compelled to kiss you, and that, I would appreciate so much more."

My heart skipped along in my chest, standing there with him so close. I was suddenly fourteen, on my parents' front stoop with my first crush, and looking toward my living room window, I could almost see the apparition of my mother's eyes, spying on me and the cute boy from school. I found I wanted Roman to kiss me. I wanted to know if he kissed the way I thought he would, with power and control and the slightest touch of sensitivity, and I wanted to do it without guilt.

I hoped I could.

I nodded. "Okay."

"Is that an okay for a hug, or a kiss?"

With a nervous smile, I whispered, "Both."

29

sebastian

Me: I am not meant for this type of shit.
Devin: Elaborate?
Me: Tabby went on a date with some fucking suit from the city.

Ty: Shit, dude. Fucker's moving in on your territory. Gotta mark her, man.

Me: Are you saying I should piss on her? Because I'm not sure she's into that, but   I'm down.

Devin: You're so fucked up, lol.

Chad: Why haven't you put a ring on that yet?

Me: Shut the hell up, Chaddington Bear. You can't say shit to me until you're engaged AND married.

Chad: How do you know I'm not married already?

Ty: You would've invited us to the wedding, dick.

Chad: Well, maybe we eloped!

Me: Did you?

Chad: No …

Me: Okay. So, like I said, Chaddington—shut the hell up.

To put it lightly, I was irritable. It had been five days since I'd seen Tabby and four since I had spoken to her. She wasn't answering my messages or calls, but I knew she was at the very least alive, because Greyson seemed to be on the phone with her regularly. So, there was some solace in that, but not enough to put a smile on my face at the idea of being ignored.

Greyson walked into the kitchen with his thumbs tapping away at the screen of his phone and I glanced over his shoulder. He narrowed his eyes petulantly, backing away from my line of sight.

"How's your aunt?" I asked casually.

"That's the second time you've asked today," he pointed out, not bothering to look up at me as he continued to type.

"Well, I was hoping I'd get an answer this time," I shot back, opening the fridge and grabbing a beer.

"Text her yourself."

Like I haven't already tried that. Rolling my eyes behind his back, I popped the cap off the bottle and took a swig before asking him, "What do you wanna do today?"

Greyson shrugged, stuffing his phone into the pocket of his shorts. "Travis and Johnny wanted to hang out, but I dunno. I might just play some *Street Fighter*."

"You and that freakin' game," I teased, throwing my head back with a groan. "That's all you ever wanna do."

313

"You can't talk. I've seen your save file," he laughed, sitting at the island and grabbing an apple from the fruit bowl on the counter. "By the way, nice win-loss ratio, Dad. You kinda suck."

"Whoa, man," I spread my arms out wide, "don't bring *my* game into this. We're talking about you here."

With another chuckle, he shook his head and took a bite, and his phone chimed. I wanted to ask if it was Tabby. I wanted to demand to see his phone, to know what she was saying, but God, what kind of overbearing lunatic would that make me?

"So, you wanna invite Travis and Johnny over?" I offered, grabbing an apple for myself. "At least then you'll have some company."

Greyson glanced up from his phone and nodded with enthusiasm. "Yeah, sure. That would be cool."

"I'll call Mel," I decided, and grabbed my phone to do something, *anything*, other than obsessively check to see if Tabby had replied.

***

"And just when I thought I've seen everything there is to see, my baby brother went and set up a playdate," Mel sing-songed as she and her four kids walked through the front door.

"First time for everything," I grumbled, patting the heads of her two youngest and hugging Johnny and Travis. "Greyson's in the basement, guys."

It didn't seem likely that two teenaged boys could sound so much like a herd of elephants, but there they were, rattling my entire house. I turned to my sister, not sure if I should be startled or impressed.

"One of *you* sounds worse than that," she teased, taking a look around the living room. Greyson's sneakers, laptop, phone charger, iPad, and sweatshirt were scattered haphazardly throughout the room, and although it wasn't a ton of stuff, the disorder gave it the appearance of being more. Mel laughed. "Your house is starting to look like mine."

"One kid can't be as bad as four," I said pointedly, grabbing the remote and turning on the TV. I looked down at my niece and nephew and asked, "What would you guys like to watch?"

"*PJ Masks*," they shouted in unison, and I snorted.

"Wow, this *PJ Masks* shi—*stuff* must be awesome to get a reaction like *that*," I eyed Mel, and she laughed.

"It's on Disney. It's the big thing in our house right now," she smiled, ruffling the hair of the two little kids before heading into the kitchen. "You got any beer?"

"Yep." I set them up with the TV before following my sister to the refrigerator. "Yo, I need to talk to you."

"Oh, and suddenly the reason for the playdate comes out," she crooned, grabbing a bottle from the fridge.

I pulled my phone from the wall charger. "Tabby went out on a date the other day with this guy she's working for. I can't stand the sleaze-bucket, but apparently she sees something in him. Anyway, I've been trying to get in touch with her, but she won't answer my calls or texts. What does it mean?"

Mel slid onto one of the chairs at the kitchen island and handed the beer to me, soundlessly asking for me to open it, and I obliged as she asked, "She went out with another guy?"

I nodded, hoping the hurt in my heart wasn't as visible as I felt it was. "She's selling his house, selling *him* a house, whatever. He's a rich guy—"

"*You're* a rich guy, Bastian," she gently pointed out.

I hardened my glare, pushing my point. "*Not* like this dude. He smells like he showers in cash every morning."

"You've smelled him?" She raised an inquisitive brow.

"I've met him a couple times, yeah. He's a douche."

"Ooh, a pissing contest. I love it." She grinned gleefully.

"Oh, good, I'm glad *someone* does, because I can't stand it. Not to mention this silent treatment crap is pissing me off." I dropped my phone to the counter for emphasis.

"Um, can I ask what happened before she stopped answering your texts?"

"I told you, she went on a date with Roman," I reminded her with exasperation.

"Oh God, that's a rich name," Mel commented, and I nodded fervently.

"See! Everything about this guy screams money."

After taking a sip of her beer, Mel wiped her mouth with the back of her hand and directed a stony glare at me. "Okay, let me ask the question again; what happened *between you two* before she went out with him and stopped talking to you?"

I faltered as I sat beside her. I hadn't told anybody about that night. Hell, I'd scarcely *thought* about it. It felt best kept only between us, a night that felt so symbolic and sentimental to me on more than just one level. I wanted it to remain untouched by others, unsullied. But Mel saw the melancholy in my eyes and pressed to know more.

"Saturday was fucking heavy," I told her, and briefly explained the conversation with Greyson in the car. Him officially calling me his dad for the first time. How I had kept myself together until I got to Tabby's house, where I'd completely lost my shit and cried in a way I hadn't in … I can't even remember how long. The things I said to her that night, the next morning, and while I spared my sister the painful, bitter details, she seemed to get the gist of it.

"So, um …" Her long nail flicked at the open mouth of her bottle. "You poured your heart out."

"That's putting it lightly," I muttered, laying my face in my hands. "You know what?"

"Yeah?"

"This shit fucking blows." I sighed into my palms. "Why the fuck does anybody do this to themselves? I feel like a psychopath."

"Yeah, love does that," and with that, I dropped my hands to the counter and she asked, "What?"

"Don't put words like that in my mouth, Melanie," I growled, setting my jaw and glaring at her like suddenly she was the enemy and the reason why that damn woman wasn't answering my goddamn texts.

"Then what do *you* call it?" She smirked knowingly, the way she did when she knew she had proven a point.

"I will admit I like her. I will even admit I like her a lot, but *love*? Definitely not."

"I really don't understand why not," she replied softly. "What's so bad about it?"

And the worst thing of all was, I didn't have an answer to that. I couldn't think what was so bad about admitting I could love someone and want to be with them exclusively. What was so bad about having a life shared with someone else who loves you back? Someone to come home to, someone to sleep with and argue with about what to have for dinner. What the hell was so bad about it? What the hell had kept me away from it for so goddamn long?

"Nothing," I deflated against the back of my seat. "God, I want there to be *something* wrong with it. But fucking hell, the only thing I can think of is how it makes me want to throw myself through a fucking window, knowing she's not talking to me."

"Well, *that's* dramatic," she mumbled, steering her eyes off toward the refrigerator. "You sound like a teenaged girl."

"Oh, good. Maybe I'll get my period soon," I grumbled with a roll of my eyes. "Whatever. And I still need help," I told her. "I mean, you're a chick, so … give me some insight. Why is she doing this?"

Sighing, Mel leaned back in her seat and twisted her lips thoughtfully. "Okay, so this guy, Roman; he's pretty put together, right?"

"He most likely sleeps in a suit, yes," I agreed, bobbing my head slowly and rubbing a hand over my chin.

"Well, Bastian, um … Tabby's pretty put together, too," Mel delicately added, grimacing the way she had that time she told me that my hamster had escaped into the barn cat's mouth.

"Yeah, okay," I snickered. "She's got her tits pierced. Don't tell me she's put together."

Mel groaned impatiently, pinching between her brows. "But does she wear a t-shirt *advertising* her pierced nipples?" I didn't reply. Instead, I bit my lips, silently marinating in her words. "Okay then. Can I tell you what I think?"

"Knock yourself out," I grumbled, getting up to grab myself a beer. I had a feeling I would need it.

"Okay, so you came into her life when shit was hitting the fan. She needed some fun, and you're a fun guy. You know, the type of guy you get wasted and fool around with. And that's great for a little while, until someone comes along that you can actually see yourself settling down with." Mel eyed me with caution, like I would pounce in a fit of violent rage any second.

"So, wait," I began, breathing deeply, "are you saying that when I started talking feelings, I scared her off because I'm not boyfriend material?"

Startled, Mel widened her eyes and shrugged. "Um, yeah, that … that's actually exactly what I'm saying. I mean, I don't know for sure. I'm not in her head or anything, but … it could be."

I grabbed my phone and typed a quick message. Mel watched me with acute skepticism before asking what the hell I was up to.

"I'm gonna show that lady that I'm perfectly capable of classing up my act," I stated simply, and I was going to need a little help from my friends.

30

tabby

"Are you excited?" I asked Mrs. Worthington.

"Excited for what, honey?"

The woman had been trying to sell her house for nearly a year, and now that we were close to finalizing the deal, she couldn't remember what there was to be excited about?

I sighed, laughing softly. "The sale."

"Oh." Mrs. Worthington tightened her lips, clicking her knitting needles together as Sandy scurried across the living room floor. "Of course, honey."

I was skeptical of her response, but continued, "I'm thinking we'll be closing by the end of August."

"Mm-hmm," she nodded, only half-listening as Mozart played his symphony on the old record player.

I sighed, resting into the armchair as my phone chimed for what felt like the fiftieth time that day, and of course, it was Sebastian. I wasn't intending to ignore him. With every text that came through, I made a mental note to reply later, and later would come and go, taking with it the courage to reply.

I didn't know how to be honest with him about Roman, about our kiss. Hell, I didn't know if I needed to be honest at all. Was it any of Sebastian's business that we had kissed, or that I had enjoyed it? It wasn't the same, that was for sure, but it had been sweet and pleasant. But it wasn't without guilt, as I had hoped, and I wondered if maybe that also played into my reluctance to talk to Sebastian.

With a pull of bravery into my lungs, I lifted my phone to read his messages.

> **Sebastian**: Hey, so I was talking to Devin and Kylie and they wanted to get together this weekend. They told me to bring a date, and since I don't know anybody else, I figured I'd ask you.
>
> **Sebastian**: You ARE still planning on coming this weekend, right?
>
> **Sebastian**: Because I could ask one of my sisters, that's cool, but I figured if you were around, you'd like to come. I mean, fancy dinner in the city. Who doesn't love that shit, right?

I had to stare at the texts for a few minutes, reading them multiple times to analyze and dissect them until they made sense. Was he asking me on a date? Or was it simply that he needed someone to go with him, to avoid being the third wheel? Sebastian didn't seem like the type of guy who cared about being the loner, he'd find fun wherever he went. But, on the other hand, I knew Devin and Kylie were a married couple who might feel more comfortable double-dating, as opposed to hanging out with a bachelor and some one-night stand.

Me: Yeah, sure, it sounds like fun. What should I wear?

Sebastian: Nothing. HAHAHA. God, I'm funny. No, for real, don't worry about it, Thumbelina. I'll handle this shit.

Me: Uh, excuse me? You're not deciding what I wear.

Sebastian: Why? You don't trust me?

Me: I probably shouldn't.

Sebastian: Okay, how about this? Bring your own dress. Something nice, just in case you don't like what I pick out. That way, you'll have options. Sound good?

Me: Yeah. Okay. I guess I can handle that.

When I put the phone down on the arm of the chair, Mrs. Worthington glanced up from her knitting and asked, "What are you smiling about?"

"Nothing," I lied.

The truth was, it'd been several days since I had smiled, and it felt good.

Free, even.

***

When I arrived at Sebastian's house that weekend, I carried my garment bag up the walkway and to the porch, preparing myself to tell him that Roman and I were making an attempt at dating. *Real* dating. Not casual sex, not feisty flirtation, but the potential for a real relationship. I knew Sebastian and I could be friends, I enjoyed his company, but this … what we were doing …

It wasn't working anymore, not when there was something else on the horizon, and I couldn't help that.

It just is.

Greyson opened the door. "Hey, Aunt Tabs."

"Hey, Grey!" I wrapped him in my arms and kissed him twice on the cheek.

I had missed him. The house was too quiet, and the distance felt too big. I'd seen him nearly every day since he was born, and not seeing him for such long periods of time was now throwing me off to the point that I couldn't pinpoint what exactly was different about him.

"Did you change something?"

"Huh?" he asked, stepping back and letting me into the house. "What do you mean?"

"You look different," I mentioned, stepping inside and noticing immediately the changes in the house.

Greyson's things were everywhere. There was no mistaking that a teenager lived here, so unlike my own house, and something in me whispered, *Sebastian's so much better at this than me.*

For a minute, I resented him for it.

"Oh, I got a haircut," Greyson told me, jumping over the back of the couch, and I noticed the other boy. I recognized him as one of Sebastian's nephews, one of Greyson's cousins, and I smiled at him.

"Hi," I greeted, and he nodded with a quickly blurted, "Oh, hey."

"So, wait. You got a haircut?" I asked Greyson, looking for confirmation, even though the sight of his hair was proof enough. The length I had grown so accustomed to was gone, leaving behind this purposefully messy look that suited him so much more. "It looks really good."

"Thanks," Greyson turned to me, smiling happily.

Every gesture, every word, every look … everything told me he was so much better off with his father. He had friends, family. He had a house that allowed him to live and thrive, and what was I providing for him? A stick-up-the-ass aunt that wouldn't let him play his drums when I was trying to concentrate.

"Where's Sebastian?" I asked, my throat tightening with the realization that I had failed my sister tremendously.

"Dad's upstairs," he told me before turning back to the movie playing on the TV.

Dad. God, I didn't know if I'd ever get used to hearing him say that. Fifteen years was a lot of time to overwrite.

The boys laughed at whatever they were watching and I felt dismissed. I decided to head upstairs and change in what had been assigned as my room. An eruption of butterflies struck me hard and fast in the gut—why was I so nervous? This was just a dinner with

Sebastian's friends, to keep him from being the third wheel. Nothing more, nothing less.

But when I landed on the top step, and saw his bedroom door open, my poor, battered heart—abused from a year of relentless heartbreak—took a startled leap into the constricting cavern of my throat.

Before me stood a stranger.

"Y-you cut your hair," I stammered, clutching my garment bag to my chest.

Sebastian ran his fingers through the short, lifted strands of blonde, mussing it up in a way that looked effortlessly unkempt and styled. "Yeah, Greyson wanted a haircut, so I thought, hell, why not?"

"*Greyson* wanted a haircut?" I asked doubtfully. He hadn't gotten his hair cut in well over a couple years.

He laughed, and his cheeks pinked just a little. "Okay, fine. You got me. *I* wanted to go, but I was freaking out, so he went first."

"W-why did you want to cut your hair?" I hated that I was horrified. I hated that I was shocked. Because, while it was certainly an unexpected change, Sebastian had taken a sharp turn from beautiful to undeniably gorgeous.

He shrugged so nonchalantly, like it wasn't a big deal whatsoever to change the hairstyle he'd kept for decades. "Just felt like it was time."

"Does it feel weird when you're drumming?" I asked.

He looked *so* different, so unlike himself, that I hesitated to reach up and touch it.

"Hell yeah, but I'll get used to it. It's kinda nice being able to see what I'm doing, actually," he laughed, and cleared his throat. "Uh, anyway, so …" He stepped forward, opening the door to the guest room. "Greyson gave me Jess's number, and I got your sizes from her—"

"You talked to Jess?"

Nodding, he replied, "Yeah, I wasn't just gonna buy you a dress and guess your size, Tabby. That's a good way to get myself castrated." He walked into the room and opened the closet, removing a garment bag from Nordstrom and laying it on the bed. "You can check it out. Mel and Dinah helped pick it out because, for some fucking reason, they didn't trust me. Jen took it upon herself to handle the shoes, so blame her if they're hideous."

"O-oh, um … okay," I nodded, taking it all in and processing. "Are you wearing that?"

I stupidly gestured toward his ripped jeans and t-shirt with its sleeves cut off. Of course he wasn't wearing that. Why would he have gone through the trouble of finding me something nice to wear, only for him to go out in some old beat-up shit he'd probably had for the past fifteen years?

But of course, Sebastian looked down at his clothes and back to me with an expression so sincere, I almost laughed just looking at him. "Well, I thought I'd throw on a tie, but yeah. Why? You don't like this?"

"Oh, God, shut up," I laughed. "Get out of here and let me get dressed."

"Yeah, me too," he sighed, nodding and heading toward the door. "Oh, and don't worry about your hair. Just leave it down."

***

Open-backed with a sweetheart neckline, the dress was stunning in a way that teetered on the fine line between dress casual and formal. A jersey-knit, swing-style dress that would have looked great on a modern-day Lucille Ball, and I found that it suited me just as well. I noted how it showed off my tattoo, and wondered if he'd done that on purpose, knowing I never would've picked it for myself.

With a swipe of black eyeliner, a sweep of mascara, and some red lipstick, I called myself finished. For the first time in a very long while, I felt satisfied without trying too hard.

He sets me free.

Slipping my feet into the red Converse that made me giggle when I opened the shoebox, I pulled in a breath, for courage, for reassurance. I pulled the door open to find Sebastian's room empty. With a quick glance down the hall, I determined that the bathroom and his drum studio were also vacant, so with a deep breath that did nothing to satisfy my nerves, I slowly made my way down the stairs.

I felt like I was in another life, another me, another prom. I descended with the anticipation of greeting my date for the first time, regardless of that little voice insisting that this was most definitely *not a date*.

I found him in the living room working with Greyson, who I was sure had even less experience than him, trying to figure out how to properly put on a tie. They were consulting the other boy's phone, looking at a diagram, when I cleared my throat and the three of them looked up from their tedious work.

"Fuck. Me." Sebastian uttered lazily under his breath, unblinking with his jaw unhinged.

"Wow, Aunt Tabs. You look *good*," Greyson complimented before turning back to Sebastian's neck.

"Grey, you have no idea what you're doing," I said, brushing him away and undoing the knots he was making.

"I was getting there," he insisted, crossing his arms and watching over my shoulder.

"Mm-hmm," I grumbled, lifting my eyes to catch Sebastian's.

He was watching me with a heart-tugging intensity, lifting the corner of his mouth into a lopsided smile. "Do you like the shoes?"

I nodded as I looped the tie. "I do, but I have a feeling your sisters didn't help pick them out at all."

Shaking his head, he grinned. "Nah, I lied; that was all me."

"But are they appropriate for where we're going?" I raised my eyebrows, tightening the black-and-red silk to his collar and smoothing it down over his chest.

"Thumbelina, tonight you're going out with a couple of rock stars. There's no such thing as appropriate or inappropriate. It just is," he said, pointing down to his own feet, and I saw that he was also wearing red Chuck Taylors. "But we do match, and that's cute, right?"

I couldn't help but giggle, shaking my head as I stood back to take him in. "Very cute," I agreed, scanning the all-black suit and black button-down shirt underneath. "You clean up nicely."

Tugging at the knot of his tie, he flashed me with a cocky grin. "Oh, baby, you have no idea."

31

sebastian

"You rented a *limo*?" Tabby stared out the front window, shock evident in her widened eyes.

"We're traveling in style tonight, babe," I told her before turning to my sister and brother-in-law. "Thanks for letting Greyson stay here tonight."

Mel smiled knowingly, passing a look between Tabby and me. "Yeah, it's no problem. Have a good time tonight." Then, she stepped closer to me, lowering her voice to say, "Don't screw this up."

"I'll try not to," I muttered in reply.

"You look so weird, man," Steve laughed, shaking his head, still staring at my hair.

"Yeah, I know," I agreed, pushing my fingers through the short blonde strands. I hoped that eventually they'd stop having phantom pains, and I'd recognize myself in the mirror. "Okay, Greyson, behave. Don't set anything on fire and don't steal anything, got it?"

Greyson rolled his eyes. "Uh-huh."

"Hey, I have to say this shit, because true story, that happened, and my parents couldn't leave me anywhere," I informed him. Mel nodded in corroboration. "See? I have back-up."

We said our goodbyes and were out the door, being let into the limo and having the door close behind us. Tabby adjusted the dress over her lap, crossing her legs and staring out the window as we pulled away from the curb. An excited little smile tugged at her red lips.

"So, you're going all out tonight, huh?" she commented quietly, as if she didn't want the driver to overhear.

"Hold on," I smirked, pressing a button to roll up the partition window. "There, now it's like we're in our own little world."

"Being around you *is* like being in my own little world." She shook her head, a flush creeping up from her neck. "What's with all the bells and whistles?"

I shrugged, leaning back in my seat and making myself comfortable. "I figured it'd be nice. I haven't really gone out since being off, and once the fall-winter tour starts up in September, I'm going to wish I had."

"I bet that's tough for you." She tipped her head, an almost sympathetic glimmer in her eyes. "To go from being such a party animal to living the single dad life."

The comment reminded me of what Mel had said. About Tabby probably being attracted to Roman for his sense of responsibility, as though she was under the impression that I had none. Despite owning a house, cooking regularly, and doing my own laundry.

I furrowed my brow and shook my head. "I really don't know what you think I do when I'm on tour. I mean, is there some drinking and having a good time? Sure, but I am nowhere near what I used to be like back in the day. I tour with a married couple with a baby, for crying out loud. We don't exactly snort lines of coke off the asses of strippers."

"Have you ever?" She was testing me, eyeing me studiously and flashing me a pinched smile.

"Snorted lines off a stripper's ass?" I chuckled, shaking my head. "Thumbelina, that's one thing I've never done."

"Which part?"

"All of it." I narrowed my glare. "Drugs have always been a hard no for me. A little weed here and there, I could get down with, but the hard shit? Fuck no. I value my life, thanks."

"Hm," she nodded, diverting her gaze to the window. "I really like the dress, by the way."

"So do I," I commented, laying my head against the back of the seat.

Her hair was pulled to the side, cascading in waves over one shoulder and leaving her back exposed. With a hand in desperate need of possessing her, I reached out, pressing my palm between her shoulder blades, touching my fingertips to the nape of her neck and into the nest of her hair.

"I've missed you." My mouth said the words, but it was my heart doing the talking.

She turned to glance over her shoulder, smiling sweetly and nodding. "Yeah, I guess I've missed you too," and she moved toward me, nestling under my arm and against my side. Her palm pressed over my thundering heart. "Can I be honest about something?"

"You better be," I smirked, finding a comfortable spot in her gaze and staying there.

"I'm not sure I miss your hair." She bit her lip, lifting her hand to touch the freshly-cut ends. "It looks so fucking good. It's like … like you've been hiding underneath it."

Laughing hoarsely, I snickered. "I had it up more than half of the time."

"Yeah, I know, but I think it kind of distracted the eye from everything else. Like your eyes—"

"What about my eyes?"

"Well," she swallowed, and I pulled her deeper into my gaze, edging my mouth closer, "they're just unusually dark, and so pretty."

"That's what every man wants to hear; that he has *pretty eyes*," I teased, batting my eyelashes.

"Shut up." She smacked my chest playfully. "You asked."

"I did," I submitted. "What else?"

"Oh, fishing for compliments, huh?"

"I'm a little self-conscious right now," I reasoned, reaching up to touch my hair and everything that was missing. "You've gotta stroke my ego a little bit before I face my friends. They have no idea I did this."

"Okay," she conceded, her voice conditioning and soothing as she slid her fingers between the lapels of my

334

jacket and down over my stomach. "Well, it makes your jawline look really good." Her head tilted, pressing her lips to the complimented region. "And your neck …" Her fingers slid lower, resting over my groin as her mouth moved to my throat.

I groaned, closing my eyes to the wetness of her tongue and the gentle rubbing of her hand. "For the record, I wasn't suggesting that you *literally* stroke my ego."

"Should I stop then?" Her question was muffled against my neck, her fingers stopping to unzip my fly.

I shook my head. "Fuck no."

***

I'd say I've been a very lucky man.

My career took off at an early age. I made a good, honest living doing what I love most. I've played with some incredibly talented people, made a lot of friends, and fucked a lot of amazing women. I've seen the world and everything in between.

I thought there wasn't anything more I could see that could impress me. But, in the backseat of the limo, on our way to the restaurant, I watched Tabby reapply her deep-red lipstick, and all of those things I'd seen—the Grand Canyon, the Northern Lights, Stonehenge, the pyramids … Suddenly, they didn't matter. They paled in comparison, mere postcard prints in my memory, someone else's photo album, and this …

This was what it was like to be in awe.

335

"That was probably the dirtiest thing I've *ever* done," she confessed, glancing at me before coating her bottom lip.

"Oh, come on. People have done *way* dirtier things in the back of limos," I teased, unable to take my eyes from her lips. Her warm, wet mouth.

"People meaning you?" she asked, accusing and smiling, as she capped her lipstick and stuffed it in her bag.

With an embarrassed smirk, I tipped my head toward her. "I don't want to talk about that shit tonight, okay?" My voice was gruff and sincere.

"Why not? You never have a problem talking."

"Yeah, but talking about it also requires thinking about it," I explained, reaching to her lap and threading my fingers between hers, "and the only woman I want to think about right now is you."

The only woman I ever *want to think about ... is you.*

She lifted her eyes to mine. The limo slowed to a halt, the city lights reflected in the emerald greens, and she shook her head in what could've been a protest.

"Sebastian, I need to tell—"

"Excuse me, sir," the driver spoke through the intercom. "We've arrived."

"Awesome," I replied, and he got out of the car to open our door.

I got out first, then held my hand out to Tabby, helping her from the car and onto the sidewalk. I slipped the driver a fifty and wished him a good night, and Tabby asked if he was meeting us later, after dinner.

"Nah, we're not going back to my house tonight," I told her, waggling my brows and leading her inside and to the elevator.

***

"Ho-ly *shit*," Devin uttered in awe.

He stood from the table the moment he spotted us approaching. I towed Tabby along with me to greet him, but the minute I was within hugging distance, I released her and threw my arms around my friend. I clapped his back and realized all at once just how much I'd missed him in the months we'd been apart.

Kylie was standing behind him, her purple hair hanging in loose tendrils, framing her face. I let go of Devin, pushing him aside, and spread my arms. "Get the hell over here, Ky."

"You can't demand hugs and not tell me what the hell you did to your hair," she demanded, pointing at my head. "Babe, did you even notice what he *did*? What the fuck!"

Devin's hands were in my hair immediately, messing it all up as he shook his head. "What happened, man? You become a dad and so you get a dad haircut?"

I chuckled, pulling out of his grasp and smoothing my hair back. "Something like that," and Kylie's accusatory expression softened as she raised her arms up, stepping around her husband so I could wrap my arms around her waist. "I've missed the fuck out of you guys, you have no idea."

"Yeah, I think we know," she said softly, tightening her arms around my neck. "I like the look, by the way. You can stop stealing my hair ties now."

Reluctantly letting go, I stepped back and outstretched an arm to Tabby, waiting patiently behind me. As she moved forward, my hand laid against the small of her back, and I said, "Guys, this is Tabby. Tabby, Devin and Kylie."

"Hello," Tabby greeted them, stepping forward with polite handshakes, but Kylie wasn't having any of that. She wrapped her arms around Tabby in a tight hug. Devin's eyes met mine, as he gave his brows a little jump as his lips curled into an approving smile.

"We've been hearing so much about you," Kylie told Tabby, stepping back to grip her shoulders. "And can I just say, I freakin' *love* your dress?"

"Thank you," Tabby replied. "And I hope you've only heard good things, although knowing this guy …"

Devin tipped his head to her. "They've been good things … mostly."

Rolling her eyes toward me with a playful groan, she said, "You're the famous Devin O'Leary. My nephew Greyson is a big fan."

Looking to me and then back at her, he asked, "He is? Why didn't you tell me that?"

I laughed. "Yeah. That's why I stuffed him in the basement. I can only hear so much of your fucking voice."

We sat—Devin next to me and across from his wife, me across from Tabby—and perused the menu in a comfortable silence before embarking in rousing conversation without a lull in sight. Tabby and Kylie got along better than I ever expected, while Devin and I talked shop and the upcoming tour. They told me how Livy was doing, about the new home studio Devin was putting into their garage, and about how Richard and Grace, Kylie's parents, were doing. They asked me about Greyson—what he was like, how things were going—and if he'd be accompanying me on the tour.

"Well," I began, grimacing at the question, "he's got school and I'm not sure how that would work with touring."

Tabby twisted her cloth napkin, avoiding my gaze. "He's better with you though, Sebastian."

"What?" I asked, my tone harder than intended, and Devin and Kylie shot a glance toward each other.

"Baby, you wanna go to the bar with me?" Devin asked Ky, and before she could answer the question, he stood and took her hand, leading her from the table.

"I was thinking about it earlier, and maybe now isn't the best time to bring it up, but he's doing really well at your house. You're doing well for *each other*, I think, and I mean, I don't know what exactly you would do about his schooling, but I really think he should stay with you," Tabby dropped the bomb before taking another sip of wine.

I chewed my bottom lip, tightening the hand around my fork, before saying, "He's known me for a couple of months, Tabby, and you expect him to just jump into my lap and be okay with hardly seeing you?"

"Isn't that exactly what's happening right now, though?" She finally looked at me. "I'm not mad about

339

it, Sebastian. I'm just … I'm just acknowledging that I'm not exactly needed at this point. He belongs in your world. He fits so much better there than in mine, and—"

"So, what does that mean? He sees you for, what? Christmas? His birthday?" I hated the anger bubbling through my veins. I hated this, when all I had wanted was a good night, to show her that we could easily, and happily, share one world. Together.

And maybe that Greyson wasn't just good with me, but with *both* of us.

"I'm not saying *that* infrequently, but …" She shrugged, a rueful smile in her gaze. "I was never meant to have kids, Sebastian. That's becoming more and more obvious to me. For a second today, when I walked into your house, I thought I had failed my sister by not being what Greyson needed, but then I remembered *I'm* the reason he's with you. This never would've happened if I hadn't found your letters in her closet. That was my role in this, it's what made me important, but I think I can step back now and let you guys do what you need to do."

"Tabby." I shook my head, tapping the base of my wine glass. "You are so much more important than you realize."

"To Greyson?"

My hand reached across the table to lay over hers. "What do you think?"

She smiled and took a metaphorical step back. "I think we should save the difficult, annoying conversations for another night, because this wine is going straight to my head and making me emotional."

340

With a challenging jump of my brows, I replied, "Maybe I want you to get emotional."

In the flickering glow of candlelight, and against a backdrop of hypnotically serene music, she watched me. Studying my face with a tilt of her head. "You're making this more difficult for me, you know that?"

My hand tightened around hers. "Maybe that's the idea."

32

tabby

After dinner, we left the restaurant. Devin and Sebastian shed their jackets and ties, and Kylie switched out her heels for a pair of flip flops she pulled from her bag. With love in his eyes, Devin held her shoes and her hand, while Sebastian walked along beside me with his hands stuffed in his pockets. He tipped his head up and back, taking in the lights and sounds.

"I fucking love it here," he commented quietly, beneath the breath of the city.

"Why don't you live here, then?" I asked him.

"Because I think that feeling this small all of the time would drive me insane," he admitted, pursing his lips.

"Oh, God, imagine that. Something that could *actually* humble you," I teased, poking him in the side, and he brushed me away.

"Baby, I *am* humble," he insisted. "Arrogance is just part of my charm."

"Uh-huh." I rolled my eyes playfully, while silently agreeing.

We found a bar. A little dive a few blocks from the restaurant. The bartender didn't bat a lash at the expense of our clothes, not caring about who we were or what we did, and without a word, set out to pouring beers and making martinis. While the guys waited, Kylie and I selected a table toward the back of the bar, illuminated by one overhanging light and then haloed in a darkness that could swallow us all.

"So, how long have you guys been together?" I asked Kylie and Devin, and they smiled the way long-term couples do. That *too long, not long enough* glance toward each other.

"Rumor has it," Sebastian said, tipping his beer to his lips, "Dev's been in love with her for, *how* long? Twenty years?"

"Close," Devin chuckled, wrapping an arm around Kylie's shoulders. "But we've only been together for, what? Five years?"

Kylie nodded. "Something around there, yeah."

"You guys make that second kid yet?" Sebastian grinned suggestively, and Kylie lifted her martini with a smirk. "And I'll take that as a no."

"I thought I'd knock her up again sometime in the beginning of the tour, so that by Thanksgiving, she'll be completely miserable and ready to murder me by Christmas," Devin grinned, and I couldn't help laughing. He pulled Kylie into his side, kissing her temple as she rolled her eyes beyond the light and toward the ceiling.

"He loves to say shit like that to show off," she grumbled. "You should hear him when we're alone."

"Oh, I know," Sebastian agreed. "Don't forget my bunk's right next to your room." Kicking his voice up a few notches, he mocked, "Oh, Kylie, you're my favorite dream to ever come true. Let me buy you a thousand daisies and name each of the petals after—" A loud thud jostled the table and Sebastian responded with an *oof*. "Ow, dude. Totally unnecessary."

"We don't need to know what else you're listening in on, you perv," Kylie grumbled, laughter lighting her eyes.

"Oh, don't worry about *that*." He shook his head. "When you guys start necking, I kick the music up. I *do* respect your privacy, believe it or not."

Devin and Kylie hung around for another half an hour before declaring the night over for them. They were beat and needed to head back to Connecticut early the next morning. With warm hugs and cheek-kisses, they bid us farewell. But, before they left, I took note of Devin pulling Sebastian in for an extra hug. He whispered something to him, and my curiosity ran wild.

"What did he say to you?" I asked as Sebastian sat back down.

A crimson flush flourished over his cheeks. "Just that he likes you."

344

I knew he was leaving something out, omitting minor details to keep me from overthinking, and so I left it alone.

We finished our second round of drinks and ordered a third. I'd always been firm about not being a drinker, but tonight was different. Tonight felt like a special occasion, and what was I celebrating?

Freedom.

No grief. No kid. No work. Just life, in the big city, with this guy who drove me crazy in the worst ways, while also making me wild in ways I could barely understand.

"I think I'm drunk," I declared, finishing off my third martini and placing the glass on the table. I reached across the table and grabbed his bottle of beer, tipping the mouth to my lips and finishing that too.

"Round four?" he offered, folding his arms on the table. His shirt sleeves were rolled to his elbows, the colorful works of art on full display.

Ignoring the question, I took his hand in mine, pulling his arm toward me, and peered through bleary eyes at the ink etched into his skin. "I've never asked what they all mean."

"They don't mean a whole lot of anything, actually," he admitted with a shrug. "I get tattoos because I want them. I find something I like, or I get an idea that I think is cool, and I get it done."

Even his body art was a testament to how he lived his life. Reckless and in the moment.

I nodded. "It's crazy how different we are."

345

"How do you figure? Does *this* have some crazy, deep philosophical meaning behind it?" He reached across the table with his opposite hand and tapped my exposed shoulder. It felt like a jab, but I still nodded. "Oh, so you're telling me you weren't some little goth kid who just really liked *The Crow*?"

"No." I shook my head, smiling and wishing it didn't feel so sad.

"Oh, well," he tipped his chair back, wobbling on the back two legs, "you can't leave a guy hanging, Thumbelina. You've gotta tell me what insight you're carrying around on your back, hidden from the world."

"It's stupid," I insisted. "I was really young when I got it."

"How old?" he asked, cocking his head.

"Sixteen," I stated matter-of-factly.

"Shit, I was sixteen when I got my first too." He uttered the words as though this bit of information was another piece to connect us to each other. "Mine doesn't look nearly as good as that does, though. Do you get it touched up?"

I nodded. "Yeah, I've had it redone since then."

"Huh." He eyed me with the glare of someone who was impressed. "So, tell me. I don't care how dumb it is. I gotta know."

With a sigh, I rolled my eyes and said, "I got it to symbolize my freedom."

"Your freedom?" He narrowed his eyes. "What do you mean?"

Oh, we're going here, I guess. "My parents were pretty oppressive. They hated that Sam and I were into

346

all this loud music and going to concerts. I only got to go because she took me." Talking about Sam felt hard in the moment, remembering the fun we used to have, the things we used to do. I bit my lip to choke down the bubbling emotion. "Getting the tattoo was sort of an act of rebellion, I guess, but it really meant something, too. I felt free when I was with her. She didn't give a fuck about anything. She never did."

"I'm sorry," Sebastian replied, and I looked up to find sympathy darkening his eyes. "I don't know if I've ever said it, but I am. I'm so fucking sorry for everything that you've been through, and I'm even more sorry that you haven't been given the chance to cope."

I shook my head, clutching his hand. "I have though, in a way. With you. You remind me of her." It was the closest I could let myself go, to tell him what he did for me. "You remind me of the life I wanted."

Lifting the corner of his mouth into a rueful smile, he stood up and tugged me to my feet. "Too much booze makes you emotional," he noted pointedly, repeating my earlier sentiment.

"Maybe that's the idea," I whispered, my voice passing over a boulder of fought emotion. "Where are we going?"

He pulled me toward the door, carrying his jacket and balled-up tie. "Does it matter?"

And I found that, tonight, it didn't. Not as long as I was with him.

***

Sebastian hailed a cab with the deft of someone who knew what they were doing. I never could without feeling overwhelmed, but he raised his hand with a confidence I would've envied had I not been with him. But I was.

The driver asked, "Where to?"

"Central Park," Sebastian replied, and the cabbie ran the meter as we barreled forward.

I hated cabs. They always felt like certain death. But tonight Sebastian wrapped his arm around my shoulders, pulled me into him, and I laid my head against his shoulder. I felt safe in his arms, against him, and I questioned for a fleeting moment if I was willing to let that end.

"Doesn't the park close?" I looked to his eyes, shooing my thoughts away long enough to ask, and he nodded.

"But not until one in the morning. We have a couple of hours," he clarified.

A few minutes passed in silence, spent listening to my worried mind, telling me we shouldn't be doing this. This was beyond sex, albeit lovely, but I couldn't afford to do this. Not with him, not when I knew I needed to end it. But before I could relent, before I could tell him it was all a bad idea and we should turn around and go home, we pulled up to the gates of Central Park and Sebastian was paying the driver.

He helped me from the car and led me to the open gateway.

"Can we play a game for a little while?" Sebastian asked, taking my hand in his and fitting his fingers between mine.

My stomach rolled with unforgiving nerves. "What kind of game?"

"Let's pretend that we're together," he suggested. And immediately, I knew I was right in thinking this was a bad idea.

I shook my head. "This feels so much like a trap," I muttered, yet I found myself giggling and tugging my bottom lip between my teeth with something that felt a little like excitement.

"It's not, I swear. I just want to see what it'd feel like."

Surrounded by gardens, fountains, and monuments, I pulled in a breath of summer air. "Why?"

"Because you said I remind you of the life you wanted, so let's pretend that it's the life we both wanted. What kind of life would we have?"

Tightening my hand around his, I pinched my lips together and nodded. "Okay, um ... speaking completely hypothetically, right?"

Sebastian nodded assuredly. "Oh, yeah. *Completely* hypothetically."

"Okay," I relented. "Um, I think we'd live in a really nice house."

"What does it look like?"

"Um, it's big, but not so big that it's overwhelming. We have enough space for your drums and my records, with plenty of space for Greyson to do his thing. And your damn chinchilla." What I didn't tell him was, I

349

pictured Mrs. Worthington's house. The only place I could consider to be my dream home, if I ever had one.

"We don't have much of a backyard," he mused, nodding to himself. "I don't know if you like that shit, but I hate taking care of it. So, I laid down some brick, built some raised gardens, put in a pool, and there's a place for the dog to shit. That's it."

I laughed. "We have a dog? Dogs are a lot of work."

"Greyson and I take care of the dog, so you don't have to deal with him, but we definitely have a dog. Grey loves him," Sebastian persisted.

I agreed, nodding thoughtfully. "Okay, so we have a dog. What kind is it?"

"Labrador. His name is Dweezil."

"Oh G—"

His hand squeezed mine as he tipped his mouth toward my ear. "It's not up for debate, Thumbelina. This is our life, so don't fight it."

I groaned. "Fine, whatever. Are we married?"

I couldn't believe I said it. The question brought a moment of hesitation, and I glanced up toward him. I expected to see fear and dread creasing the lines on his face, but all I saw was a wistful gaze toward the New York City skyline, as we continued to walk along the shrouded pathways.

"Yeah." He nodded thoughtfully. "Of course. My mom bugged us forever until we finally got it over with."

"Your sisters, Jess, and Alex were my bridesmaids, and uh, brides-man."

"Greyson was my best man."

"He loved that," I said, surprised to find my throat constricting.

We approached a bridge, passing over a lake. Walking slowly, hand in hand, I watched the life we could have playing before my eyes like a movie I'd never want to stop watching. I knew then that I'd rewatch it every chance I got, whenever my world stopped feeling good enough. Whenever I felt like a stranger to myself, I'd have these false memories of another life, another time, where this all fit.

Reaching the center of the bridge, Sebastian stopped walking and pulled me into his body. "We never have to hide that we're together," he said, pressing a palm to my cheek. His fingers slid up and into my hair, gripping with desperation.

"Freedom," I whispered, nodding.

"You never have to hide your tattoo, or your black and red toenails." He lowered his forehead to mine, taking my hand and pressing it to his chest. "And I tell you all the time that I have never felt like this about anybody before in my fucking life, and it scares the shit out of me."

I closed my eyes, breathing in the night. "I never feel like I can't have this."

"I never feel like I can't have *you*," he replied, and captured my lips with the tail end of his words.

Beneath my hand I felt the prominence of his heartbeat. Every reverberation, channeling the most inner part of myself I kept trying to shush with pant suits and nude nail polish. I wanted this, this life we built, but I knew, as his tongue took mine and tangoed between our lips, I'd never be kissed like this again.

33

tabby

With the new haircut, I almost didn't recognize Sebastian when I woke up the next morning. I had grown accustomed to the wash of blonde hair, sprayed across the pillow to blend into mine. A thought crossed my mind, as I laid there under the outstretched fingers of sunshine—had he cut it for me? To trap himself into the societal box I had stuffed myself in?

I rolled over onto my stomach and laid a hand over his back. Knowledge unraveled in my gut, telling me this would be our last time together. My last time waking up with him by my side. My last time enjoying the type of sleep he helped me to have. I wanted to close my eyes and go back there, back to my world of sweet dreams, to enjoy just a few more minutes of this free life I had only with him.

But we weren't some late-night fairytale, and he could never be mine. Not with the separate lives we kept.

Leaning over to press my lips between his tattooed shoulder blades, I climbed out of bed and went to use the bathroom. When I returned, I found him sitting up and waiting for me, arms reaching out and beckoning for me to come back, but I shook my head. He immediately appeared wounded.

"I have to get back," I insisted regrettably. "I told Mrs. Worthington I'd help her pack some of her things. She's moving into her niece's house in a couple weeks and doesn't trust the movers to handle everything, and—"

"Do you need help? Grey and I can come and give you a hand." he cut me off, swinging his legs out of bed.

"No, I ..." I swallowed my remorse and shook my head. "I can handle it."

"Okay," he relented, and in unabashed naked glory, he walked to me, wrapping his arms around my shoulders and pulling me against him. His erection pressed urgently against my stomach, and I could've cried, knowing I'd never enjoy him again. "But maybe first, we can handle this, uh, hard and pressing issue I'm dealing with right now."

I let myself laugh. "I'd love to, but I really can't."

He didn't speak again as his chin touched the top of my head, breathing deeply and tightening his arms around me. I wondered if he knew, if he could sense where this was headed, and I imagined I could hear the tiniest sound of his heart splintering.

We stopped for coffee before the limo picked us up. I thought it couldn't hurt to indulge in one last moment together, alone, with the emotional effects of the night before still clinging to our skin and hearts.

I entered the coffee shop first and inhaled the rich, bitter scent of the morning's brew. The shop was cheery, a stark and welcomed contrast to the melancholy sting in my chest.

We walked hand-in-hand to stand in line, and Sebastian began to order for us both, when a familiar voice interrupted him.

Another fated meeting, destined to destroy.

"Tabitha?" Roman greeted me with a question, cocking his head and taking in the dress and sneakers I had worn the night before. "What a surprise." Then, with what could only be described as a sneer, his eyes drifted from my face to take in Sebastian. "Fancy meeting you here, Sebastian. Nice haircut."

Sebastian's hand lifted to touch his hair. Every mention of the cut seemed to remind him of what was missing. "Oh, thanks, man. Thought it was time for a change."

Realizing Sebastian and I were still linked together, I yanked my hand away from his and held it to my chest. "Roman, it's so nice to see you."

"Mm," he uttered through lips pinched tightly. His scrutinizing gaze was pinned to Sebastian. "What are the two of you up to today? Going to a party?"

"Nah, just heading home," Sebastian answered, before I had the chance to reply.

"Sebastian," I warned him, tightening my hands to my chest.

"We have nothing to hide from him, right?" Sebastian said in protest before turning back to Roman. "We went out to dinner with a couple friends of mine and stayed in the city overnight."

I could've killed him, if Roman's steely glare didn't threaten to do it for me.

"I see." The two little words had enough impact, enough disgust, to set my face ablaze with my shame. "Well, I hope you two are very happy—"

"I'm not with him," I interjected with an urgent desire to shove Sebastian away.

"That's none of my business, apparently," Roman dismissed me, accepting a cup the barista handed to him with a thankful nod.

A knot of dread festered in my gut. "Roman, just let me—"

"I will *not* talk about this here," Roman cut me off in a voice that made me feel our eight-year difference had grown by twenty. "You can call my office on Monday. Leave a message with my secretary."

"I, um, I could call your cell later?" I offered weakly, gripping my hands to my chest and twisting my fingers together.

"There won't be any need for that. In fact, you should delete my number altogether. Have a good day." And with that, he straightened his tie in a clichéd manner and hurried around us to enter the bustling world outside.

Quickly realizing what had happened, Sebastian released a wheezing breath before shaking his head. "Fucking hell, Tabby," he grumbled before turning around and hurrying outside.

I ran after him.

34

sebastian

"Roman!" I called. The fucking guy walked faster than I expected as I followed him into a parking garage. "Jesus fucking *Christ*, man. Slow the hell down!"

Whirling on his heel, he turned to face me. "What do *you* want?" he spat at me. "I'm an incredibly busy man and I have places I need to be right now."

"Oh, I'm sure," I snickered. "I'm sure there's an army of people just itching to hear from the infamous Roman Dolecki, and I am the lucky low-life that you're devoting your precious—"

"I *really* don't have fucking time for this," he interrupted with a patronizing chuckle. "Congratulations, by the way."

I squinted my eyes, stepping toward him. "Congratulations for what?"

"For getting to her first." There was that crocodile grin of his, cracking away at his all-business façade, revealing the fractured pride underneath. "You will never *win* with her, though. I hope you realize that. Women of her stature deserve to be won by men who *deserve* them."

"I don't want to fucking *win*," I let slip through my lips, and Roman laughed.

"No, I guess you wouldn't. Men like *you* don't know what it's like to win pussy like *that*." He snickered, tipping his head back to glare at the concrete rafters. "Oh my God. I can't believe I just called you a *man*."

"Dude, why are you such a piece of shit?" I took another step toward him, noting the way he flinched.

Roman shook his head. "I'm not. I'm a good man, and I care about her. The last thing I want is to see her being dragged down to your level of trash."

I snickered. "You know what? I really don't give a fuck what you think of me, Roman. Because I'm always going to be around. And the second you do something to hurt her, that's when I'll be there to kick your fucking ass."

"Oh?" His sinister laugh echoed throughout the parking garage. "You're threatening me?"

"Yeah, I fucking am," I growled. I took one final step, my eyes an inch or two above his.

I heard her footsteps behind me, but I didn't turn around. "Sebastian, get away from him *right now*. Roman, I am so—"

"Is this the type of miscreant you want associated with your company?" Roman spoke around me but never took his eyes away from mine.

"Dude, you can't call *me* a fucking miscreant when you just talked about her like she's a *prize* you can fucking win." I held his fiery gaze and shook my head.

"Don't you *dare* put words like that into my mouth," Roman shouted, prodding a finger against my shoulder.

"You asshole." I shook my head, snorting. "You were *just* talking about winning pussy—"

Tabby gasped. "Is he serious?"

Roman uttered a disgusted sound and turned his gaze from mine to shake his head at her. "I hope you know I would never use language like that when speaking about a lady, and especially not you."

"No, I don't believe that you would," she stated. Her voice was a knife, slicing me open as I turned on my heel to stare at her, disbelieving and so gut-wrenchingly hurt, I could hardly breathe.

"You're fucking kidding me, Tabby," I wheezed, my fists clenching and unclenching with the power of my fury.

She held her palm up and out, stopping me from speaking any further as she stepped toward us. "Roman, I'm so, so sorry about this. I hope you know—"

He shook his head and folded his arms over his chest. "I understand that your connection to him is a difficult one to sever. But I hope that you will also understand my hesitation to continue our business relationship, as well as our, ah ... *personal* one."

The tone of his voice made my skin crawl as I wondered what he meant by that. Was she screwing him? Nausea steamrolled over me at the thought.

Tabby's face fell, and she shook her head as she rushed toward him. "Roman, you can't possibly expect me to cut *all* ties with him, just for us to continue …" Her words trailed off, and I felt the slightest bit of triumph in knowing that she would at least stand firmly against removing me from her life.

"Well, then, I'm sorry, but—"

"Are you kidding me?" Her voice was shrill, strained against her frustration and anger. "Roman, I will understand if you never want to go on another date with me, but are you seriously going to destroy our working relationship because of *him*?" She thrust a trembling hand in my direction and her fingertips brushed against my chest. Her voice was wavering—she was going to cry—and all I wished to do was hug her. Or punch him. Whichever.

"There are other houses and other realtors out there," he stated firmly.

I was immediately stunned by his willingness to throw everything away. The house, the partnership. The girl. "You're un-fucking-believable, you know that?" I growled, turning to face him. "Everything is *that* disposable to you?"

He shook his head and straightened his tie, but he was silent as he walked away into the parking garage. And then, Tabby and I were alone. Her tears fell silently over her cheeks, dripping from her chin and onto the concrete floor.

I touched her shoulder. "Tabby, I'm—"

She stepped away from my touch, glaring at me with a watery, cold stare. "You had no right, Sebastian. You had *no right* to talk to him the way you did. Hell, you had no right to talk to him *at all*!"

"I didn't like the way he was talking to you," I reasoned, pulling my hand back, crossing my arms and clutching at my sides. "He can't treat you like a piece of garbage because of who you decide to spend time with, Tabby. Is that *really* the type of guy you want?"

"You don't get to decide how people talk to me, Sebastian. Nobody gets to decide that but me," she snapped.

"Yeah, well, maybe someone *should*," I spat back, "and maybe that someone should be *me*."

Shaking her head, she took a step back toward the street. "It will never be you, and this is exactly why. You're incapable of biting your tongue and being an adult. You just can't do it, and maybe in your world, that's fine, but in mine? It's not."

"If this is about what happened with Roman, then I will fix—"

"Fuck Roman," she replied bitterly. "But fuck you also, for ruining my business deal after I've been trying to sell that goddamn house for nearly a year. That was my last shot at it. Did you know that? I told Alex that if I couldn't sell it to Roman, I'd give it up to him, so I guess that's that. Thank you so much."

Guilt stricken, I thrust a hand through my hair. "Tabby …"

She uttered a groan of frustration. "*God*, Sebastian, why couldn't you just*,* for *once,* keep your mouth shut?" With that, she turned around and hurried toward the street.

I clenched my eyes shut, shaking my head as I struggled for the words that would make her stop, and just like that, they came to me.

"Because I fucking love you, Tabby!" I called after her, and she did stop. She turned around and took one apprehensive step back toward me.

"You *what*?" she asked, narrowing her eyes. Was she angry?

"I love you," I repeated, finding it easier to say now that it was out in the open.

Tabby pulled her lips between her teeth as another tear slipped over her cheek. She shook her head and raked her fingers through her wild red hair. "Sebastian, you need to stop."

"Stop loving you?" I laughed bitterly. "Trust me, if I could've stopped this from happening, I would've. I'm not supposed to want one woman for the rest of my life. I'm not supposed to want a fucking picket fence and family dinners and … I don't know, *date night*. But here I am, ready to throw everything away and start over, and I *want* that, Tabby. I want it so fucking badly, and I want it with you, and Greyson, and—"

"I'll say it again." Her voice was trembling, and her hands were held out as though bracing herself against my affectionate assault. "You *need* to stop."

I was serving my heart to her on a platter, and she was turning it away. Fucking hell. Why did this have to hurt so much? And why the fuck would anybody wish for this, in the way people always seem to?

Fuck love. Fuck *this*.

"You can't make me stop," I told her, shaking my head and wondering how I still had the strength to stand.

"Yes, I can." She said it as a warning, taking another step forward to press her hand to my chest. Pressing it against my heart, as though with one little push, she could thrust her bones through mine and squeeze the organ that begged to die. She tipped her head back, finding my gaze, and whispered, "When."

***

When.

I wasn't aware a single word could ever have the power to obliterate my heart. Not until that moment. What hurt more than her saying it, was she knew what she was doing when she said it. She knew exactly what it would do to me, and yet she did it anyway. Because Tabitha Clarke was a witch, I was convinced of it then, and I stood there in the parking garage, frozen, as she walked away.

I couldn't call after her. I couldn't grab her and force her to witness the combustion of my soul, forcing her to look at what she'd done. I could only slump against the concrete wall, struck down from the impact of one fucking word, until she was gone and out of my sight.

"Jesus Christ," I finally breathed, pressing a hand over my heart.

How could two women from the same family be so cruel? How was it possible that they'd both have a hand in breaking my heart and tearing it open?

I called a car to take me home, where I waited for Greyson to be dropped off by my sister. Mel brought him to the door and when she saw me, her face fell with somber recollection. I was in more pain than I'd ever felt before in my life, but one look at Greyson's face told me I'd be okay. It'd take some time, but I knew I'd be fine.

I had my son, and anything beyond that was a bonus.

Still, I knew the reality of what was going to happen, and he needed to understand why I wouldn't be hanging out with his aunt anytime soon. Things would be weird, they'd be uncomfortable, and he deserved to know.

"Come in here, kid," I told him, leading him into the dining room where I had laid out dinner. "I grabbed Chinese."

"You hardly ever get takeout," Greyson said pointedly, and I chuckled.

"Yeah, I know, but I'm not in the mood to cook." I sighed, scrubbing my hands over my face as I sat down. "I gotta talk to you about something."

He took his seat beside me and began spooning rice and lo mein onto his plate. "I already know what you're going to say, Dad. It's cool."

"Oh yeah?" I cocked my head, eyeing him skeptically. "And what am I gonna say, smartass?"

"You're going to tell me that you and Aunt Tabs are dating." Greyson shrugged, as he grabbed an eggroll. "It's fine. It's not weird or anything."

Stunned, I dropped my eyes to the empty plate in front of me. "So, uh, you'd be okay with that?"

He scoffed. "Dad, I've known you guys were together for a while. I'm not stupid." Shoveling a forkful of fried rice into his mouth, he added, "Plus, I went to knock on your door at Aunt Tabs' place like, last month and you didn't answer. So, I opened the door and—"

I looked up, my eyes widened with shock. "Dude, why would you just walk into my room?"

"Um, I mean, you weren't in there, so I didn't—"

"Okay," I laid my hands down on the table, huffing a sigh, "we're laying down a rule right now. Unless it's an emergency—and I mean, house is burning down, someone's breaking in, you can't fucking *breathe* emergency—you and I will never barge into each other's rooms, got it?"

"Why not? Mom and Aunt Tabs never saw the big deal."

God, the kid had been raised by women for way too long. "Kid, trust me. I don't wanna see you," I jerk-off gestured with my fist, "any more than you wanna see me. So, just … knock first, and if I don't answer right away, assume shit's going down."

"What if something's wrong and you can't answer?" he countered, smirking as he picked up his eggroll.

Jesus, he was killing me. "Then … give me a couple of minutes before you come in, just to be sure."

"What if you stop breathing in that time? Is it really that important for me to never see you jacking off, that you're willing to risk your life?"

"Greyson," I groaned, laying my hands over my face and somehow finding my laugh. "God, I don't think I've ever been more sure that you're my kid than in this moment."

He snickered, continuing to eat. "Anyway, I don't care if you're dating Aunt Tabs, if it makes you guys happy. It's actually pretty cool, I think."

His approval felt like a harsh stab between my ribs. "You know, kid … I wish I had known that about two months ago."

"Why?" he asked, quirking a brow as his chewing slowed.

I nodded. "Uh … well, I don't think we'll be seeing each other very much for a while."

"What happened?"

I could've lied to him, I guess, and maybe I should have. Maybe that was the right thing to do, to keep us both looking good in the eyes of Greyson. But I was cursed with the inability to lie, unless I was bullshitting, and I couldn't bullshit about this.

"One thing you're gonna learn about me, kid, is that nobody takes me very seriously, and—"

"*I* take you seriously," Greyson interrupted, shaking his head and pinching his brows.

I fought myself to smile. "Thanks. I appreciate that, but your aunt Tabby, she, uh …" I shook my head, reconsidering my words, to spare her his wrath. So, I settled on, "I think she and I are just too different, and I needed to fuck up to realize that."

"How did you fuck up?" He leaned his elbows against the table, watching me intently.

367

Sighing heavily, I threw my head back. "Jesus, kid …" I shook my head, staring at the ceiling and gripping the back of my neck. "I'm really trying hard to sound neutral here, okay? I don't know exactly *what* I did. I know I said some shit to that Roman guy and I'm pretty sure I fucked up the sale of Jane's house." The idea that I could singlehandedly screw her out of that deal caused my stomach to curdle, and I uttered, "That fucking son of a bitch …"

"I hated that guy, anyway," Greyson shrugged like it wasn't a big deal.

"Yeah, me too," I agreed, raising my fist and he pounded his knuckles against mine.

"Maybe Jane's husband made it happen," he suggested, beginning to eat again.

"Yeah," I nodded. "Maybe."

It seemed cruel that Tom would use me as the vessel to get rid of Roman, especially if that meant Tabby would refuse my request to at the very least give this a shot. Still, I couldn't help but find a bit of solace in knowing that the scum-bucket was out of the picture, and I found it in me to eat.

35

tabby

The whole thing was a mess. My life, my job—*everything*.

When I got into work, Alex suggested that I give Roman a call. "Maybe he reacted out of anger," he had offered with more sympathy than I felt I deserved. "Maybe he just needs some time to cool off."

And now, three days later, I felt he'd had enough time. I would give it one more shot and if it didn't work out, I'd throw in the towel and hand the house over to Alex.

In truth, I was thinking about doing that anyway, even if I did get Roman back as a client. Emotionally, I wasn't sure I had it in me to continue with this house any further. I loved Mrs. Worthington, and I loved that house, but it was starting to feel like a bad omen. Just look at everything that had come to pass since I took it on. That

369

couldn't be a coincidence. Or maybe it is, and life is just cruel.

I hadn't thought much about Sam in weeks. A little trickle of a thought here and there, but I'd been busy. I'd almost been too sidetracked to notice how fucking horribly I missed her, and God, I wished I could talk to her now. She had more experience with men than anybody I knew, and while I might've frowned upon her methods, her advice was unparalleled. She would've known what to do, about both Roman and Sebastian.

But I didn't have her. All I had was my phone and my wits, so I picked them up and utilized them both.

"Roman," I said in the calmest voice I could muster the moment he answered the phone.

"Tabitha," he responded coolly. "I thought I instructed you to lose my cell phone number."

"Yes, you did," I nodded toward my desk, "but it takes a lot more than that to get me to back down."

"I see that, and I admire your persistence."

"Good," I replied, leaning back in my chair, knowing I had at least hooked him into the conversation. "Now, I understand that you might want to proceed only on a professional basis, which I am completely open to. I—"

"Can I ask you a question, Tabitha? And please. Be honest with me."

I swallowed around my words and nodded to nobody. "Yes, of course."

"Were you already sleeping with him when you and I went on our date?"

The harshness in his words slapped me across the face. My lips fell open, struggling for an answer, but all I could settle on was a simple, "Yes."

"Hm." I knew him well enough to know he was nodding, maybe pursing his lips. "I never would've taken you to be the type of woman to settle for trash, but it wouldn't be the first time I was attracted to a woman who was … how should I put it? Easy?"

"Excuse me?"

"Hell, if I knew how easy it would've been, I should've just pursued you the first day we met."

"Roman," I kept the control in my voice, despite the shaking of my hands, "you might want to consider what you're saying before I am forced to terminate *all* of my dealings with you. Should I remind you that we were only a few signatures away from closing the deal? You said so yourself, you loved Mrs. Worthington's house. It—"

"And what would you say if I told you I'd already found another house?"

Something between a gasp and a grunt passed through my lips. My hand laid over my eyes. "How did you manage that so fast?"

"Like I said, Tabitha; there would be other agents, and there would be other houses. Now, unless you can make me an offer I won't be able to refuse—maybe something along the lines of what you've been offering to your *friend*—then I'm going to end this call."

My eyes flooded with hot tears. I had never in my life felt so used, so belittled and small, and for what? For making a choice to enjoy myself with a man?

With clenched fists, I gripped the edge of my desk, and said, "How's this for an offer, Roman? Go fuck yourself. Fuck yourself hard. Fuck yourself so hard, your dick snaps off and no woman will ever be subjected again to you or your vile ass." And with that final word, I hung up, slamming my phone onto my desk as Jess appeared in my doorway.

"Wow. I think you've been spending too much time with Thor," she quipped, biting her lips and unsuccessfully hiding her grin.

"Yeah, well … let's just say I got a taste of how Sam was treated her entire fucking life," I muttered, shaking my head and wiping a finger under an eye, catching one rogue tear.

It took me all of ten minutes to realize that Sam was never wrong in choosing to spend her free time with various bed companions. She was just an adult, enjoying herself with another adult, and what the hell was so terrible about that? It didn't make her immature, it didn't make her wrong, so who the hell was I to exile her from my list of admired people because of it? She was my fucking sister. She had been unafraid to be herself, she was always loyal to her family, and she had loved her son.

I stood up from my desk and kicked off my heels. Pulling the red Chucks out from the dark space underneath, I stuffed my feet into them and declared, "I'm taking some time off, guys."

Alex showed his face in the doorway and tipped his head. "How long?"

"I don't know," I admitted. It was nice being the boss sometimes—I could say things like that and get away with it. "I'm only a phone call away, though, so if you need me for anything, I'll answer. I just need to take some time. I haven't, and … I think I'm ready to do that."

They both understood, as they nodded solemnly. And I grabbed my bag and left.

***

Before I went home, I stopped by Mrs. Worthington's house to give her the bad news about Roman.

"Oh, thank Heavens!" She raised her hands to the sky, as she sat on her emptied front porch.

"Um, excuse me?" I shook my head, worrying my bottom lip between my teeth. "I thought you wanted to sell the house."

Reaching over to clasp my knee beneath her palm, she shook her head enthusiastically. "Oh, honey, what gave you that idea?"

Frustrated, I pressed the heels of my hands to my eyes. "Because we've been at this for almost a year, Mrs. Worthington."

"No, no, Tabitha; I *need* to sell the house. I don't *want* to," she corrected me. "I would die here, if I could. But I'm afraid I'm going to be around for quite a while, and I don't think I'd be able to stand the quiet, even with Sandy here." She ran her hand over the back of the chinchilla.

I nodded, with thoughts of my own empty house weighing heavily on my mind. "I guess I can understand that."

"Someone will come along," she assured me. "But I don't think you're quite right for the job."

"I don't think I'm quite right for *any* job right now, to be honest with you," I laughed sadly.

"You're good at what you do, honey." Mrs. Worthington squeezed my knee. "I thought surely you'd be able to sell this place, but maybe you're too close to it. Maybe you want it too much."

"Yeah." I nodded. "Maybe that's what it is. Maybe …" I sighed, shaking my head and looking out toward the fence rounding the perimeter of the yard. "Maybe I've finally reached my limit."

"Everybody needs a break sometimes." She nodded affirmatively. "Take a trip. Do something you've always wanted to do. Let yourself mourn. Buy a chinchilla." She waved her hands into the air. "Do whatever it is you need to do, and then come back. I think you'll find you're a lot better off."

Take a trip. My lips stretched into a smile, and I nodded. "Yeah, you know … I think I'll do that."

36

sebastian

"You got everything?" I asked Greyson, as I leaned against the doorframe of his room.

He was still there, but given the condition of his room, it felt like he was already gone. The dirty clothes usually strewn across the floor were missing, his closet was empty, and his laptop was gone from the desk. I was glad I wouldn't be here to witness him really being gone. I wasn't sure I'd be able to handle the quiet. After two months, I'd forgotten what it was like.

"Yeah," he replied, nodding and slinging his backpack over his shoulder. "I still wish I was going with you, though."

"I know, kid."

I wrapped my arm around his shoulders and steered him out of the bedroom, shutting off the light and heading to the basement stairs.

After what Tabby had said about him being better off with me, even on tour, I did consider it. But thanks to the courts taking their time to grant me my paternal rights, I still wasn't legally allowed to make any decisions regarding his schooling. It fucking sucked, but the law is the law.

"How does your aunt feel about taking Dweezil until I get home?" I asked, chuckling to myself about the idea of Tabby having to take care of a ten-week-old puppy.

"Oh, she's *thrilled*. Can't wait," and he laughed as we reached the top of the stairs and the yellow Lab began to yap tirelessly from his living room crate. "She's going to especially love that sound. Maybe she'll be cooler about letting me play my drums when she's listening to Dweezy all night."

I couldn't get Greyson a tattoo for his sixteenth birthday—not without legal guardianship. So, I got him a puppy instead, although I will admit the dog was mostly for me. Greyson's just the guy I use to clean up after him, under the guise of him needing more chores around the house. Greyson had disagreed with that sentiment, but he was happy to have Dweezil.

"I wouldn't hold my breath on that one, kid," I laughed, entering the living room and releasing Dweezil from his crate. The puppy took off in a yellow blur toward the kitchen. "Take him out and let him pee before we hit the road, okay?"

"Yep," Greyson replied, grabbing Dweezil's leash and chasing after him.

Dropping down to the couch, I let my head fall back as I grabbed my phone and checked for messages. My sisters were teasing me about seeing Tabby for the first time since the shit hit the fan. Asking if I was ready to have my balls handed back to me yet, to which I replied, "She never had them in the first place," but that was a lie and we all knew it. Still, they were kind and didn't rub it in too much.

The guys were all excited to be back on the road, especially Dev and Ky, but it was easier for them. What were they leaving behind? Even their cat went on the road with us. I fantasized about my time of having no strings attached, with nothing to ground me back home, and I can't say I missed it. But, fuck, it hurt to think I wouldn't see Greyson, outside of video chatting, until Halloween.

I had promised I'd see him, and that we could do something cool. I was going to keep that promise.

Scrolling through my phone, there was a message from Tabby. I opened it with a touch of reluctance, the way I always opened her messages. They never said anything other than a question about Greyson, or a curt "how are you," but I always imagined that maybe one day, she'd tell me she changed her mind. Or maybe that she'd take back that one little word that had crushed my soul weeks ago. She never did though, and every time, I'd still find myself disappointed, but at least she was talking to me. As long as she was talking, I told myself there was hope.

Tabby: Drive safe. Can't wait to see you guys.

I stared at the message for way longer than necessary. A well wish. A *can't wait to see you*. It might've meant nothing, and yet, it felt as though it could mean everything.

Greyson came in from the backyard with Dweezil leading the way. I asked if he peed, and Greyson nodded. "He pooped too," he informed me, and I breathed a sigh of relief.

"Thank God. The last thing I wanted was for my car to smell like dog shit."

***

We drove into Hog Hill like it was a memory from a long time ago. It felt hazy, and yet, all too familiar. Greyson confirmed he felt the same way, commenting on how it was weird being back, after spending virtually the entire summer in my house and with my family.

"It'll feel normal again in a few days," I assured him. "It always feels weird coming home from the road, but before I know it, I'm happy as fuck to be sleeping in my own bed again. And cooking. Shit, I'm *really* going to miss cooking all the time."

"I don't think there's any way I'm going to be happy sleeping in that crappy old bed again," Greyson mumbled.

Passing through main street and driving by TC Real Estate, I thought of popping in, the way I had that first day. I wanted to say hi to Jess and Alex, for no other reason than to ask how Tabby had been all this time, if she and Roman had seen each other. Fuck, maybe they were even together, dating exclusively and getting ready to elope on some private island somewhere.

I never asked Greyson about what she'd been doing, and he never told me. It was better I didn't know, but that never stopped me from wondering, and right now, I was wondering a lot.

We pulled up to her house and Greyson sighed. "I'm not ready," he mumbled, and I reached out to grip the back of his neck.

"It's going to be fine," I promised, but what was I promising? That school wouldn't suck? That it wouldn't be weird readjusting to his aunt's house? I didn't know that either of those things wouldn't happen, so the promise felt empty and cruel.

"What if she talks shit about you?" he asked, not a question I was expecting. "What am I supposed to do?"

"She won't," I told him, knowing her better than that. "She wouldn't put you in that position."

"She better not," he grumbled.

I hated that he had taken sides. "Don't give her a hard time, kid," I warned.

"Well, then she better not talk shit about you," he reasoned with a nonchalant shrug.

Getting out of the car and grabbing Greyson's stuff from the trunk, I looked out toward the house of the woman I loved. God, it was still weird to say that—that I loved someone. It felt so serious, so *real*. It gave her so much power over me. She was in every movie I watched,

379

every song I listened to. I couldn't sleep without imagining her in my bed, or shower without imagining her long, red hair between my fingers.

I felt obsessed and fucked up. Why the hell is this feeling coveted? I didn't feel complete, or good; I felt ruined.

Greyson grabbed Dweezil and his leash, and we took the daunting walk up to the front door. I used the key I still had and pushed the door open, allowing Greyson to lead the way.

"Aunt Tabs?" He called into the house and up the stairs, as I walked into the living room.

It looked different. Lived-in. I took in the Converse laying on the floor, tucked into little pockets of space beside the couch or under the coffee table. The records, lying on the end tables or on the mantel. There was a small pile of discarded matches beside the Fresh Linen candle and even a half-full glass of something beside the couch, a red lip-print on its brim.

I couldn't help but smile. I didn't know if this was a tailspin, or just the evidence of her relaxing, but I appreciated the humanity of it. Knowing I had played a part. Should I have felt guilty for that? Because I didn't.

I turned around to catch Greyson bend over to unleash Dweezil, and I shook my head, stepping forward. "Wait. Don't let him off until he's—"

"He's fine."

Whirling on my heel, I turned around to see Tabby emerging from the back of the house.

Something I had learned about love was, I couldn't discern between reality and fantasy, not when I was

380

thinking about her. Was her hair really as gorgeous as I remembered? Were her eyes really such a vibrant green? Was fucking her really that incredible? But here, I could answer two of those questions with a resounding *yes*, and that last one, well … I would've thrown her down right there to find out, if I knew she wouldn't knee me in the nuts.

Her long, red hair was hanging in curtained waves over her t-shirt. God, I couldn't help but smile at the simple fact that she was wearing a *t-shirt*, and a Breaking Benjamin one at that. It was a tour shirt that read the current year, and I began to wonder, until I noticed her leg-emphasizing shorts and the cursive font etched into her flesh. I couldn't read it from where I stood, but I was dying to know what it said.

"Hey, Thumbelina." I didn't mean to use the nickname, but my tongue had a mind of its own.

"Hi," she uttered the simple word. It felt so good to hear her voice. Like taking a breath of air, after being suffocated nearly to the brink of death.

"You look good," I commented, completely forgetting that Greyson was standing right behind me with Dweezil itching to get the hell off his leash.

"Greyson," she said, speaking around me and ignoring the compliment, "I said you can let him off his leash. Just watch where he's going and make sure he doesn't chew on anything, okay?"

I didn't know if Greyson nodded, smiled, or gave her the finger. I couldn't take my eyes off her. That little witch … It had been weeks and she still had me under her spell.

"Do you still have stuff in the car?"

I didn't know who she was asking, but I nodded. "Yeah, I'll bring in the rest."

"I'll help." I realized she must have been talking to me, because she began to walk toward the door, as though leading the way. When I didn't follow, too busy shamelessly watching her ass move in those tight, hip-hugging shorts, she turned and narrowed her steely glare. "Let's go."

With a single nod, I looked at Greyson, who was already looking at me with sympathy, and I gave him an encouraging lopsided grin that I couldn't feel if I tried. "We'll be right back."

Tabby and I walked to the car in silence, and it wasn't until we stood next to the open trunk that she looked up into my gaze. The anger in her eyes was unrelenting.

"I know you told Greyson about us."

"Oh." It was all I could say, as I diverted my stare to the car.

"You had absolutely no right to do that without consulting me first," she lectured, her tone cold and even.

I bobbed my head solemnly. "I know, and I'm sorry if that puts you into an awkward-as-hell position, but I knew the likelihood of us being civil with one another for a while was unlikely. So, I did what I thought was best."

With a tight breath through her nose, I was relieved to find her nodding. "I understand that, but you still had no right to talk shit about me behind my—"

I held up a hand, making her stop. "Tabby, I have *never* talked shit about you. You can ask Greyson. I never wanted him to take sides, and I think I've been really good in trying to enforce that. So, whatever problems he gives you, if any, that has absolutely nothing to do with me."

"You know, as much as I'd love to believe that, you'll understand why I'm finding that really difficult to do right now."

"Sure. I already know better than to expect you'll listen to anything I have to say," I jabbed lightly.

Allowing me the final word, she turned to face the open the trunk and looked at my pile of suitcases. "Are all of these coming in?"

"Nah, just this. The rest of his stuff is already inside." I reached into the trunk, pulling out a bag of Greyson's dirty laundry. "I didn't have time to wash these before we left."

"It's fine. I'll do them." She nodded, taking the bag from me.

I closed the trunk and rounded to the backseat, pulling out the puppy's fold-away crate, and I was rewarded with an airy chuckle from her.

"I gotta tell you, I didn't expect you'd actually get a dog," she mentioned lightly, folding her arms over her chest.

"I wasn't lying about the life I wanted," I said, taking her back to that last night in Central Park. "Just because I couldn't have some of it, doesn't mean I wouldn't try for the rest."

She hummed thoughtfully, and asked, "Are you okay?"

I snorted, lifting the corner of my mouth into a rueful crooked smile. "I will be eventually. Some time on the road will be good, I think. How about you?"

She reluctantly nodded. "I took some time off work and did a little traveling. It helped a little bit. I just, um …" She scraped her teeth over her bottom lip, dropping her gaze and fumbling with her hands before looking back to me. "I really just needed some time to deal with things myself, I think. I was drowning my sadness in work, and distractions, and … *you* … And I really just needed to clear my head and cope on my own, in my own way."

"Yeah, I get that," I told her.

"Thanks for being so cool about this," she continued quietly. "I didn't think you would be, after everything …"

"Well, I'm a pretty cool guy." I smiled. "Thank *you* for not hating me."

The noticeable bob in her throat told me far more than she was willing to emit. "I am far from hating you, Sebastian."

***

"Okay, kid, give me a hug," I finally said to Greyson after stalling for way too long, "I have to hit the road. Gotta get to Devin's."

Tabby asked the question with her eyes, and I replied, "I'm driving to his place and staying the night. We have a show in Hartford tomorrow night, and he doesn't live too far from there."

She nodded. "Okay, well, break a leg."

"Don't say that shit to me," I glowered at her, standing up.

"What? It's meant to be for good luck," she insisted incredulously.

"I know what it means, but it'd be my fucking luck that I actually would break my legs and I need these fuckers to actually do my job." I smacked my thighs. "Otherwise, I'd be back home and pissed off and nobody wants to deal with that."

"Okay, fine …" She rolled her eyes. "Well, then, good luck."

"Thank you," I bowed my head to her, wishing I could just grab her and make out right there. Instead, I turned to Greyson and outstretched my arms. He hesitated, pulling his lips between his teeth and dropping his gaze to the floor. "Come on, Grey. Don't make it harder for me here."

Stepping forward, he pushed against my chest, wrapping his arms around me and pressing his head to my shoulder. I hugged him, imprinting this feeling to my bones. My throat strangled around a surge of emotion and my chest pulled tight.

"Fuck," I swallowed, tightening my arms against his shoulders. "I'm gonna miss you, kid."

"I'm going to miss you too, Dad," he breathed. "Can I call you tonight?"

I grabbed his shoulders, pushing him away from me to glare directly into his eyes. "Don't *ever* ask me that question. You call me whenever the fuck you want, okay?"

"What if you're playing?"

"Then I'll call back as soon as I can," I promised, and he nodded.

I pulled him to me again, kissing his forehead in a way that would've had me rolling my eyes at my own parents. But Greyson didn't even flinch. His throat bobbed again, his eyes brimming with tears.

"I love you, kid."

"Love you too, Dad."

Pushing an exhale from my lips, I shook my head. "Okay, we need to stop. You're going to make me all emotional and I can't deal with that shit."

We laughed as I clapped him on the shoulder, before turning to Tabby. "Thumbelina, am I getting a hug from you, or is that completely out of the question?"

Rolling her eyes, she muttered, "You get one hug and that's it."

She stepped forward and blessed me with her touch as she wrapped her arms around my waist. I know she didn't give me permission, I know she probably didn't even want it, but I tipped my lips to kiss the top of her hair, and I swore I felt her arms hold me a little tighter.

"You know, I don't want to be a presumptuous dick or anything, but I think you're going to miss me," I mumbled against the top of her head.

That's when she unwrapped her arms, folded them over her chest, and stepped away from me. "Then don't be a presumptuous dick. Drive safe."

"Yep." I nodded, offering her a small smile.

I looked between the two of them, realizing that having someone to come home to, also meant having someone to leave, and God, that made it all so much harder. But so worth it.

"Shit." I cleared my throat. "If I don't get the fuck out of here, I'll be calling those guys and telling them to find another drummer. Okay, I'm leaving."

With quick goodbyes and one last hug to Greyson, I forced myself to leave, hoping the next two months would fly by as fast as the summer had. Time on the road usually seemed to move quickly, but that was before I had people to rely on me and people to miss, and that … Well, that made the drive alone to Devin's house drag, and I could only imagine how the rest of my time away would be.

37

tabby

Two weeks after school had started, and two weeks back to work, I asked Alex how the sale of Mrs. Worthington's house was going. His response was irritatingly vague, mentioning that he'd found a few potential buyers via the internet listing, but that he didn't want me to be involved with it.

"Why the hell not?" I demanded, all but stomping my foot. "I was invested in that house for the past *year*!"

"Yes, and look at what it did to you," he responded with a pleading look in his eyes. "Hell, honey, look at you *now*. What are you even wearing?"

"What's wrong with what she's wearing?" Jess asked, gesturing toward my leather blazer and Pearl Jam t-shirt. "I think she looks badass."

"I just want to know where my sweet Tabitha went and why she had to leave Joan Jett in her place," he groused, tipping his nose into the air and leaving my office in a somber huff.

Jess turned to me. "I don't think he even knows who Joan Jett is," she muttered through the side of her mouth, and I laughed, shaking my head. Then, she added, "I like this new you, by the way."

I laughed inwardly at that. There really wasn't much about this side of me that was new at all. I was finally just letting her come out and play, instead of telling her to sit down and keep quiet while the grown-ups went about their business.

After years of constantly fighting an internal battle, I had finally decided I could be myself while still remaining professional. And two weeks back on the job, told me that was true. I'd already taken on a couple of new clients in the area, neither of which batted a lash when I met them with my fingernails painted dark grey.

I never liked nude nail polish, anyway.

"Is this what a month of going to concerts does to a girl?" Jess asked, crossing her legs and grinning.

"Oh my God, Jess, it was *amazing*," I sighed, tipping my head back and reminiscing about the four weeks I spent maxing out one of my credit cards, dipping into my savings account, and seeing shows I never thought I'd ever let myself see.

Most of the tickets had been purchased through scalpers, since I was buying them last minute. Normally, that's not the type of thing even the younger me would've done. But this time was different and it was special. I dedicated those weeks to Sam, and I learned to find freedom on my own.

"So you've said … about a hundred times," she teased, rolling her eyes playfully as she stood up and left my office. I guess I had that coming, after I'd spent the past two weeks talking endlessly about how awesome my sojourn had been.

I checked the clock and noticed that it was already time to head over to Greyson's school. I braced myself as I grabbed my briefcase and headed out the door. Every day since the start of school, I waited for him to show up with an in-school suspension notice or a detention slip. I was on edge, thinking it was all too good to be true for a few months with his father to have cured him.

Pulling up to the school, I found him already waiting for me, and like every other day, a feeling of trepidation sat heavily in my gut as he got into the car.

"Hey, how was school?" I asked him, driving away from the curb.

"It was good."

I glanced at him skeptically. The short, curt answers didn't convince me. "What was so good exactly?"

"I don't know," he shrugged, grabbing his phone out of his backpack. "It was just a good day, I guess."

"Well … are you still liking your teachers?"

"Just as much as yesterday." He eyed me sidelong, smirking in a way that immediately reminded me of his father.

"Sorry." I held my hands up in momentary surrender before gripping the wheel. "I'm allowed to ask."

"Mm-hmm." He shook his head and looked back to his phone, typing away and smiling to himself.

"Who are you talking to? Sebastian?" He nodded. "How's he doing? How's the tour?"

"You could ask him yourself, you know," Greyson muttered, continuing to type.

I sighed, tapping my fingers against the wheel. "Well, maybe I'm just trying to make conversation. I want to make sure you're okay."

Greyson groaned, laying the phone in his lap and turning to me. "I'm okay. Seriously."

"Are you *positive*? Because we could go back to the therapist, or—"

"Aunt Tabs." He cocked his head, and my eyes met his to find his pressing glare. "I'm *fine*."

Sam's memory clung to the walls of my mind as I hesitated on my words. I wanted to ask him about her, and if he thought about her anymore. He seldom brought her up, if at all, and it broke my heart to imagine he was struggling internally. Alone. Refusing to bring her up for some adolescent reason.

"Grey," I uttered on a shaking breath. "I just want you to know that you *can* talk to me, if you wanted to. If you ever wanted to talk about—"

"I miss Mom, okay?" he blurted without warning, surprising me with his apparent ability to read my mind. "I'm *not* okay that she's not here. It really sucks, and I hate it. But I *swear*, I'm okay. Just like you say that you are, too."

I tightened my grip around the steering wheel and pursed my lips. I *was* okay, while still allowing myself the freedom to miss my sister and my parents, and I considered it was possible he was also. But the question begged to be asked.

"Did he really help that much?"

"Who? You mean Dad?"

I couldn't help but smile as the tears collected in the brim of my eyes. God, he said it so easily now, like he'd been calling him that every day of his life. There was no hesitation, no awkwardness.

I nodded. "Yeah. I'm just … I'm just having a really hard time believing that he could've turned things around so much in such a short period of time." Greyson was quiet for a moment and I thought I might've upset him by questioning the positive effect his father had on him. I reached out and laid a hand on his thigh. "I don't mean that he *shouldn't* help to make things better, Grey. I'm just—"

He shook his head. "Sometimes bad things happen, and good things come along to balance them out. Not to like, *erase* the bad things, or to make you less sad that they happened or anything, but just to, you know, make them easier to deal with."

The words struck a chord within my heart and I glanced at him. "Who told you that?"

He smirked with an accompanying shrug. "Oh, I dunno. Just some guy you thought wasn't good enough for you, or something like that."

With a tip of my head toward the window, I scoffed. "Greyson …"

"I'm staying out of it," he declared, lifting his phone from his lap. "I'm just saying, Dad's one of the good things, Aunt Tabs."

392

I didn't nod, because to nod would be to admit that I agreed. And if I agreed, well ... wouldn't that be to admit that I was wrong about Sebastian? And I wasn't ready to do that.

Not yet.

***

Me: Hey.

Sebastian: Whoa. Am I dreaming, or are you actually initiating a conversation with me right now?

Me: Might want to pinch yourself really, really hard. Just to make sure.

Sebastian: Nah, no need. If I was dreaming, I'd already have a pic of your tits.

Me: Lovely.

Sebastian: So, Ms. Clarke, what did I do to deserve the gift of your attention on this fine September evening?

Me: Well, for one, your dog ate my shoes. So, you owe me a pair of heels.

Sebastian: Sorry. I told him to do that in a fit of rage. Didn't think he'd actually do it. My bad. (But also, please tell him I said, "Good boy.")

Me: So funny.

Me: Anyway, I wanted to thank you for what you've done for Greyson. I don't think I ever did, and I just think you deserved it.

Sebastian: ...

Sebastian: Still not sure that I'm not dreaming.

393

Me: Shut up. Seriously. Greyson's been doing really well. I mean, it's only the beginning of the schoolyear, but he's doing great so far.

Sebastian: Yeah, I know. He told me. He's been hanging out with a few different kids too. Did he tell you that? Kid's making some new friends who aren't little dickheads.

Me: No, he didn't tell me that. He's not telling me too much.

Sebastian: I wouldn't take it personally. He's not mad at you. I think he's just more comfortable talking to a guy.

Me: I never thought that could be a possibility.

Sebastian: Yeah. Trust me. If something was wrong, he'd tell you.

Me: Okay.

Me: Anyway, I won't keep you. I just wanted to say I really do appreciate everything you've done for him. You've really helped a lot.

Sebastian: Well, it's why you recruited me in the first place, remember?

Me: I do. I guess you did your job well.

Sebastian: I guess so.

Sebastian: And by the way, you could totally keep me. If you wanted.

I read his message a handful of times before laying the phone down for the night. There were so many things I wanted to say, but I couldn't say them, not yet. I didn't feel ready, or maybe it was that I wasn't yet convinced that what he felt—what *I* felt—was real.

38

sebastian

Standing in the airport with Chad and Ty, I felt like a kid waiting for Christmas. Practically dancing on the spot, I eagerly awaited Greyson's flight, watching the screens and checking the time.

"You guys didn't have to come," I told my friends for the thousandth time. "I would've been fine on my own."

"I gotta be sure this kid exists," Ty chuckled, dropping into a chair beside Chad. "This *could* just be one elaborate story to convince us you're not a lonely motherfucker."

"I have a puppy, dude. You can't be lonely with a puppy." I shook my head, glancing at the monitor again. Estimated time of arrival: Ten minutes. "Fucking hell. This is taking forever."

Chad rolled his eyes. "We've only been here for like, fifteen minutes."

But that's not entirely what I meant. My time before Greyson had felt like forever, the time I spent away from him now though, felt like an eternity.

I paced for a few more minutes, shaking my hands out and tapping my fingers against my thighs, before Ty finally hit me.

"Dude, did you just smack my ass?" I raised an eyebrow at him. "'Cause I didn't hate it and I'm not sure what that means for me."

"I …" Ty shook his head and ran his hand over his cropped hair. "I might've. It's what I could reach. Sit down. You're making me nervous."

"I can't sit still!" I shouted, gritting my teeth and glancing back at the monitor. "Oh, fucking hell. Five minutes. Oh my God … what if he doesn't recognize me? What if he's decided he doesn't like me anymore?"

"Carrie never decides she doesn't like me in the time I'm away," Ty pointed out, bringing up his daughter, and I rolled my eyes.

"You've known her since birth," I groused, flopping into the seat beside him. "Greyson has only known me for a handful of months. He can change his mind."

"That's all the more reason for him *not* to change his mind, man," Chad butted in, looking around Ty to glance at me. "He's got a lot of time to make up for."

Rolling my lips between my teeth, I nodded. "You know, Chaddington, for a guy so afraid of commitment, you're pretty wise."

"I'm not …" He groaned, slumping back in his chair. "Never mind."

I tapped away the minutes against the armrests of my chair, while Ty scrolled through his phone and Chad read something on his Kindle. My excitement was a tornado, making me dizzy and wreaking havoc on my nerves. It certainly didn't help when I glanced up to the monitor and saw his plane had landed.

I was so close.

My phone vibrated, and I jumped from the chair, pulling it out to find a message from Greyson. "He's here," I announced, to myself and my friends. "Holy fuck. This is crazy."

"Yeah, it is crazy, thinking you have a kid," Ty agreed, nodding and standing up. "Come on, boys. Let's go find him."

***

We waited just outside the terminal gates, watching the passengers come out and greet their loved ones. I was jealous, wishing Greyson would come out sooner. I wondered what was taking him so long, what was holding him up. If he was okay, if he needed me, if …

"There he is." I shoved my backpack at Ty's chest before moving my way through the crowd toward my son. It'd been nearly eight weeks since I'd seen him outside of our video chats. His hair was getting a little longer, but so was mine. He looked older, different, and I wished I could say I wouldn't ever take that much time away from him again, but I'd be a liar.

397

He ran to me, thrusting himself into my arms and nearly knocking me off my feet. I squeezed him, held on tight, and said, "Shit, I'm so happy you're here."

"Yeah, me too," he replied, his voice muffled by my shoulder before he stepped back and grinned. "That was my first time in a plane."

"Get the fuck out, seriously? Why didn't you tell me that?"

He shrugged. "I didn't think about it, I guess."

"Dude, you should've said something. I wouldn't have made you go alone," I persisted, immediately worried he had spent the entire flight freaking out.

"Really, Dad; it was fine," he assured me with a grin. I stopped blinking, stopped breathing, and stared at him for a few moments, before he asked, "What?"

"Nothing." I shook my head, snapping myself out of it. "I'm just really fucking happy you're here."

Greyson nodded. "Yeah, me too."

"Come on," I said, throwing his bag over my shoulder and leading the way to where Ty and Chad stood waiting.

Greyson didn't even wait for me to make the introductions. "You're Tyler Meade, and you're Chad Wilcox." He held out his hand to each of them as they both looked to me with impressed bewilderment.

"I told you he knows his shit." I beamed with pride.

"Nice to meet you, Greyson," Ty said, taking his hand and shaking heartily. "I hope you keep those manners and don't let this guy rub off on you too much."

"Trust me, Aunt Tabs wouldn't let that happen," Grey replied, darting a teasing glare in my direction.

"Ha-ha," I chided bitterly, while my heart plummeted to my stomach at the mention of her name.

"You guys ready?" Ty asked. "We've gotta get to soundcheck."

"Uh, soundcheck?" Grey questioned, a nervous tremor lacing through his words. "I'm not allowed to be there, right?"

"No, it's cool." I shrugged. "You're coming with us." We began moving toward the airport door, and he practically skipped along beside me.

"Seriously?"

"Hell yeah." I wrapped my arm around his shoulders. "Maybe you can jam with us too, if these guys are cool with it."

Ty looked over his shoulder at me and said, "I dunno if you wanna do that, bro. I mean, if the kid has chops, we might be dumping your ass to bring him on board."

"He's already less annoying," Chad muttered.

"Yo," I tightened my arm around Greyson's shoulders, "I wouldn't even care. Grey is talented as hell. I mean, he has to be, when he has my genes swimming around in there."

***

I stood at the edge of the stage, as I waited for Devin to get his perfectionist ass situated. I looked out to the rows of seats, then the dual balconies, and belted out a few bars from Collective Soul's "Needs." The acoustics in the old theater were out of this world, and my voice floated through the aisles.

"Shit, that's beautiful. I think I just got hard," I muttered to the front row.

Greyson cocked his head. "I didn't know you could sing, too."

"What can I say?" I shrugged. "I'm fucking gifted."

I stepped onto an amp and sang the first verse to Soundgarden's "Black Hole Sun." Devin uttered a "fuck yes" from behind me, and picked up at the chorus, strumming his acoustic in time with the song. I clapped my hands in self-applause as our voices and the guitar faded into the auditorium.

"You're good, but not Chris Cornell good," Chad assessed with a scrutinizing nod.

"Damn straight, Chaddington," I agreed. "Nobody sings like him anymore." And I tipped my head back, to send a salute toward the ceiling and beyond.

"Okay, you guys ready?" Devin asked, turning to glance at Ty, Chad, and me.

"Oh, well, I should probably be sitting behind these things over here first." I jumped off the amp and ran over to the drums in the back. Sitting on the throne and grabbing my sticks, I shouted, "Aye, aye, captain!"

Devin gave me a thumbs up and then pointed. "Count me in." And I did, hitting my sticks together—*one, two, three*—and I rolled into the beat for his song, "Edge of a Blue Existence."

Looking out from behind the jungle of drums and cymbals, past Devin, Ty, and Chad, I could see the head of Greyson, sitting beside Kylie. I watched him as he listened, bopping his head to the music, and I was instantly pumped full of pride for what I do. I felt the encouragement to hit harder, play better, and I imagined this must be exactly how Devin feels, every time he looks into the front row and sees Kylie.

It was the best feeling in the world.

One song flowed into the next, until Kylie apologetically interrupted and told Devin she needed to take the antsy Olivia out for a bit.

"No problem, baby," Dev answered, blowing Olivia a kiss before his two leading ladies left. Then, Dev crooked his finger, beckoning Greyson up onto the stage. "Kid, get up here."

"Seriously?" Greyson asked, his eyes searching to meet mine from behind the drums.

"If the boss tells you to get up here, then you get up here," I told him, and with a nervous look in his eyes, Greyson complied.

"So, your dad tells us you play," Devin said, placing his hand on Greyson's shoulder and steering him toward where I sat.

Grey nodded, staring at Devin like he was a god. "Yeah, I've been playing for like, five years now."

Glancing at me, Devin asked, "He any good?"

I got up from the kit, walked around to them and handed Greyson the sticks. "You okay playing righty?"

Greyson looked from Devin's face to mine with uncertainty. "Uh, I think so, but …"

"Show him what you got."

He looked at the sticks as though they might explode if he even laid his hand on them. "Are you sure?" he asked, looking from me to Devin, and Devin nodded encouragingly. "Uh, what should I play?"

"What's your favorite song to practice to?" Devin asked, swinging his guitar from his back to front.

Greyson took the sticks from me as he replied, "'Everlong.'"

My brow pinched. "Why didn't I know you could play that song?" And Greyson's smug smirk was accompanied by a shrug as he rounded the kit to sit down.

"Awesome. Dad, you're sitting out on this one," Devin directed at me, walking toward the mic, and I sat down on an amp. "Whenever you're ready, Greyson."

I watched Grey shake out his wrists and take a few deep breaths as he familiarized himself with the set-up while keeping his eyes on Devin. He was nervous, and I smiled affectionately, as his breaths became more unsteady, and I stood up from the amp.

"Hey," I said gently, walking around to crouch beside the stool. "You freaking out over here?"

"He's Devin O'Leary," Greyson gritted out through his teeth.

"So what?" I shrugged, shooting a look at Dev. "He's just a guy who plays a guitar. No biggie."

Greyson scoffed. "Yeah, okay. What if you got to play with the Foo Fighters?"

I pursed my lips and thought about that for a moment. How *would* I feel if I was ever given the opportunity to rock a song with Dave Grohl? Even given the amount of experience I had, would I ever feel worthy of an honor like that?

The answer was obvious. "They're no different than I am, kid. I mean, I love the fuck out of them, and they're

402

certainly more popular. But, when you take away the popularity, they're just a bunch of guys who really love making music, like me," I nudged my knuckles against his knee, "and *you*."

He considered that for a moment, and nodded. "But what if I screw up?"

"Then you screw up."

"But Devin's opened for one of the most famous guitarists in the *world*," Greyson pressed, darting an incredulous glance toward me before pinning his gaze back on Devin.

I barked a laugh that encouraged Chad and Ty to turn toward us, and they smiled. I imagined it was pretty bizarre for my friends to watch me handle a kid. Hell, it was still bizarre for me.

"So have I," I replied, still laughing. "And you don't mind playing with me."

Greyson rolled his eyes. "Yeah, but you're just my dad."

I know the comment should've been sobering, in the way movies and TV always makes it seem. That moment you realize you're no longer Superman and you're *just* the dad. The guy your kid doesn't want around when he's trying to impress the cute girl, in fear that you might embarrass him. I know I should've been hurt and shuffled off somewhere to feel old and unwanted. But instead, my throat clenched, squeezing around the instant burst of emotion, at knowing I was *just his dad*.

That felt so much better than being his hero.

Clearing my throat, I nodded. "Yeah, I am." I stood up, squeezing a hand against his shoulder. "But I'm still a fucking badass."

With a final deep breath, Greyson told Devin he was ready, and with a one, two, three count, Devin kicked the song off with the strumming of his guitar. Greyson kept his cool, concentrating as the sticks tapped against the hi-hat, and I nodded approvingly when he glanced toward me.

He slipped up a couple times, missing a few beats, but still, he was perfect. Because even though he gritted his teeth and shook his head at himself, he kept going. He pushed through, and when he reached the first chorus, he breathed out a sigh of relief, and his smile broke through.

"You're doing good, kid," I called to him, holding my two thumbs up.

It was with that chorus though, that I stopped paying attention to them playing. My ears picked up on the lyrics, listening to the words that I hadn't allowed myself to listen to since Tabby told me we were done. Those words now emphasized an ache I couldn't forget, couldn't let go of, and I huffed through the inflation of my cheeks.

What if nothing else feels as real as what I had with her?

What if nothing is ever that good again?

The ache spread deeper and hugged my stomach with a tightened squeeze. I emptied with another deep breath as I headed toward the edge of the stage, sitting down to let my feet dangle over the side. Fuck, I hated this feeling, and what I hated more was not knowing what to do about it. Don't they say that if you love something, you should let it go? Does anybody ever talk about what happens after that? Because I had let her go, but I couldn't *stop*.

I'm not sure I ever could.

39

tabby

Halloween was lonely, with Greyson away in Florida. It wasn't a major holiday, but it was my first alone. It reminded me of other days of importance looming ahead that. Days where I'd also likely find myself alone. Thanksgiving, Christmas, New Year's … I knew I shouldn't begrudge Greyson for possibly choosing Sebastian over me. He'd had fifteen years of holidays with me, but these would be his first with his father. He had memories to make and new traditions to create. But still, my heart hurt with every too-early Christmas song played.

I tried keeping myself busy with the steady stream of trick-or-treaters visiting the agency. Princesses and unicorns, superheroes and zombies, all begging for candy with shy smiles. Jess had taken off for the day, to spend it with her kids, leaving Alex and me to drop miniature candy bars into pumpkin buckets and canvas totes.

"Trick-or-treat!" A gaggle of elementary school children announced in unison, stepping into the office with their pillowcases extended.

"Well, let's see here," Alex scrutinized in a teasing voice and grabbed for the plastic cauldron of candy. "We have a witch, a Cinderella, a *very* cool Wolverine, and … hmm, what's your costume?"

I poked my head out from my office to look at the little girl, dressed in a plaid flannel shirt, dirty jeans, and tool belt. She beamed up at the tall Dracula and announced proudly, "I'm a carpenter, just like my daddy."

"I told her girls can't be carpenters," Wolverine grumbled disapprovingly.

Stepping out of my office, I challenged the little superhero with a cock of my brow and said, "Girls can be whatever they want." I turned my attention to her, crouching down to meet my eyes with hers before saying, "I love your costume."

"I like yours, too," the little girl whispered shyly, triumph glimmering in her hazel eyes.

Glancing down at my Foo Fighters t-shirt, fitted black jeans, and red Converse, I smiled and said, "Oh, thank you so much, honey."

"What are you even supposed to be?" Cinderella asked, wrinkling her nose.

I chuckled lightly, wishing I had remembered to throw on my cape and witch's hat before greeting them, and replied, "I'm a real estate agent."

The carpenter's lips curled into an approving grin. "Real estate agents are cool."

Remembering the pencil skirts and uncomfortable heels cluttering my closet at home, I forced the ruefulness from my smile as I nodded. "Yeah, we are."

The kids left, and I headed back into my office. Work was quiet, a usual downside to living in such a small town. The amount of people moving in or out of Hog Hill was minimal, especially during the holidays, and I found myself now with an empty workload. I wondered if I should take my lunch break, maybe call up Mrs. Worthington and see how she was doing in her new living arrangement.

Heaving a sigh, I grabbed my phone and quickly tapped out a message to Greyson.

Me: Hey kiddo. How's it going?

Seconds passed before it chimed with his reply, and I smiled as I read:

Greyson: So cool. Devin's AWESOME.
Me: Yeah, he's a really nice guy.
Greyson: They just did soundcheck and I got to play "Everlong" with them.

I stared at the message longer than I'd like to admit, mostly at the title of the song I had begun to think of as Sebastian's and mine—*ours*. I hadn't listened to it since I'd walked away from him months before in that parking garage. Not after what I had said—what I had *done*. How could I?

Before I could reply, the door to the office opened. I listened as Alex asked in a terrible Transylvanian accent, "What can I do for you today, sir?"

"I'm here to see Tabitha. Is she here?"

The rich sound of velvet floated into my office, and I couldn't help the chills that traveled the length of my spine. His voice was nearly foreign, but I could still recognize that decadent depth anywhere.

Roman Dolecki.

"She is," Alex admitted, and at the sound of his chair scraping against the wooden floor, he added, "Let me see if she's busy."

At that, he hurried into my office, quietly closing the door behind him. His grey-shadowed eyes stared with urgency as he muttered through gritted teeth, "That fine slab of rich man meat is standing out there. What should I do with him?"

I rolled my eyes, pushed away from my desk, and said, "I'll go see him."

"Are you *sure*? Do you even remember what he said to you last time you spoke with him? God, Tabitha, I wouldn't talk to him again, if I were you."

"Yes, I remember," I grumbled with a heated groan. Truthfully, the last thing I wanted was to talk to Roman Dolecki. Not after what he had said to me on the phone following his altercation with Sebastian and me. But I was still a professional, and I would hear him out.

Moving past a dumbfounded Alex, I left my office to find Roman, predictably wearing an expensive suit and standing with his watch aimed toward his gaze. Always busy. Always somewhere more important to be.

"Roman." I alerted him to my presence with a razor's edge tacked onto my voice, and he turned to face me.

"Tabitha," he replied with a formal nod of his chin, and I immediately noted the apology washing over his brown eyes. "Can we maybe speak in your office?" His gaze slid to meet Alex, now standing protectively nearby. "Privately?"

With a hastened nod, I hurried back into my office, with Roman following close at my heels. I waited for him to be seated, noting Alex's warning glare shooting daggers at the back of his head, and I closed the door.

"Well, I'd be lying if I said this wasn't a surprise," I said immediately, hurrying around the desk to my chair. "What can I do for you?"

"I'm surprised you'd even agree to speak with me again, after the awful things I said to you," he admitted, bowing his head with shame. "Which is exactly why I came here. To apologize."

"It's been months," I said, dismissing his words with a wave of my hand. "I haven't thought about all of that in weeks." It was the truth. Thoughts of Roman Dolecki had remained dormant, until he had walked through the door several minutes ago.

He smiled with remorse despite the dismissal. "I'm glad to hear it, but Tabitha, the way I spoke to you was inexcusable. Truthfully, I was hurt and rejected, but taking it out on you in that way was completely out of character. I wanted you to know that I really am sorry for what I said. I had no right."

I pursed my lips tersely, accepting the apology with a nod. "Thank you. I appreciate it, I just …" I cocked my head, narrowing my gaze with question. "I just don't entirely understand why you're doing this *now*."

"Ah, well …" Roman ran his hand over the back of his head, smoothing his dark hair as he hesitated. "I've been meaning to, but I wasn't sure how, and then so much time had passed … But, then, I received a phone call—"

Every extremity froze, every vertebra locked. "A phone call?"

Shame and embarrassment shadowed his features as he nodded. "Yes, uh … I received a phone call the other day, asking if I ever apologized to you. When I said no, I was asked why not, and I didn't have a good answer."

A blend of affection and anger coalesced in my gut. My lips pinched and then rolled together as I shook my head, and then said, "I'm sure I can guess who it was."

With a brief nod, he forced a smile. "I was taken aback, but I can't say I blame him either. He was just making sure I did the right thing by you, and …"

Roman's words dissipated into the air, and I glanced back to his face to find a wistful gaze in his eyes. The faintest of affectionate smiles curved his lips, and I asked what he was smiling about.

"O-oh," he stuttered, coming back from his day dream. "It's just, I couldn't understand before why you'd choose him over me. I understand the relationship to him, but romantically, it didn't make any sense to me at the

411

time. But," he locked his eyes with mine as his smile broadened, "if I'm being honest, I'm not sure I would have defended you the way he did. Truthfully, I've never felt that way toward anybody before, not even my ex-wife, which is probably why she's my ex."

"Roman ..." I swallowed, deflating with my exhale.

He lifted his hand to stop my words. "You don't need to explain anything to me, Tabitha. I know I never could've been what he is for you. Hell, I wonder if I can be that for anybody sometimes." His eyes crinkled with a rueful smile. "And I am sorry about what happened to our professional relationship. That was ..." His head shook with his personal disdain. "Unforgivable."

"Yeah, well," I sucked at my teeth, feeling the bitter bite of that reminder, "it is what it is."

Roman tapped his fingers against the armrests of the chair. Something was still hanging in the air. Unspoken words, unfinished business. I was tempted to ask what else was on his mind, but I left it alone. What was the point?

He reached across the desk, touching his fingers to mine. "Have a good life, Tabitha." His smile was reluctant as he stood, sighing with finality. "I hope it's everything you wanted."

"You too, Roman," I rasped through a dry throat, as I watched him leave.

40

tabby

"What do you mean you *sold it*?" I hissed into the phone.

Alex sighed. "It means what it sounds like, honey; I sold the house."

The potato masher hung from my limp fingers, until I lost my grip and it clattered to the floor. I could hardly make sense of the emotions weaving around my heart, encasing my spirit with a sense of failure and sadness and a longing I wish I could erase. It was so final, so devastating.

"To who?" I finally asked, after moments of being locked in a dumbfounded stupor.

"Would it really make you feel any better if you knew?"

I bent to grab the masher from the floor, shaking myself from my trance. "Was it Roman?"

"No, not Roman."

"Then—"

"Tabitha, I just wanted to let you know that it's done. The sale will be finalized in about a week and Mrs. Worthington will be free of it. No more worrying on your part, or hers."

"A *week*?" I squeaked. "That's so—"

"It's done, honey," Alex pressed gently.

I pushed my head to nod at nobody. "Yeah. Yeah, I know you're right. Um … thanks for letting me know."

"Happy Thanksgiving, honey. Give that blonde Adonis' ass a squeeze for me." He giggled girlishly as I rolled my eyes.

"Have a happy Thanksgiving, Alex," I grumbled, and hung up the phone.

I took a deep breath and found the determination to have a good day. I should've been focused on how grateful I was that Greyson had wanted to spend the holiday with me. I couldn't allow myself to mourn Mrs. Worthington's house. Not today.

Grabbing the remote for my sound system, I hit play and was immediately treated to the distorted electric guitar of my favorite Seether song, "Fake It." I sang along, mashing the potatoes and bopping my head to the music, when I realized the irony in the lyrics. Of faking it to fit into society, to meet the expectations of others.

I snorted as I set the potatoes aside. Next, I grabbed a carving knife and set to work on the turkey. Golden and not the slightest bit dry, the bird had been cooked to perfection. Cutting into it, I inhaled, taking in the rich aroma with pride as I sang along to Seether's "Here And Now."

I missed Sam.

I hoped she could see Greyson, excelling in school and forging an incredible relationship with his father. I was done trying to guess why she never wanted Sebastian in his life. Those were questions we would never have answers to, and that was something we just had to accept. But I hoped she was happy with the way things had turned out. I hoped she knew I was doing the best I could, and I hoped she was proud.

But more than all of that, I just wished she was still here.

As I held onto one of the legs and began to cut, the front door swung open. With a jolt, I whipped my head to face the intruder, and an instantaneous sting of pain swept through my hand and up my arm. The knife clattered to the floor and I clutched my fingers to my chest, as Sebastian walked into the kitchen with aluminum trays bundled in his arms.

"Honey, I'm ho—hey, are you okay?" He slid the trays onto the counter. "Jesus, Tabby, you're bleeding. Let me see."

I winced as he took my hand in his, the throbbing escalating with every pulse. Blood swelled from the back of my pointer and middle fingers, and I immediately felt faint at the sight.

"Oh my God," I uttered, with the wash of lightheadedness.

I reached for the counter with my other hand as Sebastian grabbed for a towel, squeezing the cloth around my fingers and ordering me to hold my hand above my head.

"Where's your Band-aids and shit?" His words came to me through a warbled effect as my eyes fluttered and my hand drooped to my side. "Oh boy," he grumbled and pulled me toward a chair, forcing me to sit down. His fingers snapped in front of my spotting eyes. "Hey, ground control to Major Tabby, are you listening to me?"

"Uh-huh," I mumbled, nodding weakly.

"Yeah, okay, this is going well. Hold on a second … Hey Grey! Got a situation down here, kid!"

***

When did I get on the couch?

My eyes blinked open to the brightness of the living room, and I turned my head to find Sebastian sitting on the coffee table, wrapping gauze and bandages around my fingers.

"Did I pass out?" I mumbled, laying a hand over my forehead.

"Yep," he confirmed with a smirk. "You could've told me you can't deal with blood."

"I can," I defended. "Just not my own."

He cocked his head and smirked. "Must make that time of the month really difficult, huh?" Rolling my eyes, I attempted to jerk my hand from his grasp. "Hey, I'm not done here yet. Relax."

"Well, you don't have to be so disgusting," I scolded.

416

Chuckling, his lips quirked into a lopsided smile as his eyes met mine. "No, you're right. I'm sorry."

The immediate rush of tension dissipated just as quickly as it came. "You don't think I need stitches?"

"Nah." He shook his head, wrapping the final strip of bandage tape around my pointer finger. "They might scar a little, but they're not deep enough to rush you down to the emergency room."

Trusting him, I nodded. "How'd you find the first aid kit?"

"Greyson got it while I carried you in here," he said, and patted his hand over mine before gently laying it over my stomach. "Okay. You're good. Time for me to butcher the bird."

"Wait, you don't—"

His deep brown eyes widened with laughter. "Tabby. You almost chopped your fingers off! There's no fucking way I'm letting you wield any more weapons."

"You startled me!" I defended myself, as he stood up and headed into the kitchen.

"You knew I was coming!" he laughed in reply.

I slowly got up from the couch, testing my legs before trusting them enough to walk after him, and when I did, I found him already set to the task. The breath was stolen from my lungs at the sound of his powerful voice, singing along to Seether's "Rise Above This." A deep, melodic growl, nearly matching that of Shaun Morgan himself. I leaned against the door frame, losing myself in the bang of his head and the sway of his hips, and before I could stop, I found myself thinking that I would be perfectly content if this was my life.

417

This could be the life I've always wanted.

"Hey, by the way," he tossed over his shoulder, "thanks for inviting me for dinner. You really didn't have to do that."

Feeling as though I'd been caught doing something I shouldn't have, I cleared my throat and pushed away from the door. "Oh, stop," I brushed him off, walking to stand beside him as he continued to carve. "It's really not a big deal."

"Uh, yes, it is," he laughed, smirking and holding my gaze. "It *is* a big deal when the woman you have history with invites you over for fucking Thanksgiving dinner."

"Well, whatever," I dismissed the comment with a purse of my lips. "Thanksgiving is for family, and guess what, Sebastian? That's what you are. As weird as this all might be. You're family."

He lowered the knife, laying it on the counter as his eyes searched mine for an answer to the question I sensed he was thinking but wouldn't ask. *What the hell are we doing here?* I stood frozen, wondering the same thing. I found myself wishing that he would lay his hand against my cheek and kiss me, telling me to forget dinner before carrying me up to my room. And along with my fantasy, I finally succumbed to the proclamation of my heart.

I love him.

The self-admission struck me deep, rattling my soul, and I turned away from him, wide-eyed and bitten-lipped.

"This isn't weird," he finally spoke. "It just kinda feels like us."

I begged my heart to relax as I replied, "It just is, right?"

"Yeah." I looked to him again and watched him nod with acknowledgment. "Exactly."

***

"This is *so* freakin' good," Greyson declared, spooning another helping of sweet potato casserole onto his plate. "Aunt Tabs, you should let Dad cook more often."

"Okay, for the record, I didn't *let him* cook," I pointed out, glancing at Sebastian with a taunting smirk. "He just *showed up* with this stuff."

"Hey, I told you I'd bring something," Sebastian reminded me.

"Yes, you told me you'd bring *something*." I gestured toward a plate of homemade buttermilk biscuits, the tray of marshmallow-covered sweet potatoes, and a dish of cranberry stuffing. "You didn't tell me you'd blow my green bean casserole out of the water with food Martha Stewart would be proud of."

He let out a throaty chuckle, reaching out for another serving of said casserole. "Hey, don't diss the green beans. This shit is good."

Greyson wrinkled his nose. "Yeah, whatever. Nobody eats that crap."

Sebastian squinted his eyes with a warning glare aimed at his son. "Come on, man. Be nice."

"It's okay," I insisted. "I've made this thing every year since I was … God, twenty or so. And I only did it because my mom loved it so much. She was *the* only person who ate it though, so I guess I didn't *have* to make it this year …"

"Well, *I'm* glad you did," Sebastian said, keeping his stern glare on Greyson. "Because *I* think it's fucking good."

Greyson smirked. "You're just trying to—"

My cheeks ignited as Sebastian pointed a finger at the smug teen. "Hey. I'd keep my mouth shut if I were you."

"Oh yeah?" Greyson challenged, continuing to smirk as he cocked his head and darted his eyes toward me. "Why?"

"Because Christmas is coming, that's why," Sebastian shot back, before dropping his fork as he pushed his hands into his hair, eyes wide with horror. "Oh my fucking God. I'm turning into my mother."

I bubbled with giggles. I didn't bother to say it, as the moment had passed and eating had recommenced, but I found it astonishing. The effortless way the two of them had fallen into their roles as father and son. The expected awkward phase had lasted a meager month, if that, and then it was *this*: a relaxed balance between parenting and friendship. Sebastian was a natural, more than I ever expected, and dammit if it didn't make him that much more attractive.

"So, uh, speaking of Christmas," Sebastian said, reigniting the conversation as he darted his eyes toward me. "I was wondering if—"

420

"You don't need to ask if Greyson can be with you for Christmas," I interjected with my assumption. "I'm sure Grey would want to be at your place anyway. Right?" I turned to my nephew, who responded with an eager nod, and my heart flinched.

"Yeah, but that's not all I was going to say," Sebastian replied with a chuckle. "I was asking if you'd *both* like to come to my place."

"Yes!" Greyson shouted before I could answer for myself. "Aunt Tabs, you have to."

I shook my head, immediately awkward and reluctant to accept. "Sebastian, you don't need to invite me."

"But you invited me here today," he said pointedly, darting his eyes between Greyson and me.

"It's not the same thing. You'll have all your family there, and—"

"And I thought we established that *we*," he circled his finger, pointing at Greyson, himself and me, "*are* a family."

Swallowing, I nodded, grounding myself by flattening my hands against the table. "We *are*, but I—"

"Come *on*, Aunt Tabs," Greyson blurted, slumping into his chair. He pleaded with his eyes. "You'll be all alone if you don't come, and I want you there."

That's all it took for me to give in. "Okay, okay. I'll go."

"Excellent," Sebastian replied with a grin. "And you better be bringing one of those green bean casseroles with you. The Morrisons are gonna go apeshit over that stuff."

421

41

sebastian

It was torture, but I was proud of myself, as I spent the evening with Tabby, cleaning up after dinner. Greyson was upstairs, practicing his paradiddles, and there was no sign of him coming down any time soon. There was no reason for me not to make a move—God knows I wanted to. Hell, I probably could've and gotten away with it, especially with all of the flirting she kept tossing my way.

But I was laying low. Waiting. I still wasn't entirely sure she was convinced that I could be the man she deserved. And maybe I wasn't entirely convinced that I was worthy of her. Still, I was going to try. It just wasn't the right time. Not yet.

For now, I was enjoying this. Even while my dick screamed obscenities as I watched her bend into the refrigerator with another armful of leftovers.

"I *really* hope you'll be taking some of this home," she laughed, stepping aside to showcase the packed shelves. "The two of us aren't going to eat all of this."

"Maybe Jess and Alex would want some," I suggested.

"Why? You don't want any? Not even this delicious green bean casserole I apparently made just for you?" Tabby held out the foil-covered dish and shot me a look with a pair of big, hopeful eyes.

She was trying to take care of me, I noted. Either that or pawning off some food nobody else would touch.

I smiled apologetically. "Seriously, I would, but I'm leaving tomorrow, and I won't be home for another couple of weeks. There's no reason to load the fridge up with food I won't eat. And trust me, coming back to the stench of rotten food isn't something I wanna do for a *long* time."

Conceding with a nod, she put the dish back and closed the refrigerator door. "Fair enough. Can't blame me for trying, but that shit does look nasty when it goes bad."

"All the more reason for me to leave it with you," I laughed, heading to the sink and turning on the faucet. "You want me to wash these now, or load up the dishwasher?"

"Um." She hesitated as I eyed her questioningly. She didn't want to ask for my help, but I could tell the offer was tempting the hell out of her. "If you could just rinse them off, I'll put them in the dishwasher."

"*Or*," I opened the washer, rinsed off a dish, and slid it into the rack, "I could rinse them off *and* load them in."

"You really don't have to do that," Tabby insisted, heading over to stand beside me.

"Eh," I shrugged, rinsing the other dishes, "it's not a big deal."

Then, I don't know why, but she blurted out, "Sebastian, I'm really sorry that I hurt you. I know I've said it before, but I want you to know how much I mean it." I turned to face her, and she knew she had my attention. "I really didn't want for that to happen. I just thought you were, uh … immune to that kind of thing."

"That makes two of us," I said as lightheartedly as possible. "Why are you bringing this up now?"

Crossing her arms over her chest, she leaned against the counter and let go of a rueful sigh. "I don't know. I guess it's just that we had such a good time today, and I'm really happy you came, and—"

"And *you* thought it'd be awkward as fuck because we used to bone," I offered, smirking as I dropped a fork into the utensil holder.

The mention of sex was enough to deepen the rosy glow on her cheeks, and if I knew I had the permission, I would've leaned down and kissed them.

Tabby laughed airily. "Well, since you put it so eloquently … yes, I thought it'd be weird. But it's not, and I'm honestly really surprised with how mature you are about all of this. I didn't think you'd ever want to talk to me again."

I snorted, shaking my head. "Tabby, you realize we basically have a kid together, right?"

Her brows knitted, and her lips pinched. Worry settled into her eyes. "No, we don't. I mean, once you get your parental rights from the courts, you'll have the right to never let Greyson see—"

A quick burst of anger ignited in the pit of my stomach as I dropped the spoon I was holding. "*Hey*," I interjected, turning my head to flash her with a stony glare. "Listen to me right now. When his mother died, *you* took on that role, never mind the fact that you've been a part of his entire fucking life. So, I don't give a shit how you feel about me, okay? What I care about is how *you* feel—how *Greyson* feels—and there is *no way* in Hell I would *ever* take him away from what he has with you. So, do yourself a favor and stop thinking that bullshit."

Her breaths were shallow, and her fingers worked to pick away her black nail polish. I watched her until she had worked her way beyond being startled and nodded.

"O-okay," she whispered. "Thank you."

I guffawed, turning back to the sink. "God, Tabby, don't fucking thank me for that. *I* should be the one thanking *you*."

"Why?"

"Because you changed my life," I stated simply with a nonchalant shrug.

It was her turn to snort. "Oh, come on—"

"Hey, I could've gone my entire stupid life without ever knowing I had this badass kid in the world. You didn't *need* to get me involved. I mean, I know you

426

needed the help at the time, but you guys would've been fine eventually. You brought me into it because deep down, underneath all that beige, you felt it was the right thing to do. And because of that, you changed my fucking life."

"Yeah," she chuckled with a shake of her head. "I'm sure you're thrilled that I helped make it harder for you to get laid while at home."

A low chuckle rumbled through my chest. There was so much irony in that statement. She thought it was Greyson who'd made it difficult for me to get women, but really? It was her.

"I would've given up all the pussy in the world to have known him sooner," I replied honestly.

Because it would've meant knowing her as well.

***

Dressed in her pajamas, Tabby passed a cup of coffee into my hands before dropping down beside me on the couch. "Anything you wanna listen to, or are you good with this?"

I read between the lines as an acoustic version of "Everlong" played through the speakers. The song held meaning, memories and feelings, and with the diversion of her eyes and the tapping of her bandaged fingers against her own mug, I had the suspicion that it was mutual.

"Nah, this is fine. It's almost over anyway." I sipped my coffee and slid the cup onto the table. "So, hey, did Jane's house ever sell?"

Her gaze remained on the coffee in her hands as she twisted her lips and released a sad, weighted breath. "Yeah. Alex actually called me today about that."

"Oh," I raised my eyebrows, "that's a good thing, right?"

"I guess. It just feels really, um … over."

I quirked my lips into a half-smile. "So, why is this something to look so sad about?"

Shrugging, she continued to pout. "I guess it just feels like the end. I mean, you know I had such a hard year, and trying to sell that damn house followed me throughout all of it. So, knowing it's now gone is like …" She hesitated, cocking her head and considering her words. "It's like saying goodbye to the whole freakin' year."

My arm stretched out over the back of the couch. My fingers sat inches away from touching her hair. "I would've thought you'd be relieved about that."

"I know," she said with a slight bob of her head. "I guess I am, but in a way, saying goodbye to that house feels like saying goodbye to every other difficult thing I've dealt with this year. Losing my parents, losing Sam, the break-up with my fiancé … getting over all that pain is almost as bad as the pain itself."

I nodded, relating her situation to the only thing I understood. "I guess I can kinda understand that. I mean, when I thought Sam had gotten an abortion, I mourned for a while. It sucked because nobody else knew about it, so I was left to deal with the whole thing on my own. But in a way, I think not having anybody to talk to about it kinda helped in not thinking about it, you know?" I looked toward her eyes and she nodded, so I continued: "I'd go all day, not giving it any thought. But then, at night, it's all I could think about. Like, what kinda person would he have become if he'd been given the chance, or would he have looked like me or her, and it hurt so fucking badly, thinking I'd never know. And it felt like I'd never move past that feeling, but one day, I just stopped thinking about it all that much. I don't even know when it was, but it sucked to suddenly realize that I couldn't remember the last time I thought about my unborn kid."

Tabby was silent as she nodded, clenching her fingers tighter around the mug. I wondered what was on her mind, or at the tip of her tongue.

"But I think we're *supposed* to continue with our lives, Tabby," I went on, "and I think that's why we let go when we're not even aware that we're doing it. It's *survival*. So, I get why you're kinda down about the house, and the year being over, but I think it's also a good thing that you're moving forward. Because that means you're surviving, and there's not much that's more important than that."

For the first time since sitting down, Tabby turned to me. A mist glazed over her eyes and the corners of her mouth lifted with a smile.

"You know, I think I'm finally starting to realize that Greyson was right about you," she whispered.

I narrowed my eyes. "What the hell did that little shit say about me? Because if he mentioned my stash of porn, it's not *my* fault he—"

"Oh my God," she groaned, laying a hand over her eyes and laughing before letting it drop to her lap. "No, that's not what he mentioned, and for the record, I have no idea why you'd even have a *stash of porn* when you can get everything for free on the internet."

I shrugged nonchalantly and grabbed for my cup of coffee. "Attachment issues."

Tabby laughed with a roll of her eyes, running her fingers through her long, red hair, now kept loose and hanging long over her back. "Greyson said you were one of our good things, and despite comments like that, I think he's probably right."

I took a long, slow sip of coffee and watched her intently from over the brim. This moment … it *almost* felt right. To tell her I was never going to stop loving her, that she was it for me, that a life with her and Greyson was the only life I wanted. But there was still that word, *probably*. Greyson was *probably* right.

With the mug empty, I placed it back on the coffee table and nodded. "Only probably, huh?"

Her smile was almost apologetic. "Don't push it, Sebastian."

"Nah, you're right." I nodded slowly, pulling my arm away from the back of the couch and laying my hand beside her bare thigh.

My eyes dropped to the script etched into her skin, the tattoo I had noticed months before. With a bold touch of my fingers, I traced a line over the cursive text, and read, "'She is freedom.'"

I thought about that, about her, about what the words might've meant.

"Hm," I grunted with a single bob of my head. "You got it over the summer?"

"In August, yeah. While I was in Pennsylvania, after seeing Breaking Benjamin."

"You were by yourself?" She nodded, and then, I was reading between the lines. Nodding and knowing what they meant. It was her gift, a tribute, to her sister. And the permanent reminder of what Tabby wanted for herself. "I like it. It suits you."

"You don't even know why I got it." Her laugh was awkward. Choked.

"It's really none of my business," I replied with a shrug. "And for the record, you are."

"I am what?" I gave her leg another pat and stood up. Grabbing my jacket off the chair, I headed toward the door, with Tabby hurrying behind me. "Hey, answer the question!"

"Tabby," I groaned playfully, turning on my heel. "It's past my bedtime and I still need to drive home."

The Foo Fighters' "Walking After You" filtered through the air. In a moment of spontaneity, the acoustic notes drove me to drop my jacket to the floor and wrap my arm around her waist, pulling her close. She was startled as I took her hand, careful not to hurt her injured fingers, and persuaded her body to sway in time with mine. It took a few seconds and then her feet moved on their own, her head pressed against my chest and her hand rested on my shoulder.

She was surrendering, I could feel it, but it still wasn't time yet. I just needed this, to dance with her, before leaving again and not seeing her for another month.

"You *are* freedom," I finally answered, when the song ended and I let her go.

"I'm trying," she rasped through a throat tight with surprise and conviction.

"Well, you are," I persisted.

She didn't press further as I picked up my jacket and ran upstairs to give Greyson a hug. He was already sleeping, passed out on his bed with Dweezil under one arm. Crouching down, I kissed his forehead and smoothed his hair back, wishing I didn't have to leave again so soon.

Opening his eyes a crack, he mumbled, "Hey Dad. You leaving?"

I nodded regretfully. "Yeah, kid. I gotta get home and try to sleep for a while before hitting the road tomorrow night."

"Why don't you just stay here?" His arm tightened around Dweezil as the yellow Lab snuggled closer.

"I'd love to, but uh … I'm not sure it's the right time for sleepovers again, if you catch my drift."

"Mm," he shrugged, burrowing his face further into the pillow. "You could stay in here if you're too chicken shit."

Chuckling, I shook my head. "I'll take a rain check, okay? I'll see you soon."

He muttered a "love you, Dad" before closing his eyes. "I love you too, kid," I replied, kissing his forehead again and pulling his blanket up over his and Dweezil's shoulders. I left the room and took the stairs again, to where Tabby waited for me by the front door.

"At the risk of sounding cheesy as hell, I'm most thankful for you this year," she said as she opened the door.

The pounding from my chest rang in my ears like church bells, telling me to seize the moment. To make it mine. But I ignored the thunderous booms, as I smiled and wrapped her in a hug, breathing in her scent one more time before depriving myself for the month.

"At the risk of sounding like a pervert, I'm most thankful to say I've slept with you," I muttered quietly in her ear, and she groaned, shoving me away. I chuckled, cocking my head and rolling my eyes, as I said, "And I guess I'm thankful to know you, too. But you know, not to make you feel bad, but, I'm most thankful for Greyson."

Her palm smoothed over the leather against my chest. "You should be."

"I'll see you soon, Tabby," I said, turning to head out the door, while wishing I could leave her with a *love you* and a kiss. But I had been honest when I told her she was freedom. She was mine; the freedom to love, the freedom to break out of my cycle of casual fucking. The freedom to wait and be patient.

The freedom to give her the life we all, not just wanted, but deserved to have.

42

tabby

"Greyson!" I called up the stairs for what felt like the hundredth time. "Let's *go*!"

Thrusting a hand into my hair, I groaned and hurried to pull on a pair of ankle boots that hovered somewhere between dressy and casual. Sebastian had been excruciatingly vague when telling me about Christmas at his place. All he said was to come. Not what kind of clothes we were expected to wear, not what we should bring … He just wanted us to be there, which was both sweet and irritating.

Just like him.

Greyson thundered down the stairs with Dweezil at his heels. He was wearing the sweater vest and shirt I insisted he put on and he scowled, despite the jeans and sneakers I told him were fine.

"I feel ridiculous," he complained, as I reached out to fix his hair. "Come on, Aunt Tabs! I'm *fine*!"

"This is your first Christmas with your father. Your grandparents, aunts, uncles, and God knows how many cousins will also be there, and you're going to look nice," I ordered, smoothing down the tufts that were already brushing the tops of his ears. "Maybe you should get a haircut over winter break."

"Hell no. I'm growing it out again." He swatted my hands away and grabbed Dweezil's leash from off a hook near the door. "Come here, Dweezy," he commanded, and the dog listened obediently.

"Okay, you go get Dweezil into the—"

I was interrupted by a knock on the door. Curiously, I answered, swinging it open to reveal a man in a chauffeur's hat. I narrowed my eyes, glancing between the driver and Greyson, before asking, "Um, can I help you?"

"Miss Tabitha Clarke?" I nodded my reply and he smiled kindly. "Merry Christmas, ma'am. I'm here to drive you and Greyson to Mr. Moore's residence."

Flabbergasted, I stared at him for one, two seconds. Blinking and stunned. "Uh, th-thank you very much, but I think I can—"

"Mr. Moore gave me very specific instructions to not let you talk me out of taking you to his home," the driver interrupted apologetically, turning down the corners of his mouth. "I'm sorry."

"Oh, he did, huh?" I grumbled, crossing my arms and shaking my head.

Greyson shrugged and grabbed his coat, leading Dweezil past the driver and to the sleek black car parked in the driveway. I was tempted to refuse, to call Sebastian and tell him he had absolutely no right to demand I do *anything* against my will.

"Mr. Moore told me you might be a little hesitant, so he wanted me to tell you that, um …" The driver pursed his lips and inhaled deeply. "That you should just get your gorgeous ass in the car and trust him." Then he winced and added, "His words, not mine."

"Yeah, I bet they are," I muttered begrudgingly. But still, I was unable to fight the smile pulling at my lips.

***

"We're just about there," Ted, the driver, announced.

Huh? Sebastian's house was roughly a few hours away from mine. I knew I had spaced out a bit, scrolling through my phone and chatting idly with Greyson, but could I have really lost entire hours of my life in what only felt like twenty minutes?

I glanced out the window to find that we weren't far from home. In fact, we were just off of Hog Hill's tiny main street, driving through the wealthier side of town. A realization crept over me, but acceptance wasn't yet catching up with reality. I laid a hand over my mouth as the car came to a stop outside of the house.

"All right, here we are," Ted said with a smile. "I'll just grab your bags from the back and carry them in."

"Grey," I managed to say through my clenched throat as I stared out the window.

436

"Yeah?" He turned to me, his lips upturned in a mischievous smile.

"Did *you* know about this?"

He shrugged smugly. "Maybe." He didn't wait for my reply as he got out of the car, leading Dweezil up the walkway to the familiar porch.

I was hesitating, my hand resting on the door handle. I was too stunned, too shocked to react with anything but a blank stare toward the house I thought I'd never step foot in again. Not after Alex had sold it, and …

"Oh God," I uttered, shaking my head. "Fucking Alex."

He had known, and I didn't know if I should go straight to his house and kiss him, or beat him senseless for allowing me to believe it was completely gone.

With the packages under his arm and green bean casserole in his hands, Ted knocked on the window, breaking me out of my shock-induced paralysis. I pushed the door open and he asked, "Are you ready, ma'am?"

I wanted to tell him that there was no way I was ever going to be ready to face the grandest of gestures, but I knew I also couldn't sit in that car forever. So, I nodded and put on a brave smile, hoping I could keep it in place.

***

"Tabby!" Ronnie, Sebastian's mother, called the moment I stepped into the foyer. "Merry Christmas, honey. Can I take your coat?"

"Uh, y-yeah, sure," I said, flashing her a weak smile.

437

I slid my arms from the sleeves and allowed her to hurry off as I surveyed the room. God, it looked the same, but of course it did. It hadn't been that long since I was last here, and yet, it felt like forever. Mrs. Worthington's belongings were gone, replaced with things from Sebastian's old house hours away.

When the fuck did he have the time to move? He hadn't been home. He'd been on tour. When did he manage to accomplish all of this? How did I never catch on?

The questions were abundant, and they dizzied my mind as I tightened my arms around myself, strolling into the living room to greet Sebastian's brothers-in-law with hugs and forced smiles.

"Hey, Tabby, good to see you again," they each seemed to say, and to each I replied, "Yeah, you too. Merry Christmas." It was all I could manage, when the place was already starting to lose the floral smell of Mrs. Worthington, adopting the scents of leather, sandalwood, and man.

Sebastian's dad, John, stopped me on the way to the kitchen. "Merry Christmas, young lady," he greeted me with a one-armed hug, a beer occupying his other hand. "How do you like Bastian's new digs?"

I chuckled awkwardly, raising my eyes to the vaulted ceilings. "Uh, well, it's, um …" An emotional blockade jammed my words, and I swallowed. "It's very surprising."

He nodded in agreement. "We were a little shocked ourselves, when he told us he was selling the house. He's had that place since … God, since he started making money, I guess. Bought it for a song back then. But he put in an offer on this old girl months ago."

"*Months* ago?" I cocked an eyebrow and eyed him suspiciously.

"Yeah. I think it was back in August? He hired my sons-in-law to move his stuff over when the sale was finalized at the end of September."

September? On Thanksgiving, Alex had told me the sale would be finalized in a week.

He'd been working on this plan for months, since our fight. Since I ended things. "Why?" I asked aloud. "Why would he do this?"

"Uh, well, he said he wanted to be closer to Greyson, and—"

"Dad! What the hell!" Sebastian interrupted, wrapping an arm around his dad's shoulders. "You're not supposed to give away *all* of the secrets! Jesus Christ …" He turned to me, rolling his eyes and shaking his head. "I swear, I can't take this old man anywhere."

At the sight of him, I immediately thought I might cry. My bottom lip began to lose control, quivering and quaking despite my resolve to remain calm.

"C-can we talk?" I whispered, my voice hoarse.

"Oh, yeah, sure," Sebastian replied casually, as if he hadn't just knocked me dead with the most elaborate scheme to win me over. "You gotta come to the kitchen, though. I can't leave all that shit for too long, unless you wanna eat some burnt-ass ham and over-boiled potatoes."

I followed him through the swinging kitchen door, only to find his sisters crowded around the table. They turned to me, then immediately looked to each other with wide-eyed stares and excited grins. Mel was the first to open her mouth to speak, when Sebastian reached between them to smack his hand on the table.

"Hey! You three. Get the fuck out of here right now."

"Oh, that's really the nicest way you could've asked?" Dinah groaned, shooting him with an angry side-eye.

"Get the fuck out of here right now, *please*?" he corrected, narrowing his glare at his older sisters.

"I thought you wanted us to help you get dinner ready," Mel threw in, teasing with a pinch of her lips and a jump of her brows. "Remember? You distinctly said for us to get in here and—"

"Yeah, well, that was before I was about to …" He nudged his head toward me, and I huffed a sigh. "*You know*. So, for fuck's sake, get out."

Jen turned to me, with exhaustion hooding her eyelids. "Tabby, please, we're begging you. Take him back. He's been driving us all insane."

"Go!" Sebastian growled, nudging them toward the door. They obeyed with begrudged grumbles and teasing jabs, and then, we were alone. He turned to me, smiling sweetly. "There. Now, what were you going to say?"

"You, uh … y-you bought Mrs. Worthington's house," I stammered, suddenly shy and unable to find the right words to express just how I was feeling.

"Yep." He nodded astutely, walking with purpose to the stove. Lifting a lid off a large pot, he took a peek inside and held out his hand. "Hey, you wanna grab me that wooden spoon from the counter over there?"

"Uh, sure." I immediately found the one he was asking for and passed it into his waiting palm.

"Thank you," he replied, and stirred. "How do you like your mashed potatoes, by the way? You like them creamy or lumpy?"

"L-lumpy."

Glancing at me, his lips curled into a small smile. "Me too."

I stood beside him, picking at my fingernails, while every question I wanted to ask jumped up my throat and fizzled out on my tongue. For the first time ever, I was rendered speechless and absolutely dumbfounded in his presence. I watched with a knotted gut as he stirred the potatoes, then sprinkled a pinch of salt into the water before closing the pot again. With every wasted, awkward moment that passed, I imagined the conversation we could've been having, mentally kicking myself for being too much of a coward to just ask *why*.

Then, when the spoon was placed beside the stove, I found my courage.

"W—"

"Did you know this house is seriously haunted?" He turned against the counter, leaning against the granite with an amused smirk tugging at his lips. "Like, okay. Last night, I was finally done cleaning and wrapping presents, right? And while I was heading up the stairs to go to bed, I swear on my right hand, I felt like I was being watched. I even turned around to make sure someone wasn't following me. And I was like, whoa, calm the fuck down, because I was the only one here, obviously. Anyway, I finally get upstairs, piss, go to bed, and as I'm falling asleep, I swear to you, I felt someone sit at the edge of the bed."

A chill dodged through me and the hairs on my arms stood on end. "Get the hell out."

Holding up his hands, palms out, he said, "I *swear*. Weirdest shit that's ever happened to me. But what was even weirder was that, I wasn't even freaked out. Like, you hear something like that and you think you'd be scared out of your fucking mind, right?"

His eyes sought mine, widened with expectation, and I nodded. "Uh, yes."

"Right, but you know, I really wasn't. I was so … *cool with it*, and you know what I did?"

"Got the hell out of there?" I laughed, aware of the tension releasing from my fingers down to my toes.

"Not even. All I did was say, 'Night, Tom.' Without even thinking. I just blurted it out, rolled over, and went the hell to sleep." He spread his arms out and eyed me with a startled look that made me giggle. "I mean, what the fuck? I'm whispering to ghosts now or something? I told Jane to take her hubby with her when she left, but I guess he failed to get the memo."

"I guess you have a roommate then, huh?" I bit my bottom lip while the nerves twisted again around my stomach.

"Not the one I want, but I guess so," Sebastian shrugged, crossing his arms. "I guess it's good that there's nothing malevolent about him—right, T?" He raised his eyes to the ceiling, and when, expectedly, his question went unanswered, his brows dropped and his eyes narrowed. "Well, we're clearly not on speaking terms yet, but we'll get there."

Finally, with enough courage to spare, I asked, "When did you make an offer?"

Cocking his head, he pursed his lips with thought as though he were doing the math. "Uh, pretty much right after Roman pulled out of the deal."

"But *how*? I don't understand how you did all of this without me ever finding out."

He lifted his mouth into a lopsided smile. "It was all done over the phone, Tabby. Alex hooked me up. Greyson and I spent August packing my house, and pretty much as soon as I left, my sisters' husbands moved my shit over. You didn't have any reason to come by this part of town, since Jane was already living with her niece, so when would you have ever found out?"

A shroud was lifted from my eyes, allowing the light of realization in. "You've been living in this house for—"

"A couple of weeks," he finished with a smug grin. "And you had absolutely no idea. I fucking played your ass."

The room felt small and hot. Too tight and stifled to breathe. I moved to sit down at the small breakfast table he once had in his old kitchen.

"Why didn't you tell me?"

"Eh," he shrugged casually, "why would I do that and blow the most amazing Christmas present *ever*?"

I couldn't wrap my head around it. He'd had a life in his old house, with his family only a short distance away.

It was lost on me why he'd give all of that up, to live in this tiny, nowhere town. I know what he said he felt for me, but that was months ago. That was when I turned him down and told him to put a stop to whatever it was he thought he felt, after we'd only slept together a handful of times. Hadn't enough time now passed for him to put it all behind him?

Have I put it behind me?

"Don't make a big deal out of it, Tabby," he stated in an even tone.

Whipping my head to stare at him incredulously, I nearly shouted, "How can I *not*?"

"Uh, by just accepting it for what it is?"

"And what is *it*, Sebastian? Because for months, you've been telling me it isn't *anything*, but this feels a lot like *something*," I snapped, gritting my teeth and hoping I could make it through the rest of this discussion without breaking down.

"Yeah, you know, you're right about that," he agreed with a nod. "I never should've told you that, because I'm pretty sure I knew from the beginning that this was more than just us fucking around."

A tremored breath rasped through my throat as I asked, "How did you know that?"

With a one-shouldered shrug, he chuckled. "Because I've slept with only one woman multiple times in my life, and that's you."

"That is ... so oddly romantic," I grumbled, tipping my head back to look at the ceiling as Sebastian turned to stir the potatoes again. "I don't—"

He sighed heavily. "Look, Tabby," he stopped me with my name, and I closed my mouth. "I know you wanna continue this conversation, okay, and we will. We have to, I get it, but let's just get through today first, okay? Can we do that?"

I dropped my gaze to the tiled floor. "Why can't we talk now?"

"Because I need a *chance*," he blurted as though the line had been rehearsed. I raised my eyes back to his and found them pleading with me. "I just want to show you that I *can* give you everything you want, okay? That's all."

Without another word, I conceded with a single nod, and set out to help him in the kitchen. We finished the cooking together, laughing and sharing flirty comments and gentle touches on the arm or hip. A number of times, within the span of only a few minutes, I almost kissed him, or maybe it was Sebastian who almost kissed me, but neither of us took the chance. Not yet, but I knew it was coming.

Because, what I never told him, was that I already knew he could give me everything I wanted.

He already had.

43

sebastian

"This has got to be the most elaborate scheme to get some pussy *ever*," Greg muttered, sidling up beside me with a glass of eggnog in hand. "And by the way, man, this eggnog is out of this freakin' world. You made this stuff?"

"I was up *all* fucking night making that shit," I grumbled, kneeling in front of the tree. "And for the millionth time, it's not a *scheme*."

"If she turns you down after all of this, I'd say you're officially on her shit list," Matt chuckled against the rim of his glass.

I shook my head as I twisted one of the burnt-out, multicolored lights. Whoever said putting lights on a tree was a good idea was obviously high as a fucking kite, because it truly was a special kind of torture, trying to get them all to stay lit and all at the same time.

"Hell, if she turns you down after all of this, *she* should be on *your* shit list," Steve chimed in from the couch.

"Oh my God," Jen groaned, swatting at Steve's arm. "Can you guys just leave him alone?"

"And can we please remember that *she's here*?" Dinah tacked on in a whispered growl.

For months, my brothers-in-law had teased me for buying the old Worthington house in Hog fucking Hill. Although I'd successfully recruited them to help move my crap, they couldn't understand why I'd want to pack up and leave the house I'd been living in for sixteen years, seemingly at the drop of a hat. They immediately assumed it was to win Tabby over, to show her that I was willing to go the distance to get her back, and sure, that was a big part of it.

But it was only a bonus.

Because, even though I loved her and there was no way in Hell I was ever going to stop, I bought this house for Greyson. Apart from the time spent on the road, I didn't want to go another day without seeing him, and the only way to accomplish that was to move closer to him. I wanted to keep him in his school, to keep him close to everything he'd ever known and to bring the members of *his* family closer together. Because above everything else, I loved *him*, and when you love someone, you do what's best for them.

And for Greyson, that was this: a father and a mother figure who loved him, a dog to chill with, a big fucking family to call his own. It was not only the life I knew he wanted, but the life *he* deserved.

The life I would've given him from the very beginning, had I been given the chance.

I twisted the light again and the entire strand went out. "Son of a bitch."

"You know, we have this thing at our house that basically repairs those stupid little shits," Greg commented, kneeling beside me. "I mean, I have Jen handle these things, so *I* never have to worry about them, but she says it works pretty well."

"Wow, Greg, that's fucking awesome, man. Hey, did you happen to bring it with you?" I turned to face him.

"Uh," his jaw shifted uncomfortably before he met my eyes again, "let's pretend I didn't say anything."

"Yeah, that's a great idea," I grumbled, shaking my head.

Greyson ran into the living room with Travis and Johnny on his heels. "Hey, Dad?"

"What's up, dude?" I stood up, resigning myself to having only a partially lit tree and making a mental note to get one of those gadgets Greg was talking about.

"Can we go jam in the basement? I wanna show Trav and Johnny your drums."

Every one of my brothers-in-law eyed each other with dread at the mention of drums. I felt their pain. Three teenaged boys, two of which didn't know what the hell they were doing, beating on the skins sounded like the worst idea on the planet, even to me.

I put my hands on my hips and chuckled. "Uh … Yeah, that's not happening."

Grey threw his head back dramatically. "Oh, *come on*, Dad. It's *Christmas*."

"Yeah? Is there a point you're trying to make here, or …?" I shrugged and raised a brow.

Countering with an equal amount of disbelief as I was using on him, he shot me with an exhausted glare. "Jesus would've wanted it this way. I mean, you know the little drummer boy?"

The corners of my mouth lifted with reluctant amusement. "Yeah, I've heard of him."

Johnny and Travis flanked Greyson, their newly adopted ring leader, as he continued, "Well, the little drummer boy didn't have a, uh, a gift to bring him, right? So, he played his drums—"

"*Drum*," Jen interjected helpfully. "He only had one drum, Grey."

"Thanks, Aunt Jen," Grey nodded gratefully, pointing his finger at my sister. "Okay, so he played his *drum* for Jesus as a birthday present, so *we* were thinking that it'd be an awesome way to celebrate the birth of Christ by *also* playing drums. Except we have a lot of them, so really, it's a better present."

I bobbed my head, as if considering his argument while quelling my urge to laugh. "You know, I hear you, but, uh, yeah, still not happening."

My son groaned as disappointment overshadowed the excitement in Johnny and Travis' eyes. "Why not?" Grey asked, his brows lowering to darken his eyes.

"Well," I reached an arm out to wrap around his shoulders, "there's a few reasons. One," I held up a finger, "Jesus is a pretty old guy, so I think he'd probably

449

just like to spend his birthday taking a nap. Two," I held up another, "dinner's gonna be on the table in about two seconds. And three," another finger, "and this is probably the most important of them all—I'm not entirely convinced that basement isn't a meeting ground for ghosts. Got some weird fucking vibes down there the other night, man, and I really don't wanna use you as the sacrificial lamb, you know what I'm saying?"

Greyson's tired expression grew even more impatient. "There aren't any ghosts in the basement, Dad," he drawled.

I steered him from the living room and toward the dining room, where Tabby was helping Mel to lay out the dishes and utensils. "Yeah, well, you can be sure about that if you want, but I'm not so convinced. So, no drums today, and instead, you can help your aunts set the table. How's that for a deal?"

"Whatever," he grumbled in reply, but his argument stopped there as he set out to place forks at every chair.

Tabby's eyes met mine as one side her mouth lifted into a smile. "You need any more help in the kitchen?"

"Nah, my parents have it covered." I returned the smile, stuffing my hands into my pockets. From the corner of my eye, I caught Mel's hopeful glance in our direction.

Tabby nodded. "Okay. Um, can I do anything else?"

There was a laundry list of things I could've given her. Move in with me, marry me, give me another kid or three … but I wasn't pushing my luck just yet.

"Nah, I've got this covered," I replied with a confident grin, because you know what? I did. All of it.

450

I've got this.

***

"You guys can crash here tonight, if you don't wanna drive back this late," I offered my parents as we headed into the living room to collect their coats.

"You say that, but you really don't want us getting in your way," Dad replied with a wink, darting a suggestive glare in Tabby's direction. "You better seal this deal, or else you're out of the will. Greyson will get everything we're leaving you, you got it?"

"Wow. Harsh," I grumbled, watching as my mother leaned over Greyson, sleeping on the couch, and pressed a kiss to his temple.

He stirred, opening his eyes to narrow slits. Muttering something incoherent, Mom smiled, smoothing her palm over his cheek. "We're heading home, sweetheart."

Greyson nodded sleepily. "Bye, Grandma. See you soon."

I chewed at the corner of my lip, breathing through a wave of tear-inducing emotion. Moments like this did it for me—the use of titles, the little pieces that pushed us closer to becoming even more of a family.

Mom beamed with joy and kissed him again before straightening up and touching my gaze with hers. She flattened her palms to her chest as she walked toward me, outstretching her arms and pulling me in for a hug.

"Have I ever told you how proud I am of the man you've become?"

451

Shit. I swallowed relentlessly at another wave and buried my face against her shoulder. "Nope, can't say I've ever heard that one before."

"Well, you're hearing it now." She ran her fingers over the back of my head and turned to kiss my cheek. "I love you, honey. Take care of that boy of yours."

"Will do." I nodded, standing up and stepping back to wipe at my eyes. "Love you too, Mom. Give me a call when you get home."

Dad approached me with an extended hand, and when I accepted his firm grip, he pulled me in for a hug and a pat on the back. "Your first holiday was a success, kiddo. Kinda can't believe you didn't burn the house down."

"Eh, T wouldn't let that happen. That old dude's too attached to let this place go down in flames," I scoffed, shooting an incredulous glare at Tabby and she burst with a melodic giggle. I drowned in that sound, and I hoped it'd never stop.

"Who's *T*?" Dad asked, stepping back and squeezing my hand.

"Oh, just the ghost of Jane's dead husband," I replied nonchalantly, waving my hand dismissively in the air.

"Huh. Right. Well, we'll call as soon as we're back with the piggies. God, they're going to be so angry with us for leaving them home alone …" He tipped his head toward Mom, eyeing her with worry, and she nodded sympathetically.

They turned to Tabby with hopeful grins and wistful eyes. I saw in them every wish I had left. For her to take

452

me back, for her to be mine. To recognize that what we had wasn't something to question, but something to accept as being *right*.

"Merry Christmas, Tabby," Mom said, pulling her into an encompassing hug. "I'm so glad you could join us."

"Me too," Tabby spoke quietly against Mom's shoulder. Squeezing her and sighing. "Get home safe.

Dad was next to wrap his arms around her. "Give him a chance," he said, a little too loudly and I groaned, shaking my head.

"Thanks a lot, Dad. Now she's onto my master plan," I groused with a stony glare in his direction.

Tabby laughed, kissing my father on the cheek. "We'll see," she whispered, but loud enough for me to also hear. "Merry Christmas."

My parents left with encouraging glances in my direction before closing the door behind them. And then, Tabby and I were alone, save for Greyson and Dweezil sleeping on the couch. I sucked in a breath of determination and bravery, as I crossed the living room to grab a blanket, laying it over Greyson and smoothing the hair off his forehead.

"You touch him like he's a baby," Tabby commented gently, coming to stand beside me.

I had never thought about it like that before, catching my fingers as they delicately brushed over his hairline. "I guess because, for me, he kinda is. I missed out on that shit, you know?"

Tabby worried her lower lip between her teeth and nodded with understanding. "Yeah, I know," she whispered, and then she took my hand. "Come on. I have a present for you."

I let her lead me from the living room before I asked, "Is it a blowjob?"

Looking over her shoulder, she huffed with exasperation. "Not *that* kind of present."

Before I could express my disappointment, we were in the backroom, the room I would always consider Sandy's room, now cluttered with boxes and things needing to be put away. Tabby released my hand to grab a small wrapped gift from a pile of boxes.

"I hid it in here when we were unwrapping gifts earlier. I thought you'd prefer to open it in private," she explained, and my lips lifted into a suggestive grin.

"Is it a picture of you, naked? Because, Thumbelina, I would really appreciate the fuck out of that."

Rolling her eyes, she bit her bottom lip before saying, "Maybe one day, but that's—"

My brows jumped to my hairline. "Whoa. You didn't say no."

"Just open the damn present," she pressed impatiently with a light giggle. "Then we'll talk."

Taking a deep breath, I sat down on a spare drum throne. "Okay, let's see what we have in here," I muttered, tearing the corner to reveal a hint of baby blue, and I froze. My throat worked, my jaw shifted, and I looked back to Tabby with hesitation. She nodded, urging me to continue, and I tore the paper from the glass window.

An immediate rush of tears flooded my eyes at the sight of a tiny baby boy, swaddled in blue, with a little cap on his head. His eyes were closed, and I imagined I could hear him breathing. I imagined I could smell the new scent of his skin, could feel the fragile knuckles of every tiny finger. I imagined that I knew what it was like to hold him in the crook of my arm, the way I'd hold Devin's Olivia, except Greyson was *mine*. To cherish. To protect.

"He, uh … he was such a good baby," Tabby said, filling the space with something other than the sound of my running nose and dripping eyes. "He loved to cuddle, and was one of those rare babies that slept through the night. Sam used to think there was something wrong with him because he was *so* freakishly good, until he was a toddler and all Hell broke loose."

I laughed, nodding through my breakdown. "Talk to my mom. Supposedly I was a real asshole when I was three."

"Oh, I can only imagine."

"Thank you," I said hoarsely, gripping the picture frame between shaking hands. "For this. This is probably the best fucking present you could've ever given me."

She moved toward me, and a flash of déjà vu struck me from that night in my drum studio. The time she had first kissed me. But tonight there was no music playing, there was no urgent desperation to feed on her passion. All there was, was the searing, throbbing knowledge that this wasn't an *it just is* situation. It never was. It was my salvation, her freedom—it was *everything*.

"Sebastian, I never wanted to get into real estate. It wasn't like, this dream of mine to sell houses. But when Sam got pregnant, I felt so much pressure to be the good daughter, and to be a stable figure in Greyson's life. So, I forced myself to change. I went to college, I got this boring fucking job that I turned out being pretty good at, and I met a guy I cared for who never felt entirely right."

I shook my head, lowering the frame to my lap. "I already know this shit, Tabby. You don't need to explain it to me."

She held a hand out and I closed my lips. "It was so fucking exhausting being someone I was never comfortable with. But I'd just look at my sister and think, well, that's the alternative. And then, when she died, I just ..." She looked off, beyond me, her bottom lip trembling. "I just couldn't figure out what purpose a life like that has in the world, you know? Working these menial jobs, screwing men for fun, jumping from apartment to apartment, and mooching off people ... all for it to end, leaving behind a fucking mess for someone else to clean up."

The tremoring anger in her voice stabbed at my heart, at my lungs, until my hands clenched tightly around the painted wood frame. It was all I had, all I could do, to keep myself from reaching out and pulling her to me.

"I loved her. I loved her so goddamn much, and the amount of anger I felt toward her was ... God, it was *crushing*, because I think I kinda saw it coming, you know? The road she was on, it felt like it could've only led there, and then, when I met you ..." She laughed without an iota of humor. "You were *exactly* who I envisioned her being with, and you were *exactly* what I didn't want you to be. This cocky, obnoxious asshole

456

who didn't know how to keep his mouth shut." I smirked morosely and dropped my gaze to the picture of baby Greyson. "But while you were everything I had hoped you wouldn't be, you were also everything that Greyson needed, and it's taken me all this time to realize you're also exactly what *I* need."

I brought my gaze to hers. "So, does that mean you're sorry you called me a man-child?"

Tabby laughed with a subtle shake of her head, as one hand reached out to brush over my cheek. "It means I'm sorry I walked away. And that I thought I couldn't be with you because of some stupid job. And that you thought you had to cut your fucking hair to win me over. Because I really do love your hair when it's long."

Throwing my head back, I reached out, wrapping my arms around her waist and pulling her to stand between my thighs. "Oh, thank you, baby Jesus. I miss my hair so goddamn much."

Tabby laughed, and I pressed my cheek against her chest as I held her in my arms. "Apology accepted, Thumbelina. You can say it now," I muttered breathlessly, listening to the sound of her booming heart.

"Say what?" she asked, threading her fingers through the hair I was never cutting that short again.

"That you love me, that you'll move in here and save me from the ghosts, that you'll let me give you everything you want, that you'll never let me stop." She bent to kiss the top of my head and whispered something I didn't quite hear. I pulled away from her chest to narrow my gaze at her bitten lips and soulful eyes, and asked, "What was that?"

457

Unraveling my arms from her waist, she took my hands and led me out of the room. "I want to see your haunted bedroom."

"That's definitely *not* what you just said," I said pointedly, smirking with excitement for what I knew was coming. She pulled me toward the bottom of the staircase. "And whatever you have going on in that head of yours, I'm not sure T's really gonna appreciate it. He may or may not be a little old-fashioned."

"Well," she whispered, stepping onto the first step and leaning forward to lightly brush her lips over mine, "you'll just have to tell your ghost buddy to close his eyes."

44

tabby

"Yes," I whispered against his lips, my back pressed to the door of the master suite I'd grown to know well in the months I'd spent showing and attempting to sell.

With one quick peck on my mouth, Sebastian leaned back, eyeing me skeptically. "Wait, what?"

"Yes. That's my answer."

He cocked his head, looking all at once intrigued and perplexed. As though the rush of blood from his brain to groin had made him forgetful. I rolled my eyes and pressed my hands to his chest, pushing him gently toward the bed.

"I'll move in here and protect you from the ghosts, even though I'm still not convinced they're here—"

"Oh, baby, they fucking are. You don't get that vibe in here?" His eyes widened, his head nodded subtly. "Just wait until you feel something watch you while you sleep."

"Shut up!" I laughed, pushing him down to the mattress. "I'm trying to do a romantic thing right now and you're ruining it."

"Okay, okay," he let up, reaching out to grab my hands and pulling me down to lay with him. "You continue while I get these things off you," and he set to work, unzipping my jeans and sliding them off my legs.

The chilled air in his room hit my skin and I bit my lip with anticipation as he dipped his head, pressing his lips over the black lace of my underwear. His eyes swept up over my body, locking with mine, and encouraged me to continue as his thumbs hooked under the waistband.

I swallowed. "I'll let you give me everything I want," I gasped as he threw the lace to the floor and swept his tongue over me with a hungry groan. "Jesus, you're distracting me!" I whined, throwing my head back against the mattress.

"Then I'll remind you," he responded with another long, languorous lick. "You were gonna make me promise not to stop, even if you say when."

"Oh, God …" I groaned at the suction of his lips. "I'm never saying when again," and two fingers slipped inside the cleft between my legs.

"You promise?" he asked, his voice muffled by my skin, vibrating and coaxing my fingers to thread into the mess of his hair.

"I promise." My eyes met his and I nodded with affirmation and encouragement, my hips rising and falling with the heat of his mouth and the deftness of his hand.

He brought me to the edge, when my head was thrown back and my breath was tripped and ragged. His hand left me empty as he sat back, tearing away at his cumbersome clothes and revealing the body of ink I had missed too much over the months we were apart. My hands grappled for him, fingers digging into his shoulders as I pulled him forcefully to me, and he laid over me to wrestle his tongue against mine.

"I fucking love you." He broke the kiss to say the words and resumed before I had the chance to reply.

As I waited with eager anticipation for his body to align with mine, I wondered if he just didn't think I'd say it back. That I was willing to give up my home to live with him without reciprocating the feelings he had for me. Maybe, I considered, he just didn't think he could be loved, not by someone like me, who once abhorred the idea of interacting with him. The thought sliced at my heart, and my gaze sought his, as my hands reached out to press their palms to his cheeks.

"Sebastian," I said, with a choked gasp as one thrust of his hips brought me to a place I never wanted to leave again.

He groaned his response, touching his forehead to mine. "Holy fuck … I'm never going that long without this again."

The long, salacious strokes reminded me that he, a reformed playboy of sorts, had gone months without being touched by anybody but himself. If anything could be a testament of his honest devotion to me, it was that, and my fingers clasped tighter to his scruffy cheeks.

"I love you," I whispered, nodding my confirmation.

A broken gasp touched my lips as his eyes squeezed shut. "Fuck, Tabby … say it again …"

I choked on a surprising sob, hooked a leg around his waist, and repeated, "I love you, Sebastian. I love you so fucking much, you have no idea."

And as though the lack of confession had been the pin holding his composure together, he broke into a fervent fit of kisses and deep, delving thrusts of his hips. Hands grasped and fingers clawed. Tongues tied and hair pulled. I came undone, gasping and begging for more, and he came after, touching his forehead to my shoulder and pleading me to *don't stop, don't stop, don't stop.*

When it was over, Sebastian collapsed, tangling his fingers into my hair and peppering lazy kisses against my lips before rolling over and laying face-up on the bed, his arm wrapped around my shoulders.

"So, I gotta ask," he said, after catching his breath, "what did it for you?"

My arm wrapped around his waist, and I laughed. "What?"

"You're the first woman aside from my mom and sisters to say you love me, so what the hell did it? Was it my dashing good looks or was it the unparalleled wit?"

I looked toward his eyes, finding them trained on me, as they always seemed to be. "It, um …" I shrugged against him. "I guess it was Greyson. The way you are with him, how easily he fell in love with you. How

462

quickly you fell in love with him and immediately assumed your role, like you were always meant for it. The way ..." I hesitated, taking a deep breath and exhaling as I continued, "The way you broke down when he first called you his dad. I think that's when I really fell for you."

Sebastian nodded, tightening his arm around my shoulders. "That's a good answer," he replied, his tone rasped with heavy emotion. Then, he admitted, "I never stopped wanting him."

"I know." I flattened my palm, smoothing over the nest of blonde hair.

His heart pulsed beneath my hand, thundering with the power of a man who had everything in his grasp. Triumph and pride, swelling his lungs with every rise and fall of his chest, as though he had won a battle after years of defeat.

He finally had everything he had ever wanted; the life, and love, of his son.

"And you," he added, nodding affirmatively. "I've secretly wanted you for years. A little witch who could finally tame this beast."

I nuzzled my cheek against his shoulder, silently thanking him for setting me free, and whispered, "I love you, Sebastian."

"I love you too," he replied. "And that's never going to stop."

My eyes closed to the ghosts of the past, whispering their goodbyes, and with them came the peace of settling into this new life—the life we wanted. Together.

epilogue

sebastian

"Anyway, I decided to get rid of it."

I woke with a jolt. My hair was matted to the sweat dotting along my forehead, and I brushed the growing lengths back. Lifting up onto an elbow, I reached over to the nightstand and flipped the switch on the ugliest piece of shit lamp I had ever seen.

Tabby liked them, and what Tabby liked, Tabby got.

She slept soundly beside me, unstartled by my rude awakening. I watched her for a minute, debating whether I should wake her or not.

Fuck, she was beautiful, even as she slept. Some people can't look good while sleeping. They revert to a weird state of childlike innocence, with puffed cheeks and puckered lips. But Tabby maintained the beauty that made me want to stare at her and wonder how the hell an immature bastard like myself managed to get so lucky.

464

I decided to let her sleep, but knowing I needed to do something to take my mind off the sudden return of that dream, I climbed out of bed and quietly left our room. I was tempted to step into my drum studio and beat the skins to rid myself of the adrenaline, but I headed downstairs instead. Some TV might do me some good, I figured, and I swung into the living room, only to find Greyson sitting on the couch.

"Hey kid," I greeted him, hopping over the back of the sofa and landing next to him. "Can't sleep either?"

He shrugged. "Not really."

I noted a book in his lap, and nudged my chin toward it, as I asked, "What's that?"

Wordlessly, Greyson flipped the cover open, to present me with the first page of photographs, and my interest piqued. I leaned closer to look at the baby pictures of Greyson, a younger Tabby, and a vaguely familiar face. His mother.

"God, you were cute." My mouth had a mind of its own as the corners of my lips lifted into a warm smile. "Turn the page."

Grey complied, and my eyes focused on one large picture of Sam, holding a swaddled bundle of blue. She was lying in a hospital bed, gorgeous green eyes pointed directly at the camera and a bright, deliriously happy smile affixed to her young, pretty face.

"That was right after you were born, I guess," I muttered, nodding slowly.

"Do you hate her?" Greyson asked, finally speaking in a low, gruff tone.

I tore my eyes from the picture and turned to the tormented look on his face, and I shook my head. "No. I don't hate your mom. There's some shit I wish I knew, sure, but …" I pursed my lips, looking back to the picture and wishing I could remember more about her. "Nah, I don't hate her."

"Why not?"

Pulling in a deep breath, I leaned into the back of the couch and wrapped my arm around his shoulders. "Because all of this, Grey?" I lifted my hand and gestured out toward the living room. "All of this never would've happened if it weren't for her."

He nodded and looked down to the picture. "She would've liked you."

"You think she would've approved of me marrying your aunt tomorrow?" I chuckled, squeezing his shoulder.

Greyson snorted at that. "Oh, yeah. Definitely. She would've been like, '*Finally*, someone's gonna make her chill out.'"

I laughed. "That's good to know."

"Yeah," he replied, nodding. "She couldn't stand the guy Aunt Tabs was with before. He was so …" He uttered a sound of disgust.

"Well, I, for one, am glad she dodged that freakin' bullet," I mumbled, and squeezed his shoulder once again before standing. "Come on, kid. Big day tomorrow, and you know if you're not awake bright and early, your aunt is gonna rip you a new one."

His nod was accompanied by a forlorn sigh as his eyes met those of his mom once again. "I wish she was gonna be there."

"Me too, kid."

***

Tabby wrapped her arm around my waist as I laid back down. She lifted her head and pressed her ear to my chest.

"Too excited to sleep?" she teased, and I felt her smile in the dark.

"That, and I had a bad dream," I gently mentioned.

She hummed as her fingers came up to thread between the hairs on my chest. "About me leaving you at the alter?"

I snorted a chuckle. "Baby, even dream me knows there's no way that'd ever happen."

Her lips pressed to my skin. "Well, what was it about, then?"

My fingers slid into the lengths of her auburn hair. Stroking, combing, as I revisited the nightmare that haunted me every now and then. I told her about the phone call, the memory of her sister telling me she was going to have an abortion. Tabby stroked her fingers over my chest, nodding solemnly, until I was done, and she lifted her head to kiss my jaw.

"At least it's just a dream," she offered gently.

"I thought it was the truth for a long time," I reminded her, as our eyes met in the darkness.

Tabby nodded, lifting her hand to lay against my cheek. "I know."

"Do you know why she didn't get rid of him?" I asked without intending to say the words aloud.

She lifted herself higher, brushed her nose against mine, and kissed my lips in a way that steadied my hammering heart. My arm tightened around her, pulling her closer and finding a calm amidst the anxiety.

"I talked her out of it," she whispered, and my brow furrowed.

"But I thought you judged the hell out of her when she told you," I cautiously mentioned.

Tabby's lips met mine again before her sad smile took over. "I did, and I knew I didn't want to be anything like her." The regret in her voice swallowed any remnants of joy from the air, and she sighed, as her fingers kept stroking over my chest.

"But she was *pregnant*," she continued, "and there was something really happy in that, too. I mean, I think part of me really hoped that having a baby would calm her down a little, but deep down, I knew that wouldn't happen. I just kept thinking about the baby in there, and even while she kept saying she had made a mistake, I couldn't think of him like that. I kept thinking he happened for a reason, and that he deserved a chance to be something, you know?"

I nodded, knowing the rest of that story. How she had changed the course of her own life, to serve as the stability she knew Greyson would need. She was selfless, the polar opposite of how I had lived much of my life, and I shook my head as I floated somewhere between adoration and awe.

"I fucking love you, you know that?" I whispered, molding my palm to her cheek.

"Well, I'd hope so," she laughed lightly, pushing her fingers into my hair. "I mean, in just a few hours, I'm going to be your wife. You *better* love me."

I grinned, reveling in that word. *Wife*. Fuck, who would've imagined me ever being married, with a family of my own? A year ago, I didn't even know I had a son, let alone a woman just waiting for me to come along and mess her up.

Commitment was so far from my vocabulary then, and now, I wished I could chain myself to their sides. Just so I would never know what it was like to be without them again. They changed me—they *tamed* me.

And although Sam might've been the one to carry Greyson for nine months, it all came down to *this* woman. Her sister. The one to convince her that having a baby was the right call. The one to give my son the sturdy foundation he needed throughout the first fifteen years of his life, to give him a home and a mother when his was no longer there. The one who brought me into their lives, introduced me to this house and a life I never knew I could have but never stopped wanting.

All of this never would've happened, if it weren't for her.

That little witch.
My Thumbelina.

acknowledgements

First, I need to thank the Foo Fighters. For "Everlong," for giving me a concert I will never forget, for everything, but mostly, for being fucking awesome.

Second, everybody else:

My family—for their patience and understanding. The endless amount of encouragement and faith. I don't know where I'd be without them.

Danny—for everything, but mostly, right now, I need to talk about this cover! His ability to know exactly what I'm talking about with minimal detail is honestly mind-blowing. I guess that's why we've been together for so goddamn long. Never gonna stop. Never saying when.

Jess—for her time, her enthusiasm, and the ridiculous praise for this book. Never thought I'd impress that woman so much, but I did it with this one. Onto the next!

My betas—for adoring Sebastian. That's all I can say. This character was unlike anything I've ever written, and I feared what they'd think of him. But their enthusiasm was so surprising, and *that* gave me the confidence to believe in this book.

Laura and Amanda—for listening, for advising, for picking me up when I needed it. I'm blessed to know them and call them my friends.

The indie ladies—for the support and every iota of advice they have ever given me. I am who I am because of them. I can never repay what they've done for me, and I hope that one day I'll feel worthy of it all.

Lastly, my dear readers—for reading my words, for believing in me. It is never taken for granted.